THE BEST SHORT STORIES

OF

W. Somerset Maugham

D1575957

THE BEST
SHORT STORIES OF
W. Somerset Maugham

SELECTED, AND WITH AN INTRODUCTION, BY John Beecroft

The Modern Library · New York

Contents

Contents

Introduction

Though he claims he is a mere teller of tales and only a good craftsman, William Somerset Maugham has become universally recognized as a master in the modern world of arts and letters. He has triumphed as a dramatist, his novels have been read by untold numbers of people, and he has produced some of the finest short stories in modern literature.

Born in Paris in 1874, where his father was connected with the British Embassy, Maugham learned to speak French before he learned English and did not live in England until he was ten years old. Thus he had instilled in him two modes of life, two liberties, two points of view, with a sense of never wholly belonging to either country. This detached attitude has given him an analytical and critical quality that emerges in his depiction of character and study of human behavior.

When his home was broken by the death of his parents, Maugham, the youngest of the children, was taken to England to live with an uncle. Uncle Henry was a clergyman and apparently not too interested in children or not too eager to assume responsibility for the rearing of a nephew. Maugham pictures these years in *Of Human Bondage,* a book which is now regarded as one of the most important novels of our time.

Young Maugham escaped from his uncle's authority and English universities by going to Heidelberg. After two years in Germany he returned to England to study medicine. In 1892, he entered St. Thomas' Medical School. When he completed the course set for him, he emerged as a member of the Royal College of Surgeons and Licentiate of the Royal College of Physicians, but, taking what little money he had left from his patrimony, he turned his back on his profession and went to the Continent to write.

He received little encouragement from publishers or the public for the novels and plays he wrote during this period. However, in 1907 a producer took Maugham's play, *Lady Frederick,* as a stopgap in an emergency. It was a crashing success and Maugham had a demand for all the plays he could produce. *The Circle, Our Betters, The Constant Wife, The Letter* are among his better known dramas that are still seen on stage and screen.

Of Human Bondage was published in 1915. It was not until after *The Moon and Sixpence* came out in 1919, however, that Maugham's great autobiographical novel began to receive attention. Since then there has been a large and steady demand for it in many editions.

When World War I started, Maugham was forty years old. His war service was in the Intelligence Department as a secret agent operating for a part of the time out of Geneva. During the Russian Revolution he was sent on a special mission to Petrograd. His experiences during these exciting and active years were used in the Ashenden series—a superb collection of spy stories.

After years of living in various countries and travelling the world over, Maugham bought the house which he still considers his home. It is a villa on the French Riviera that was built by a retired bishop who had lived most of his life in Morocco. Maugham took out as much of the Oriental decoration as he could without rebuilding and moved in his own furniture and his fine collection of modern French paintings. There he entertained many of the social and literary celebrities who flocked to the Riviera during its gayest days. At the outbreak of World War II Maugham had to flee from his villa with only the few possessions he could carry. On a crowded and badly provisioned tramp steamer he managed to get to England. The British government sent Maugham to America—again in government service. During the war years he lived in New York, spending the winters on the Nelson Doubleday plantation in South Carolina, where he wrote *The Razor's Edge,* his last full length novel. After the war Maugham reclaimed his home, which had been looted by the Italians, occupied by the Germans and damaged by the French and Americans.

Many of Maugham's stories—all have now been gathered into two volumes, *East and West* and *The World Over*—are the result of his travels in China, Indo-China, Malaya, Borneo, Siam and Burma. His most famous short story, first titled *Miss Sadie Thompson* and now known as *Rain,* has had a spectacular success. Here are his own comments on the source of this story: "I was travelling from Honolulu to Pago Pago and, hoping they might at some time be of service, I jotted down as usual my impressions of such of my fellow-passengers as attracted my attention. This is what I said of Miss Thompson: 'Plump, pretty in a coarse fashion, perhaps not more than twenty-seven. She wore a white dress and a large white hat, long white boots from which the calves bulged in cotton stockings.' There had been a raid on the Red Light district in Honolulu just before we sailed and the gossip of the ship spread the report that she was making the journey to escape arrest. My notes go on: '*W. The Missionary.* He was a tall thin man, with long limbs loosely jointed, he had hollow cheeks and high cheek bones, his fine, large, dark eyes were deep in their sockets, he had full sensual lips, he wore his hair rather long. He had a cadaverous air and a look of supressed fire. His hands were large, with long fingers, rather finely shaped. His naturally pale skin was deeply burned by the tropical sun. *Mrs. W. His Wife.* She was a little woman with her hair very elaborately done, New England; not prominent blue eyes behind gold-rimmed pince-nez, her face was long like a sheep's, but she gave no impression of foolishness, rather of extreme alertness. She had the quick movements of a bird. The most noticeable thing about her was her voice, high, metallic, and without inflection; it fell on the ear with a hard monotony, irritating to the nerves like the ceaseless clamour of a pneumatic drill.

She was dressed in black and wore round her neck a gold chain from which hung a small cross. She told me that W. was a missionary on the Gilberts and his district consisting of widely separated islands he frequently had to go distances by canoe. During this time she remained at headquarters and managed the mission. Often the seas were very rough and the journeys were not without peril. She spoke of the depravity of the natives with a vehement, unctuous horror, telling me of their marriage customs which were obscene beyond description. She inveighed against dancing.' I talked with the missionary and his wife but once, and with Miss Thompson not at all. Here is the note for the story: 'A prostitute, flying from Honolulu after a raid, lands at Pago Pago. There lands there also a missionary and his wife. Also the narrator. All are obliged to stay there owing to an outbreak of measles. The missionary finding out her profession persecutes her. He reduces her to misery, shame, and repentance, he has no mercy on her. He induces the governor to order her return to Honolulu. One morning he is found with his throat cut by his own hand and she is once more radiant and self-possessed. She looks at men and scornfully exclaims: dirty pigs.' "

The technique of the short story has always interested Maugham. De Maupassant and Chekhov influenced him but he developed a form of story that has the unmistakable Maugham flavor. "I like a story that fits. I did not take to writing stories seriously till I had had much experience as a dramatist, and this experience taught me to leave out everything that did not service the dramatic value of my story. It taught me to make incident follow incident in such a manner as to lead up to the climax I had in mind . . ." Maugham has stated repeatedly that a story must have a beginning, a middle and an end. "I should define a short story as a piece of fiction that has unity of impression and that can be read at a single sitting. I should be inclined to say that the only test of its excellence is that it interests . . . let no one think that entertainment is a cheap and shoddy thing, let him leave such a belief to the most snobbish and vulgar of highbrows; entertainment is a form of pleasure and pleasure is in itself good . . . However great a work is commonly agreed to be, if it bores you, to read it is futile; it must entertain you, or so far as you are concerned it is valueless."

The stories in this book will, I believe, provide every reader with many hours of pleasure. The qualities that distinguish Maugham in all his writings—variety of material, lucidity of plot, sharpness of characterization, naturalness of dialogue, absence of pretentious straining—these and many other desirable qualities will be found abundantly here. And it is such qualities that assure Maugham of an enduring place in the annals of literature and in the hearts of all who love good stories.

JOHN BEECROFT

Conway, Massachusetts

THE BEST

SHORT STORIES OF

W. Somerset Maugham

The Letter

OUTSIDE on the quay the sun beat fiercely. A stream of motors, lorries and buses, private cars and hirelings, sped up and down the crowded thoroughfare, and every chauffeur blew his horn; rickshaws threaded their nimble path amid the throng, and the panting coolies found breath to yell at one another; coolies, carrying heavy bales, sidled along with their quick jog-trot and shouted to the passer-by to make way; itinerant vendors proclaimed their wares. Singapore is the meeting-place of a hundred peoples; and men of all colours, black Tamils, yellow Chinks, brown Malays, Armenians, Jews and Bengalis, called to one another in raucous tones. But inside the office of Messrs. Ripley, Joyce & Naylor it was pleasantly cool; it was dark after the dusty glitter of the street and agreeably quiet after its unceasing din. Mr. Joyce sat in his private room, at the table, with an electric fan turned full on him. He was leaning back, his elbows on the arms of the chair, with the tips of the outstretched fingers of one hand resting neatly against the tips of the outstretched fingers of the other. His gaze rested on the battered volumes of the Law Reports which stood on a long shelf in front of him. On the top of a cupboard were square boxes of japanned tin on which were painted the names of various clients.

There was a knock at the door.

"Come in."

A Chinese clerk, very neat in his white ducks, opened it.

"Mr. Crosbie is here, sir."

He spoke beautiful English, accenting each word with precision, and Mr. Joyce had often wondered at the extent of his vocabulary. Ong Chi Seng was a Cantonese, and he had studied law at Gray's Inn. He was spending a year or two with Messrs. Ripley, Joyce & Naylor in order to prepare himself for practice on his own account. He was industrious, obliging, and of exemplary character.

"Show him in," said Mr. Joyce.

He rose to shake hands with his visitor and asked him to sit down. The light fell on him as he did so. The face of Mr. Joyce remained in shadow. He was by nature a silent man, and now he looked at Robert Crosbie for quite a minute without speaking. Crosbie was a big fellow well over six feet high, with broad shoulders, and muscular. He was a rubber-planter, hard with the constant exercise of walking over the estate and with the tennis which was his relaxation when the day's work was over. He was deeply sunburned. His hairy hands, his feet in clumsy boots, were enormous, and Mr. Joyce found himself thinking that a blow of that great fist would easily kill the fragile Tamil. But there was no fierceness in his blue eyes; they were confiding and gentle; and his face, with its big, undistinguished features, was open, frank and honest. But at this moment it bore a look of deep distress. It was drawn and haggard.

"You look as though you hadn't had much sleep the last night or two," said Mr. Joyce.

"I haven't."

Mr. Joyce noticed now the old felt hat, with its broad double brim, which Crosbie had placed on the table; and then his eyes travelled to the khaki shorts he wore, showing his red hairy thighs, the tennis shirt open at the neck, without a tie, and the dirty khaki jacket with the ends of the sleeves turned up. He looked as though he had just come in from a long tramp among the rubber trees. Mr. Joyce gave a slight frown.

"You must pull yourself together, you know. You must keep your head."

"Oh, I'm all right."

"Have you seen your wife to-day?"

"No, I'm to see her this afternoon. You know, it is a damned shame that they should have arrested her."

"I think they had to do that," Mr. Joyce answered in his level, soft tone.

"I should have thought they'd have let her out on bail."

"It's a very serious charge."

"It is damnable. She did what any decent woman would do in her place. Only, nine women out of ten wouldn't have the pluck. Leslie's the best woman in the world. She wouldn't hurt a fly. Why, hang it all, man, I've been married to her for twelve years, do you think I don't know her? God, if I'd got hold of the man I'd have wrung his neck. I'd have killed him without a moment's hesitation. So would you."

"My dear fellow, everybody's on your side. No one has a good word to say for Hammond. We're going to get her off. I don't suppose either the assessors or the judge will go into court without having already made up their minds to bring in a verdict of not guilty."

"The whole thing's a farce," said Crosbie violently. "She ought never to have been arrested in the first place, and then it's terrible, after all the poor girl's gone through, to subject her to the ordeal of a trial. There's not a soul I've met since I've been in Singapore, man or woman, who hasn't told me that Leslie was absolutely justified. I think it's awful to keep her in prison all these weeks."

"The law is the law. After all, she confesses that she killed the man. It is terrible, and I'm dreadfully sorry both for you and for her."

"I don't matter a hang," interrupted Crosbie.

"But the fact remains that murder has been committed, and in a civilized community a trial is inevitable."

"Is it murder to exterminate noxious vermin? She shot him as she would have shot a mad dog."

Mr. Joyce leaned back again in his chair and once more placed the tips of his ten fingers together. The little construction he formed looked like the skeleton of a roof. He was silent for a moment.

"I should be wanting in my duty as your legal adviser," he said at last, in an even voice, looking at his client with his cool, brown eyes, "if I did not tell you that there is one point which causes me just a little anxiety. If your wife had only shot Hammond once, the whole thing would be absolutely plain sailing. Unfortunately she fired six times."

"Her explanation is perfectly simple. In the circumstances any one would have done the same."

"I daresay," said Mr. Joyce, "and of course I think the explanation is very reasonable. But it's no good closing our eyes to the facts. It's always a good plan to put yourself in another man's place, and I can't deny that if I were prosecuting for the Crown that's the point on which I should centre my enquiry."

"My dear fellow, that's perfectly idiotic."

Mr. Joyce shot a sharp glance at Robert Crosbie. The shadow of a smile hovered over his shapely lips. Crosbie was a good fellow, but he could hardly be described as intelligent.

"I daresay it's of no importance," answered the lawyer, "I just thought it was a point worth mentioning. You haven't got very long to wait now, and when it's all over I recommend you to go off somewhere with your wife on a trip and forget all about it. Even though we are almost dead certain to get an acquittal, a trial of that sort is anxious work and you'll both want a rest."

For the first time Crosbie smiled, and his smile strangely changed his face. You forgot the uncouthness and saw only the goodness of his soul.

"I think I shall want it more than Leslie. She's borne up wonderfully. By God, there's a plucky little woman for you."

"Yes, I've been very much struck by her self-control," said the lawyer. "I should never have guessed that she was capable of such determination."

His duties as her counsel had made it necessary for him to have a good many interviews with Mrs. Crosbie since her arrest. Though things had been made as easy as could be for her, the fact remained that she was in jail, awaiting her trial for murder, and it would not have been surprising if her nerves had failed her. She appeared to bear her ordeal with composure. She read a great deal, took such exercise as was possible, and by favour of the authorities worked at the pillow lace which had always formed the entertainment of her long hours of leisure. When Mr. Joyce saw her she was neatly dressed in cool, fresh, simple frocks, her hair was carefully arranged, and her nails were manicured. Her manner was collected. She was able even to jest upon the little inconveniences of her position. There was something casual about the way in which she spoke of the tragedy, which suggested to Mr. Joyce that only her good breeding prevented her from finding something a trifle ludicrous in a situation which was eminently serious. It surprised him, for he had never thought that she had a sense of humour.

He had known her off and on for a good many years. When she paid visits to Singapore she generally came to dine with his wife and himself, and once or twice she had passed a week-end with them at their bungalow by the sea. His wife had spent a fortnight with her on the estate and had met Geoffrey Hammond several times. The two couples had been on friendly, if not on intimate, terms, and it was on this account that Robert Crosbie had rushed over to Singapore immediately after the catastrophe and begged Mr. Joyce to take charge personally of his unhappy wife's defence.

The story she told him the first time he saw her, she had never varied in the smallest detail. She told it as coolly then, a few hours after the tragedy, as she told it now. She told it connectedly, in a level, even voice, and her only sign of confusion was when a slight colour came into her cheeks as she described one or two of its incidents. She was the last woman to whom one would have expected such a thing to happen. She was in the early thirties, a fragile creature, neither short nor tall, and graceful rather than pretty. Her wrists and ankles were very delicate, but she was extremely thin and you could see the bones of her hands through the white skin, and the veins were large and blue. Her face was colourless, slightly sallow, and her lips were pale. You did not notice the colour of her eyes. She had a great deal of light brown hair and it had a slight natural wave; it was the sort of hair that with a little touching-up would have been very pretty, but you could not imagine that Mrs. Crosbie would think of resorting to any such device. She was a quiet, pleasant, unassuming woman. Her manner was engaging and if she was not very popular it was because she suffered from a certain shyness. This was comprehensible enough, for the planter's life is lonely, and in her own house, with people she knew, she was in her quiet way charming. Mrs. Joyce after her fortnight's stay had told her husband that Leslie was a very agreeable hostess. There was more in her, she said, than people thought; and when you came to know her you were surprised how much she had read and how entertaining she could be.

She was the last woman in the world to commit murder.

Mr. Joyce dismissed Robert Crosbie with such reassuring words as he could find and, once more alone in his office, turned over the pages of the brief. But it was a mechanical action, for all its details were familiar to him. The case was the sensation of the day, and it was discussed in all the clubs, at all the dinner tables, up and down the Peninsula from Singapore to Penang. The facts that Mrs. Crosbie gave were simple. Her husband had gone to Singapore on business and she was alone for the night. She dined by herself, late, at a quarter to nine, and after dinner sat in the sitting-room working at her lace. It opened on to the verandah. There was no one in the bungalow, for the servants had retired to their own quarters at the back of the compound. She was surprised to hear a step on the gravel path in the garden, a booted step which suggested a white man rather than a native, for she had not heard a motor drive up and she could not imagine who could be coming to see her at that time of night. Someone ascended the few stairs that led up to the bungalow, walked across the verandah, and appeared at the door of the room in which she sat. At the first moment she did not recognize the visitor. She sat with a shaded lamp and he stood with his back to the darkness.

"May I come in?" he said.

She did not even recognize the voice.

"Who is it?" she asked.

She worked with spectacles, and she took them off as she spoke.

"Geoff. Hammond."

"Of course. Come in and have a drink."

She rose and shook hands with him cordially. She was a little surprised to see him, for though he was a neighbour neither she nor Robert had been lately on very intimate terms with him, and she had not seen him for some weeks. He was the manager of a rubber estate nearly eight miles from theirs and she wondered why he had chosen this late hour to come and see them.

"Robert's away," she said. "He had to go to Singapore for the night."

Perhaps he thought his visit called for some explanation, for he said:

"I'm sorry. I felt rather lonely to-night, so I thought I'd just come along and see how you were getting on."

"How on earth did you come? I never heard a car."

"I left it down the road. I thought you might both be in bed and asleep."

This was natural enough. The planter gets up at dawn in order to take the roll-call of the workers, and soon after dinner he is glad to go to bed. Hammond's car was in point of fact found next day a quarter of a mile from the bungalow.

Since Robert was away there was no whisky and soda in the room. Leslie did not call the boy, since he was probably asleep, but fetched it herself. Her guest mixed himself a drink and filled his pipe.

Geoff. Hammond had a host of friends in the colony. He was at this time in the late thirties, but he had come out as a lad. He had been one of the first to volunteer on the outbreak of war, and had done very well. A wound in the knee caused him to be invalided out of the army after two years, but he returned to the Federated Malay States with a D.S.O. and an M.C. He was one of the best billiard players in the colony. He had been a beautiful dancer and a fine tennis player, but, though able no longer to dance, and his tennis, with a stiff knee, was not so good as it had been, he had the gift of popularity and was universally liked. He was a tall, good-looking fellow, with attractive blue eyes and a fine head of black, curling hair. Old stagers said his only fault was that he was too fond of the girls, and after the catastrophe they shook their heads and vowed that they had always known this would get him into trouble.

He began now to talk to Leslie about the local affairs, the forthcoming races in Singapore, the price of rubber, and his chances of killing a tiger which had been lately seen in the neighbourhood. She was anxious to finish by a certain date the piece of lace on which she was working, for she wanted to send it home for her mother's birthday, and so put on her spectacles again and drew towards her chair the little table on which stood the pillow.

"I wish you wouldn't wear those great horn-spectacles," he said. "I don't know why a pretty woman should do her best to look plain."

She was a trifle taken aback at this remark. He had never used that tone with her before. She thought the best thing was to make light of it.

"I have no pretensions to being a raving beauty, you know, and, if you ask me point blank, I'm bound to tell you that I don't care two pins if you think me plain or not."

"I don't think you're plain. I think you're awfully pretty."

"Sweet of you," she answered ironically. "But in that case I can only think you half-witted."

He chuckled. But he rose from his chair and sat down in another by her side.

"You're not going to have the face to deny that you have the prettiest hands in the world," he said.

He made a gesture as though to take one of them. She gave him a little tap.

"Don't be an idiot. Sit down where you were before and talk sensibly, or else I shall send you home."

He did not move.

"Don't you know that I'm awfully in love with you?" he said.

She remained quite cool.

"I don't. I don't believe it for a minute, and even if it were true I don't want you to say it."

She was the more surprised at what he was saying, since during the seven years she had known him he had never paid her any particular attention. When he came back from the war they had seen a good deal of one another, and once when he was ill Robert had gone over and brought him back to their bungalow in his car. He had stayed with them then for a fortnight. But their interests were dissimilar and the acquaintance had never ripened into friendship. For the last two or three years they had seen little of him. Now and then he came over to play tennis, now and then they met him at some planter's who was giving a party, but it often happened that they did not set eyes on him for a month at a time.

Now he took another whisky and soda. Leslie wondered if he had been drinking before. There was something odd about him, and it made her a trifle uneasy. She watched him help himself with disapproval.

"I wouldn't drink any more if I were you," she said, good-humouredly still.

He emptied his glass and put it down.

"Do you think I'm talking to you like this because I'm drunk?" he asked abruptly.

"That is the most obvious explanation, isn't it?"

"Well, it's a lie. I've loved you ever since I first knew you. I've held my tongue as long as I could, and now it's got to come out. I love you, I love you, I love you."

She rose and carefully put aside the pillow.

"Good-night," she said.

"I'm not going now."

At last she began to lose her temper.

"But, you poor fool, don't you know that I've never loved any one but Robert, and even if I didn't love Robert you're the last man I should care for."

"What do I care? Robert's away."

"If you don't go away this minute I shall call the boys and have you thrown out."

"They're out of earshot."

She was very angry now. She made a movement as though

to go on to the verandah from which the house-boy would certainly hear her, but he seized her arm.

"Let me go," she cried furiously.

"Not much. I've got you now."

She opened her mouth and called "Boy, boy," but with a quick gesture he put his hand over it. Then before she knew what he was about he had taken her in his arms and was kissing her passionately. She struggled, turning her lips away from his burning mouth.

"No, no, no," she cried. "Leave me alone. I won't."

She grew confused about what happened then. All that had been said before she remembered accurately, but now his words assailed her ears through a mist of horror and fear. He seemed to plead for her love. He broke into violent protestations of passion. And all the time he held her in his tempestuous embrace. She was helpless, for he was a strong, powerful man, and her arms were pinioned to her sides; her struggles were unavailing and she felt herself growing weaker; she was afraid she would faint, and his hot breath on her face made her feel desperately sick. He kissed her mouth, her eyes, her cheeks, her hair. The pressure of his arms was killing her. He lifted her off her feet. She tried to kick him, but he only held her more closely. He was carrying her now. He wasn't speaking any more, but she knew that his face was pale and his eyes hot with desire. He was taking her into the bedroom. He was no longer a civilized man, but a savage. And as he ran he stumbled against a table which was in the way. His stiff knee made him a little awkward on his feet, and with the burden of the woman in his arms he fell. In a moment she had snatched herself away from him. She ran round the sofa. He was up in a flash and flung himself towards her. There was a revolver on the desk. She was not a nervous woman, but Robert was to be away for the night and she had meant to take it into her room when she went to bed. That was why it happened to be there. She was frantic with terror now. She did not know what she was doing. She heard a report. She saw Hammond stagger. He gave a cry. He said something, she didn't know what. He lurched out of the room on to the verandah. She was in a frenzy now, she was beside herself, she followed him out, yes, that was it, she must have followed him out, though she remembered nothing of it, she followed firing automatically shot after shot till the six chambers were empty. Hammond fell down on the floor of the verandah. He crumpled up into a bloody heap.

When the boys, startled by the reports, rushed up, they found her standing over Hammond with the revolver still in her hand, and Hammond lifeless. She looked at them for a moment without speaking. They stood in a frightened, huddled bunch. She let the revolver fall from her hand and without a word turned and went into the sitting-room. They watched her go into her bedroom and turn the key in the lock. They dared not touch the dead body, but looked at it with terrified eyes, talking excitedly to one another in undertones. Then the head-boy collected himself; he had been with them for many years, he was Chinese and a level-headed fellow. Robert had gone into Singapore on his motor-cycle and the car stood in the garage. He told the seis to get it out; they must go at once to the Assistant District Officer and tell him what had happened. He picked up the revolver and put it in his pocket. The A.D.O., a man called Withers, lived on the outskirts of the nearest town, which was about thirty-five miles away. It took them an hour and a half to reach him. Every one was asleep, and they had to rouse the boys. Presently Withers came out and they told him their errand. The head-boy showed him the revolver in proof of what he said. The A.D.O. went into his room to dress, sent for his car, and in a little while was following them back along the deserted road. The dawn was just breaking as he reached the Crosbies' bungalow. He ran up the steps of the verandah, and stopped short as he saw Hammond's body lying where he fell. He touched the face. It was quite cold.

"Where's mem?" he asked the house-boy.

The Chinese pointed to the bedroom. Withers went to the door and knocked. There was no answer. He knocked again.

"Mrs. Crosbie," he called.

"Who is it?"

"Withers."

There was another pause. Then the door was unlocked and slowly opened. Leslie stood before him. She had not been to bed and wore the tea-gown in which she had dined. She stood and looked silently at the A.D.O.

"Your house-boy fetched me," he said. "Hammond. What have you done?"

"He tried to rape me and I shot him."

"My God! I say, you'd better come out here. You must tell me exactly what happened."

"Not now. I can't. You must give me time. Send for my husband."

Withers was a young man, and he did not know exactly what to do in an emergency which was so out of the run of his duties. Leslie refused to say anything till at last Robert arrived. Then she told the two men the story, from which since then, though she had repeated it over and over again, she had never in the slightest degree diverged.

The point to which Mr. Joyce recurred was the shooting. As a lawyer he was bothered that Leslie had fired not once but six times, and the examination of the dead man showed that four of the shots had been fired close to the body. One might almost have thought that when the man fell she stood over him and emptied the contents of the revolver into him. She confessed that her memory, so accurate for all that had preceded, failed her here. Her mind was blank. It pointed to an uncontrollable fury; but uncontrollable fury was the last thing you would have expected from this quiet and demure woman. Mr. Joyce had known her a good many years, and had always thought her an unemotional person; during the weeks that had passed since the tragedy her composure had been amazing.

Mr. Joyce shrugged his shoulders.

"The fact is, I suppose," he reflected, "that you can never tell what hidden possibilities of savagery there are in the most respectable of women."

There was a knock at the door.

"Come in."

The Chinese clerk entered and closed the door behind him. He closed it gently, with deliberation, but decidedly, and advanced to the table at which Mr. Joyce was sitting.

"May I trouble you, sir, for a few words' private conversation?" he said.

The elaborate accuracy with which the clerk expressed himself always faintly amused Mr. Joyce, and now he smiled.

"It's no trouble, Chi Seng," he replied.

"The matter on which I desire to speak to you, sir, is delicate and confidential."

"Fire away."

Mr. Joyce met his clerk's shrewd eyes. As usual Ong Chi Seng was dressed in the height of local fashion. He wore very shiny patent-leather shoes and gay silk socks. In his black tie was a pearl and ruby pin, and on the fourth finger of his left hand a diamond ring. From the pocket of his neat white coat protruded a gold fountain pen and a gold pencil. He wore a gold wrist-watch, and on the bridge of his nose invisible pince-nez. He gave a little cough.

"The matter has to do with the case R. v. Crosbie, sir."

"Yes?"

"A circumstance has come to my knowledge, sir, which seems to me to put a different complexion on it."

"What circumstance?"

"It has come to my knowledge, sir, that there is a letter in existence from the defendant to the unfortunate victim of the tragedy."

"I shouldn't be at all surprised. In the course of the last seven years I have no doubt that Mrs. Crosbie often had occasion to write to Mr. Hammond."

Mr. Joyce had a high opinion of his clerk's intelligence and his words were designed to conceal his thoughts.

"That is very probable, sir. Mrs. Crosbie must have communicated with the deceased frequently, to invite him to dine with her for example, or to propose a tennis game. That was my first thought when the matter was brought to my notice. This letter, however, was written on the day of the late Mr. Hammond's death."

Mr. Joyce did not flicker an eyelash. He continued to look at Ong Chi Seng with the smile of faint amusement with which he generally talked to him.

"Who has told you this?"

"The circumstances were brought to my knowledge, sir, by a fliend of mine."

Mr. Joyce knew better than to insist.

"You will no doubt recall, sir, that Mrs. Crosbie has stated that until the fatal night she had had no communication with the deceased for several weeks."

"Have you got the letter?"

"No, sir."

"What are its contents?"

"My fliend gave me a copy. Would you like to peruse it, sir?"

"I should."

Ong Chi Seng took from an inside pocket a bulky wallet. It was filled with papers, Singapore dollar notes and cigarette cards. From the confusion he presently extracted a half sheet of thin note-paper and placed it before Mr. Joyce. The letter read as follows:

R. will be away for the night. I absolutely must see you. I shall expect you at eleven. I am desperate and if you don't come I won't answer for the consequences. Don't drive up.—L.

It was written in the flowing hand which the Chinese were taught at the foreign schools. The writing, so lacking in character, was oddly incongruous with the ominous words.

"What makes you think that this note was written by Mrs. Crosbie?"

"I have every confidence in the veracity of my informant, sir," replied Ong Chi Seng. "And the matter can very easily be put to the proof. Mrs. Crosbie will no doubt be able to tell you at once whether she wrote such a letter or not."

Since the beginning of the conversation Mr. Joyce had not taken his eyes off the respectful countenance of his clerk. He wondered now if he discerned in it a faint expression of mockery.

"It is inconceivable that Mrs. Crosbie should have written such a letter," said Mr. Joyce.

"If that is your opinion, sir, the matter is of course ended. My fliend spoke to me on the subject only because he thought, as I was in your office, you might like to know of the existence of this letter before a communication was made to the Deputy Public Prosecutor."

"Who has the original?" asked Mr. Joyce sharply.

Ong Chi Seng made no sign that he perceived in this question and its manner a change of attitude.

"You will remember, sir, no doubt, that after the death of Mr. Hammond it was discovered that he had had relations with a Chinese woman. The letter is at present in her possession."

That was one of the things which had turned public opinion most vehemently against Hammond. It came to be known that for several months he had had a Chinese woman living in his house.

For a moment neither of them spoke. Indeed everything had been said and each understood the other perfectly.

"I'm obliged to you, Chi Seng. I will give the matter my consideration."

"Very good, sir. Do you wish me to make a communication to that effect to my fliend?"

"I daresay it would be as well if you kept in touch with him," Mr. Joyce answered with gravity.

"Yes, sir."

The clerk noiselessly left the room, shutting the door again with deliberation, and left Mr. Joyce to his reflections. He stared at the copy, in its neat, impersonal writing, of Leslie's letter. Vague suspicions troubled him. They were so disconcerting that he made an effort to put them out of his mind. There must be a simple explanation of the letter, and Leslie without doubt could give it at once, but, by heaven, an explanation was needed. He rose from his chair, put the letter

in his pocket, and took his topee. When he went out Ong
Chi Seng was busily writing at his desk.

"I'm going out for a few minutes, Chi Seng," he said.

"Mr. George Reed is coming by appointment at twelve
o'clock, sir. Where shall I say you've gone?"

Mr. Joyce gave him a thin smile.

"You can say that you haven't the least idea."

But he knew perfectly well that Ong Chi Seng was aware
that he was going to the jail. Though the crime had been
committed in Belanda and the trial was to take place at Belanda Bharu, since there was in the jail there no convenience
for the detention of a white woman Mrs. Crosbie had been
brought to Singapore.

When she was led into the room in which he waited she
held out her thin, distinguished hand, and gave him a pleasant smile. She was as ever neatly and simply dressed and her
abundant, pale hair was arranged with care.

"I wasn't expecting to see you this morning," she said
graciously.

She might have been in her own house, and Mr. Joyce almost expected to hear her call the boy and tell him to bring
the visitor a gin pahit.

"How are you?" he asked.

"I'm in the best of health, thank you." A flicker of amusement flashed across her eyes. "This is a wonderful place for a
rest cure."

The attendant withdrew and they were left alone.

"Do sit down," said Leslie.

He took a chair. He did not quite know how to begin. She
was so cool that it seemed almost impossible to say to her the
thing he had come to say. Though she was not pretty there
was something agreeable in her appearance. She had elegance,
but it was the elegance of good breeding in which there was
nothing of the artifice of society. You had only to look at
her to know what sort of people she had and what kind of
surroundings she had lived in. Her fragility gave her a singular refinement. It was impossible to associate her with the
vaguest idea of grossness.

"I'm looking forward to seeing Robert this afternoon," she said, in her good-humoured, easy voice. (It was a pleasure to hear her speak, her voice and her accent were so distinctive of her class.) "Poor dear, it's been a great trial to his nerves. I'm thankful it'll all be over in a few days."

"It's only five days now."

"I know. Each morning when I awake I say to myself, 'one less.'" She smiled then. "Just as I used to do at school and the holidays were coming."

"By the way, am I right in thinking that you had no communication whatever with Hammond for several weeks before the catastrophe?"

"I'm quite positive of that. The last time we met was at a tennis-party at the MacFarrens'. I don't think I said more than two words to him. They have two courts, you know, and we didn't happen to be in the same sets."

"And you haven't written to him?"

"Oh, no."

"Are you quite sure of that?"

"Oh, quite," she answered, with a little smile. "There was nothing I should write to him for except to ask him to dine or to play tennis, and I hadn't done either for months."

"At one time you'd been on fairly intimate terms with him. How did it happen that you had stopped asking him to anything?"

Mrs. Crosbie shrugged her thin shoulders.

"One gets tired of people. We hadn't anything very much in common. Of course, when he was ill Robert and I did everything we could for him, but the last year or two he'd been quite well, and he was very popular. He had a good many calls on his time, and there didn't seem to be any need to shower invitations upon him."

"Are you quite certain that was all?"

Mrs. Crosbie hesitated for a moment.

"Well, I may just as well tell you. It had come to our ears that he was living with a Chinese woman, and Robert said he wouldn't have him in the house. I had seen her myself."

Mr. Joyce was sitting in a straight-backed arm-chair, resting his chin on his hand, and his eyes were fixed on Leslie. Was it his fancy that as she made this remark her black pupils were filled on a sudden, for the fraction of a second, with a dull red light? The effect was startling. Mr. Joyce shifted in his chair. He placed the tips of his ten fingers together. He spoke very slowly, choosing his words.

"I think I should tell you that there is in existence a letter in your handwriting to Geoff. Hammond."

He watched her closely. She made no movement, nor did her face change colour, but she took a noticeable time to reply.

"In the past I've often sent him little notes to ask him to something or other, or to get me something when I knew he was going to Singapore."

"This letter asks him to come and see you because Robert was going to Singapore."

"That's impossible. I never did anything of the kind."

"You'd better read it for yourself."

He took it out of his pocket and handed it to her. She gave it a glance and with a smile of scorn handed it back to him.

"That's not my handwriting."

"I know, it's said to be an exact copy of the original."

She read the words now, and as she read a horrible change came over her. Her colourless face grew dreadful to look at. It turned green. The flesh seemed on a sudden to fall away and her skin was tightly stretched over the bones. Her lips receded, showing her teeth, so that she had the appearance of making a grimace. She stared at Mr. Joyce with eyes that started from their sockets. He was looking now at a gibbering death's head.

"What does it mean?" she whispered.

Her mouth was so dry that she could utter no more than a hoarse sound. It was no longer a human voice.

"That is for you to say," he answered.

"I didn't write it. I swear I didn't write it."

"Be very careful what you say. If the original is in your handwriting it would be useless to deny it."

"It would be a forgery."

"It would be difficult to prove that. It would be easy to prove that it was genuine."

A shiver passed through her lean body. But great beads of sweat stood on her forehead. She took a handkerchief from her bag and wiped the palms of her hands. She glanced at the letter again and gave Mr. Joyce a sidelong look.

"It's not dated. If I had written it and forgotten all about it, it might have been written years ago. If you'll give me time, I'll try and remember the circumstances."

"I noticed there was no date. If this letter were in the hands of the prosecution they would cross-examine the boys. They would soon find out whether someone took a letter to Hammond on the day of his death."

Mrs. Crosbie clasped her hands violently and swayed in her chair so that he thought she would faint.

"I swear to you that I didn't write that letter."

Mr. Joyce was silent for a little while. He took his eyes from her distraught face, and looked down on the floor. He was reflecting.

"In these circumstances we need not go into the matter further," he said slowly, at last breaking the silence. "If the possessor of this letter sees fit to place it in the hands of the prosecution you will be prepared."

His words suggested that he had nothing more to say to her, but he made no movement of departure. He waited. To himself he seemed to wait a very long time. He did not look at Leslie, but he was conscious that she sat very still. She made no sound. At last it was he who spoke.

"If you have nothing more to say to me I think I'll be getting back to my office."

"What would anyone who read the letter be inclined to think that it meant?" she asked then.

"He'd know that you had told a deliberate lie," answered Mr. Joyce sharply.

"When?"

"You have stated definitely that you had had no communication with Hammond for at least three months."

"The whole thing has been a terrible shock to me. The

events of that dreadful night have been a nightmare. It's not very strange if one detail has escaped my memory."

"It would be very unfortunate when your memory has re-produced so exactly every particular of your interview with Hammond, that you should have forgotten so important a point as that he came to see you in the bungalow on the night of his death at your express desire."

"I hadn't forgotten. After what happened I was afraid to mention it. I thought you'd none of you believe my story if I admitted that he'd come at my invitation. I daresay it was stupid of me; but I lost my head, and after I'd said once that I'd had no communication with Hammond I was obliged to stick to it."

By now Leslie had recovered her admirable composure, and she met Mr. Joyce's appraising glance with candour. Her gentleness was very disarming.

"You will be required to explain, then, *why* you asked Hammond to come and see you when Robert was away for the night."

She turned her eyes full on the lawyer. He had been mis-taken in thinking them insignificant, they were rather fine eyes, and unless he was mistaken they were bright now with tears. Her voice had a little break in it.

"It was a surprise I was preparing for Robert. His birth-day is next month. I knew he wanted a new gun and you know I'm dreadfully stupid about sporting things. I wanted to talk to Geoff. about it. I thought I'd get him to order it for me."

"Perhaps the terms of the letter are not very clear to your recollection. Will you have another look at it?"

"No, I don't want to," she said quickly.

"Does it seem to you the sort of letter a woman would write to a somewhat distant acquaintance because she wanted to consult him about buying a gun?"

"I daresay it's rather extravagant and emotional. I do express myself like that, you know. I'm quite prepared to admit it's very silly." She smiled. "And after all, Geoff. Hammond wasn't quite a distant acquaintance. When he was ill I'd nursed him like a mother. I asked him to come when Robert was away, because Robert wouldn't have him in the house."

Mr. Joyce was tired of sitting so long in the same position. He rose and walked once or twice up and down the room, choosing the words he proposed to say; then he leaned over the back of the chair in which he had been sitting. He spoke slowly in a tone of deep gravity.

"Mrs. Crosbie, I want to talk to you very, very seriously. This case was comparatively plain sailing. There was only one point which seemed to me to require explanation: as far as I could judge, you had fired no less than four shots into Hammond when he was lying on the ground. It was hard to accept the possibility that a delicate, frightened, and habitually self-controlled woman, of gentle nurture and refined instincts, should have surrendered to an absolutely uncontrolled frenzy. But of course it was admissible. Although Geoffrey Hammond was much liked and on the whole thought highly of, I was prepared to prove that he was the sort of man who might be guilty of the crime which in justification of your act you accused him of. The fact, which was discovered after his death, that he had been living with a Chinese woman gave us something very definite to go upon. That robbed him of any sympathy which might have been felt for him. We made up our minds to make use of the odium which such a connection cast upon him in the minds of all respectable people. I told your husband this morning that I was certain of an acquittal, and I wasn't just telling him that to give him heart. I do not believe the assessors would have left the court."

They looked into one another's eyes. Mrs. Crosbie was strangely still. She was like a little bird paralyzed by the fascination of a snake. He went on in the same quiet tones.

"But this letter has thrown an entirely different complexion on the case. I am your legal adviser, I shall represent you in Court. I take your story as you tell it me, and I shall conduct your defence according to its terms. It may be that I believe your statements, and it may be that I doubt them. The duty of counsel is to persuade the Court that the evidence

placed before it is not such as to justify it in bringing in a
verdict of guilty, and any private opinion he may have of
the guilt or innocence of his client is entirely beside the
point."

He was astonished to see in Leslie's eyes the flicker of a
smile. Piqued, he went on somewhat dryly.

"You're not going to deny that Hammond came to your
house at your urgent, and I may even say, hysterical, invitation?"

Mrs. Crosbie, hesitating for an instant, seemed to consider.

"They can prove that the letter was taken to his bungalow
by one of the house-boys. He rode over on his bicycle."

"You mustn't expect other people to be stupider than
you. The letter will put them on the track of suspicions which
have entered nobody's head. I will not tell you what I personally thought when I saw the copy. I do not wish you to
tell me anything but what is needed to save your neck."

Mrs. Crosbie gave a shrill cry. She sprang to her feet,
white with terror.

"You don't think they'd hang me?"

"If they came to the conclusion that you hadn't killed
Hammond in self-defence, it would be the duty of the as-
sessors to bring in a verdict of guilty. The charge is murder.
It would be the duty of the judge to sentence you to death."

"But what can they prove?" she gasped.

"I don't know what they can prove. You know. I don't
want to know. But if their suspicions are aroused, if they begin
to make enquiries, if the natives are questioned—what is it
that can be discovered?"

She crumpled up suddenly. She fell on the floor before he
could catch her. She had fainted. He looked round the room
for water, but there was none there, and he did not want to
be disturbed. He stretched her out on the floor and kneeling
beside her waited for her to recover. When she opened her
eyes he was disconcerted by the ghastly fear that he saw in
them.

"Keep quite still," he said. "You'll be better in a moment."

"You won't let them hang me," she whispered.

She began to cry, hysterically, while in undertones he sought to quieten her.

"For goodness' sake, pull yourself together," he said.

"Give me a minute."

Her courage was amazing. He could see the effort she made to regain her self-control, and soon she was once more calm.

"Let me get up now."

He gave her his hand and helped her to her feet. Taking her arm, he led her to the chair. She sat down wearily.

"Don't talk to me for a minute or two," she said.

"Very well."

When at last she spoke it was to say something which he did not expect. She gave a little sigh.

"I'm afraid I've made rather a mess of things," she said.

He did not answer, and once more there was a silence.

"Isn't it possible to get hold of the letter?" she said at last.

"I do not think anything would have been said to me about it if the person in whose possession it is was not pre-pared to sell it."

"Who's got it?"

"The Chinese woman who was living in Hammond's house."

A spot of colour flickered for an instant on Leslie's cheek-bones.

"Does she want an awful lot for it?"

"I imagine that she has a very shrewd idea of its value. I doubt if it would be possible to get hold of it except for a very large sum."

"Are you going to let me be hanged?"

"Do you think it's so simple as all that to secure possession of an unwelcome piece of evidence? It's no different from suborning a witness. You have no right to make any such suggestion to me."

"Then what is going to happen to me?"

"Justice must take its course."

She grew very pale. A little shudder passed through her body.

"I put myself in your hands. Of course I have no right to ask you to do anything that isn't proper."

Mr. Joyce had not bargained for the little break in her voice which her habitual self-restraint made quite intolerably moving. She looked at him with humble eyes and he thought that if he rejected their appeal they would haunt him for the rest of his life. After all, nothing could bring poor Hammond back to life again. He wondered what really was the explanation of that letter. It was not fair to conclude from it that she had killed Hammond without provocation. He had lived in the East a long time and his sense of professional honour was not perhaps so acute as it had been twenty years before. He stared at the floor. He made up his mind to do something which he knew was unjustifiable, but it stuck in his throat and he felt dully resentful towards Leslie. It embarrassed him a little to speak.

"I don't know exactly what your husband's circumstances are?"

Flushing a rosy red, she shot a swift glance at him.

"He has a good many tin shares and a small share in two or three rubber estates. I suppose he could raise money."

"He would have to be told what it was for."

She was silent for a moment. She seemed to think.

"He's in love with me still. He would make any sacrifice to save me. Is there any need for him to see the letter?"

Mr. Joyce frowned a little, and, quick to notice, she went on.

"Robert is an old friend of yours. I'm not asking you to do anything for me, I'm asking you to save a rather simple, kind man who never did you any harm from all the pain that's possible."

Mr. Joyce did not reply. He rose to go and Mrs. Crosbie, with the grace that was natural to her, held out her hand. She was shaken by the scene, and her look was haggard, but she made a brave attempt to speed him with courtesy.

"It's so good of you to take all this trouble for me. I can't begin to tell you how grateful I am."

Mr. Joyce returned to his office. He sat in his own room, quite still, attempting to do no work, and pondered. His imagination brought him many strange ideas. He shuddered a little. At last there was the discreet knock on the door which he was expecting. Ong Chi Seng came in.

"I was just going out to have my tiffin, sir," he said.

"All right."

"I didn't know if there was anything you wanted before I went, sir."

"I don't think so. Did you make another appointment for Mr. Reed?"

"Yes, sir. He will come at three o'clock."

"Good."

Ong Chi Seng turned away, walked to the door, and put his long slim fingers on the handle. Then, as though on an afterthought, he turned back.

"Is there anything you wish me to say to my fliend, sir?"

Although Ong Chi Seng spoke English so admirably he had still a difficulty with the letter r, and he pronounced it "fliend."

"What friend?"

"About the letter Mrs. Crosbie wrote to Hammond deceased, sir."

"Oh! I'd forgotten about that. I mentioned it to Mrs. Crosbie and she denies having written anything of the sort. It's evidently a forgery."

Mr. Joyce took the copy from his pocket and handed it to Ong Chi Seng. Ong Chi Seng ignored the gesture.

"In that case, sir, I suppose there would be no objection if my fliend delivered the letter to the Deputy Public Prosecutor."

"None. But I don't quite see what good that would do your friend."

"My fliend, sir, thought it was his duty in the interests of justice."

"I am the last man in the world to interfere with any one who wishes to do his duty, Chi Seng."

The eyes of the lawyer and of the Chinese clerk met. Not the shadow of a smile hovered on the lips of either, but they understood each other perfectly.

"I quite understand, sir," said Ong Chi Seng, "but from my

study of the case R. v. Crosbie I am of opinion that the pro-
duction of such a letter would be damaging to our client."

"I have always had a very high opinion of your legal acu-
men, Chi Seng."

"It has occurred to me, sir, that if I could persuade my
fliend to induce the Chinese woman who has the letter to
deliver it into our hands it would save a great deal of trouble."

Mr. Joyce idly drew faces on his blotting-paper.

"I suppose your friend is a business man. In what circumstances do you think he would be induced to part with the
letter?"

"He has not got the letter. The Chinese woman has the
letter. He is only a relation of the Chinese woman. She is an
ignorant woman; she did not know the value of the letter
till my fliend told her."

"What value did he put on it?"

"Ten thousand dollars, sir."

"Good God! Where on earth do you suppose Mrs. Crosbie
can get ten thousand dollars! I tell you the letter's a forgery."

He looked up at Ong Chi Seng as he spoke. The clerk was
unmoved by the outburst. He stood at the side of the desk,
civil, cool and observant.

"Mr. Crosbie owns an eighth share of the Betong Rubber
Estate and a sixth share of the Selantan River Rubber Estate.
I have a fliend who will lend him the money on the security
of his properties."

"You have a large circle of acquaintance, Chi Seng."

"Yes, sir."

"Well, you can tell them to go to hell. I would never advise Mr. Crosbie to give a penny more than five thousand for
a letter that can be very easily explained."

"The Chinese woman does not want to sell the letter, sir.
My fliend took a long time to persuade her. It is useless to
offer her less than the sum mentioned."

Mr. Joyce looked at Ong Chi Seng for at least three minutes. The clerk bore the searching scrutiny without embar-

rassment. He stood in a respectful attitude with downcast
eyes. Mr. Joyce knew his man. Clever fellow, Chi Seng, he
thought, I wonder how much he's going to get out of it.

"Ten thousand dollars is a very large sum."

"Mr. Crosbie will certainly pay it rather than see his wife
hanged, sir."

Again Mr. Joyce paused. What more did Chi Seng know
than he had said? He must be pretty sure of his ground if he
was obviously so unwilling to bargain. That sum had been
fixed because whoever it was that was managing the affair
knew it was the largest amount that Robert Crosbie could
raise.

"Where is the Chinese woman now?" asked Mr. Joyce.

"She is staying at the house of my fliend, sir."

"Will she come here?"

"I think it more better if you go to her, sir. I can take you
to the house to-night and she will give you the letter. She is
a very ignorant woman, sir, and she does not understand
cheques."

"I wasn't thinking of giving her a cheque. I will bring
banknotes with me."

"It would only be waste of valuable time to bring less than
ten thousand dollars, sir."

"I quite understand."

"I will go and tell my fliend after I have had my tiffin, sir."

"Very good. You'd better meet me outside the club at ten
o'clock to-night."

"With pleasure, sir," said Ong Chi Seng.

He gave Mr. Joyce a little bow and left the room. Mr.
Joyce went out to have luncheon too. He went to the club
and here, as he had expected, he saw Robert Crosbie. He was
sitting at a crowded table, and as he passed him, looking for
a place, Mr. Joyce touched him on the shoulder.

"I'd like a word or two with you before you go," he said.

"Right you are. Let me know when you're ready."

Mr. Joyce had made up his mind how to tackle him. He
played a rubber of bridge after luncheon in order to allow
time for the club to empty itself. He did not want on this

particular matter to see Crosbie in his office. Presently Crosbie came into the card-room and looked on till the game was finished. The other players went on their various affairs, and the two were left alone.

"A rather unfortunate thing has happened, old man," said Mr. Joyce, in a tone which he sought to render as casual as possible. "It appears that your wife sent a letter to Hammond asking him to come to the bungalow on the night he was killed."

"But that's impossible," cried Crosbie. "'She's always stated that she had had no communication with Hammond. I know from my own knowledge that she hadn't set eyes on him for a couple of months."

"The fact remains that the letter exists. It's in the possession of the Chinese woman Hammond was living with. Your wife meant to give you a present on your birthday, and she wanted Hammond to help her to get it. In the emotional excitement that she suffered from after the tragedy, she forgot all about it, and having once denied having any communication with Hammond, she was afraid to say that she had made a mistake. It was of course very unfortunate, but I daresay it was not unnatural."

Crosbie did not speak. His large, red face bore an expression of complete bewilderment, and Mr. Joyce was at once relieved and exasperated by his lack of comprehension. He was a stupid man, and Mr. Joyce had no patience with stupidity. But his distress since the catastrophe had touched a soft spot in the lawyer's heart; and Mrs. Crosbie had struck the right note when she asked him to help her, not for her sake, but for her husband's.

"I need not tell you that it would be very awkward if this letter found its way into the hands of the prosecution. Your wife has lied, and she would be asked to explain the lie. It alters things a little if Hammond did not intrude, an unwanted guest, but came to your house by invitation. It would be easy to arouse in the assessors a certain indecision of mind."

Mr. Joyce hesitated. He was face to face now with his

decision. If it had been a time for humour, he could have smiled at the reflection that he was taking so grave a step, and that the man for whom he was taking it had not the smallest conception of its gravity. If he gave the matter a thought, he probably imagined that what Mr. Joyce was doing was what any lawyer did in the ordinary run of business.

"My dear Robert, you are not only my client, but my friend. I think we must get hold of that letter. It'll cost a good deal of money. Except for that I should have preferred to say nothing to you about it."

"How much?"

"Ten thousand dollars."

"That's a devil of a lot. With the slump and one thing and another it'll take just about all I've got."

"Can you get it at once?"

"I suppose so. Old Charlie Meadows will let me have it on my tin shares and on those two estates I'm interested in."

"Then will you?"

"Is it absolutely necessary?"

"If you want your wife to be acquitted."

Crosbie grew very red. His mouth sagged strangely.

"But . . ." He could not find words, his face now was purple. "But I don't understand. She can explain. You don't mean to say they'd find her guilty? They couldn't hang her for putting a noxious vermin out of the way."

"Of course they wouldn't hang her. They might only find her guilty of manslaughter. She'd probably get off with two or three years."

Crosbie started to his feet and his red face was distraught with horror.

"Three years."

Then something seemed to dawn in that slow intelligence of his. His mind was darkness across which shot suddenly a flash of lightning, and though the succeeding darkness was as profound, there remained the memory of something not seen but perhaps just descried. Mr. Joyce saw that Crosbie's big red hands, coarse and hard with all the odd jobs he had set them to, trembled.

"What was the present she wanted to make me?"

"She says she wanted to give you a new gun."

Once more that great red face flushed a deeper red.

"When have you got to have the money ready?"

There was something odd in his voice now. It sounded as though he spoke with invisible hands clutching at his throat.

"At ten o'clock to-night. I thought you could bring it to my office at about six."

"Is the woman coming to you?"

"No, I'm going to her."

"I'll bring the money. I'll come with you."

Mr. Joyce looked at him sharply.

"Do you think there's any need for you to do that? I think it would be better if you left me to deal with this matter by myself."

"It's my money, isn't it? I'm going to come."

Mr. Joyce shrugged his shoulders. They rose and shook hands. Mr. Joyce looked at him curiously.

At ten o'clock they met in the empty club.

"Everything all right?" asked Mr. Joyce.

"Yes. I've got the money in my pocket."

"Let's go then."

They walked down the steps. Mr. Joyce's car was waiting for them in the square, silent at that hour, and as they came to it Ong Chi Seng stepped out of the shadow of a house. He took his seat beside the driver and gave him a direction. They drove past the Hotel de l'Europe and turned up by the Sailors' Home to get into Victoria Street. Here the Chinese shops were open still, idlers lounged about, and in the road way rickshaws and motor-cars and gharries gave a busy air to the scene. Suddenly their car stopped and Chi Seng turned round.

"I think it more better if we walk here, sir," he said.

They got out and he went on. They followed a step or two behind. Then he asked them to stop.

"You wait here, sir. I go in and speak to my fliend."

He went into a shop, open to the street, where three or four Chinese were standing behind the counter. It was one of those strange shops where nothing was on view and you wondered what it was they sold there. They saw him address a stout man in a duck suit with a large gold chain across his breast and the man shot a quick glance out into the night. He gave Chi Seng a key and Chi Seng came out. He beckoned to the two men waiting and slid into a doorway at the side of the shop. They followed him and found themselves at the foot of a flight of stairs.

"If you wait a minute I will light a match," he said, always resourceful. "You come upstairs, please."

He held a Japanese match in front of them, but it scarcely dispelled the darkness and they groped their way up behind him. On the first floor he unlocked a door and going in lit a gas-jet.

"Come in, please," he said.

It was a small square room, with one window, and the only furniture consisted of two low Chinese beds covered with matting. In one corner was a large chest, with an elaborate lock, and on this stood a shabby tray with an opium pipe on it and a lamp. There was in the room the faint, acrid scent of the drug. They sat down and Ong Chi Seng offered them cigarettes. In a moment the door was opened by the fat Chinaman whom they had seen behind the counter. He bade them good evening in very good English and sat down by the side of his fellow-countryman.

"The Chinese woman is just coming," said Chi Seng.

A boy from the shop brought in a tray with a tea-pot and cups and the Chinaman offered them a cup of tea. Crosbie refused. The Chinese talked to one another in undertones, but Crosbie and Mr. Joyce were silent. At last there was the sound of a voice outside; some one was calling in a low tone; and the Chinaman went to the door. He opened it, spoke a few words, and ushered a woman in. Mr. Joyce looked at her. He had heard much about her since Hammond's death, but he had never seen her. She was a stoutish person, not very young, with a broad, phlegmatic face. She was powdered and rouged and her eyebrows were a thin black line, but she gave you the impression of a woman of character. She wore a pale blue jacket and a white skirt, her costume was not quite European nor quite Chinese, but on her feet were little Chinese silk slippers. She wore heavy gold chains round her neck, gold bangles on her wrists, gold ear-rings and elaborate gold pins in her black hair. She walked in slowly, with the air of a woman sure of herself, but with a certain heaviness of tread, and sat down on the bed beside Ong Chi Seng. He said something to her and nodding she gave an incurious glance at the two white men.

"Has she got the letter?" asked Mr. Joyce.

"Yes, sir."

Crosbie said nothing, but produced a roll of five-hundred-dollar notes. He counted out twenty and handed them to Chi Seng.

"Will you see if that is correct?"

The clerk counted them and gave them to the fat Chinaman.

"Quite correct, sir."

The Chinaman counted them once more and put them in his pocket. He spoke again to the woman and she drew from her bosom a letter. She gave it to Chi Seng who cast his eyes over it.

"This is the right document, sir," he said, and was about to give it to Mr. Joyce when Crosbie took it from him.

"Let me look at it," he said.

Mr. Joyce watched him read and then held out his hand for it.

"You'd better let me have it."

Crosbie folded it up deliberately and put it in his pocket.

"No, I'm going to keep it myself. It's cost me enough money."

Mr. Joyce made no rejoinder. The three Chinese watched the little passage, but what they thought about it, or whether they thought, it was impossible to tell from their impassive countenances. Mr. Joyce rose to his feet.

"Do you want me any more to-night, sir?" said Ong Chi Seng.

"No." He knew that the clerk wished to stay behind in

order to get his agreed share of the money, and he turned to Crosbie. "Are you ready?"

Crosbie did not answer, but stood up. The Chinaman went to the door and opened it for them. Chi Seng found a bit of candle and lit it in order to light them down, and the two Chinese accompanied them to the street. They left the woman sitting quietly on the bed smoking a cigarette. When they reached the street the Chinese left them and went once more upstairs.

"What are you going to do with that letter?" asked Mr. Joyce.

"Keep it."

They walked to where the car was waiting for them and here Mr. Joyce offered his friend a lift. Crosbie shook his head.

"I'm going to walk." He hesitated a little and shuffled his feet. "I went to Singapore on the night of Hammond's death partly to buy a new gun that a man I knew wanted to dispose of. Good-night."

He disappeared quickly into the darkness.

Mr. Joyce was quite right about the trial. The assessors went into court fully determined to acquit Mrs. Crosbie. She gave evidence on her own behalf. She told her story simply and with straightforwardness. The D.P.P. was a kindly man and it was plain that he took no great pleasure in his task. He asked the necessary questions in a deprecating manner. His speech for the prosecution might really have been a speech for the defence, and the assessors took less than five minutes to consider their popular verdict. It was impossible to prevent the great outburst of applause with which it was received by the crowd that packed the court-house. The judge congratulated Mrs. Crosbie and she was a free woman.

No one had expressed a more violent disapprobation of Hammond's behaviour than Mrs. Joyce; she was a woman loyal to her friends and she had insisted on the Crosbies staying with her after the trial, for she in common with every one else had no doubt of the result, till they could make arrangements to go away. It was out of the question for poor, dear, brave Leslie to return to the bungalow at which the horrible catastrophe had taken place. The trial was over by half-past twelve and when they reached the Joyces' house a grand luncheon was awaiting them. Cocktails were ready, Mrs. Joyce's million-dollar cocktail was celebrated through all the Malay States, and Mrs. Joyce drank Leslie's health. She was a talkative, vivacious woman, and now she was in the highest spirits. It was fortunate, for the rest of them were silent. She did not wonder, her husband never had much to say, and the other two were naturally exhausted from the long strain to which they had been subjected. During luncheon she carried on a bright and spirited monologue. Then coffee was served.

"Now, children," she said in her gay, bustling fashion, "you must have a rest and after tea I shall take you both for a drive to the sea."

Mr. Joyce, who lunched at home only by exception, had of course to go back to his office.

"I'm afraid I can't do that, Mrs. Joyce," said Crosbie. "I've got to get back to the estate at once."

"Not to-day?" she cried.

"Yes, now. I've neglected it too long and I have urgent business. But I shall be very grateful if you will keep Leslie until we have decided what to do."

Mrs. Joyce was about to expostulate, but her husband prevented her.

"If he must go, he must, and there's an end of it."

There was something in the lawyer's tone which made her look at him quickly. She held her tongue and there was a moment's silence. Then Crosbie spoke again.

"If you'll forgive me, I'll start at once so that I can get there before dark." He rose from the table. "Will you come and see me off, Leslie?"

"Of course."

They went out of the dining-room together.

"I think that's rather inconsiderate of him," said Mrs. Joyce. "He must know that Leslie wants to be with him just now."

"I'm sure he wouldn't go if it wasn't absolutely necessary."

"Well, I'll just see that Leslie's room is ready for her.

She wants a complete rest, of course, and then amusement."

Mrs. Joyce left the room and Joyce sat down again. In a short time he heard Crosbie start the engine of his motorcycle and then noisily scrunch over the gravel of the garden path. He got up and went into the drawing-room. Mrs. Crosbie was standing in the middle of it, looking into space, and in her hand was an open letter. He recognized it. She gave him a glance as he came in and he saw that she was deathly pale.

"He knows," she whispered.

Mr. Joyce went up to her and took the letter from her hand. He lit a match and set the paper afire. She watched it burn. When he could hold it no longer he dropped it on the tiled floor and they both looked at the paper curl and blacken. Then he trod it into ashes with his foot.

"What does he know?"

She gave him a long, long stare and into her eyes came a strange look. Was it contempt or despair? Mr. Joyce could not tell.

"He knows that Geoff. was my lover."

Mr. Joyce made no movement and uttered no sound.

"He'd been my lover for years. He became my lover almost immediately after he came back from the war. We knew how careful we must be. When we became lovers I pretended I was tired of him, and he seldom came to the house when Robert was there. I used to drive out to a place we knew and he met me, two or three times a week, and when Robert went to Singapore he used to come to the bungalow late, when the boys had gone for the night. We saw one another constantly, all the time, and not a soul had the smallest suspicion of it. And then lately, a year ago, he began to change. I didn't know what was the matter. I couldn't believe that he didn't care for me any more. He always denied it. I was frantic. I made him scenes. Sometimes I thought he hated me. Oh, if you knew what agonies I endured. I passed through hell. I knew he didn't want me any more and I wouldn't let him go. Misery! Misery! I loved him. I'd given him everything. He was all my life. And then I heard he was living with a

Chinese woman. I couldn't believe it. I wouldn't believe it. At last I saw her, I saw her with my own eyes, walking in the village, with her gold bracelets and her necklaces, an old, fat, Chinese woman. She was older than I was. Horrible! They all knew in the kampong that she was his mistress. And when I passed her, she looked at me and I knew that she knew I was his mistress too. I sent for him. I told him I must see him. You've read the letter. I was mad to write it. I didn't know what I was doing. I didn't care. I hadn't seen him for ten days. It was a lifetime. And when last we'd parted he took me in his arms and kissed me and told me not to worry. And he went straight from my arms to hers."

She had been speaking in a low voice, vehemently, and now she stopped and wrung her hands.

"That damned letter. We'd always been so careful. He always tore up any word I wrote to him the moment he'd read it. How was I to know he'd leave that one? He came and I told him I knew about the Chinawoman. He denied it. He said it was only scandal. I was beside myself. I don't know what I said to him. Oh, I hated him then. I tore him limb from limb. I said everything I could to wound him. I insulted him. I could have spat in his face. And at last he turned on me. He told me he was sick and tired of me and never wanted to see me again. He said I bored him to death. And then he acknowledged that it was true about the Chinawoman. He said he'd known her for years, before the war, and she was the only woman who really meant anything to him, and the rest was just pastime. And he said he was glad I knew, and now at last I'd leave him alone. And then I don't know what happened, I was beside myself, I saw red. I seized the revolver and I fired. He gave a cry and I saw I'd hit him. He staggered and rushed for the verandah. I ran after him and fired again. He fell, and then I stood over him and I fired and fired till the revolver went click, click, and I knew there were no more cartridges."

At last she stopped, panting. Her face was no longer human, it was distorted with cruelty, and rage and pain. You would never have thought that this quiet, refined woman was capable of such a fiendish passion. Mr. Joyce took a step backwards. He was absolutely aghast at the sight of her. It was not a face, it was a gibbering, hideous mask. Then they heard a voice calling from another room, a loud, friendly, cheerful voice. It was Mrs. Joyce.

"Come along, Leslie darling, your room's ready. You must be dropping with sleep."

Mrs. Crosbie's features gradually composed themselves. Those passions, so clearly delineated, were smoothed away as with your hand you would smooth a crumpled paper, and in a minute the face was cool and calm and unlined. She was a trifle pale, but her lips broke into a pleasant, affable smile. She was once more the well-bred and even distinguished woman.

"I'm coming, Dorothy dear. I'm sorry to give you so much trouble."

The Verger

THERE had been a christening that afternoon at St. Peter's, Neville Square, and Albert Edward Foreman still wore his verger's gown. He kept his new one, its folds as full and stiff as though it were made not of alpaca but of perennial bronze, for funerals and weddings (St. Peter's, Neville Square, was a church much favoured by the fashionable for these ceremonies) and now he wore only his second-best. He wore it with complacence, for it was the dignified symbol of his office, and without it (when he took it off to go home) he had the disconcerting sensation of being somewhat insufficiently clad. He took pains with it; he pressed it and ironed it himself. During the sixteen years he had been verger of this church he had had a succession of such gowns, but he had never been able to throw them away when they were worn out and the complete series, neatly wrapped up in brown paper, lay in the bottom drawers of the wardrobe in his bedroom.

The verger busied himself quietly, replacing the painted wooden cover on the marble font, taking away a chair that had been brought for an infirm old lady, and waited for the vicar to have finished in the vestry so that he could tidy up in there and go home. Presently he saw him walk across the chancel, genuflect in front of the high altar and come down the aisle; but he still wore his cassock.

"What's he 'anging about for?" the verger said to himself. "Don't 'e know I want my tea?"

The vicar had been but recently appointed, a red-faced energetic man in the early forties, and Albert Edward still regretted his predecessor, a clergyman of the old school who preached leisurely sermons in a silvery voice and dined out a great deal with his more aristocratic parishioners. He liked things in church to be just so, but he never fussed; he was not like this new man who wanted to have his finger in every pie. But Albert Edward was tolerant. St. Peter's was in a very good neighbourhood and the parishioners were a very nice class of people. The new vicar had come from the East End and he couldn't be expected to fall in all at once with the discreet ways of his fashionable congregation.

"All this 'ustle," said Albert Edward. "But give 'im time, he'll learn."

When the vicar had walked down the aisle so far that he could address the verger witout raising his voice more than was becoming in a place of worship he stopped.

"Foreman, will you come into the vestry for a minute. I have something to say to you."

"Very good, sir."

The vicar waited for him to come up and they walked up the church together.

"A very nice christening, I thought, sir. Funny 'ow the baby stopped cryin' the moment you took him."

"I've noticed they very often do," said the vicar, with a little smile. "After all I've had a good deal of practice with them."

It was a source of subdued pride to him that he could nearly always quiet a whimpering infant by the manner in which he held it and he was not unconscious of the amused admiration with which mothers and nurses watched him settle the baby in the crook of his surpliced arm. The verger knew that it pleased him to be complimented on his talent.

The vicar preceded Albert Edward into the vestry. Albert Edward was a trifle surprised to find the two churchwardens there. He had not seen them come in. They gave him pleasant nods.

"Good-afternoon, my lord. Good-afternoon, sir," he said to one after the other.

They were elderly men, both of them, and they had been

churchwardens almost as long as Albert Edward had been verger. They were sitting now at a handsome refectory table that the old vicar had brought many years before from Italy and the vicar sat down in the vacant chair between them. Albert Edward faced them, the table between him and them, and wondered with slight uneasiness what was the matter. He remembered still the occasion on which the organist had got into trouble and the bother they had all had to hush things up. In a church like St. Peter's, Neville Square, they couldn't afford a scandal. On the vicar's red face was a look of resolute benignity, but the others bore an expression that was slightly troubled.

"He's been naggin' them, he 'as," said the verger to himself. "He's jockeyed them into doin' something, but they don't 'alf like it. That's what it is, you mark my words."

But his thoughts did not appear on Albert Edward's clean-cut and distinguished features. He stood in a respectful but not obsequious attitude. He had been in service before he was appointed to his ecclesiastical office, but only in very good houses, and his deportment was irreproachable. Starting as a page-boy in the household of a merchant-prince, he had risen by due degrees from the position of fourth to first footman, for a year he had been single-handed butler to a widowed peeress and, till the vacancy occurred at St. Peter's, butler with two men under him in the house of a retired ambassador. He was tall, spare, grave and dignified. He looked, if not like a duke, at least like an actor of the old school who specialised in dukes' parts. He had tact, firmness and self-assurance. His character was unimpeachable.

The vicar began briskly.

"Foreman, we've got something rather unpleasant to say to you. You've been here a great many years and I think his lordship and the general agree with me that you've fulfilled the duties of your office to the satisfaction of everybody concerned."

The two churchwardens nodded.

"But a most extraordinary circumstance came to my knowledge the other day and I felt it my duty to impart it to the churchwardens. I discovered to my astonishment that you could neither read nor write."

The verger's face betrayed no sign of embarrassment.

"The last vicar knew that, sir," he replied. "He said it didn't make no difference. He always said there was a great deal too much education in the world for 'is taste."

"It's the most amazing thing I ever heard," cried the general. "Do you mean to say that you've been verger of this church for sixteen years and never learned to read or write?"

"I went into service when I was twelve, sir. The cook in the first place tried to teach me once, but I didn't seem to 'ave the knack for it, and then what with one thing and another I never seemed to 'ave the time. I've never really found the want of it. I think a lot of these young fellows waste a rare lot of time readin' when they might be doin' something useful."

"But don't you want to know the news?" said the other churchwarden. "Don't you ever want to write a letter?"

"No, me lord, I seem to manage very well without. And of late years now they've all these pictures in the papers I get to know what's goin' on pretty well. Me wife's quite a scholar and if I want to write a letter she writes it for me. It's not as if I was a bettin' man."

The two churchwardens gave the vicar a troubled glance and then looked down at the table.

"Well, Foreman, I've talked the matter over with these gentlemen and they quite agree with me that the situation is impossible. At a church like St. Peter's, Neville Square, we cannot have a verger who can neither read nor write."

Albert Edward's thin, sallow face reddened and he moved uneasily on his feet, but he made no reply.

"Understand me, Foreman, I have no complaint to make against you. You do your work quite satisfactorily; I have the highest opinion both of your character and of your capacity; but we haven't the right to take the risk of some accident that might happen owing to your lamentable ignorance. It's a matter of prudence as well as of principle."

"But couldn't you learn, Foreman?" asked the general.

"No, sir, I'm afraid I couldn't, not now. You see, I'm not as young as I was and if I couldn't seem able to get the letters in me 'ead when I was a nipper I don't think there's much chance of it now."

"We don't want to be harsh with you, Foreman," said the vicar. "But the churchwardens and I have quite made up our minds. We'll give you three months and if at the end of that time you cannot read and write I'm afraid you'll have to go."

Albert Edward had never liked the new vicar. He'd said from the beginning that they'd made a mistake when they gave him St. Peter's. He wasn't the type of man they wanted with a classy congregation like that. And now he straightened himself a little. He knew his value and he wasn't going to allow himself to be put upon.

"I'm very sorry, sir, I'm afraid it's no good. I'm too old a dog to learn new tricks. I've lived a good many years without knowin' 'ow to read and write, and without wishin' to praise myself, self-praise is no recommendation, I don't mind sayin' I've done my duty in that state of life in which it 'as pleased a merciful providence to place me, and if I *could* learn now I don't know as I'd want to."

"In that case, Foreman, I'm afraid you must go."

"Yes, sir, I quite understand. I shall be 'appy to 'and in my resignation as soon as you've found somebody to take my place."

But when Albert Edward with his usual politeness had closed the church door behind the vicar and the two church-wardens he could not sustain the air of unruffled dignity with which he had borne the blow inflicted upon him and his lips quivered. He walked slowly back to the vestry and hung up on its proper peg his verger's gown. He sighed as he thought of all the grand funerals and smart weddings it had seen. He tidied everything up, put on his coat, and hat in hand walked down the aisle. He locked the church door be-hind him. He strolled across the square, but deep in his sad thoughts he did not take the street that led him home, where a nice strong cup of tea awaited him; he took the wrong turning. He walked slowly along. His heart was heavy. He did not know what he should do with himself. He did not fancy the notion of going back to domestic service; after being his own master for so many years, for the vicar and churchwardens could say what they liked, it was he that had run St. Peter's, Neville Square, he could scarcely demean himself by accepting a situation. He had saved a tidy sum, but not enough to live on without doing something, and life seemed to cost more every year. He had never thought to be troubled with such questions. The vergers of St. Peter's, like the popes of Rome, were there for life. He had often thought of the pleasant reference the vicar would make in his sermon at evensong the first Sunday after his death to the long and faithful service, and the exemplary character of their late verger, Albert Edward Foreman. He sighed deeply. Albert Edward was a non-smoker and a total abstainer, but with a certain latitude; that is to say he liked a glass of beer with his dinner and when he was tired he enjoyed a cigarette. It occurred to him now that one would comfort him and since he did not carry them he looked about him for a shop where he could buy a packet of Gold Flakes. He did not at once see one and walked on a little. It was a long street, with all sorts of shops in it, but there was not a single one where you could buy cigarettes.

"That's strange," said Albert Edward.

To make sure he walked right up the street again. No, there was no doubt about it. He stopped and looked reflectively up and down.

"I can't be the only man as walks along this street and wants a fag," he said. "I shouldn't wonder but what a fellow might do very well with a little shop here. Tobacco and sweets, you know."

He gave a sudden start.

"That's an idea," he said. "Strange 'ow things come to you when you least expect it."

He turned, walked home, and had his tea.

"You're very silent this afternoon, Albert," his wife remarked.

"I'm thinkin'," he said.

He considered the matter from every point of view and next day he went along the street and by good luck found a little shop to let that looked as though it would exactly suit him. Twenty-four hours later he had taken it and when a month after that he left St. Peter's, Neville Square, for ever, Albert Edward Foreman set up in business as a tobacconist and newsagent. His wife said it was a dreadful come-down after being verger of St. Peter's, but he answered that you had to move with the times, the church wasn't what it was, and 'enceforward he was going to render unto Cæsar what was Cæsar's. Albert Edward did very well. He did so well that in a year or so it struck him that he might take a second shop and put a manager in. He looked for another long street that hadn't got a tobacconist in it and when he found it, and a shop to let, took it and stocked it. This was a success too. Then it occurred to him that if he could run two he could run half a dozen, so he began walking about London, and whenever he found a long street that had no tobacconist and a shop to let he took it. In the course of ten years he had acquired no less than ten shops and he was making money hand over fist. He went round to all of them himself every Monday, collected the week's takings and took them to the bank.

One morning when he was there paying in a bundle of notes and a heavy bag of silver the cashier told him that the manager would like to see him. He was shown into an office and the manager shook hands with him.

"Mr. Foreman, I wanted to have a talk to you about the money you've got on deposit with us. D'you know exactly how much it is?"

"Not within a pound or two, sir; but I've got a pretty rough idea."

"Apart from what you paid in this morning it's a little over thirty thousand pounds. That's a very large sum to have on deposit and I should have thought you'd do better to invest it."

"I wouldn't want to take no risk, sir. I know it's safe in the bank."

"You needn't have the least anxiety. We'll make you out a list of absolutely gilt-edged securities. They'll bring you in a better rate of interest than we can possibly afford to give you."

A troubled look settled on Mr. Foreman's distinguished face. "I've never 'ad anything to do with stocks and shares and I'd 'ave to leave it all in your 'ands," he said.

The manager smiled. "We'll do everything. All you'll have to do next time you come in is just to sign the transfers."

"I could do that all right," said Albert uncertainly. "But 'ow should I know what I was signin'?"

"I suppose you can read," said the manager a trifle sharply.

Mr. Foreman gave him a disarming smile.

"Well, sir, that's just it. I can't. I know it sounds funny-like, but there it is, I can't read or write, only me name, an' I only learnt to do that when I went into business."

The manager was so surprised that he jumped up from his chair.

"That's the most extraordinary thing I ever heard."

"You see, it's like this, sir, I never 'ad the opportunity until it was too late and then some'ow I wouldn't. I got obstinate-like."

The manager stared at him as though he were a prehistoric monster.

"And do you mean to say that you've built up this important business and amassed a fortune of thirty thousand pounds without being able to read or write? Good God, man, what would you be now if you had been able to?"

"I can tell you that, sir," said Mr. Foreman, a little smile on his still aristocratic features. "I'd be verger of St. Peter's, Neville Square."

The Vessel of Wrath

THERE are few books in the world that contain more meat than the Sailing Directions published by the Hydrographic Department by order of the Lords Commissioners of the Admiralty. They are handsome volumes, bound (very flimsily) in cloth of different colours, and the most expensive of them is cheap. For four shillings you can buy the Yangtse Kiang Pilot, "containing a description of, and sailing directions for, the Yangtse Kiang from the Wusung River to the highest navigable point, including the Han Kiang, the Kialing Kiang, and the Min Kiang"; and for three shillings you can get Part III of the Eastern Archipelago Pilot, "comprising the N. E. end of Celebes, Molucca and Gilolo passages, Banda and Arafura Seas, and North, West, and South-West coasts of New Guinea." But it is not very safe to do so if you are a creature of settled habits that you have no wish to disturb or if you have an occupation that holds you fast to one place. These businesslike books take you upon enchanted journeys of the spirit; and their matter-of-fact style, the admirable order, the concision with which the material is set before you, the stern sense of the practical that informs every line, cannot dim the poetry that, like the spice-laden breeze that assails your senses with a more than material languor when you approach some of those magic islands of the Eastern seas, blows with so sweet a fragrance through the printed pages. They tell you the anchorages and the landing places, what supplies you can get at each spot, and where you can get water; they tell you the lights and buoys, tides, winds and weather that you will find there. They give you brief information about the population and the trade. And it is strange when you think how sedately it is all set down, with no words wasted, that so much else is given you besides. What? Well, mystery and beauty, romance and the glamour of the unknown. It is no common book that offers you casually turning its pages such a paragraph as this: "Supplies. A few jungle fowl are preserved, the island is also the resort of vast numbers of sea birds. Turtle are found in the lagoon, as well as quantities of various fish, including grey mullet, shark, and dog-fish; the seine cannot be used with any effect; but there is a fish which may be taken on a rod. A small store of tinned provisions and spirits is kept in a hut for the relief of shipwrecked persons. Good water may be obtained from a well near the landing place." Can the imagination want more material than this to go on a journey through time and space?

In the volume from which I have copied this passage, the compliers with the same restraint have described the Alas Islands. They are composed of a group or chain of islands, "for the most part low and wooded, extending about 75 miles east and west, and 40 miles north and south." The information about them, you are told, is very slight; there are channels between the different groups, and several vessels have passed through them, but the passages have not been thoroughly explored, and the positions of many of the dangers not yet determined; it is therefore advisable to avoid them. The population of the group is estimated at about 8000, of whom 200 are Chinese and 400 Mohammedans. The rest are heathen. The principal island is called Baru, it is surrounded by a reef, and here lives a Dutch Controleur. His white house with its red roof on the top of a little hill is the most prominent object that the vessels of the Royal Netherlands Steam Packet Company see when every other month on their way up to Macassar and every four weeks on their way down to Merauke in Dutch New Guinea they touch at the island.

At a certain moment of the world's history the Controleur was Mynheer Evert Gruyter and he ruled the people who inhabited the Alas Islands with firmness tempered by a keen sense of the ridiculous. He had thought it a very good joke to be placed at the age of twenty-seven in a position of such consequence and at thirty he was still amused by it. There was no cable communication between his islands and Batavia, and the mail arrived after so long a delay that even if he asked advice, by the time he received it, it was useless, and so he equably did what he thought best and trusted to his good fortune to keep out of trouble with the authorities. He was very short, not more than five feet four in height, and extremely fat; he was of a florid complexion. For coolness' sake he kept his head shaved and his face was hairless. It was round and red. His eyebrows were so fair that you hardly saw them; and he had little twinkling blue eyes. He knew that he had no dignity, but for the sake of his position made up for it by dressing very dapperly. He never went to his office, nor sat in court, nor walked abroad but in spotless white. His stengah-shifter, with its bright brass buttons, fitted him very tightly and displayed the shocking fact that, young though he was, he had a round and protruding belly. His good-humoured face shone with sweat and he constantly fanned himself with a palm-leaf fan.

But in his house Mr. Gruyter preferred to wear nothing but a sarong and then with his white podgy little body he looked like a fat funny boy of sixteen. He was an early riser and his breakfast was always ready for him at six. It never varied. It consisted of a slice of papaia, three cold fried eggs, Edam cheese, sliced thin, and a cup of black coffee. When he had eaten it, he smoked a large Dutch cigar, read the papers if he had not read them through and through already, and then dressed to go down to his office.

One morning while he was thus occupied his head boy came into his bedroom and told him that Tuan Jones wanted to know if he could see him. Mr. Gruyter was standing in front of a looking-glass. He had his trousers on and was admiring his smooth chest. He arched his back in order to throw it out and throw in his belly and with a good deal of satisfaction gave his breast three or four resounding slaps. It was a manly chest. When the boy brought the message he looked at his own eyes in the mirror and exchanged a slightly ironic smile with them. He asked himself what the devil his visitor could want. Evert Gruyter spoke English, Dutch and Malay with equal facility, but he thought in Dutch. He liked to do this. It seemed to him a pleasantly ribald language.

"Ask the Tuan to wait and say I shall come directly." He put on his tunic, over his naked body, buttoned it up, and strutted into the sitting-room. The Rev. Owen Jones got up.

"Good-morning, Mr. Jones," said the Controleur. "Have you come in to have a peg with me before I start my day's work?"

Mr. Jones did not smile.

"I've come to see you upon a very distressing matter, Mr. Gruyter," he answered.

The Controleur was not disconcerted by his visitor's gravity nor depressed by his words. His little blue eyes beamed amiably.

"Sit down, my dear fellow, and have a cigar."

Mr. Gruyter knew quite well that the Rev. Owen Jones neither drank nor smoked, but it tickled something prankish in his nature to offer him a drink and a smoke whenever they met. Mr. Jones shook his head.

Mr. Jones was in charge of the Baptist Mission on the Alas Islands. His headquarters were at Baru, the largest of them, with the greatest population, but he had meeting-houses under the care of native helpers in several other islands of the group. He was a tall, thin melancholy man, with a long face, sallow and drawn, of about forty. His brown hair was already white on the temples and it receded from the forehead. This gave him a look of somewhat vacuous intellectuality. Mr. Gruyter both disliked and respected him. He disliked him because he was narrow-minded and dogmatic. Himself a cheerful pagan who liked the good things of the flesh and was determined to get as many of them as his circumstances permitted, he had no patience with a man who disapproved of them all. He thought the customs of the country suited its inhabitants and had no

patience with the missionary's energetic efforts to destroy
a way of life that for centuries had worked very well. He
respected him because he was honest, zealous and good. Mr.
Jones, an Australian of Welsh descent, was the only qualified
doctor in the group and it was a comfort to know that if you
fell ill you need not rely only on a Chinese practitioner,
and none knew better than the Controleur how useful to all
Mr. Jones's skill had been and with what charity he had
given it. On the occasion of an epidemic of influenza the
missionary had done the work of ten men and no storm short
of a typhoon could prevent him from crossing to one
island or another if his help was needed.

He lived with his sister in a little white house about half a
mile from the village and when the Controleur had arrived,
came on board to meet him and begged him to stay till he
could get his own house in order. The Controleur had accepted and soon saw for himself with what simplicity the
couple lived. It was more than he could stand. Tea at three
sparse meals a day and when he lit his cigar Mr. Jones
politely but firmly asked him to be good enough not to
smoke since both his sister and he strongly disapproved of
it. In twenty-four hours Mr. Gruyter moved into his own
house. He fled, with panic in his heart, as though from a
plague-stricken city. The Controleur was fond of a joke and
he liked to laugh; to be with a man who took your nonsense
in deadly earnest and never even smiled at your best story
was more than flesh and blood could stand. The Rev. Owen
Jones was a worthy man, but as a companion he was impossible. His sister was worse. Neither had a sense of
humour, but whereas the missionary was of a melancholy
turn, doing his duty so conscientiously, with the obvious
conviction that everything in the world was hopeless, Miss
Jones was resolutely cheerful. She grimly looked on the
bright side of things. With the ferocity of an avenging angel
she sought out the good in her fellow men. Miss Jones taught
in the mission school and helped her brother in his medical
work. When he did operations she gave the anæsthetic and

was matron, dresser and nurse of the tiny hospital which on his own initiative Mr. Jones had added to the mission. But the Controleur was an obstinate little fellow and he never lost his capacity of extracting amusement from the Rev. Owen's dour struggle with the infirmities of human nature, and Miss Jones's ruthless optimism. He had to get his fun where he could. The Dutch boats came in three times in two months for a few hours and then he could have a good old crack with the captain and chief engineer, and once in a blue moon a pearling lugger came in from Thursday Island or Port Darwin and for two or three days he had a grand time. They were rough fellows, the pearlers, for the most part, but they were full of guts, and they had plenty of liquor on board, and good stories to tell, and the Controleur had them up to his house and gave them a fine dinner and the party was only counted a success if they were all too drunk to get back on the lugger again that night. But besides the missionary the only white man who lived on Baru was Ginger Ted, and he, of course, was a disgrace to civilization. There was not a single thing to be said in his favour. He cast discredit on the white race. All the same, but for Ginger Ted the Controleur sometimes thought he would find life on the island of Baru almost more than he could bear.

Oddly enough it was on account of this scamp that Mr. Jones, when he should have been instructing the pagan young in the mysteries of the Baptist faith, was paying Mr. Gruyter this early visit.

"Sit down, Mr. Jones," said the Controleur. "What can I do for you?"

"Well, I've come to see you about the man they call Ginger Ted. What are you going to do now?"

"Why, what's happened?"

"Haven't you heard? I thought the sergeant would have told you."

"I don't encourage the members of my staff to come to my private house unless the matter is urgent," said the Controleur rather grandly. "I am unlike you, Mr. Jones, I only work in order to have leisure and I like to enjoy my leisure without disturbance."

But Mr. Jones did not care much for small talk and he was not interested in general reflections.

"There was a disgraceful row in one of the Chinese shops last night. Ginger Ted wrecked the place and half killed a Chinaman."

"Drunk again, I suppose," said the Controleur placidly.

"Naturally. When is he anything else? They sent for the police and he assaulted the sergeant. They had to have six men to get him to the gaol."

"He's a hefty fellow," said the Controleur.

"I suppose you'll send him to Macassar."

Evert Gruyter returned the missionary's outraged look with a merry twinkle. He was no fool and he knew already what Mr. Jones was up to. It gave him considerable amusement to tease him a little.

"Fortunately my powers are wide enough to enable me to deal with the situation myself," he answered.

"You have power to deport anyone you like, Mr. Gruyter, and I'm sure it would save a lot of trouble if you got rid of the man altogether."

"I have the power of course, but I am sure you would be the last person to wish me to use it arbitrarily."

"Mr. Gruyter, the man's presence here is a public scandal. He's never sober from morning till night; it's notorious that he has relations with one native woman after another."

"That is an interesting point, Mr. Jones. I had always heard that alcoholic excess, though it stimulated sexual desire, prevented its gratification. What you tell me about Ginger Ted does not seem to bear out this theory."

The missionary flushed a dull red.

"These are physiological matters which at the moment I have no wish to go into," he said, frigidly. "The behaviour of this man does incalculable damage to the prestige of the white race, and his example seriously hampers the efforts that are made in other quarters to induce the people of these islands to lead a less vicious life. He's an out and out bad lot."

"Pardon my asking, but have you made any attempts to reform him?"

"When he first drifted here I did my best to get in touch with him. He repelled all my advances. When there was that first trouble I went to him and talked to him straight from the shoulder. He swore at me."

"No one has a greater appreciation than I of the excellent work that you and other missionaries do on these islands, but are you sure that you always exercise your calling with all the tact possible?"

The Controleur was rather pleased with this phrase. It was extremely courteous and yet contained a reproof that he thought worth administering. The missionary looked at him gravely. His sad brown eyes were full of sincerity.

"Did Jesus exercise tact when he took a whip and drove the money-changers from the Temple? No, Mr. Gruyter. Tact is the subterfuge the lax avail themselves of to avoid doing their duty."

Mr. Jones's remark made the Controleur feel suddenly that he wanted a bottle of beer. The missionary leaned forward earnestly.

"Mr. Gruyter, you know this man's transgressions just as well as I do. It's unnecessary for me to remind you of them. There are no excuses for him. Now he really has overstepped the limit. You'll never have a better chance than this. I beg you to use the power you have and turn him out once for all."

The Controleur's eyes twinkled more brightly than ever. He was having a lot of fun. He reflected that human beings were much more amusing when you did not feel called upon in dealing with them to allot praise or blame.

"But Mr. Jones, do I understand you right? Are you asking me to give you an assurance to deport this man before I've heard the evidence against him and listened to his defence?"

"I don't know what his defence can be."

The Controleur rose from his chair and really he managed to get quite a little dignity into his five feet four inches.

"I am here to administer justice according to the laws of the Dutch Government. Permit me to tell you that I am exceedingly surprised that you should attempt to influence me in my judicial functions."

The missionary was a trifle flustered. It had never occurred to him that this little whipper-snapper of a boy, ten years younger than himself, would dream of adopting such an attitude. He opened his mouth to explain and apologize, but the Controleur raised a podgy little hand.

"It is time for me to go to my office, Mr. Jones. I wish you good-morning."

The missionary, taken aback, bowed and without another word walked out of the room. He would have been surprised to see what the Controleur did when his back was turned. A broad grin broke on his lips and he put his thumb to his nose and cocked a snook at the Rev. Owen Jones.

A few minutes later he went down to his office. His head clerk, who was a Dutch half-caste, gave him his version of the previous night's row. It agreed pretty well with Mr. Jones's. The Court was sitting that day.

"Will you take Ginger Ted first, sir?" asked the clerk.

"I see no reason to do that. There are two or three cases held over from the last sitting. I will take him in his proper order."

"I thought perhaps as he was a white man you would like to see him privately, sir."

"The majesty of the law knows no difference between white and coloured, my friend," said Mr. Gruyter, somewhat pompously.

The Court was a big square room with wooden benches on which, crowded together, sat natives of all kinds, Polynesians, Bugis, Chinese, Malays, and they all rose when a door was opened and a sergeant announced the arrival of the controleur. He entered with his clerk and took his place on a little dais at a table of varnished pitch pine. Behind him was a large engraving of Queen Wilhelmina. He dispatched half a dozen cases and then Ginger Ted was brought in. He stood in the dock, handcuffed, with a warder on either side of him. The Controleur looked at him with a grave face, but he could not keep the amusement out of his eyes.

Ginger Ted was suffering from a hangover. He swayed a little as he stood and his eyes were vacant. He was a man still young, thirty perhaps, of somewhat over the middle height, rather fat, with a bloated red face and a shock of curly red hair. He had not come out of the tussle unscathed. He had a black eye and his mouth was cut and swollen. He wore khaki shorts, very dirty and ragged, and his singlet had been almost torn off his back. A great rent showed the thick mat of red hair with which his chest was covered, but showed also the astonishing whiteness of his skin. The Controleur looked at the charge sheet. He called the evidence. When he had heard it, when he had seen the Chinaman whose head Ginger Ted had broken with a bottle, when he had heard the agitated story of the sergeant who had been knocked flat when he tried to arrest him, when he had listened to the talk of the havoc wrought by Ginger Ted who in his drunken fury had smashed everything he could lay hands on, he turned and addressed the accused in English.

"Well, Ginger, what have you got to say for yourself?"

"I was blind. I don't remember a thing about it. If they say I half killed 'im I suppose I did. I'll pay the damage if they'll give me time."

"You will, Ginger," said the Controleur, "but it's me who'll give you time."

He looked at Ginger Ted for a minute in silence. He was an unappetizing object. A man who had gone completely to pieces. He was horrible. It made you shudder to look at him and if Mr. Jones had not been so officious, at that moment the Controleur would certainly have ordered him to be deported.

"You've been a trouble ever since you came to the islands, Ginger. You're a disgrace. You're incorrigibly idle. You've been picked up in the street dead drunk time and time again. You've kicked up row after row. You're hopeless. I told you the last time you were brought here that if you were arrested

again I should deal with you severely. You've gone the
limit this time and you're for it. I sentence you to six months'
hard labour."

"Me?"

"You."

"By God, I'll kill you when I come out."

He burst into a string of oaths both filthy and blasphemous. Mr. Gruyter listened scornfully. You can swear much
better in Dutch than in English and there was nothing that
Ginger Ted said that he could not have effectively capped.

"Be quiet," he ordered. "You make me tired."

The Controleur repeated his sentence in Malay and the
prisoner was led struggling away.

Mr. Gruyter sat down to tiffin in high good humour. It was
astonishing how amusing life could be if you exercised a little
ingenuity. There were people in Amsterdam, and even in Batavia and Surabaya, who looked upon his island home as a place
of exile. They little knew how agreeable it was and what
fun he could extract from unpromising material. They asked
him whether he did not miss the club and the races and
the cinema, the dances that were held once a week at the
Casino and the society of Dutch ladies. Not at all. He liked
comfort. The substantial furniture of the room in which he
sat had a satisfying solidity. He liked reading French novels
of a frivolous nature and he appreciated the sensation of reading one after the other without the uneasiness occasioned by
the thought that he was wasting his time. It seemed to
him a great luxury to waste time. When his young man's
fancy turned to thoughts of love his head boy brought to the
house a little dark-skinned bright-eyed creature in a sarong.
He took care to form no connection of a permanent nature.
He thought that change kept the heart young. He enjoyed
freedom and was not weighed down by a sense of responsibility. He did not mind the heat. It made a sluice over with
cold water half a dozen times a day a pleasure that had almost
an æsthetic quality. He played the piano. He wrote letters
to his friends in Holland. He felt no need for the conversation of intellectual persons. He liked a good laugh, but he

could get that out of a fool just as well as out of a professor of philosophy. He had a notion that he was a very wise little man.

Like all good Dutchmen in the Far East he began his lunch with a small glass of Hollands gin. It has a musty acrid flavour, and the taste for it must be acquired, but Mr. Gruyter preferred it to any cocktail. When he drank it he felt besides that he was upholding the traditions of his race. Then he had *rystafel*. He had it every day. He heaped a soup-plate high with rice, and then, his three boys waiting on him, helped himself to the curry that one handed him, to the fried egg that another brought, and to the condiment presented by the third. Then each one brought another dish, of bacon, or bananas, or pickled fish, and presently his plate was piled high in a huge pyramid. He stirred it all together and began to eat. He ate slowly and with relish. He drank a bottle of beer.

He did not think while he was eating. His attention was applied to the mass in front of him and he consumed it with a happy concentration. It never palled on him. And when he had emptied the great plate it was a compensation to think that next day he would have *rystafel* again. He grew tired of it as little as the rest of us grow tired of bread. He finished his beer and lit his cigar. The boy brought him a cup of coffee. He leaned back in his chair then and allowed himself the luxury of reflection.

It tickled him to have sentenced Ginger Ted to the richly deserved punishment of six months' hard labour, and he smiled when he thought of him working on the roads with the other prisoners. It would have been silly to deport from the island the one man with whom he could occasionally have a heart-to-heart talk, and besides, the satisfaction it would have given the missionary would have been bad for that gentleman's character. Ginger Ted was a scamp and a scallywag, but the Controleur had a kindly feeling for him. They had drunk many a bottle of beer in one another's company and when the pearl fishers from Port Darwin came in and they all made a night of it, they had got gloriously tight together. The Controleur liked the reckless way in which Ginger Ted squandered the priceless treasure of life.

Ginger Ted had wandered in one day on the ship that was going up from Merauke to Macassar. The captain did not know how he had found his way there, but he had travelled steerage with the natives, and he stopped off at the Alas Islands because he liked the look of them. Mr. Gruyter had a suspicion that their attraction consisted perhaps in their being under the Dutch flag and so out of British jurisdiction. But his papers were in order, so there was no reason why he should not stay. He said that he was buying pearl-shell for an Australian firm, but it soon appeared that his commercial undertakings were not serious. Drink, indeed, took up so much of his time that he had little left over for other pursuits. He was in receipt of two pounds a week, paid monthly, which came regularly to him from England. The Controleur guessed that this sum was paid only so long as he kept well away from the persons who sent it. It was anyway too small to permit him any liberty of movement. Ginger Ted was reticent. The Controleur discovered that he was an Englishman, this he learnt from his passport, which described him as Edward Wilson, and that he had been in Australia. But why he had left England and what he had done in Australia he had no notion. Nor could he ever quite tell to what class Ginger Ted belonged. When you saw him in a filthy singlet and a pair of ragged trousers, a battered topi on his head, with the pearl fishers and heard his conversation, coarse, obscene and illiterate, you thought he must be a sailor before the mast who had deserted his ship, or a labourer, but when you saw his handwriting you were surprised to find that it was that of a man not without at least some education, and on occasion when you got him alone, if he had had a few drinks but was not yet drunk, he would talk of matters that neither a sailor nor a labourer would have been likely to know anything about. The Controleur had a certain sensitiveness and he realized that Ginger Ted did no speak to him as an inferior to a superior but as an equal. Most of his remittance was mortgaged before he received it.

and the Chinamen to whom he owed money were standing at his elbow when the monthly letter was delivered to him, but with what was left he proceeded to get drunk. It was then that he made trouble, for when drunk he grew violent and was then likely to commit acts that brought him into the hands of the police. Hitherto Mr. Gruyter had contented himself with keeping him in gaol till he was sober and giving him a talking to. When he was out of money he cadged what drink he could from anyone who would give it him. Rum, brandy, arak, it was all the same to him. Two or three times Mr. Gruyter had got him work on plantations run by Chinese in one or other of the islands, but he could not stick to it, and in a few weeks was back again at Baru on the beach. It was a miracle how he kept body and soul together. He had, of course, a way with him. He picked up the various dialects spoken on the islands, and knew how to make the natives laugh. They despised him, but they respected his physical strength, and they liked his company. He was as a result never at a loss for a meal or a mat to sleep on. The strange thing was, and it was this that chiefly outraged the Rev. Owen Jones, that he could do anything he liked with a woman. The Controleur could not imagine what it was they saw in him. He was casual with them and rather brutal. He took what they gave him, but seemed incapable of gratitude. He used them for his pleasure and then flung them indifferently away. Once or twice this had got him into trouble, and Mr. Gruyter had had to sentence an angry father for sticking a knife in Ginger Ted's back one night, and a Chinese woman had sought to poison herself by swallowing opium because he had deserted her. Once Mr. Jones came to the Controleur in a great state because the beachcomber had seduced one of his converts. The Controleur agreed that it was very deplorable, but could only advise Mr. Jones to keep a sharp eye on these young persons. The Controleur liked it less when he discovered that a girl whom he fancied a good deal himself and had been seeing for several weeks had all the time been according her favours also to Ginger Ted. When he thought of this particular incident he smiled again at the thought of Ginger Ted doing six months' hard labour. It is seldom in this life that in the process of doing your bounden duty you can get back on a fellow who has played you a dirty trick.

A few days later Mr. Gruyter was taking a walk, partly for exercise and partly to see that some job he wanted done was being duly proceeded with, when he passed a gang of prisoners working under the charge of a warder. Among them he saw Ginger Ted. He wore the prison sarong, a dingy tunic called in Malay a baju, and his own battered topi. They were repairing the road, and Ginger Ted was wielding a heavy pick. The way was narrow and the Controleur saw that he must pass within a foot of him. He remembered his threats. He knew that Ginger Ted was a man of violent passion and the language he had used in the dock made it plain that he had not seen what a good joke it was of the Controleur's to sentence him to six months' hard labour. If Ginger Ted suddenly attacked him with the pick, nothing on God's earth could save him. It was true that the warder would immediately shoot him down, but meanwhile the Controleur's head would be bashed in. It was with a funny little feeling in the pit of his stomach that Mr. Gruyter walked through the gang of prisoners. They were working in pairs a few feet from one another. He set his mind on neither hastening his pace nor slackening it. As he passed Ginger Ted, the man swung his pick into the ground and looked up at the Controleur and as he caught his eye winked. The Controleur checked the smile that rose to his lips and with official dignity strode on. But that wink, so lusciously full of sardonic humour, filled him with satisfaction. If he had been the Caliph of Bagdad instead of a junior official in the Dutch Civil Service, he would forthwith have released Ginger Ted, sent slaves to bathe and perfume him, and having clothed him in a golden robe entertained him to a sumptuous repast.

Ginger Ted was an exemplary prisoner and in a month or two the Controleur, having occasion to send a gang to do some work on one of the outlying islands, included him in it.

There was no gaol there, so the ten fellows he sent, under the charge of a warder, were billeted on the natives and after their day's work lived like free men. The job was sufficient to take up the rest of Ginger Ted's sentence. The Controleur saw him before he left.

"Look here, Ginger," he said to him, "here's ten guilder for you so that you can buy yourself tobacco when you're gone."

"Couldn't you make it a bit more? There's eight pounds a month coming in regularly."

"I think that's enough. I'll keep the letters that come for you, and when you get back you'll have a tidy sum. You'll have enough to take you anywhere you want to go."

"I'm very comfortable here," said Ginger Ted.

"Well, the day you come back, clean yourself up and come over to my house. We'll have a bottle of beer together."

"That'll be fine. I guess I'll be ready for a good crack then."

Now chance steps in. The island to which Ginger Ted had been sent was called Maputiti, and like all the rest of them it was rocky, heavily wooded and surrounded by a reef. There was a village among coconuts on the sea-shore opposite the opening of the reef and another village on a brackish lake in the middle of the island. Of this some of the inhabitants had been converted to Christianity. Communication with Baru was effected by a launch that touched at the various islands at irregular intervals. It carried passengers and produce. But the villagers were seafaring folk, and if they had to communicate urgently with Baru, manned a prahu and sailed the fifty miles or so that separated them from it. It happened that when Ginger Ted's sentence had but another fortnight to run the Christian headman of the village on the lake was taken suddenly ill. The native remedies availed him nothing and he writhed in agony. Messengers were sent to Baru imploring the missionary's help; but as ill luck would have it Mr. Jones was suffering at the moment from an attack of malaria. He was in bed and unable to move. He talked the matter over with his sister.

"It sounds like acute appendicitis," he told her.

"You can't go, Owen," she said.

"I can't let the man die."

Mr. Jones had a temperature of a hundred and four. His head was aching like mad. He had been delirious at night. His eyes were shining strangely and his sister felt that he was holding on to his wits by a sheer effort of will.

"You couldn't operate in the state you're in."

"No, I couldn't. Then Hassan must go."

Hassan was the dispenser.

"You couldn't trust Hassan. He'd never dare to do an operation on his own responsibility. And they'd never let him. I'll go. Hassan can stay here and look after you."

"You can't remove an appendix?"

"Why not? I've seen you do it. I've done lots of minor operations."

Mr. Jones felt he didn't quite understand what she was saying.

"Is the launch in?"

"No, it's gone to one of the islands. But I can go in the prahu the men came in."

"You? I wasn't thinking of you. You can't go."

"I'm going, Owen."

"Going where?" he said.

She saw that his mind was wandering already. She put her hand soothingly on his dry forehead. She gave him a dose of medicine. He muttered something and she realized that he did not know where he was. Of course she was anxious about him, but she knew that his illness was not dangerous, and she could leave him safely to the mission boy who was helping her nurse him and to the native dispenser. She slipped out of the room. She put her toilet things, a night-dress, and a change of clothes into a bag. A little chest with surgical instruments, bandages and antiseptic dressings was kept always ready. She gave them to the two natives who had come over from Maputiti, and telling the dispenser what she was going to do gave him instructions to inform her brother when he was able to listen. Above all he was not to be anxious about her. She put on her topi and sallied forth.

The mission was about half a mile from the village. She walked quickly. At the end of the jetty the prahu was waiting. Six men manned it. She took her place in the stern and they set off with a rapid stroke. Within the reef the sea was calm, but when they crossed the bar they came upon a long swell. But this was not the first journey of the sort Miss Jones had taken and she was confident in the sea-worthiness of the boat she was in. It was noon and the sun beat down from a sultry sky. The only thing that harassed her was that they could not arrive before dark, and if she found it necessary to operate at once she could count only on the light of hurricane lamps.

Miss Jones was a woman of hard on forty. Nothing in her appearance would have prepared you for such determination as she had just shown. She had an odd drooping gracefulness, which suggested that she might be swayed by every breeze; it was almost an affectation; and it made the strength of char-acter which you soon discovered in her seem positively mon-strous. She was flat-chested, tall and extremely thin. She had a long sallow face and she was much afflicted with prickly heat. Her lank brown hair was drawn back straight from her fore-head. She had rather small eyes, grey in colour, and be-cause they were somewhat too close they gave her face a shrewish look. Her nose was long and thin and a trifle red. She suffered a good deal from indigestion. But this infirmity availed nothing against her ruthless determination to look upon the bright side of things. Firmly persuaded that the world was evil and men unspeakably vicious, she extracted any little piece of decency she could find in them with the modest pride with which a conjurer extracts a rabbit from a hat. She was quick, resourceful and competent. When she arrived on the island she saw that there was not a moment to lose if she was to save the headman's life. Under the greatest dif-ficulties, showing a native how to give the anæsthetic, she operated, and for the next three days nursed the patient with anxious assiduity. Everything went very well and she realized that her brother could not have made a better job of it. She waited long enough to take out the stitches and then prepared to go home. She could flatter herself that she had not wasted her time. She had given medical attention to such as needed it, she had strengthened the small Christian community in its faith, admonished such as were lax and cast the good seed in places where it might be hoped under divine providence to take root.

The launch, coming from one of the other islands, put in somewhat late in the afternoon, but it was full moon and they expected to reach Baru before midnight. They brought her things down to the wharf and the people who were seeing her off stood about repeating their thanks. Quite a little crowd collected. The launch was loaded with sacks of copra, but Miss Jones was used to its strong smell and it did not incommode her. She made herself as comfortable a place to sit in as she could, and waiting for the launch to start, chatted with her grateful flock. She was the only passenger. Suddenly a group of natives emerged from the trees that embowered the little village on the lagoon and she saw that among them was a white man. He wore a prison sarong and a baju. He had long red hair. She at once recognized Ginger Ted. A policeman was with him. They shook hands and Ginger Ted shook hands with the villagers who accompanied him. They bore bundles of fruit and a jar which Miss Jones guessed contained native spirit, and these they put in the launch. She discovered to her surprise that Ginger Ted was coming with her. His term was up and instructions had arrived that he was to be returned to Baru in the launch. He gave her a glance, but did not nod—indeed Miss Jones turned away her head—and stepped in. The mechanic started his engine and in a moment they were jug-jugging through the channel in the lagoon. Ginger Ted clambered on to a pile of sacks and lit a cigarette.

Miss Jones ignored him. Of course she knew him very well. Her heart sank when she thought that he was going to be once more in Baru, creating a scandal and drinking, a peril to the women and a thorn in the flesh of all decent people. She knew the steps her brother had taken to have him deported and she had no patience with the Controleur, who would not see a duty that stared him so plainly in the face. When they had crossed the bar and were in the open sea Ginger Ted took the stopper out of the jar of arak and putting his mouth to it took a long pull. Then he handed the jar to the two mechanics who formed the crew. One was a middle-aged man and the other a youth.

"I do not wish you to drink anything while we are on the journey," said Miss Jones sternly to the elder one.

He smiled at her and drank.

"A little arak can do no one any harm," he answered. He passed the jar to his companion, who drank also.

"If you drink again I shall complain to the Controleur," said Miss Jones.

The elder man said something she could not understand, but which she suspected was very rude, and passed the jar back to Ginger Ted. They went along for an hour or more. The sea was like glass and the sun set radiantly. It set behind one of the islands and for a few minutes changed it into a mystic city of the skies. Miss Jones turned round to watch it and her heart was filled with gratitude for the beauty of the world.

"And only man is vile," she quoted to herself.

They went due east. In the distance was a little island which she knew they passed close by. It was uninhabited. A rocky islet thickly grown with virgin forest. The boatman lit his lamps. The night fell and immediately the sky was thick with stars. The moon had not yet risen. Suddenly there was a slight jar and the launch began to vibrate strangely. The engine rattled. The head mechanic, calling to his mate to take the helm, crept under the housing. They seemed to be going more slowly. The engine stopped. She asked the youth what was the matter, but he did not know. Ginger Ted got down from the top of the copra sacks and slipped under the housing. When he reappeared she would have liked to ask him what had happened, but her dignity prevented her. She sat still and occupied herself with her thoughts. There was a long swell and the launch rolled slightly. The mechanic emerged once more into view and started the engine. Though it rattled like mad they began to move. The launch vibrated from stem to stern. They went very slowly. Evidently something was amiss, but Miss Jones was exasperated rather than alarmed. The launch was supposed to do six knots, but now it was just crawling along; at that rate they would not get into Baru till long, long after midnight. The mechanic, still busy under the housing, shouted out something to the man at the helm. They spoke in Bugi, of which Miss Jones knew very little. But after a while she noticed that they had changed their course and seemed to be heading for the little uninhabited island a good deal to the lee of which they should have passed.

"Where are we going?" she asked the helmsman with sudden misgiving.

He pointed to the islet. She got up and went to the housing and called to the man to come out.

"You're not going there? Why? What's the matter?"

"I can't get to Baru," he said.

"But you must. I insist. I order you to go to Baru."

The man shrugged his shoulders. He turned his back on her and slipped once more under the housing. Then Ginger Ted addressed her.

"One of the blades of the propeller has broken off. He thinks he can get as far as that island. We shall have to stay the night there and he'll put on a new propeller in the morning when the tide's out."

"I can't spend the night on an uninhabited island with three men," she cried.

"A lot of women would jump at it."

"I insist on going to Baru. Whatever happens we must get there to-night."

"Don't get excited, old girl. We've got to beach the boat to put a new propeller on, and we shall be all right on the island."

"How dare you speak to me like that! I think you're very insolent."

"You'll be O.K. We've got plenty of grub and we'll have a

snack when we land. You have a drop of arak and you'll feel like a house on fire."

"You're an impertinent man. If you don't go to Baru I'll have you all put in prison."

"We're not going to Baru. We can't. We're going to that island and if you don't like it you can get out and swim."

"Oh, you'll pay for this."

"Shut up, you old cow," said Ginger Ted.

Miss Jones gave a gasp of anger. But she controlled herself. Even out there, in the middle of the ocean, she had too much dignity to bandy words with that vile wretch. The launch, the engine rattling horribly, crawled on. It was pitch dark now, and she could no longer see the island they were making for. Miss Jones, deeply incensed, sat with lips tight shut and a frown on her brow; she was not used to being crossed. Then the moon rose and she could see the bulk of Ginger Ted sprawling on the top of the piled sacks of copra. The glimmer of his cigarette was strangely sinister. Now the island was vaguely outlined against the sky. They reached it and the boatman ran the launch on to the beach. Suddenly Miss Jones gave a gasp. The truth had dawned on her and her anger changed to fear. Her heart beat violently. She shook in every limb. She felt dreadfully faint. She saw it all. Was the broken propeller a put-up job or was it an accident? She could not be certain; anyhow, she knew that Ginger Ted would seize the opportunity. Ginger Ted would rape her. She knew his character. He was mad about women. That was what he had done, practically, to the girl at the mission, such a good little thing she was and an excellent sempstress; they would have prosecuted him for that and he would have been sentenced to years of imprisonment only very unfortunately the innocent child had gone back to him several times and indeed had only complained of his ill usage when he left her for somebody else. They had gone to the Controleur about it, but he had refused to take any steps, saying in that coarse way of his that even if what the girl said was true, it didn't look very much as though it had been

an altogether unpleasant experience. Ginger Ted was a
scoundrel. And she was a white woman. What chance was
there that he would spare her? None. She knew men. But
she must pull herself together. She must keep her wits about
her. She must have courage. She was determined to sell her
virtue dearly, and if he killed her—well, she would rather
die than yield. And if she died she would rest in the arms
of Jesus. For a moment a great light blinded her eyes and
she saw the mansions of her Heavenly Father. They were
a grand and sumptuous mixture of a picture palace and a
railway station. The mechanics and Ginger Ted jumped out
of the launch and, waist deep in water, gathered round the
broken propeller. She took advantage of their preoccupation
to get her case of surgical instruments out of the box. She
took out the four scalpels it contained and secreted them in
her clothing. If Ginger Ted touched her she would not
hesitate to plunge a scalpel in his heart.

"Now then, miss, you'd better get out," said Ginger Ted.
"You'll be better off on the beach than in the boat."

She thought so too. At least there she would have
freedom of action. Without a word she clambered over the
copra sacks. He offered her his hand.

"I don't want your help," she said coldly.

"You can go to hell," he answered.

It was a little difficult to get out of the boat without
showing her legs, but by the exercise of considerable ingenuity she managed it.

"Damned lucky we've got something to eat. We'll make a
fire and then you'd better have a snack and a nip of arak."

"I want nothing. I only want to be left alone."

"It won't hurt me if you go hungry."

She did not answer. She walked, with head erect, along
the beach. She held the largest scalpel in her closed fist. The
moon allowed her to see where she was going. She looked
for a place to hide. The thick forest came down to the very
edge of the beach; but, afraid of its darkness (after all, she
was but a woman), she dared not plunge into its depth. She
did not know what animals lurked there or what dangerous

snakes. Besides, her instinct told her that it was better to
keep those three bad men in sight; then if they came towards
her she would be prepared. Presently she found a little hollow.
She looked round. They seemed to be occupied with their
own affairs and they could not see her. She slipped in. There
was a rock between them and her so that she was hidden
from them and yet could watch them. She saw them go to
and from the boat carrying things. She saw them build a fire.
It lit them luridly and she saw them sit around it and eat, and
she saw the jar of arak passed from one to the other. They
were all going to get drunk. What would happen to her
then? It might be that she could cope with Ginger Ted,
though his strength terrified her, but against three she would
be powerless. A mad idea came to her to go to Ginger Ted
and fall on her knees before him and beg him to spare
her. He must have some spark of decent feeling in him
and she had always been so convinced that there was good
even in the worst of men. He must have had a mother. Perhaps he had a sister. Ah, but how could you appeal to a man
blinded with lust and drunk with arak? She began to feel
terribly weak. She was afraid she was going to cry. That
would never do. She needed all her self-control. She bit
her lip. She watched them, like a tiger watching his prey;
no, not like that, like a lamb watching three hungry wolves.
She saw them put more wood on the fire and Ginger Ted,
in his sarong, silhouetted by the flames. Perhaps after he had
had his will of her he would pass her on to the others.
How could she go back to her brother when such a thing
had happened to her? Of course he would be sympathetic,
but would he ever feel quite the same to her again? It
would break his heart. And perhaps he would think that she
ought to have resisted more. For his sake perhaps it would
be better if she said nothing about it, naturally the men
would say nothing. It would mean twenty years in prison
for them. But then supposing she had a baby. Miss Jones
instinctively clenched her hands with horror and nearly cut
herself with the scalpel. Of course it would only infuriate
them if she resisted.

"What shall I do?" she cried. "What have I done to deserve this?"

She flung herself down on her knees and prayed to God to save her. She prayed long and earnestly. She reminded God that she was a virgin and just mentioned, in case it had slipped the divine memory, how much St. Paul had valued that excellent state. And then she peeped round the rock again. The three men appeared to be smoking and the fire was dying down. Now was the time that Ginger Ted's lewd thoughts might be expected to turn to the woman who was at his mercy. She smothered a cry, for suddenly he got up and walked in her direction. She felt all her muscles grow taut, and though her heart was beating furiously she clenched the scalpel firmly in her hand. But it was for another purpose that Ginger Ted had got up. Miss Jones blushed and looked away. He strolled slowly back to the others and sitting down again raised the jar of arak to his lips. Miss Jones, crouching behind the rock, watched with straining eyes. The conversation round the fire grew less and presently she divined, rather than saw, that the two natives wrapped themselves in blankets and composed themselves to slumber. She understood. This was the moment Ginger Ted had been waiting for. When they were fast asleep he would get up cautiously and without a sound, in order not to wake the others, creep stealthily towards her. Was it that he was unwilling to share her with them or did he know that his deed was so dastardly that he did not wish them to know of it? After all, he was a white man and she was a white women. He could not have sunk so low as to allow her to suffer the violence of natives. But his plan, which was so obvious to her, had given her an idea; when she saw him coming she would scream, she would scream so loudly that it would wake the two mechanics. She remembered now that the elder, though he had only one eye, had a kind face. But Ginger Ted did not move. She was feeling terribly tired. She began to fear that she would not have the strength now to resist him. She had gone through too much. She closed her eyes for a minute.

When she opened them it was broad daylight. She must have fallen asleep and, so shattered was she by emotion, have slept till long after dawn. It gave her quite a turn. She sought to rise, but something caught in her legs. She looked and found that she was covered with two empty copra sacks. Someone had come in the night and put them over her. Ginger Ted. She gave a little scream. The horrible thought flashed through her mind that he had outraged her in her sleep. No. It was impossible. And yet he had had her at his mercy. Defenceless. And he had spared her. She blushed furiously. She raised herself to her feet, feeling a little stiff, and arranged her disordered dress. The scalpel had fallen from her hand and she picked it up. She took the two copra sacks and emerged from her hiding-place. She walked towards the boat. It was floating in the shallow water of the lagoon.

"Come on, Miss Jones," said Ginger Ted. "We've finished. I was just going to wake you up."

She could not look at him, but she felt herself as red as a turkey cock.

"Have a banana?" he said.

Without a word she took it. She was very hungry, and ate it with relish.

"Step on this rock and you'll be able to get in without wetting your feet."

Miss Jones felt as though she could sink into the ground with shame, but she did as he told her. He took hold of her arm—good heavens, his hand was like an iron vice, never, never could she have struggled with him—and helped her into the launch. The mechanic started the engine and they slid out of the lagoon. In three hours they were at Baru.

That evening, having been officially released, Ginger Ted went to the Controleur's house. He wore no longer the prison uniform, but the ragged singlet and the khaki shorts in which he had been arrested. He had had his hair cut and it fitted his head now like a little curly red cap. He was thinner. He had lost his bloated flabbiness and looked younger and better. Mr. Gruyter, a friendly grin on his round face, shook hands

with him and asked him to sit down. The boy brought two
bottles of beer.

"I'm glad to see you hadn't forgotten my invitation, Ginger," said the Controleur.

"Not likely. I've been looking forward to this for six
months."

"Here's luck, Ginger Ted."

"Same to you, Controleur."

They emptied their glasses and the Controleur clapped his
hands. The boy brought two more bottles.

"Well, you don't bear me any malice for the sentence I
gave you, I hope."

"No bloody fear. I was mad for a minute, but I got over
it. I didn't have half a bad time, you know. Nice lot of girls
on that island, Controleur. You ought to give 'em a look
over one of these days."

"You're a bad lot, Ginger."

"Terrible."

"Good beer, isn't it?"

"Fine."

"Let's have some more."

Ginger Ted's remittance had been arriving every month
and the Controleur now had fifty pounds for him. When
the damage he had done to the Chinaman's shop was paid for
there would still be over thirty.

"That's quite a lot of money, Ginger. You ought to do
something useful with it."

"I mean to," answered Ginger. "Spend it."

The Controleur sighed.

"Well, that's what money's for, I guess."

The Controleur gave his guest the news. Not much had
happened during the last six months. Time on the Alas
Islands did not matter very much and the rest of the world
did not matter at all.

"Any wars anywhere?" asked Ginger Ted.

"No. Not that I've noticed. Harry Jervis found a pretty
big pearl. He says he's going to ask a thousand quid for it."

"I hope he gets it."

"And Charlie McCormack's married."

"He always was a bit soft."

Suddenly the boy appeared and said Mr. Jones wished to know if he might come in. Before the Controleur could give an answer Mr. Jones walked in.

"I won't detain you long," he said. "I've been trying to get hold of this good man all day and when I heard he was here I thought you wouldn't mind my coming."

"How is Miss Jones?" asked the Controleur politely. "None the worse for her night in the open, I trust."

"She's naturally a bit shaken. She had a temperature and I've insisted on her going to bed, but I don't think it's serious."

The two men had got up on the missionary's entrance, and now the missionary went up to Ginger Ted and held out his hand.

"I want to thank you. You did a great and noble thing. My sister is right, one should always look for the good in their fellow men; I am afraid I misjudged you in the past: I beg your pardon."

He spoke very solemnly. Ginger Ted looked at him with amazement. He had not been able to prevent the missionary taking his hand. He still held it.

"What the hell are you talking about?"

"You had my sister at your mercy and you spared her. I thought you were all evil and I am ashamed. She was defenceless. She was in your power. You had pity on her. I thank you from the bottom of my heart. Neither my sister nor I will ever forget. God bless and guard you always."

Mr. Jones's voice shook a little and he turned his head away. He released Ginger Ted's hand and strode quickly to the door. Ginger Ted watched him with a blank face.

"What the blazes does he mean?" he asked.

The Controleur laughed. He tried to control himself, but the more he did the more he laughed. He shook and you saw the folds of his fat belly ripple under the sarong. He leaned back in his long chair and rolled from side to side. He did not laugh only with his face, he laughed with his whole body,

and even the muscles of his podgy legs shook with mirth.
He held his aching ribs. Ginger Ted looked at him frowning,
and because he did not understand what the joke was he
grew angry. He seized one of the empty beer bottles by the
neck.

"If you don't stop laughing, I'll break your bloody head
open," he said.

The Controleur mopped his face. He swallowed a mouthful
of beer. He sighed and groaned because his sides were hurt-
ing him.

"He's thanking you for having respected the virtue of
Miss Jones," he spluttered at last.

"Me?" cried Ginger Ted.

The thought took quite a long time to travel through his
head, but when at last he got it he flew into a violent rage.
There flowed from his mouth such a stream of blasphemous
obscenities as would have startled a marine.

"That old cow," he finished. "What does he take me for?"

"You have the reputation of being rather hot stuff with
the girls, Ginger," giggled the little Controleur.

"I wouldn't touch her with the fag end of a barge-pole.
It never entered my head. The nerve. I'll wring his blasted
neck. Look here, give me my money, I'm going to get drunk."

"I don't blame you," said the Controleur.

"That old cow," repeated Ginger Ted. "That old cow."

He was shocked and outraged. The suggestion really shattered his sense of decency.

The Controleur had the money at hand and having got
Ginger Ted to sign the necessary papers gave it to him.

"Go and get drunk, Ginger Ted," he said, "but I warn you,
if you get into mischief it'll be twelve months next time."

"I shan't get into mischief," said Ginger Ted sombrely. He
was suffering from a sense of injury. "It's an insult," he
shouted at the Controleur. "That's what it is, it's a bloody
insult."

He lurched out of the house, and as he went he muttered
to himself: "dirty swine, dirty swine." Ginger Ted remained[1]

drunk for a week. Mr. Jones went to see the Controleur again.

"I'm very sorry to hear that poor fellow has taken up his evil course again," he said. "My sister and I are dreadfully disappointed. I'm afraid it wasn't very wise to give him so much money at once."

"It was his own money. I had no right to keep it back."

"Not a legal right, perhaps, but surely a moral right."

He told the Controleur the story of that fearful night on the island. With her feminine instinct, Miss Jones had realized that the man, inflamed with lust, was determined to take advantage of her, and, resolved to defend herself to the last, had armed herself with a scalpel. He told the Controleur how she had prayed and wept and how she had hidden herself. Her agony was indescribable, and she knew that she could never have survived the shame. She rocked to and fro and every moment she thought he was coming. And there was no help anywhere and at last she had fallen asleep; she was tired out, poor thing, she had undergone more than any human being could stand, and then when she awoke she found that he had covered her with copra sacks. He had found her asleep, and surely it was her innocence, her very helplessness that had moved him, he hadn't the heart to touch her; he covered her gently with two copra sacks and crept silently away.

"It shows you that deep down in him there is something sterling. My sister feels it's our duty to save him. We must do something for him."

"Well, in your place I wouldn't try till he's got through all his money," said the Controleur, "and then if he's not in gaol you can do what you like."

But Ginger Ted didn't want to be saved. About a fortnight after his release from prison he was sitting on a stool outside a Chinaman's shop looking vacantly down the street when he saw Miss Jones coming along. He stared at her for a minute and once more amazement seized him. He muttered to himself and there can be little doubt that his mutterings

were disrespectful. But then he noticed that Miss Jones had
seen him and he quickly turned his head away; he was
conscious, notwithstanding, that she was looking at him. She
was walking briskly, but she sensibly diminished her pace as
she approached him. He thought she was going to stop and
speak to him. He got up quickly and went into the shop. He
did not venture to come out for at least five minutes. Half an
hour later Mr. Jones himself came along and he went
straight up to Ginger Ted with outstretched hand.

"How do you do, Mr. Edward? My sister told me I should
find you here."

Ginger Ted have him a surly look and did not take the
proffered hand. He made no answer.

"We'd be so very glad if you'd come to dinner with us
next Sunday. My sister's a capital cook and she'll make you a
real Australian dinner."

"Go to hell," said Ginger Ted.

"That's not very gracious," said the missionary, but with a
little laugh to show that he was not affronted. "You go and
see the Controleur from time to time, why shouldn't you
come and see us? It's pleasant to talk to white people now
and then. Won't you let bygones be bygones? I can assure
you of a very cordial welcome."

"I haven't got clothes fit to go out in," said Ginger Ted
sulkily.

"Oh, never mind about that. Come as you are."

"I won't."

"Why not? You must have a reason."

Ginger Ted was a blunt man. He had no hesitation in
saying what we should all like to when we receive unwelcome
invitations.

"I don't want to."

"I'm sorry. My sister will be very disappointed."

Mr. Jones, determined to show that he was not in the least
offended, gave him a breezy nod and walked on. Forty-eight
hours later there mysteriously arrived at the house in which
Ginger Ted lodged a parcel containing a suit of ducks, a
tennis shirt, a pair of socks and some shoes. He was unac-

customed to receiving presents and next time he saw the Controleur asked him if it was he who had sent the things.

"Not on your life," replied the Controleur. "I'm perfectly indifferent to the state of your wardrobe."

"Well, then, who the hell can have?"

"Search me."

It was necessary from time to time for Miss Jones to see Mr. Gruyter on business and shortly after this she came to see him one morning in his office. She was a capable woman and though she generally wanted him to do something he had no mind to, she did not waste his time. He was a little surprised then to discover that she had come on a very trivial errand. When he told her that he could not take cognizance of the matter in question, she did not as was her habit try to convince him, but accepted his refusal as definite. She got up to go and then as though it were an afterthought said:

"Oh, Mr. Gruyter, my brother is very anxious that we should have the man they call Ginger Ted to supper with us and I've written him a little note inviting him for the day after tomorrow. I think he's rather shy, and I wonder if you'd come with him."

"That's very kind of you."

"My brother feels that we ought to do something for the poor fellow."

"A woman's influence and all that sort of thing," said the Controleur demurely.

"Will you persuade him to come? I'm sure he will if you make a point of it, and when he knows the way he'll come again. It seems such a pity to let a young man like that go to pieces altogether."

The Controleur looked up at her. She was several inches taller than he. He thought her very unattractive. She reminded him strangely of wet linen hung on a clothes-line to dry. His eyes twinkled, but he kept a straight face.

"I'll do my best," he said.

"How old is he?" she asked.

"According to his passport he's thirty-one."

"And what is his real name?"

"Wilson."

"Edward Wilson," she said softly.

"It's astonishing that after the life he's led he should be so strong," murmured the Controleur. "He has the strength of an ox."

"Those red-headed men sometimes are very powerful," said Miss Jones, but spoke as though she were choking.

"Quite so," said the Controleur.

Then for no obvious reason Miss Jones blushed. She hurriedly said good-bye to the Controleur and left his office.

"Godverdomme!" said the Controleur.

He knew now who had sent Ginger Ted the new clothes.

He met him during the course of the day and asked him whether he had heard from Miss Jones. Ginger Ted took a crumpled ball of paper out of his pocket and gave it to him. It was the invitation. It ran as follows:

Dear Mr. Wilson,—

My brother and I would be so very glad if you would come and have supper with us next Thursday at 7.30. The Controleur has kindly promised to come. We have some new records from Australia which I am sure you will like. I am afraid I was not very nice to you last time we met, but I did not know you so well then, and I am big enough to admit it when I have committed an error. I hope you will forgive me and let me be your friend.

Yours sincerely,
Martha Jones.

The Controleur noticed that she addressed him as Mr. Wilson and referred to his own promise to go, so that when she told him she had already invited Ginger Ted she had a little anticipated the truth.

"What are you going to do?"

"I'm not going, if that's what you mean. Damned nerve."

"You must answer the letter."

"Well, I won't."

"Now look here, Ginger, you put on those new clothes and you come as a favour to me. I've got to go, and damn it all, you can't leave me in the lurch. It won't hurt you just once."

Ginger Ted looked at the Controleur suspiciously, but his face was serious and his manner sincere; he could not guess that within him the Dutchman bubbled with laughter.

"What the devil do they want me for?"

"I don't know. The pleasure of your society, I suppose."

"Will there by any booze?"

"No, but come up to my house at seven, and we'll have a tiddly before we go."

"Oh, all right," said Ginger Ted sulkily.

The Controleur rubbed his little fat hands with joy. He was expecting a great deal of amusement from the party. But when Thursday came and seven o'clock Ginger Ted was dead drunk and Mr. Gruyter had to go alone. He told the missionary and his sister the plain truth. Mr. Jones shook his head.

"I'm afraid it's no good, Martha, the man's hopeless."

For a moment Miss Jones was silent and the Controleur saw two tears trickle down her long thin nose. She bit her lip.

"No one is hopeless. Everyone has some good in him. I shall pray for him every night. It would be wicked to doubt the power of God."

Perhaps Miss Jones was right in this, but the divine providence took a very funny way of effecting its ends. Ginger Ted began to drink more heavily than ever. He was so troublesome that even Mr. Gruyter lost patience with him. He made up his mind that he could not have the fellow on the islands any more and resolved to deport him on the next boat that touched at Baru. Then a man died under mysterious circumstances after having been for a trip to one of the islands and the Controleur learnt that there had been several deaths on the same island. He sent the Chinese who was the official doctor of the group to look into the matter, and very soon received intelligence that the deaths were due to cholera. Two more took place at Baru and the certainty was forced upon him that there was an epidemic.

The Controleur cursed freely. He cursed in Dutch, he cursed in English and he cursed in Malay. Then he drank a bottle of beer and smoked a cigar. After that he took thought. He knew the Chinese doctor would be useless. He was a nervous little man from Java and the natives would refuse to obey his orders. The Controleur was efficient and knew pretty well what must be done, but he could not do everything single-handed. He did not like Mr. Jones, but just then he was thankful that he was at hand, and he sent for him at once. In ten minutes Mr. Jones was in the office. He was accompanied by his sister.

"You know what I want to see you about, Mr. Jones," he said abruptly.

"Yes. I've been expecting a message from you. That is why my sister has come with me. We are ready to put all our resources at your disposal. I need not tell you that my sister is as competent as a man."

"I know. I shall be very glad of her assistance."

They set to without further delay to discuss the steps that must be taken. Hospital huts would have to be erected and quarantine stations. The inhabitants of the various villages on the islands must be forced to take proper precautions. In a good many cases the infected villages drew their water from the same well as the uninfected, and in each case this difficulty would have to be dealt with according to circumstances. It was necessary to send round people to give orders and make sure that they were carried out. Negligence must be ruthlessly punished. The worst of it was that the natives would not obey other natives, and orders given by native policemen, themselves unconvinced of their efficacy, would certainly be disregarded. It was advisable for Mr. Jones to stay at Baru where the population was largest and his medical attention most wanted; and what with the official duties that forced him to keep in touch with his headquarters, it was impossible for Mr. Gruyter to visit all the other islands himself.

Miss Jones must go; but the natives of some of the outlying islands were wild and treacherous; the Controleur had had a good deal of trouble with them. He did not like the idea of exposing her to danger.

"I'm not afraid," she said.

"I daresay. But if you have your throat cut I shall get into trouble, and besides, we're so short-handed I don't want to risk losing your help."

"Then let Mr. Wilson come with me. He knows the natives better than anyone and can speak all their dialects."

"Ginger Ted?" The Controleur stared at her. "He's just getting over an attack of D.T.'s."

"I know," she answered.

"You know a great deal, Miss Jones."

Even though the moment was so serious Mr. Gruyter could not but smile. He gave her a sharp look, but she met it coolly.

"There's nothing like responsibility for bringing out what there is in a man, and I think something like this may be the making of him."

"Do you think it would be wise to trust yourself for days at a time to a man of such infamous character?" said the missionary.

"I put my trust in God," she answered gravely.

"Do you think he'd be any use?" asked the Controleur. "You know what he is."

"I'm convinced of it." Then she blushed. "After all, no one knows better than I that he's capable of self-control."

The Controleur bit his lip.

"Let's send for him."

He gave a message to the sergeant and in a few minutes Ginger Ted stood before them. He looked ill. He had evidently been much shaken by his recent attack and his nerves were all to pieces. He was in rags and he had not shaved for a week. No one could have looked more disreputable.

"Look here, Ginger," said the Controleur, "it's about this cholera business. We've got to force the natives to take precautions and we want you to help us."

"Why the hell should I?"

"No reason at all. Except philanthropy."

"Nothing doing, Controleur. I'm not a philanthropist."

"That settles that. That was all. You can go."

But as Ginger Ted turned to the door Miss Jones stopped him.

"It was my suggestion, Mr. Wilson. You see, they want me to go to Labobo and Sakunchi, and the natives there are so funny I was afraid to go alone. I thought if you came I should be safer."

He gave her a look of extreme distaste.

"What do you suppose I care if they cut your throat?"

Miss Jones looked at him and her eyes filled with tears. She began to cry. He stood and watched her stupidly.

"There's no reason why you should." She pulled herself together and dried her eyes. "I'm being silly. I shall be all right. I'll go alone."

"It's damned foolishness for a woman to go to Labobo."

She gave him a little smile.

"I daresay it is, but you see, it's my job and I can't help myself. I'm sorry if I offended you by asking you. You must forget about it. I daresay it wasn't quite fair to ask you to take such a risk."

For quite a minute Ginger Ted stood and looked at her. He shifted from one foot to the other. His surly face seemed to grow black.

"Oh, hell, have it your own way," he said at last. "I'll come with you. When d'you want to start?"

They set out next day, with drugs and disinfectants, in the government launch. Mr. Gruyter as soon as he had put the necessary work in order was to start off in a prahu in the other direction. For four months the epidemic raged. Though everything possible was done to localize it one island after another was attacked. The Controleur was busy from morning to night. He had no sooner got back to Baru from one or other of the islands to do what was necessary there than he had to set off again. He distributed food and medicine. He cheered the terrified people. He supervised everything. He worked like a dog. He saw nothing of Ginger Ted, but he heard from Mr. Jones that the experiment was working out beyond all hopes. The scamp was behaving himself. He had a way with the natives; and by cajolery, firmness and on occasion the use of his fist, managed to make them take the steps necessary for their own safety. Miss Jones could congratulate herself on the success of the scheme. But the Controleur was too tired to be amused. When the epidemic had run its course he rejoiced because out of a population of eight thousand only six hundred had died.

Finally he was able to give the district a clean bill of health.

One evening he was sitting in his sarong on the verandah of his house and he read a French novel with the happy consciousness that once more he could take things easy. His head boy came in and told him that Ginger Ted wished to see him. He got up from his chair and shouted to him to come in. Company was just what he wanted. It had crossed the Controleur's mind that it would be pleasant to get drunk that night, but it is dull to get drunk alone, and he had regretfully put the thought aside. And heaven had sent Ginger Ted in the nick of time. By God, they would make a night of it. After four months they deserved a bit of fun. Ginger Ted entered. He was wearing a clean suit of white ducks. He was shaved. He looked another man.

"Why, Ginger, you look as if you'd been spending a month at a health resort instead of nursing a pack of natives dying of cholera. And look at your clothes. Have you just stepped out of a band-box?"

Ginger Ted smiled rather sheepishly. The head boy brought two bottles of beer and poured them out.

"Help yourself, Ginger," said the Controleur as he took his glass.

"I don't think I'll have any, thank you."

The Controleur put down his glass and looked at Ginger Ted with amazement.

"Why, what's the matter? Aren't you thirsty?"

"I don't mind having a cup of tea."

"A cup of what?"

"I'm on the wagon. Martha and I are going to be married."

"Ginger!"

The Controleur's eyes popped out of his head. He scratched his shaven pate.

"You can't marry Miss Jones," he said. "No one could marry Miss Jones."

"Well, I'm going to. That's what I've come to see you about. Owen's going to marry us in chapel, but we want to be married by Dutch law as well."

"A joke's a joke, Ginger. What's the idea?"

"She wanted it. She fell for me that night we spent on the island when the propeller broke. She's not a bad old girl when you get to know her. It's her last chance, if you understand what I mean, and I'd like to do something to oblige her. And she wants someone to take care of her, there's no doubt about that."

"Ginger, Ginger, before you can say knife she'll make you into a damned missionary."

"I don't know that I'd mind that so much if we had a little mission of our own. She says I'm a bloody marvel with the natives. She says I can do more with a native in five minutes than Owen can do in a year. She says she's never known anyone with the magnetism I have. It seems a pity to waste a gift like that."

The Controleur looked at him without speaking and slowly nodded his head three or four times. She'd nobbled him all right.

"I've converted seventeen already," said Ginger Ted.

"You? I didn't know you believed in Christianity."

"Well, I don't know that I did exactly, but when I talked to 'em and they just came into the fold like a lot of blasted sheep, well, it gave me quite a turn. Blimey, I said, I daresay there's something in it after all."

"You should have raped her, Ginger. I wouldn't have been hard on you. I wouldn't have given you more than three years and three years is soon over."

"Look here, Controleur, don't you ever let on that the

thought never entered my head. Women are touchy, you know, and she'd be as sore as hell if she knew that."

"I guessed she'd got her eye on you, but I never thought it would come to this." The Controleur in an agitated manner walked up and down the verandah. "Listen to me, old boy," he said after an interval of reflection, "we've had some grand times together and a friend's a friend. I'll tell you what I'll do, I'll lend you the launch and you can go and hide on one of the islands till the next ship comes along and then I'll get 'em to slow down and take you on board. You've only got one chance now and that's to cut and run."

Ginger Ted shook his head.

"It's no good, Controleur, I know you mean well, but I'm going to marry the blasted woman, and that's that. You don't know the joy of bringing all them bleeding sinners to repentance, and Christ, that girl can make a treacle pudding. I haven't eaten a better one since I was a kid."

The Controleur was very much disturbed. The drunken scamp was his only companion on the islands and he did not want to lose him. He discovered that he had even a certain affection for him. Next day he went to see the missionary.

"What's this I hear about your sister marrying Ginger Ted?" he asked him. "It's the most extraordinary thing I've ever heard in my life."

"It's true nevertheless."

"You must do something about it. It's madness."

"My sister is of full age and entitled to do as she pleases."

"But you don't mean to tell me you approve of it. You know Ginger Ted. He's a bum and there are no two ways about it. Have you told her the risk she's running? I mean, bringing sinners to repentance and all that sort of thing's all right, but there are limits. And does the leopard ever change his spots?"

Then for the first time in his life the Controleur saw a twinkle in the missionary's eye.

"My sister is a very determined woman, Mr. Gruyter," he replied. "From that night they spent on the island he never had a chance."

The Controleur gasped. He was as surprised as the prophet when the Lord opened the mouth of the ass, and she said unto Balaam, "What have I done unto thee, that thou hast smitten me these three times?" Perhaps Mr. Jones was human after all.

"Allejesus!" muttered the Controleur.

Before anything more could be said Miss Jones swept into the room. She was radiant. She looked ten years younger. Her cheeks were flushed and her nose was hardly red at all.

"Have you come to congratulate me, Mr. Gruyter?" she cried, and her manner was sprightly and girlish. "You see, I was right after all. Everyone has some good in them. You don't know how splendid Edward has been all through this terrible time. He's a hero. He's a saint. Even I was surprised."

"I hope you'll be very happy, Miss Jones."

"I know I shall. Oh, it would be wicked of me to doubt it. For it is the Lord who has brought us together."

"Do you think so?"

"I know it. Don't you see? Except for the cholera Edward would never have found himself. Except for the cholera we should never have learnt to know one another. I have never seen the hand of God more plainly manifest."

The Controleur could not but think that it was rather a clumsy device to bring those two together that necessitated the death of six hundred innocent persons, but not being well versed in the ways of omnipotence he made no remark.

"You'll never guess where we're going for our honeymoon," said Miss Jones, perhaps a trifle archly.

"Java?"

"No, if you'll lend us the launch, we're going to that island where we were marooned. It has very tender recollections for both of us. It was there that I first guessed how fine and good Edward was. It's there I want him to have his reward."

The Controleur caught his breath. He left quickly, for he thought that unless he had a bottle of beer at once he would have a fit. He was never so shocked in his life.

The Hairless Mexican

"Do you like macaroni?" said R.

"What do you mean by macaroni?" answered Ashenden. "It is like asking me if I like poetry. I like Keats and Wordsworth and Verlaine and Goethe. When you say macaroni, do you mean *spaghetti, tagliatelli, rigatoni, vermicelli, fettucini, tufali, farfalli,* or just macaroni?"

"Macaroni," replied R., a man of few words.

"I like all simple things, boiled eggs, oysters and caviare, *truite au bleu,* grilled salmon, roast lamb (the saddle by preference), cold grouse, treacle tart and rice pudding. But of all simple things the only one I can eat day in and day out, not only without disgust but with the eagerness of an appetite unimpaired by excess, is macaroni."

"I am glad of that because I want you to go down to Italy."

Ashenden had come from Geneva to meet R. at Lyons and having got there before him had spent the afternoon wandering about the dull, busy and prosaic streets of that thriving city. They were sitting now in a restaurant on the *place* to which Ashenden had taken R. on his arrival because it was reputed to give you the best food in that part of France. But since in so crowded a resort (for the Lyonese like a good dinner) you never knew what inquisitive ears were pricked up to catch any useful piece of information that might fall from your lips, they had contented themselves with talking of indifferent things. They had reached the end of an admirable repast.

"Have another glass of brandy?" said R.

"No, thank you," answered Ashenden, who was of an abstemious turn.

"One should do what one can to mitigate the rigours of war," remarked R. as he took the bottle and poured out a glass for himself and another for Ashenden.

Ashenden, thinking it would be affectation to protest, let the gesture pass, but felt bound to remonstrate with his chief on the unseemly manner in which he held the bottle.

"In my youth I was always taught that you should take a woman by the waist and a bottle by the neck," he murmured.

"I am glad you told me. I shall continue to hold a bottle by the waist and give women a wide berth."

Ashenden did not know what to reply to this and so remained silent. He sipped his brandy and R. called for his bill. It was true that he was an important person, with power to make or mar quite a large number of his fellows, and his opinions were listened to by those who held in their hands the fate of empires; but he could never face the business of tipping a waiter without an embarrassment that was obvious in his demeanour. He was tortured by the fear of making a fool of himself by giving too much or of exciting the waiter's icy scorn by giving too little. When the bill came he passed some hundred-franc notes over to Ashenden and said:

"Pay him, will you? I can never understand French figures."

The groom brought them their hats and coats.

"Would you like to go back to the hotel?" asked Ashenden.

"We might as well."

It was early in the year, but the weather had suddenly turned warm, and they walked with their coats over their arms. Ashenden knowing that R. liked a sitting-room had engaged one for him and to this, when they reached the hotel, they went. The hotel was old-fashioned and the sitting-room was vast. It was furnished with a heavy mahogany suite upholstered in green velvet and the chairs were set primly round a large table. On the walls, covered with a dingy paper, were large steel engravings of the battles of Napoleon, and from the ceiling hung an enormous chandelier once used for gas, but now fitted with electric bulbs. It flooded the cheerless room with a cold, hard light.

"This is very nice," said R., as they went in.

"Not exactly cosy," suggested Ashenden.

"No, but it looks as though it were the best room in the place. It all looks very *good* to me."

He drew one of the green velvet chairs away from the table and, sitting down, lit a cigar. He loosened his belt and unbuttoned his tunic.

"I always thought I liked a cheroot better than anything," he said, "but since the war I've taken quite a fancy to Havanas. Oh, well, I suppose it can't last for ever." The corners of his mouth flickered with the beginning of a smile. "It's an ill wind that blows nobody any good."

Ashenden took two chairs, one to sit on and one for his feet, and when R. saw him he said: "That's not a bad idea," and swinging another chair out from the table with a sigh of relief put his boots on it.

"What room is that next door?" he asked.

"That's your bedroom."

"And on the other side?"

"A banqueting hall."

R. got up and strolled slowly about the room and when he passed the windows, as though in idle curiosity, peeped through the heavy rep curtains that covered them, and then returning to his chair once more comfortably put his feet up.

"It's just as well not to take any more risk than one need," he said.

He looked at Ashenden reflectively. There was a slight smile on his thin lips, but the pale eyes, too closely set together, remained cold and steely. R.'s stare would have been embarrassing if Ashenden had not been used to it. He knew that R. was considering how he would broach the subject that he had in mind. The silence must have lasted for two or three minutes.

"I'm expecting a fellow to come and see me to-night,"

he said at last. "His train gets in about ten." He gave his wrist-watch a glance. "He's known as the Hairless Mexican."

"Why?"

"Because he's hairless and because he's a Mexican."

"The explanation seems perfectly satisfactory," said Ashenden.

"He'll tell you all about himself. He talks nineteen to the dozen. He was on his uppers when I came across him. It appears that he was mixed up in some revolution in Mexico and had to get out with nothing but the clothes he stood up in. They were rather the worse for wear when I found him. If you want to please him you call him General. He claims to have been a general in Huerta's army, at least I think it was Huerta; anyhow he says that if things had gone right he would be minister of war now and no end of a big bug. I've found him very useful. Not a bad chap. The only thing I really have against him is that he will use scent."

"And where do I come in?" asked Ashenden.

"He's going down to Italy. I've got rather a ticklish job for him to do and I want you to stand by. I'm not keen on trusting him with a lot of money. He's a gambler and he's a bit too fond of the girls. I suppose you came from Geneva on your Ashenden passport."

"Yes."

"I've got another for you, a diplomatic one, by the way, in the name of Somerville with visas for France and Italy. I think you and he had better travel together. He's an amusing cove when he gets going, and I think you ought to get to know one another."

"What is the job?"

"I haven't yet quite made up my mind how much it's desirable for you to know about it."

Ashenden did not reply. They eyed one another in a detached manner, as though they were strangers who sat together in a railway carriage and each wondered who and what the other was.

"In your place I'd leave the General to do most of the talking. I wouldn't tell him more about yourself than you

find absolutely necessary. He won't ask you any questions,
I can promise you that, I think he's by way of being a gentleman after his own fashion."

"By the way, what is his real name?"

"I always call him Manuel, I don't know that he likes it
very much, his name is Manuel Carmona."

"I gather by what you have not said that he's an un-
mitigated scoundrel."

R. smiled with his pale blue eyes.

"I don't know that I'd go quite so far as that. He hasn't
had the advantages of a public-school education. His ideas
of playing the game are not quite the same as yours or
mine. I don't know that I'd leave a gold cigarette case about
when he was in the neighbourhood, but if he lost money
to you at poker and had pinched your cigarette case he
would immediately pawn it to pay you. If he had half a
chance he'd seduce your wife, but if you were up against
it he'd share his last crust with you. The tears will run
down his face when he hears Gounod's 'Ave Maria' on the
gramophone, but if you insult his dignity he'll shoot you
like a dog. It appears that in Mexico it's an insult to get
between a man and his drink and he told me himself that
once when a Dutchman who didn't know passed between
him and the bar he whipped out his revolver and shot him
dead."

"Did nothing happen to him?"

"No, it appears that he belongs to one of the best families.
The matter was hushed up and it was announced in the
papers that the Dutchman had committed suicide. He did
practically. I don't believe the Hairless Mexican has a great
respect for human life."

Ashenden who had been looking intently at R. started a
little and he watched more carefully than ever his chief's
tired, lined and yellow face. He knew that he did not make
this remark for nothing.

"Of course a lot of nonsense is talked about the value of
human life. You might just as well say that the counters
you use at poker have an intrinsic value, their value is what

you like to make it; for a general giving battle men are merely counters and he's a fool if he allows himself for sentimental reasons to look upon them as human beings."

"But, you see, they're counters that feel and think and if they believe they're being squandered they are quite capable of refusing to be used any more."

"Anyhow that's neither here nor there. We've had information that a man called Constantine Andreadi is on his way from Constantinople with certain documents that we want to get hold of. He's a Greek. He's an agent of Enver Pasha and Enver has great confidence in him. He's given him verbal messages that are too secret and too important to be put on paper. He's sailing from the Piræus, on a boat called the Ithaca, and will land at Brindisi on his way to Rome. He's to deliver his dispatches at the German embassy and impart what he has to say personally to the ambassador."

"I see."

At this time Italy was still neutral; the Central Powers were straining every nerve to keep her so; the Allies were doing what they could to induce her to declare war on their side.

"We don't want to get into any trouble with the Italian authorities, it might be fatal, but we've got to prevent Andreadi from getting to Rome."

"At any cost?" asked Ashenden.

"Money's no object," answered R., his lips twisting into a sardonic smile.

"What do you propose to do?"

"I don't think you need bother your head about that."

"I have a fertile imagination," said Ashenden.

"I want you to go down to Naples with the Hairless Mexican. He's very keen on getting back to Cuba. It appears that his friends are organizing a show and he wants to be as near at hand as possible so that he can hop over to Mexico when things are ripe. He needs cash. I've brought money down with me, in American dollars, and I shall give it to you to-night. You'd better carry it on your person."

"Is it much?"

"It's a good deal, but I thought it would be easier for you if it wasn't bulky, so I've got it in thousand dollar notes. You will give the Hairless Mexican the notes in return for the documents that Andreadi is bringing."

A question sprang to Ashenden's lips, but he did not ask it. He asked another instead.

"Does this fellow understand what he has to do?"

"Perfectly."

There was a knock at the door. It opened and the Hairless Mexican stood before them.

"I have arrived. Good-evening, Colonel. I am enchanted to see you."

R. got up.

"Had a nice journey, Manuel? This is Mr. Somerville who's going to Naples with you. General Carmona."

"Pleased to meet you, sir."

He shook Ashenden's hand with such force that he winced

"Your hands are like iron, General," he murmured.

The Mexican gave them a glance.

"I had them manicured this morning. I do not think they were very well done. I like my nails much more highly polished."

They were cut to a point, stained bright red, and to Ashenden's mind shone like mirrors. Though it was not cold the General wore a fur coat with an astrakhan collar and with his every movement a wave of perfume was wafted to your nose.

"Take off your coat, General, and have a cigar," said R.

The Hairless Mexican was a tall man, and though thinnish gave you the impression of being very powerful; he was smartly dressed in a blue serge suit, with a silk handkerchief neatly tucked in the breast pocket of his coat, and he wore a gold bracelet on his wrist. His features were good, but a little larger than life-size, and his eyes were brown and lustrous. He was quite hairless. His yellow skin had the smoothness of a woman's and he had no eyebrows nor eyelashes; he wore a pale brown wig, rather long, and the locks were arranged in artistic disorder. This and the unwrinkled sallow face, combined with his dandified dress, gave him an appearance that was at first glance a trifle horrifying. He was repulsive and ridiculous, but you could not take your eyes from him. There was a sinister fascination in his strangeness.

He sat down and hitched up his trousers so that they should not bag at the knee.

"Well, Manuel, have you been breaking any hearts to-day?" said R. with his sardonic joviality.

The General turned to Ashenden.

"Our good friend, the Colonel, envies me my successes with the fair sex. I tell him he can have just as many as I if he will only listen to me. Confidence, that is all you need. If you never fear a rebuff you will never have one."

"Nonsense, Manuel, one has to have your way with the girls. There's something about you that they can't resist."

The Hairless Mexican laughed with a self-satisfaction that he did not try to disguise. He spoke English very well, with a Spanish accent, but with an American intonation.

"But since you ask me, Colonel, I don't mind telling you that I got into conversation on the train with a little woman who was coming to Lyons to see her mother-in-law. She was not very young and she was thinner than I like a woman to be, but she was possible, and she helped me to pass an agreeable hour."

"Well, let's get to business," said R.

"I am at your service, Colonel." He gave Ashenden a glance. "Is Mr. Somerville a military man?"

"No," said R., "he's an author."

"It takes all sorts to make a world, as you say. I am happy to make your acquaintance, Mr. Somerville. I can tell you many stories that will interest you; I am sure that we shall get on well together. You have a sympathetic air. I am very sensitive to that. To tell you the truth I am nothing but a bundle of nerves and if I am with a person who is anti-pathetic to me I go all to pieces."

"I hope we shall have a pleasant journey," said Ashenden.

"When does our friend arrive at Brindisi?" asked the Mexican, turning to R.

"He sails from the Piræus in the Ithaca on the fourteenth. It's probably some old tub, but you'd better get down to Brindisi in good time."

"I agree with you."

R. got up and with his hands in his pocket sat on the edge of the table. In his rather shabby uniform, his tunic unbuttoned, he looked a slovenly creature beside the neat and well-dressed Mexican.

"Mr. Somerville knows practically nothing of the errand on which you are going and I do not desire you to tell him anything. I think you had much better keep your own counsel. He is instructed to give you the funds you need for your work, but your actions are your own affair. If you need his advice of course you can ask for it."

"I seldom ask other people's advice and never take it."

"And should you make a mess of things I trust you to keep Mr. Somerville out of it. He must on no account be compromised."

"I am a man of honour, Colonel," answered the Hairless Mexican with dignity, "and I would sooner let myself be cui in a thousand pieces than betray my friends."

"That is what I have already told Mr. Somerville. On the other hand if everything pans out O. K. Mr. Somerville is instructed to give you the sum we agreed on in return for the papers I spoke to you about. In what manner you get them is no business of his."

"That goes without saying. There is only one thing I wish to make quite plain; Mr. Somerville understands of course that I have not accepted the mission with which you have entrusted me on account of the money?"

"Quite," replied R., gravely, looking him straight in the eyes.

"I am with the Allies body and soul, I cannot forgive the Germans for outraging the neutrality of Belgium, and if I

accept the money that you have offered me it is because I
am first and foremost a patriot. I can trust Mr. Somerville
implicitly, I suppose?"

R. nodded. The Mexican turned to Ashenden.

"An expedition is being arranged to free my unhappy
country from the tyrants that exploit and ruin it and every
penny that I receive will go on guns and cartridges. For
myself I have no need of money; I am a soldier and I can
live on a crust and a few olives. There are only three oc-
cupations that befit a gentleman, war, cards and women; it
costs nothing to sling a rifle over your shoulder and take
to the mountains—and that is real warfare, not this ma-
nœuvring of battalions and firing of great guns—women love
me for myself, and I generally win at cards."

Ashenden found the flamboyance of this strange creature,
with his scented handkerchief and his gold bracelet, very
much to his taste. This was far from being just the man in
the street (whose tyranny we rail at but in the end submit
to) and to the amateur of the baroque in human nature he
was a rarity to be considered with delight. He was a purple
patch on two legs. Notwithstanding his wig and his hairless
big face he had undoubtedly an air; he was absurd, but he
did not give you the impression that he was a man to be
trifled with. His self-complacency was magnificent.

"Where is your kit, Manuel?" asked R.

It was possible that a frown for an instant darkened the
Mexican's brow at the abrupt question that seemed a little
contemptuously to brush to one side his eloquent statement,
but he gave no other sign of displeasure. Ashenden suspected
that he thought the Colonel a barbarian insensitive to the
finer emotions.

"I left it at the station."

"Mr. Somerville has a diplomatic passport so that he can
get it through with his own things at the frontier without
examination if you like."

"I have very little, a few suits and some linen, but perhaps
it would be as well if Mr. Somerville would take charge

of it. I bought half a dozen suits of silk pyjamas before I left Paris."

"And what about you?" asked R., turning to Ashenden.

"I've only got one bag. It's in my room."

"You'd better have it taken to the station while there's someone about. Your train goes at one ten."

"Oh?"

This was the first Ashenden had heard that they were to start that night.

"I think you'd better get down to Naples as soon as possible."

"Very well."

R. got up.

"I'm going to bed. I don't know what you fellows want to do."

"I shall take a walk about Lyons," said the Hairless Mexican. "I'm interested in life. Lend me a hundred francs, Colonel, will you? I have no change on me."

R. took out his pocket-book and gave the General the note he asked for. Then to Ashenden:

"What are you going to do? Wait here?"

"No," said Ashenden, "I shall go to the station and read."

"You'd both of you better have a whisky and soda before you go, hadn't you? What about it, Manuel?"

"It is very kind of you, but I never drink anything but champagne and brandy."

"Mixed?" asked R. drily.

"Not necessarily," returned the other with gravity.

R. ordered brandy and soda and when it came, whereas he and Ashenden helped themselves to both, the Hairless Mexican poured himself out three parts of a tumbler of neat brandy and swallowed it in two noisy gulps. He rose to his feet and put on his coat with the astrakhan collar, seized in one hand his bold black hat and, with the gesture of a romantic actor giving up the girl he loved to one more worthy of her, held out the other to R.

"Well, Colonel, I will bid you goodnight and pleasant

dreams. I do not expect that we shall meet again so soon."

"Don't make a hash of things, Manuel, and if you do keep your mouth shut."

"They tell me that in one of your colleges where the sons of gentlemen are trained to become naval officers it is written in letters of gold: there is no such word as impossible in the British Navy. I do not know the meaning of the word failure."

"It has a good many synonyms," retorted R.

"I will meet you at the station, Mr. Somerville," said the Hairless Mexican, and with a flourish left them.

R. looked at Ashenden with that little smile of his that always made his face look so dangerously shrewd.

"Well, what d'you think of him?"

"You've got me beat," said Ashenden. "Is he a mountebank? He seems as vain as a peacock. And with that frightful appearance can he really be the lady's man he pretends? What makes you think you can trust him?"

R. gave a low chuckle and he washed his thin, old hands with imaginary soap.

"I thought you'd like him. He's quite a character, isn't he? I think we can trust him." R.'s eyes suddenly grew opaque. "I don't believe it would pay him to double-cross us." He paused for a moment. "Anyhow we've got to risk it. I'll give you the tickets and the money and then you can take yourself off; I'm all in and I want to go to bed."

Ten minutes later Ashenden set out for the station with his bag on a porter's shoulder.

Having nearly two hours to wait he made himself comfortable in the waiting-room. The light was good and he read a novel. When the time drew near for the arrival of the train from Paris that was to take them direct to Rome and the Hairless Mexican did not appear Ashenden, beginning to grow a trifle anxious, went out on the platform to look for him. Ashenden suffered from that distressing malady known as train fever: an hour before his train was due he began to have apprehensions lest he should miss it; he was

impatient with the porters who would never bring his luggage down from his room in time and he could not understand why the hotel bus cut it so fine; a block in the street
would drive him to frenzy and the languid movements of
the station porters infuriate him. The whole world seemed
in a horrid plot to delay him; people got in his way as he
passed through the barriers; others, a long string of them,
were at the ticket-office getting tickets for other trains than
his and they counted their change with exasperating care; his
luggage took an interminable time to register; and then if
he was travelling with friends they would go to buy news-
papers, or would take a walk along the platform and he
was certain they would be left behind, they would stop to
talk to a casual stranger or suddenly be seized with a desire
to telephone and disappear at a run. In fact the universe
conspired to make him miss every train he wanted to take
and he was not happy unless he was settled in his corner,
his things on the rack above him, with a good half hour
to spare. Sometimes by arriving at the station too soon he
had caught an earlier train than the one he had meant to,
but that was nerve-racking and caused him all the anguish
of very nearly missing it.

The Rome express was signalled and there was no sign
of the Hairless Mexican, it came in and he was not to be
seen. Ashenden became more and more harassed. He walked
quickly up and down the platform, looked in all the waiting-
rooms, went to the *consigne* where the luggage was left;
he could not find him. There were no sleeping-cars, but a
number of people got out and he took two seats in a first-
class carriage. He stood at the door, looking up and down
the platform and up at the clock; it was useless to go if
his travelling companion did not turn up and Ashenden
made up his mind to take his things out of the carriage as
the porter cried *en voiture;* but, by George! he would give
the brute hell when he found him. There were three minutes
more, then two minutes, then one; at that late hour there
were few persons about and all who were travelling had
taken their seats. Then he saw the Hairless Mexican, fol-

lowed by two porters with his luggage and accompanied by
a man in a bowler-hat, walk leisurely on to the platform.
He caught sight of Ashenden and waved to him.

"Ah, my dear fellow, there you are, I wondered what had
become of you."

"Good God, man, hurry up or we shall miss the train."

"I never miss a train. Have you got good seats? The
chef de gare has gone for the night; this is his assistant."

The man in the bowler-hat took it off when Ashenden
nodded to him.

"But this is an ordinary carriage. I am afraid I could not
travel in that." He turned to the station-master's assistant
with an affable smile. "You must do better for me than
that, *mon cher.*"

"*Certainement, mon général,* I will put you into a *salon-lit.*
Of course."

The assistant station-master led them along the train and
put them in an empty compartment where there were two
beds. The Mexican eyed it with satisfaction and watched
the porters arrange the luggage.

"That will do very well. I am much obliged to you." He
held out his hand to the man in the bowler-hat. "I shall
not forget you and next time I see the Minister I will tell
him with what civility you have treated me."

"You are too good, General. I shall be very grateful."

A whistle was blown and the train started.

"This is better than an ordinary first-class carriage, I think,
Mr. Somerville," said the Mexican. "A good traveller should
learn how to make the best of things."

But Ashenden was still extremely cross.

"I don't know why the devil you wanted to cut it so fine.
We should have looked a pair of damned fools if we'd
missed the train."

"My dear fellow, there was never the smallest chance of
that. When I arrived I told the station-master that I was
General Carmona, Commander-in-Chief of the Mexican Army,
and that I had to stop off in Lyons for a few hours to hold

a conference with the British Field-Marshal. I asked him to hold the train for me if I was delayed and suggested that my government might see its way to conferring an order on him. I have been to Lyons before, I like the girls here; they have not the *chic* of the Parisians, but they have something, there is no denying that they have something. Will you have a mouthful of brandy before you go to sleep?"

"No, thank you," said Ashenden morosely.

"I always drink a glass before going to bed, it settles the nerves."

He looked in his suit-case and without difficulty found a bottle. He put it to his lips and had a long drink, wiped his mouth with the back of his hand and lit a cigarette. Then he took off his boots and lay down. Ashenden dimmed the light.

"I have never yet made up my mind," said the Hairless Mexican reflectively, "whether it is pleasanter to go to sleep with the kisses of a beautiful woman on your mouth or with a cigarette between your lips. Have you ever been to Mexico? I will tell you about Mexico to-morrow. Goodnight."

Presently Ashenden heard from his steady breathing that he was asleep and in a little while himself dozed off. Presently he woke. The Mexican, deep in slumber, lay motionless; he had taken off his fur coat and was using it as a blanket; he still wore his wig. Suddenly there was a jolt and the train with a noisy grinding of brakes stopped; in the twinkling of an eye, before Ashenden could realize that anything had happened, the Mexican was on his feet with his hand to his hip.

"What is it?" he cried.

"Nothing. Probably only a signal against us."

The Mexican sat down heavily on his bed. Ashenden turned on the light.

"You wake quickly for such a sound sleeper," he said.

"You have to in my profession."

Ashenden would have liked to ask him whether this was murder, conspiracy or commanding armies, but was not sure that it would be discreet. The General opened his bag and took out the bottle.

"Will you have a nip?" he asked. "There is nothing like it when you wake suddenly in the night."

When Ashenden refused he put the bottle once more to his lips and poured a considerable quantity of liquor down his throat. He sighed and lit a cigarette. Although Ashenden had seen him now drink nearly a bottle of brandy and it was probable that he had had a good deal more when he was going about the town he was certainly quite sober. Neither in his manner nor in his speech was there any indication that he had drunk during the evening anything but lemonade.

The train started and soon Ashenden again fell asleep. When he awoke it was morning and turning round lazily he saw that the Mexican was awake too. He was smoking a cigarette. The floor by his side was strewn with burnt-out butts and the air was thick and grey. He had begged Ashenden not to insist on opening a window, for he said the night air was dangerous.

"I did not get up, because I was afraid of waking you. Will you do your toilet first or shall I?"

"I'm in no hurry," said Ashenden.

"I am an old campaigner, it will not take me long. Do you wash your teeth every day?"

"Yes," said Ashenden.

"So do I. It is a habit I learned in New York. I always think that a fine set of teeth are an adornment to a man."

There was a wash-basin in the compartment and the General scrubbed his teeth, with gurglings and garglings, energetically. Then he got a bottle of eau-de-cologne from his bag, poured some of it on a towel and rubbed it over his face and hands. He took a comb and carefully arranged his wig; either it had not moved in the night or else he had set it straight before Ashenden awoke. He got another bottle out of his bag, with a spray attached to it, and squeezing a bulb covered his shirt and coat with a fine cloud of scent, did the same to his handkerchief, and then with a beaming face, like a man who has done his duty by the world and is well pleased, turned to Ashenden and said:

"Now I am ready to brave the day. I will leave my things for you, you need not be afraid of the eau-de-cologne, it is the best you can get in Paris."

"Thank you very much," said Ashenden. "All I want is soap and water."

"Water? I never use water except when I have a bath. Nothing can be worse for the skin."

When they approached the frontier, Ashenden, remembering the General's instructive gesture when he was suddenly awakened in the night, said to him:

"If you've got a revolver on you I think you'd better give it to me. With my diplomatic passport they're not likely to search me, but they might take it into their heads to go through you and we don't want to have any bothers."

"It is hardly a weapon, it is only a toy," returned the Mexican, taking out of his hip-pocket a fully loaded revolver of formidable dimensions. "I do not like parting with it even for an hour, it gives me the feeling that I am not fully dressed. But you are quite right, we do not want to take any risks; I will give you my knife as well. I would always rather use a knife than a revolver; I think it is a more elegant weapon."

"I daresay it is only a matter of habit," answered Ashenden. "Perhaps you are more at home with a knife."

"Anyone can pull a trigger, but it needs a man to use a knife."

To Ashenden it looked as though it were in a single movement that he tore open his waistcoat and from his belt snatched and opened a long knife of murderous aspect. He handed it to Ashenden with a pleased smile on his large, ugly and naked face.

"There's a pretty piece of work for you, Mr. Somerville. I've never seen a better bit of steel in my life, it takes an edge like a razor and it's strong; you can cut a cigarette-

paper with it and you can hew down an oak. There is nothing to get out of order and when it is closed it might be
the knife a schoolboy uses to cut notches in his desk."

He shut it with a click and Ashenden put it along with
the revolver in his pocket.

"Have you anything else?"

"My hands," replied the Mexican with arrogance, "but
those I daresay the custom officials will not make trouble
about."

Ashenden remembered the iron grip he had given him
when they shook hands and slightly shuddered. They were
large and long and smooth; there was not a hair on them
or on the wrists, and with the pointed, rosy, manicured
nails there was really something sinister about them.

Ashenden and General Carmona went through the formali-
ties at the frontier independently and when they returned
to their carriage Ashenden handed back to his companion
the revolver and the knife. He sighed.

"Now I feel more comfortable. What do you say to a
game of cards?"

"I should like it," said Ashenden.

The Hairless Mexican opened his bag again and from a
corner extracted a greasy pack of French cards. He asked
Ashenden whether he played écarté and when Ashenden
told him that he did not suggested piquet. This was a game
that Ashenden was not unfamiliar with so they settled the
stakes and began. Since both were in favour of quick action
they played the game of four hands, doubling the first and
last. Ashenden had good enough cards, but the General
seemed notwithstanding always to have better. Ashenden kept
his eyes open and he was not careless of the possibility that
his antagonist might correct the inequalities of chance, but he
saw nothing to suggest that everything was not above board.
He lost game after game. He was capoted and rubiconed.
The score against him mounted up and up till he had lost
something like a thousand francs, which at that time was a
tidy sum. The General smoked innumerable cigarettes. He
made them himself with a twist of the finger, a lick of his

tongue and incredible celerity. At last he flung himself against the back of his seat.

"By the way, my friend, does the British Government pay your card losses when you are on a mission?" he asked.

"It certainly doesn't."

"Well, I think you have lost enough. If it went down on your expense account I would have proposed playing till we reached Rome, but you are sympathetic to me. If it is your own money I do not want to win any more of it."

He picked up the cards and put them aside. Ashenden somewhat ruefully took out a number of notes and handed them to the Mexican. He counted them and with his usual neatness put them carefully folded into his pocket-book. Then, leaning forward, he patted Ashenden almost affectionately on the knee.

"I like you, you are modest and unassuming, you have not the arrogance of your countrymen, and I am sure that you will take my advice in the spirit in which it is meant. Do not play piquet with people you don't know."

Ashenden was somewhat mortified and perhaps his face showed it, for the Mexican seized his hand.

"My dear fellow, I have not hurt your feelings? I would not do that for the world. You do not play piquet worse than most piquet players. It is not that. If we were going to be together longer I would teach you how to win at cards. One plays cards to win money and there is no sense in losing."

"I thought it was only in love and war that all things were fair," said Ashenden, with a chuckle.

"Ah, I am glad to see you smile. That is the way to take a loss. I see that you have good humour and good sense. You will go far in life. When I get back to Mexico and am in possession of my estates again you must come and stay with me. I will treat you like a king. You shall ride my best horses, we will go to bull-fights together, and if there are girls you fancy you have only to say the word and you shall have them."

He began telling Ashenden of the vast territories, the

haciendas and the mines in Mexico, of which he had been dispossessed. He told him of the feudal state in which he lived. It did not matter whether what he said was true or not, for those sonorous phrases of his were fruity with the rich-distilled perfumes of romance. He described a spacious life that seemed to belong to another age and his eloquent gestures brought before the mind's eye tawny distances and vast green plantations, great herds of cattle and in the moon-lit night the song of the blind singers that melted in the air and the twanging of guitars.

"Everything I lost, everything. In Paris I was driven to earn a pittance by giving Spanish lessons or showing Ameri-cans—*Americanos del Norte,* I mean—the night life of the city. I who had flung away a thousand *duros* on a dinner have been forced to beg my bread like a blind Indian. I who have taken pleasure in clasping a diamond bracelet round the wrist of a beautiful woman have been forced to accept a suit of clothes from a hag old enough to be my mother. Patience. Man is born to trouble as the sparks fly upward, but misfortune cannot last for ever. The time is ripe and soon we shall strike our blow."

He took up the greasy pack of cards and set them out in a number of little piles.

"Let us see what the cards say. They never lie. Ah, if I had only had greater faith in them I should have avoided the only action of my life that has weighed heavily on me. My conscience is at ease. I did what any man would do under the circumstances, but I regret that necessity forced upon me an action that I would willingly have avoided."

He looked through the cards, set some of them on one side on a system Ashenden did not understand, shuffled the remainder and once more put them in little piles.

"The cards warned me, I will never deny that, their warn-ing was clear and definite. Love and a dark woman, danger, betrayal and death. It was as plain as the nose on your face. Any fool would have known what it meant and I have been using the cards all my life. There is hardly an action that

I make without consulting them. There are no excuses. I was besotted. Ah, you of the Northern races do not know what love means, you do not know how it can prevent you from sleeping, how it can take your appetite for food away so that you dwindle as if from a fever, you do not understand what a frenzy it is so that you are like a madman and you will stick at nothing to satisfy your desire. A man like me is capable of every folly and every crime when he is in love, *si Señor*, and of heroism. He can scale mountains higher than Everest and swim across seas broader than the Atlantic. He is god, he is devil. Women have been my ruin."

Once more the Hairless Mexican glanced at the cards, took some out of the little piles and left others in. He shuffled them again.

"I have been loved by multitudes of women. I do not say it in vanity. I offer no explanation. It is mere matter of fact. Go to Mexico City and ask them what they know of Manuel Carmona and of his triumphs. Ask them how many women have resisted Manuel Carmona."

Ashenden, frowning a little, watched him reflectively. He wondered whether R., that shrewd fellow who chose his instruments with such a sure instinct, had not this time made a mistake, and he was uneasy. Did the Hairless Mexican really believe that he was irresistible or was he merely a blatant liar? In the course of his manipulations he had thrown out all the cards in the pack but four and these now lay in front of him face downwards and side by side. He touched them one by one but did not turn them up.

"There is fate," he said, "and no power on earth can change it. I hesitate. This is a moment that ever fills me with apprehension and I have to steel myself to turn over the cards that may tell me that disaster awaits me. I am a brave man, but sometimes I have reached this stage and not had the courage to look at the four fatal cards."

Indeed now he eyed the backs of them with an anxiety he did not try to hide.

"What was I saying to you?"

"You were telling me that women found your fascinations irresistible?" replied Ashenden dryly.

"Once all the same I found a woman who resisted me. I saw her first in a house, a *casa de mujeres* in Mexico City, she was going down the stairs as I went up; she was not very beautiful, I had had a hundred more beautiful, but she had something that took my fancy and I told the old woman who kept the house to send her to me. You will know her when you go to Mexico City; they call her La Marqueza. She said that the girl was not an inmate, but came there only from time to time and had left. I told her to have her there next evening and not to let her go till I came. But I was delayed and when I arrived La Marqueza told me that the girl had said she was not used to being kept waiting and had gone. I am a good-natured fellow and I do not mind if women are capricious and teasing, that is part of their charm, so with a laugh I sent her a note of a hundred *duros* and promised that on the following day I would be punctual. But when I went, on the minute, La Marqueza handed me back my hundred *duros* and told me the girl did not fancy me. I laughed at her impertinence. I took off the diamond ring I was wearing and told the old woman to give her that and see whether it would induce her to change her mind. In the morning La Marqueza brought me in return for my ring—a red carnation. I did not know whether to be amused or angry. I am not used to being thwarted in my passions, I never hesitate to spend money (what is it for but to squander on pretty women?), and I told La Marqueza to go to the girl and say that I would give her a thousand *duros* to dine with me that night. Presently she came back with the answer that the girl would come on the condition that I allowed her to go home immediately after dinner. I accepted with a shrug of the shoulders. I did not think she was serious. I thought that she was saying that only to make herself more desired. She came to dinner at my house. Did I say she was not beautiful? She was the most beautiful, the most exquisite creature

I had ever met. I was intoxicated. She had charm and she had wit. She had all the *gracia* of the Andalusian. In one word she was adorable. I asked her why she had treated me so casually and she laughed in my face. I laid myself out to be agreeable. I exercised all my skill. I surpassed myself. But when we finished dinner she rose from her seat and bade me good-night. I asked her where she was going. She said I had promised to let her go and she trusted me as a man of honour to keep my word. I expostulated, I reasoned, I raved, I stormed. She held me to my word. All I could induce her to do was to consent to dine with me the following night on the same terms.

"You will think I was a fool, I was the happiest man alive; for seven days I paid her a thousand silver *duros* to dine with me. Every evening I waited for her with my heart in my mouth, as nervous as a *novillero* at his first bull-fight, and every evening she played with me, laughed at me, coquetted with me and drove me frantic. I was madly in love with her. I have never loved anyone so much before or since. I could think of nothing else. I was distracted. I neglected everything. I am a patriot and I love my country. A small band of us had got together and made up our minds that we could no longer put up with the misrule from which we were suffering. All the lucrative posts were given to other people, we were being made to pay taxes as though we were tradesmen, and we were exposed to abominable affronts. We had money and men. Our plans were made and we were ready to strike. I had an infinity of things to do, meetings to go to, ammunition to get, orders to give; I was so besotted over this woman that I could attend to nothing.

"You would have thought that I should be angry with her for making such a fool of me, me who had never known what it was not to gratify my smallest whim; I did not believe that she refused me to inflame my desires, I believed that she told the plain truth when she said that she would not give herself to me until she loved me. She said it was for me to make her love me. I thought her an angel. J

was ready to wait. My passion was so consuming that sooner
or later, I felt, at last it must communicate itself to her; it
was like a fire on the prairie that devours everything around
it; and at last—at last she said she loved me. My emotion
was so terrific that I thought I should fall down and die.
Oh, what rapture, oh, what madness! I would have given
her everything I possessed in the world, I would have torn
down the stars from heaven to deck her hair; I wanted to
do something to prove to her the extravagance of my love,
I wanted to do the impossible, the incredible, I wanted to
give her myself, my soul, my honour, all, all I had and all
I was; and that night when she lay in my arms I told
her of our plot and who we were that were concerned in
it. I felt her body stiffen with attention, I was conscious of
a flicker of her eyelids, there was something, I hardly knew
what, the hand that stroked my face was dry and cold; a
sudden suspicion seized me and all at once I remembered
what the cards had told me: love and a dark woman, danger,
betrayal and death. Three times they'd said it and I wouldn't
heed. I made no sign that I had noticed anything. She
nestled up against my heart and told me that she was
frightened to hear such things and asked me if so and so
was concerned. I answered her. I wanted to make sure.
One after the other, with infinite cunning, between her
kisses she cajoled me into giving every detail of the plot,
and now I was certain, as certain as I am that you sit before me, that she was a spy. She was a spy of the president's and she had been set to allure me with her devilish
charm and now she had wormed out of me all our secrets.
The lives of all of us were in her hands and I knew that
if she left that room in twenty-four hours we should be
dead men. And I loved her, I loved her; oh, words cannot
tell you the agony of desire that burned my heart; love
like that is no pleasure, it is pain, pain, but the exquisite
pain that transcends all pleasure. It is that heavenly anguish
that the saints speak of when they are seized with a divine
ecstasy. I knew that she must not leave the room alive and
I feared that if I delayed my courage would fail me.

" 'I think I shall sleep,' she said.

" 'Sleep, my dove,' I answered.

" '*Alma de mi corazon*,' she called me. 'Soul of my heart.' They were the last words she spoke. Those heavy lids of hers, dark like a grape and faintly humid, those heavy lids of hers closed over her eyes and in a little while I knew by the regular movement of her breast against mine that she slept. You see, I loved her, I could not bear that she should suffer, she was a spy, yes, but my heart bade me spare her the terror of knowing what must happen. It is strange, I felt no anger because she had betrayed me, I should have hated her because of her vileness, I could not, I only felt that my soul was enveloped in night. Poor thing, poor thing, I could have cried for pity for her. I drew my arm very gently from around her, my left arm that was, my right was free, and raised myself on my hand. But she was so beautiful, I turned my face away when I drew the knife with all my strength across her lovely throat. Without awaking she passed from sleep to death."

He stopped and stared frowning at the four cards that still lay, their backs upward, waiting to be turned up.

"It was in the cards. Why did I not take their warning? I will not look at them. Damn them. Take them away."

With a violent gesture he swept the whole pack on to the floor.

"Though I am a free-thinker I had masses said for her soul." He leaned back and rolled himself a cigarette. He inhaled a long breathful of smoke. He shrugged his shoulders. "The Colonel said you were a writer. What do you write?"

"Stories," replied Ashenden.

"Detective stories?"

"No."

"Why not? They are the only ones I read. If I were a writer I should write detective stories."

"They are very difficult. You need an incredible amount of invention. I devised a murder story once, but the murder was so ingenious that I could never find a way of bringing it home to the murderer, and after all, one of the conventions of the detective story is that the mystery should in the end be solved and the criminal brought to justice."

"If your murder is as ingenious as you think the only means you have of proving the murderer's guilt is by the discovery of his motives. When once you have found a motive the chances are that you will hit upon evidence that till then had escaped you. If there is no motive the most damning evidence will be inconclusive. Imagine for instance that you went up to a man in a lonely street on a moonless night and stabbed him to the heart. Who would ever think of you? But if he was your wife's lover, or your brother, or had cheated or insulted you, then a scrap of paper, a bit of string or a chance remark would be enough to hang you. What were your movements at the time he was killed? Are there not a dozen people who saw you before and after? But if he was a total stranger you would never for a moment be suspected. It was inevitable that Jack the Ripper should escape unless he was caught in the act."

Ashenden had more than one reason to change the conversation. They were parting at Rome and he thought it necessary to come to an understanding with his companion about their respective movements. The Mexican was going to Brindisi and Ashenden to Naples. He meant to lodge at the Hotel de Belfast, which was a large second-rate hotel near the harbour frequented by commercial travellers and the thriftier kind of tripper. It would be as well to let the General have the number of his room so that he could come up if necessary without enquiring of the porter, and at the next stopping-place Ashenden got an envelope from the station-buffet and made him address it in his own writing to himself at the post-office in Brindisi. All Ashenden had to do then was to scribble a number on a sheet of paper and post it.

The Hairless Mexican shrugged his shoulders.

"To my mind all these precautions are rather childish. There is absolutely no risk. But whatever happens you may be quite sure that I will not compromise you."

"This is not the sort of job which I'm very familiar with,"

said Ashenden. "I'm content to follow the Colonel's instructions and know no more about it than it's essential I should."

"Quite so. Should the exigencies of the situation force me to take a drastic step and I get into trouble I shall of course be treated as a political prisoner. Sooner or later Italy is bound to come into the war on the side of the Allies and I shall be released. I have considered everything. But I beg you very seriously to have no more anxiety about the outcome of our mission than if you were going for a picnic on the Thames."

But when at last they separated and Ashenden found himself alone in a carriage on the way to Naples he heaved a great sigh of relief. He was glad to be rid of that chattering, hideous and fantastic creature. He was gone to meet Constantine Andreadi at Brindisi and if half of what he had told Ashenden was true, Ashenden could not but congratulate himself that he did not stand in the Greek spy's shoes. He wondered what sort of a man he was. There was a grimness in the notion of his coming across the blue Ionian, with his confidential papers and his dangerous secrets, all unconscious of the noose into which he was putting his head. Well, that was war, and only fools thought it could be waged with kid gloves on.

Ashenden arrived in Naples and having taken a room at the hotel, wrote its number on a sheet of paper in block letters and posted it to the Hairless Mexican. He went to the British Consulate where R. had arranged to send any instructions he might have for him and found that they knew about him and everything was in order. Then he put aside these matters and made up his mind to amuse himself. Here in the South the spring was well advanced and in the busy streets the sun was hot. Ashenden knew Naples pretty well. The Piazza di San Ferdinando, with its bustle, the Piazza del Plebiscito, with its handsome church, stirred in his heart pleasant recollections. The Strada di Chiaia was as noisy as ever. He stood at corners and looked up the narrow alleys that climbed the hill precipitously, those alleys of high houses with the washing set out to dry on lines

across the street like pennants flying to mark a feast-day;
and he sauntered along the shore, looking at the burnished
sea with Capri faintly outlined against the day, till he came
to Posilippo where there was an old, rambling and bedraggled *palazzo* in which in his youth he had spent many
a romantic hour. He observed the curious little pain with
which the memories of the past wrung his heart-strings.
Then he took a fly drawn by a small and scraggy pony and
rattled back over the stones to the *Galleria* where he sat
in the cool and drank an *americano* and looked at the people
who loitered there, talking, for ever talking with vivacious
gestures, and, exercising his fancy, sought from their appearance to divine their reality.

For three days Ashenden led the idle life that fitted so
well the fantastical, untidy and genial city. He did nothing
from morning till night but wander at random, looking, not
with the eye of the tourist who seeks for what ought to
be seen, nor with the eye of the writer who looks for his
own, (seeing in a sunset a melodious phrase or in a face
the inkling of a character,) but with that of the tramp to
whom whatever happens is absolute. He went to the museum
to look at the statue of Agrippina the Younger, which he
had particular reasons for remembering with affection, and
took the opportunity to see once more the Titian and the
Brueghel in the picture gallery. But he always came back
to the church of Santa Chiara. Its grace, it gaiety, the airy
persiflage with which it seemed to treat religion and at the
back of this its sensual emotion; its extravagance, its elegance
of line; to Ashenden it seemed to express, as it were in one
absurd and grandiloquent metaphor, the sunny, dusty, lovely
city and its bustling inhabitants. It said that life was charming and sad; it's a pity one hadn't any money, but money
wasn't everything, and anyway why bother when we are
here to-day and gone to-morrow, and it was all very exciting
and amusing, and after all we must make the best of things:
facciamo una piccola combinazione.

But on the fourth morning when Ashenden, having just
stepped out of his bath, was trying to dry himself on a

towel that absorbed no moisture, his door was quickly opened and a man slipped into his room.

"What d'you want?" cried Ashenden.

"It's all right. Don't you know me?"

"Good Lord, it's the Mexican. What have you done to yourself?"

He had changed his wig and wore now a black one, close cropped, that fitted on his head like a cap. It entirely altered the look of him and though this was still odd enough, it was quite different from that which he had borne before. He wore a shabby grey suit.

"I can only stop a minute. He's getting shaved."

Ashenden felt his cheeks suddenly redden.

"You found him then?"

"That wasn't difficult. He was the only Greek passenger on the ship. I went on board when she got in and asked for a friend who had sailed from the Piræus. I said I had come to meet a Mr. George Diogenidis. I pretended to be much puzzled at his not coming and I got into conversation with Andreadi. He's travelling under a false name. He calls himself Lombardos. I followed him when he landed and do you know the first thing he did? He went into a barber's and had his beard shaved. What do you think of that?"

"Nothing. Anyone might have his beard shaved."

"That is not what I think. He wanted to change his appearance. Oh, he's cunning. I admire the Germans, they leave nothing to chance, he's got his whole story pat, but I'll tell you that in a minute."

"By the way, you've changed your appearance too."

"Ah yes, this is a wig I'm wearing; it makes a difference, doesn't it?"

"I should never have known you."

"One has to take precautions. We are bosom friends. We had to spend the day in Brindisi and he cannot speak Italian. He was glad to have me help him and we travelled up together. I have brought him to this hotel. He says he is going to Rome to-morrow, but I shall not let him out of my sight; I do not want him to give me the slip. He says

that he wants to see Naples and I have offered to show him
everything there is to see."

"Why isn't he going to Rome to-day?"

"That is part of the story. He pretends he is a Greek business man who has made money during the war. He says he
was the owner of two coasting steamers and has just sold
them. Now he means to go to Paris and have his fling. He
says he has wanted to go to Paris all his life and at last has
the chance. He is close. I tried to get him to talk. I told him I
was a Spaniard and had been to Brindisi to arrange communications with Turkey about war material. He listened to me
and I saw he was interested, but he told me nothing and of
course I did not think it wise to press him. He has the papers
on his person."

"How do you know?"

"He is not anxious about his grip, but he feels every now
and then round his middle, they're either in a belt or in the
lining of his vest."

"Why the devil did you bring him to this hotel?"

"I thought it would be more convenient. We may want to
search his luggage."

"Are you staying here too?"

"No, I am not such a fool as that, I told him I was going
to Rome by the night train and would not take a room. But I
must go, I promised to meet him outside the barber's in fifteen minutes."

"All right."

"Where shall I find you to-night if I want you?"

Ashenden for an instant eyed the Hairless Mexican, then
with a slight frown looked away.

"I shall spend the evening in my room."

"Very well. Will you just see that there's nobody in the
passage."

Ashenden opened the door and looked out. He saw no one.
The hotel in point of fact at that season was nearly empty.
There were few foreigners in Naples and trade was bad.

"It's all right," said Ashenden.

The Hairless Mexican walked boldly out. Ashenden closed

the door behind him. He shaved and slowly dressed. The sun
was shining as brightly as usual on the square and the people
who passed, the shabby little carriages with their scrawny
horses, had the same air as before, but they did not any longer
fill Ashenden with gaiety. He was not comfortable. He went
out and called as was his habit at the Consulate to ask if there
was a telegram for him. Nothing. Then he went to Cook's and
looked out the trains to Rome: there was one soon after midnight and another at five in the morning. He wished he could
catch the first. He did not know what were the Mexican's
plans; if he really wanted to get to Cuba he would do well to
make his way to Spain, and, glancing at the notices in the
office, Ashenden saw that next day there was a ship sailing
from Naples to Barcelona.

Ashenden was bored with Naples. The glare in the streets
tired his eyes, the dust was intolerable, the noise was deafening. He went to the *Galleria* and had a drink. In the afternoon he went to a cinema. Then, going back to his hotel, he
told the clerk that since he was starting so early in the morning he preferred to pay his bill at once, and he took his luggage to the station, leaving in his room only a dispatch-case in
which were the printed part of his code and a book or two.
He dined. Then returning to the hotel, he sat down to wait
for the Hairless Mexican. He could not conceal from himself
the fact that he was exceedingly nervous. He began to read,
but the book was tiresome, and he tried another: his attention
wandered and he glanced at his watch. It was desperately
early; he took up his book again, making up his mind that he
would not look at his watch till he had read thirty pages, but
though he ran his eyes conscientiously down one page after
another he could not tell more than vaguely what it was he
read. He looked at the time again. Good God, it was only half-
past ten. He wondered where the Hairless Mexican was, and
what he was doing; he was afraid he would make a mess of
things. It was a horrible business. Then it struck him that he
had better shut the window and draw the curtains. He smoked
innumerable cigarettes. He looked at his watch and it was a
quarter past eleven. A thought struck him and his heart began

to beat against his chest; out of curiosity he counted his pulse and was surprised to find that it was normal. Though it was a warm night and the room was stuffy his hands and feet were icy. What a nuisance it was, he reflected irritably, to have an imagination that conjured up pictures of things that you didn't in the least want to see! From his standpoint as a writer he had often considered murder and his mind went to that fearful description of one in *Crime and Punishment*. He did not want to think of this topic, but it forced itself upon him; his book dropped to his knees and staring at the wall in front of him (it had a brown wall-paper with a pattern of dingy roses) he asked himself how, if one had to, one would commit a murder in Naples. Of course there was the Villa, the great leafy garden facing the bay in which stood the aquarium; that was deserted at night and very dark; things happened there that did not bear the light of day and prudent persons after dusk avoided its sinister paths. Beyond Posilippo the road was very solitary and there were byways that led up the hill in which by night you would never meet a soul, but how would you induce a man who had any nerves to go there? You might suggest a row in the bay, but the boat-man who hired the boat would see you; it was doubtful indeed if he would let you go on the water alone; there were disreputable hotels down by the harbour where no questions were asked of persons who arrived late at night without luggage; but here again the waiter who showed you your room had the chance of a good look at you and you had on entering to sign an elaborate questionnaire.

Ashenden looked once more at the time. He was very tired. He sat now not even trying to read, his mind a blank.

Then the door opened softly and he sprang to his feet. His flesh crept. The Hairless Mexican stood before him.

"Did I startle you?" he asked smiling. "I thought you would prefer me not to knock."

"Did anyone see you come in?"

"I was let in by the night-watchman; he was asleep when I rang and didn't even look at me. I'm sorry I'm so late, but I had to change."

The Hairless Mexican wore now the clothes he had travelled down in and his fair wig. It was extraordinary how different he looked. He was bigger and more flamboyant; the very shape of his face was altered. His eyes were shining and he seemed in excellent spirits. He gave Ashenden a glance.

"How white you are, my friend! Surely you're not nervous?"

"Have you got the documents?"

"No. He hadn't got them on him. This is all he had."

He put down on the table a bulky pocket-book and a passport.

"I don't want them," said Ashenden quickly. "Take them."

With a shrug of the shoulders the Hairless Mexican put the things back in his pocket.

"What was in his belt? You said he kept feeling round his middle."

"Only money. I've looked through the pocket-book. It contains nothing but private letters and photographs of women. He must have locked the documents in his grip before coming out with me this evening."

"Damn," said Ashenden.

"I've got the key of his room. We'd better go and look through his luggage."

Ashenden felt a sensation of sickness in the pit of his stomach. He hesitated. The Mexican smiled not unkindly.

"There's no risk, *amigo*," he said, as though he were reassuring a small boy, "but if you don't feel happy, I'll go alone."

"No, I'll come with you," said Ashenden.

"There's no one awake in the hotel and Mr. Andreadi won't disturb us. Take off your shoes if you like."

Ashenden did not answer. He frowned because he noticed that his hands were slightly trembling. He unlaced his shoes and slipped them off. The Mexican did the same.

"You'd better go first," he said. "Turn to the left and go straight along the corridor. It's number thirty-eight."

Ashenden opened the door and stepped out. The passage was dimly lit. It exasperated him to feel so nervous when he could not but be aware that his companion was perfectly at ease. When they reached the door the Hairless Mexican inserted the key, turned the lock and went in. He switched on the light. Ashenden followed him and closed the door. He noticed that the shutters were shut.

"Now we're all right. We can take our time."

He took a bunch of keys out of his pocket, tried one or two and at last hit upon the right one. The suitcase was filled with clothes.

"Cheap clothes," said the Mexican contemptuously as he took them out. "My own principle is that it's always cheaper in the end to buy the best. After all one is a gentleman or one isn't a gentleman."

"Are you obliged to talk?" asked Ashenden.

"A spice of danger affects people in different ways. It only excites me, but it puts you in a bad temper, *amigo.*"

"You see I'm scared and you're not," replied Ashenden with candour.

"It's merely a matter of nerves."

Meanwhile he felt the clothes, rapidly but with care, as he took them out. There were no papers of any sort in the suit-case. Then he took out his knife and slit the lining. It was a cheap piece and the lining was gummed to the material of which the suit-case was made. There was no possibility of anything being concealed in it.

"They're not here. They must be hidden in the room."

"Are you sure he didn't deposit them in some office? At one of the consulates for example?"

"He was never out of my sight for a moment except when he was getting shaved."

The Hairless Mexican opened the drawers and the cupboard. There was no carpet on the floor. He looked under the bed, in it, and under the mattress. His dark eyes shot up and down the room, looking for a hiding-place, and Ashenden felt that nothing escaped him.

"Perhaps he left them in charge of the clerk downstairs?"

"I should have known it. And he wouldn't dare. They're not here. I can't understand it."

He looked about the room irresolutely. He frowned in the attempt to guess at a solution of the mystery.

"Let's get out of here," said Ashenden.

"In a minute."

The Mexican went down on his knees, quickly and neatly folded the clothes, and packed them up again. He locked the bag and stood up. Then, putting out the light, he slowly opened the door and looked out. He beckoned to Ashenden and slipped into the passage. When Ashenden had followed him he stopped and locked the door, put the key in his pocket and walked with Ashenden to his room. When they were inside it and the bolt drawn Ashenden wiped his clammy hands and his forehead.

"Thank God, we're out of that!"

"There wasn't really the smallest danger. But what are we to do now? The Colonel will be angry that the papers haven't been found."

"I'm taking the five o'clock train to Rome. I shall wire for instructions there."

"Very well, I will come with you."

"I should have thought it would suit you better to get out of the country more quickly. There's a boat to-morrow that goes to Barcelona. Why don't you take that and if necessary I can come to see you there?"

The Hairless Mexican gave a little smile.

"I see that you are anxious to be rid of me. Well, I won't thwart a wish that your inexperience in these matters excuses. I will go to Barcelona. I have a visa for Spain."

Ashenden looked at his watch. It was a little after two. He had nearly three hours to wait. His companion comfortably rolled himself a cigarette.

"What do you say to a little supper?" he asked. "I'm as hungry as a wolf."

The thought of food sickened Ashenden, but he was terribly thirsty. He did not want to go out with the Hairless Mexican, but neither did he want to stay in that hotel by himself.

"Where could one go at this hour?"

"Come along with me. I'll find you a place."

Ashenden put on his hat and took his dispatch-case in his hand. They went downstairs. In the hall the porter was sleeping soundly on a mattress on the floor. As they passed the desk, walking softly in order not to wake him, Ashenden noticed in the pigeon-hole belonging to his room a letter. He took it out and saw that it was addressed to him. They tiptoed out of the hotel and shut the door behind them. Then they walked quickly away. Stopping after a hundred yards or so under a lamp-post Ashenden took the letter out of his pocket and read it; it came from the Consulate and said: *The enclosed telegram arrived to-night and in case it is urgent I am sending it round to your hotel by messenger.* It had apparently been left some time before midnight while Ashenden was sitting in his room. He opened the telegram and saw that it was in code.

"Well, it'll have to wait," he said, putting it back in his pocket.

The Hairless Mexican walked as though he knew his way through the deserted streets and Ashenden walked by his side. At last they came to a tavern in a blind alley, noisome and evil, and this the Mexican entered.

"It's not the Ritz," he said, "but at this hour of the night it's only in a place like this that we stand a chance of getting something to eat."

Ashenden found himself in a long sordid room at one end of which a wizened young man sat at a piano; there were tables standing out from the wall on each side and against them benches. A number of persons, men and women, were sitting about. They were drinking beer and wine. The women were old, painted, and hideous; and their harsh gaiety was at once noisy and lifeless. When Ashenden and the Hairless Mexican came in they all stared and when they sat down at one of the tables Ashenden looked away in order not to meet the leering eyes, just ready to break into a smile, that sought his insinuatingly. The wizened pianist strummed a tune and several couples got up and began to dance. Since there were not enough men to go round some of the women danced together. The General ordered two plates of spaghetti and a bottle of Capri wine. When the wine was brought he drank a glassful greedily and then waiting for the *pasta* eyed the women who were sitting at the other tables.

"Do you dance?" he asked Ashenden. "I'm going to ask one of these girls to have a turn with me."

He got up and Ashenden watched him go up to one who had at least flashing eyes and white teeth to recommend her; she rose and he put his arm round her. He danced well. Ashenden saw him begin talking; the woman laughed and presently the look of indifference with which she had accepted his offer changed to one of interest. Soon they were chatting gaily. The dance came to an end and putting her back at her table he returned to Ashenden and drank another glass of wine.

"What do you think of my girl?" he asked. "Not bad, is she? It does one good to dance. Why don't you ask one of them? This is a nice place, is it not? You can always trust me to find anything like this. I have an instinct."

The pianist started again. The woman looked at the Hairless Mexican and when with his thumb he pointed to the floor she jumped up with alacrity. He buttoned up his coat, arched his back and standing up by the side of the table waited for her to come to him. He swung her off, talking, smiling, and already he was on familiar terms with everyone in the room. In fluent Italian, with his Spanish accent, he exchanged badinage with one and the other. They laughed at his sallies. Then the waiter brought two heaped platefuls of macaroni and when the Mexican saw them he stopped dancing without ceremony and allowing his partner to get back to her table as she chose hurried to his meal.

"I'm ravenous," he said. "And yet I ate a good dinner. Where did you dine? You're going to eat some macaroni, aren't you?"

"I have no appetite," said Ashenden.

But he began to eat and to his surprise found that he was hungry. The Hairless Mexican ate with huge mouthfuls, enjoying himself vastly; his eyes shone and he was loquacious. The woman he had danced with had in that short time told him all about herself and he repeated now to Ashenden what she had said. He stuffed huge pieces of bread into his mouth. He ordered another bottle of wine.

"Wine?" he cried scornfully. "Wine is not a drink, only champagne; it does not even quench your thirst. Well, *amigo,* are you feeling better?"

"I'm bound to say I am," smiled Ashenden.

"Practice, that is all you want, practice."

He stretched out his hand to pat Ashenden on the arm.

"What's that?" cried Ashenden with a start. "What's that stain on your cuff?"

The Hairless Mexican gave his sleeve a glance.

"That? Nothing. It's only blood. I had a little accident and cut myself."

Ashenden was silent. His eyes sought the clock that hung over the door.

"Are you anxious about your train? Let me have one more dance and then I'll accompany you to the station."

The Mexican got up and with his sublime self-assurance seized in his arms the woman who sat nearest to him and danced away with her. Ashenden watched him moodily. He was a monstrous, terrible figure with that blond wig and his hairless face, but he moved with a matchless grace; his feet were small and seemed to hold the ground like the pads of a cat or a tiger; his rhythm was wonderful and you could not but see that the bedizened creature he danced with was intoxicated by his gestures. There was music in his toes and in the long arms that held her so firmly, and there was music in those long legs that seemed to move strangely from the hips. Sinister and grotesque though he was, there was in him now a feline elegance, even something of beauty, and you felt a secret, shameful fascination. To Ashenden he suggested one of those sculptures of the pre-Aztec hewers of stone, in which there is barbarism and vitality, something terrible and cruel, and yet withal a brooding and significant loveliness. All the same he would gladly have left him to finish the night by himself in that sordid dance-hall, but he knew that he must have a business conversation with him. He did not look forward to it without misgiving. He had been instructed to give

Manuel Carmona certain sums in return for certain documents. Well, the documents were not forthcoming, and as for
the rest—Ashenden knew nothing about that; it was no business of his. The Hairless Mexican waved gaily as he passed
him.

"I will come the moment the music stops. Pay the bill and
then I shall be ready."

Ashenden wished he could have seen into his mind. He
could not even make a guess at its workings. Then the Mexican, with his scented handkerchief wiping the sweat from
his brow, came back.

"Have you had a good time, General?" Ashenden asked
him.

"I always have a good time. Poor white trash, but what do I
care? I like to feel the body of a woman in my arms and see
her eyes grow languid and her lips part as her desire for me
melts the marrow in her bones like butter in the sun. Poor
white trash, but women."

They sallied forth. The Mexican proposed that they should
walk and in that quarter, at that hour, there would have been
little chance of finding a cab; but the sky was starry. It was a
summer night and the air was still. The silence walked beside
them like the ghost of a dead man. When they neared the
station the houses seemed on a sudden to take on a greyer,
more rigid line, and you felt that the dawn was at hand. A
little shiver trembled through the night. It was a moment of
apprehension and the soul for an instant was anxious; it was
as though, inherited down the years in their countless millions,
it felt a witless fear that perhaps another day would not break.
But they entered the station and the night once more en-
wrapped them. One or two porters lolled about like stage-
hands after the curtain has rung down and the scene is struck.
Two soldiers in dim uniforms stood motionless.

The waiting-room was empty, but Ashenden and the Hairless Mexican went to sit in the most retired part of it.

"I still have an hour before my train goes. I'll just see what
this cable's about."

He took it out of his pocket and from the dispatch-case

got his code. He was not then using a very elaborate one. It was in two parts, one contained in a slim book and the other, given him on a sheet of paper and destroyed by him before he left allied territory, committed to memory. Ashenden put on his spectacles and set to work. The Hairless Mexican sat in a corner of the seat, rolling himself cigarettes and smoking; he sat there placidly, taking no notice of what Ashenden did, and enjoyed his well-earned repose. Ashenden deciphered the groups of numbers one by one and as he got it out jotted down each word on a piece of paper. His method was to abstract his mind from the sense till he had finished, since he had discovered that if you took notice of the words as they came along you often jumped to a conclusion and sometimes were led into error. So he translated quite mechanically, without paying attention to the words as he wrote them one after the other. When at last he had done he read the complete message. It ran as follows:

Constantine Andreadi has been detained by illness at Piræus. He will be unable to sail. Return Geneva and await instructions.

At first Ashenden could not understand. He read it again. He shook from head to foot. Then, for once robbed of his self-possession, he blurted out, in a hoarse, agitated and furious whisper:

"You bloody fool, you've killed the wrong man."

Mr. Harrington's Washing

WHEN Ashenden went on deck and saw before him a low-lying coast and a white town he felt a pleasant flutter of excitement. It was early and the sun had not long risen, but the sea was glassy and the sky was blue; it was warm already and one knew that the day would be sweltering. Vladivostok. It really gave one the sensation of being at the end of the world. It was a long journey that Ashenden had made from New York to San Francisco, across the Pacific in a Japanese boat to Yokohama, then from Tsuruki in a Russian boat, he the only Englishman on board, up the Sea of Japan. From Vladivostok he was to take the Trans-Siberian to Petrograd. It was the most important mission that he had ever had and he was pleased with the sense of responsibility that it gave him. He had no one to give him orders, unlimited funds (he carried in a belt next to his skin bills of exchange for a sum so enormous that he was staggered when he thought of them), and though he had been set to do something that was beyond human possibility he did not know this and was prepared to set about his task with confidence. He believed in his own astuteness. Though he had both esteem and admiration for the sensibility of the human race he had little respect for their intelligence: man has always found it easier to sacrifice his life than to learn the multiplication table.

Ashenden did not much look forward to ten days on a Russian train and in Yokohama he had heard rumours that in one or two places bridges had been blown up and the line cut. He was told that the soldiers, completely out of hand, would rob him of everything he possessed and turn him out on the steppe to shift for himself. It was a cheerful prospect. But the train was certainly starting and whatever happened later (and Ashenden had always a feeling that things never turned out as badly as you expected) he was determined to get a place on it. His intention on landing was to go at once to the British Consulate and find out what arangements had been made for him; but as they neared the shore and he was able to discern the untidy and bedraggled town he felt not a little forlorn. He knew but a few words of Russian. The only man on the ship who spoke English was the purser and though he promised Ashenden to do anything he could to help him Ashenden had the impression that he must not too greatly count upon him. It was a relief then, when they docked, to have a young man, small and with a mop of untidy hair, obviously a Jew, come up to him and ask if his name was Ashenden.

"Mine is Benedict. I'm the interpreter at the British Consulate. I've been told to look after you. We've got you a place on the train to-night."

Ashenden's spirits went up. They landed. The little Jew looked after his luggage and had his passport examined and then, getting into a car that waited for them, they drove off to the Consulate.

"I've had instructions to offer you every facility," said the Consul, "and you've only got to tell me what you want. I've fixed you up all right on the train, but God knows if you'll ever get to Petrograd. Oh, by the way, I've got a travelling companion for you. He's a man called Harrington, an American, and he's going to Petrograd for a firm in Philadelphia. He's trying to fix up some deal with the Provisional Government."

"What's he like?" asked Ashenden.

"Oh, he's all right. I wanted him to come with the American Consul to luncheon, but they've gone for an excursion in the country. You must get to the station a couple of hours before the train starts. There's always an awful scrimmage and if you're not there in good time someone will pinch your seat."

The train started at midnight and Ashenden dined with Benedict at the station restaurant which was, it appeared, the only place in that slatternly town where you could get a decent meal. It was crowded. The service was intolerably slow. Then they went on to the platform, where, though they had still two hours to spare, there was already a seething mob. Whole families, sitting on piles of luggage, seemed to be camped there. People rushed to and fro, or stood in little groups violently arguing. Women screamed. Others were silently weeping. Here two men were engaged in a fierce quarrel. It was a scene of indescribable confusion. The light in the station was wan and cold and the white faces of all those people were like the white faces of the dead waiting, patient or anxious, distraught or penitent, for the judgment of the last day. The train was made up and most of the carriages were already filled to overflowing. When at last Benedict found that in which Ashenden had his place a man sprang out of it excitedly.

"Come in and sit down," he said. "I've had the greatest difficulty in keeping your seat. A fellow wanted to come in here with a wife and two children. My Consul has just gone off with him to see the station-master."

"This is Mr. Harrington," said Benedict.

Ashenden stepped into the carriage. It had two berths in it. The porter stowed his luggage away. He shook hands with his travelling companion.

Mr. John Quincy Harrington was a very thin man of somewhat less than middle height, he had a yellow, bony face, with large, pale-blue eyes and when he took off his hat to wipe his brow wet from the perturbation he had endured he showed a large, bald skull; it was very bony and the ridges and protuberances stood out disconcertingly. He wore a bowler hat, a black coat and waistcoat, and a pair of striped trousers; a very high white collar and a neat, unobtrusive tie. Ashenden did not know precisely how you should dress in order to take a ten days' journey across Siberia, but he could not but think that Mr. Harrington's costume was eccentric. He spoke with precision in a high-pitched voice and in an accent that Ashenden recognized as that of New England.

In a minute the station-master came accompanied by a bearded Russian, suffering evidently from profound emotion, and followed by a lady holding two children by the hand. The Russian, tears running down his face, was talking with quivering lips to the station-master and his wife between her sobs was apparently telling him the story of her life. When they arrived at the carriage the altercation became more violent and Benedict joined in with his fluent Russian. Mr. Harrington did not know a word of the language, but being obviously of an excitable turn broke in and explained in voluble English that these seats had been booked by the Consuls of Great Britain and the United States respectively, and though he didn't know about the King of England, he could tell them straight and they could take it from him that the President of the United States would never permit an American citizen to be done out of a seat on the train that he had duly paid for. He would yield to force, but to nothing else, and if they touched him he would register a complaint with the Consul at once. He said all this and a great deal more to the station-master, who of course had no notion what he was talking about, but with much emphasis and a good deal of gesticulation made him in reply a passionate speech. This roused Mr. Harrington to the utmost pitch of indignation, for shaking his fist in the station-master's face, his own pale with fury, he cried out:

"Tell him I don't understand a word he says and I don't want to understand. If the Russians want us to look upon them as a civilized people why don't they talk a civilized language? Tell him that I am Mr. John Quincy Harrington and I'm travelling on behalf of Messrs Crewe and Adams of Philadelphia with a special letter of introduction to Mr. Kerensky and if I'm not left in peaceful possession of this carriage, Mr. Crewe will take the matter up with the Administration in Washington."

Mr. Harrington's manner was so truculent and his gestures

so menacing that the station-master, throwing up the sponge, turned on his heel without another word and walked moodily away. He was followed by the bearded Russian and his wife arguing heatedly with him and the two apathetic children. Mr. Harrington jumped back into the carriage.

"I'm terribly sorry to have to refuse to give up my seat to a lady with two children," he said. "No one knows better than I the respect due to a woman and a mother, but I've got to get to Petrograd by this train if I don't want to lose a very important order and I'm not going to spend ten days in a corridor for all the mothers in Russia."

"I don't blame you," said Ashenden.

"I am a married man and I have two children myself. I know that travelling with your family is a difficult matter, but there's nothing that I know to prevent you from staying at home."

When you are shut up with a man for ten days in a railway carriage you can hardly fail to learn most of what there is to know about him, and for ten days (for eleven to be exact) Ashenden spent twenty-four hours a day with Mr. Harrington. It is true that they went into the dining-room three times a day for their meals, but they sat opposite to one another; it is true that the train stopped for an hour morning and afternoon so that they were able to have a tramp up and down the platform, but they walked side by side. Ashenden made acquaintance with some of his fellow-travellers and sometimes they came into the compartment to have a chat, but if they only spoke French or German Mr. Harrington would watch them with acidulous disapproval and if they spoke English he would never let them get a word in. For Mr. Harrington was a talker. He talked as though it were a natural function of the human being, automatically, as men breathe or digest their food; he talked not because he had something to say, but because he could not help himself, in a high-pitched, nasal voice, without inflection, at one dead level of tone. He talked with precision, using a copious vocabulary and forming his sentences with deliberation; he never used a short word when a longer one would do; he never paused. He went on and on. It was not a torrent, for there was nothing impetuous about it, it was like a stream of lava pouring irresistibly down the side of a volcano. It flowed with a quiet and steady force that overwhelmed everything that was in its path.

Ashenden thought he had never known as much about anyone as he knew about Mr. Harrington, and not only about him, with all his opinions, habits and circumstances, but about his wife and his wife's family, his children and their schoolfellows, his employers and the alliances they had made for three or four generations with the best families of Philadelphia. His own family had come from Devonshire early in the eighteenth century and Mr. Harrington had been to the village where the graves of his forebears were still to be seen in the churchyard. He was proud of his English ancestry, but proud too of his American birth, though to him America was a little strip of land along the Atlantic coast and Americans were a small number of persons of English or Dutch origin whose blood had never been sullied by foreign admixture. He looked upon the Germans, Swedes, Irish and the inhabitants of Central and Eastern Europe who for the last hundred years have descended upon the United States as interlopers. He turned his attention away from them as a maiden lady who lived in a secluded manor might avert her eyes from the factory chimneys that had trespassed upon her retirement.

When Ashenden mentioned a man of vast wealth who owned some of the finest pictures in America Mr. Harrington said:

"I've never met him. My great-aunt Maria Penn Warmington always said his grandmother was a very good cook. My great-aunt Maria was terribly sorry when she left her to get married. She said she never knew anyone who could make an apple pancake as she could."

Mr. Harrington was devoted to his wife and he told Ashenden at unbelievable length how cultivated and what a perfect mother she was. She had delicate health and had undergone a great number of operations all of which he described in detail. He had had two operations himself, one on his tonsils and one to remove his appendix and he took Ashenden day by day through his experiences. All his friends had had operations and his knowledge of surgery was encyclopædic. He had two sons, both at school, and he was seriously considering whether he would not be well-advised to have them operated on. It was curious that one of them should have enlarged tonsils, and he was not at all happy about the appendix of the other. They were more devoted to one another than he had ever seen two brothers be and a very good friend of his, the brightest surgeon in Philadelphia, had offered to operate on them both together so that they should not be separated. He showed Ashenden photographs of the boys and their mother. This journey of his to Russia was the first time in their lives that he had been separated from them and every morning he wrote a long letter to his wife telling her everything that had happened and a good deal of what he had said during the day. Ashenden watched him cover sheet after sheet of paper with his neat, legible and precise handwriting.

Mr. Harrington had read all the books on conversation and knew its technique to the last detail. He had a little book in which he noted down the stories he heard and he told Ashenden that when he was going out to dinner he always looked up half a dozen so that he should not be at a loss. They were marked with a G if they could be told in general society and with an M (for men) if they were more fit for rough masculine ears. He was a specialist in that peculiar form of anecdote that consists in narrating a long serious incident, piling detail upon detail, till a comic end is reached. He spared you nothing and Ashenden foreseeing the point long before it arrived would clench his hands and knit his brows in the strenuous effort not to betray his impatience and at last force from his unwilling mouth a grim and hollow laugh. If someone came into the compartment in the middle Mr. Harrington would greet him with cordiality.

"Come right in and sit down. I was just telling my friend a story. You must listen to it, it's one of the funniest things you ever heard."

Then he would begin again from the very beginning and repeat it word for word, without altering a single apt epithet.

till he reached the humorous end. Ashenden suggested once that they should see whether they could find two people on the train who played cards so that they might while away the time with a game of bridge, but Mr. Harrington said he never touched cards and when Ashenden in desperation began to play patience he pulled a wry face.

"It beats me how an intelligent man can waste his time card playing, and of all the unintellectual pursuits I have ever seen it seems to me that solitaire is the worst. It kills conversation. Man is a social animal and he exercises the highest part of his nature when he takes part in social intercourse."

"There is a certain elegance in wasting time," said Ashenden. "Any fool can waste money, but when you waste time you waste what is priceless. Besides," he added with bitterness, "you can still talk."

"How can I talk when your attention is taken up by whether you are going to get a black seven to put on a red eight? Conversation calls forth the highest powers of the intellect and if you have made a study of it you have the right to expect that the person you're talking to will give you the fullest attention he is capable of."

He did not say this acrimoniously, but with the good-humoured patience of a man who has been much tried. He was just stating a plain fact and Ashenden could take it or leave it. It was the claim of the artist to have his work taken seriously.

Mr. Harrington was a diligent reader. He read pencil in hand, underlining passages that attracted his attention and on the margin making in his neat writing comments on what he read. This he was fond of discussing and when Ashenden himself was reading and felt on a sudden that Mr. Harrington, book in one hand and pencil in the other, was looking at him with his large pale eyes he began to have violent palpitations of the heart. He dared not look up, he dared not even turn the page, for he knew that Mr. Harrington would regard this as ample excuse to break into a discourse, but remained with his eyes fixed desperately on a single word, like a chicken with its beak to a chalk line, and only ventured to breathe when he realized that Mr. Harrington, having given up the attempt, had resumed his reading. He was then engaged on a History of the American Constitution in two volumes and for recreation was perusing a stout volume that purported to contain all the great speeches of the world. For Mr. Harrington was an after-dinner speaker and had read all the best books on speaking in public. He knew exactly how to get on good terms with his audience, just where to put in the serious words that touched their hearts, how to catch their attention by a few apt stories and finally with what degree of eloquence, suiting the occasion, to deliver his peroration.

Mr. Harrington was very fond of reading aloud. Ashenden had had frequent occasion to observe the distressing propensity of Americans for this pastime. In hotel drawing-rooms at night after dinner he had often seen the father of a family seated in a retired corner and surrounded by his wife, his two sons and his daughter, reading to them. On ships crossing the Atlantic he had sometimes watched with awe the tall, spare gentleman of commanding aspect who sat in the centre of fifteen ladies no longer in their first youth and in a resonant voice read to them the history of Art. Walking up and down the promenade deck he had passed honeymooning couples lying on deck-chairs and caught the unhurried tones of the bride as she read to her young husband the pages of a popular novel. It had always seemed to him a curious way of showing affection. He had had friends who had offered to read to him and he had known women who had said they loved being read to, but he had always politely refused the invitation and firmly ignored the hint. He liked neither reading aloud nor being read aloud to. In his heart he thought the national predilection for this form of entertainment the only flaw in the perfection of the American character. But the immortal gods love a good laugh at the expense of human beings and now delivered him, bound and helpless, to the knife of the high priest. Mr. Harrington flattered himself that he was a very good reader and he explained to Ashenden the theory and practice of the art. Ashenden learned that there were two schools, the dramatic and the natural: in the first you imitated the voices of those who spoke (if you were reading a novel) and when the heroine wailed you wailed and when emotion choked her you choked too; but in the other you read as impassively as though you were reading the price-list of a mail-order house in Chicago. This was the school Mr. Harrington belonged to. In the seventeen years of his married life he had read aloud to his wife, and to his sons as soon as they were old enough to appreciate them, the novels of Sir Walter Scott, Jane Austen, Dickens, the Brontë Sisters, Thackeray, George Eliot, Nathaniel Hawthorne and W. J. Howells. Ashenden came to the conclusion that it was second nature with Mr. Harrington to read aloud and to prevent him from doing so made him as uneasy as cutting off his tobacco made the confirmed smoker. He would take you unawares.

"Listen to this," he would say, "you must listen to this," as though he were suddenly struck by the excellence of a maxim or the neatness of a phrase. "Now just tell me if you don't think this is remarkably well put. It's only three lines."

He read them and Ashenden was willing to give him a moment's attention, but having finished them, without pausing for a moment to take breath, he went on. He went right on. On and on. In his measured high-pitched voice, without emphasis or expression, he read page after page. Ashenden fidgeted, crossed and uncrossed his legs, lit cigarettes and smoked them, sat first in one positon, then in another. Mr. Harrington went on and on. The train went leisurely through the interminable steppes of Siberia. They passed villages and crossed rivers. Mr. Harrington went on and on. When he finished a great speech by Edmund Burke he put down the book in triumph.

"Now that in my opinion is one of the finest orations in the English language. It is certainly a part of our common heritage that we can look upon with genuine pride."

"Doesn't it seem to you a little ominous that the people to whom Edmund Burke made that speech are all dead?" asked Ashenden gloomily.

Mr. Harrington was about to reply that this was hardly to be wondered at since the speech was made in the eighteenth century when it dawned upon him that Ashenden (bearing up wonderfully under affliction as any unprejudiced person could not fail to admit) was making a joke. He slapped his knee and laughed heartily.

"Gee, that's a good one," he said. "I'll write that down in my little book. I see exactly how I can bring it in one time when I have to speak at our luncheon club."

Mr. Harrington was a highbrow; but that appellation, invented by the vulgar as a term of abuse, he had accepted like the instrument of a saint's martyrdom, the gridiron of Saint Laurence for instance or the wheel of Saint Catherine, as an honorific title. He gloried in it.

"Emerson was a highbrow," he said. "Longfellow was a highbrow. Oliver Wendell Holmes was a highbrow. James Russell Lowell was a highbrow."

Mr. Harrington's study of American literature had taken him no further down the years than the period during which those eminent, but not precisely thrilling, authors flourished.

Mr. Harrington was a bore. He exasperated Ashenden, and enraged him; he got on his nerves, and drove him to frenzy. But Ashenden did not dislike him. His self-satisfaction was enormous but so ingenuous that you could not resent it; his conceit was so childlike that you could only smile at it. He was so well-meaning, so thoughtful, so deferential, so polite that though Ashenden would willingly have killed him he could not but own that in that short while he had conceived for Mr. Harrington something very like affection. His manners were exquisite, formal, a trifle elaborate perhaps (there is no harm in that, for good manners are the product of an artificial state of society and so can bear a touch of the powdered wig and the lace ruffle) but though natural to his good breeding they gained a pleasant significance from his good heart. He was ready to do anyone a kindness and seemed to find nothing too much trouble if he could thereby oblige his fellow man. He was eminently *serviable*. And it may be that this is a word for which there is no exact translation because the charming quality it denotes is not very common among our practical people. When Ashenden was ill for a couple of days Mr. Harrington nursed him with devotion. Ashenden was embarrassed by the care he took of him and though racked with pain could not help laughing at the fussy attention with which Mr. Harrington took his temperature, from his neatly packed valise extracted a whole regiment of tabloids and firmly doctored him; and he was touched by the trouble he gave himself to get from the dining-car the things that he thought Ashenden could eat. He did everything in the world for him but stop talking.

It was only when he was dressing that Mr. Harrington was silent, for then his maidenly mind was singly occupied with the problem of changing his clothes before Ashenden without indelicacy. He was extremely modest. He changed his linen every day, neatly taking it out of his suit-case and neatly putting back what was soiled; but he performed miracles of dexterity in order during the process not to show an inch of bare skin. After a day or two Ashenden gave up the struggle to keep neat and clean in that dirty train, with one lavatory for the whole carriage, and soon was as grubby as the rest of the passengers; but Mr. Harrington refused to yield to the difficulties. He performed his toilet with deliberation, notwithstanding the impatient persons who rattled the door-handle, and returned from the lavatory every morning washed, shining and smelling of soap. Once dressed, in his black coat, striped trousers and well-polished shoes, he looked as spruce as though he had just stepped out of his tidy little red-brick house in Philadelphia and was about to board the street-car that would take him down town to his office. At one point of the journey it was announced that an attempt had been made to blow up a bridge and that there were disturbances at the next station over the river; it might be that the train would be stopped and the passengers turned adrift or taken prisoners. Ashenden, thinking he might be separated from his luggage, took the precaution to change into his thickest clothes so that if he had to pass the winter in Siberia he need suffer as little as necessary from the cold; but Mr. Harrington would not listen to reason; he made no preparations for the possible experience and Ashenden had the conviction that if he spent three months in a Russian prison he would still preserve that smart and natty appearance. A troop of Cossacks boarded the train and stood on the platform of each carriage with their guns loaded, and the train rattled gingerly over the damaged bridge; then they came to the station at which they had been warned of danger, put on steam and dashed straight through it. Mr. Harrington was mildly satirical when Ashenden changed back into a light summer suit.

Mr. Harrington was a keen business man. It was obvious that it would need someone very astute to over-reach him and Ashenden was sure that his employers had been well-advised to send him on this errand. He would safeguard their interests with all his might and if he succeeded in driving a bargain with the Russians it would be a hard one. His loyalty to his firm demanded that. He spoke of the partners with affectionate reverence. He loved them and was proud of them; but he did not envy them because their wealth was great. He was quite content to work on a salary and thought himself adequately paid; so long as he could educate his boys and leave his widow enough to live on what was money to him? He thought it a trifle vulgar to be rich. He looked upon culture as more important than money. He was careful of it and after every meal put down in his note-book exactly what it had cost him. His firm might be certain that he would not charge a penny more for his expenses than he had spent. But having discovered that poor people came to the station at the stopping places of the train to beg and seeing that the war had really brought them to destitution he took care before each halt to supply himself with ample small change and in a shame-faced way, mocking himself for being taken in by such impostors, distributed everything in his pocket.

"Of course I know they don't deserve it," he said, "and I don't do it for them. I do it entirely for my own peace of mind. I should feel so terribly badly if I thought some man really was hungry and I'd refused to give him the price of a meal."

Mr. Harrington was absurd, but lovable. It was inconceivable that anyone should be rude to him, it would have seemed as dreadful as hitting a child; and Ashenden, chafing inwardly but with a pretence of amiability, suffered meekly and with a truly Christian spirit the affliction of the gentle, ruthless creature's society. It took eleven days at that time to get from Vladivostok to Petrograd and Ashenden felt that he could not have borne another day. If it had been twelve he would have killed Mr. Harrington.

When at last (Ashenden tired and dirty, Mr. Harrington neat, sprightly and sententious) they reached the outskirts of Petrograd and stood at the window looking at the crowded houses of the city, Mr. Harrington turned to Ashenden and said:

"Well, I never would have thought that eleven days in the train would pass so quickly. We've had a wonderful time. I've enjoyed your company and I know you've enjoyed mine. I'm not going to pretend I don't know that I'm a pretty good conversationalist. But now we've come together like this we must take care to stay together. We must see as much of one another as we can while I'm in Petrograd."

"I shall have a great deal to do," said Ashenden. "I'm afraid my time won't be altogether my own."

"I know," answered Mr. Harrington cordially. "I expect to be pretty busy myself, but we can have breakfast together anyway and we'll meet in the evening and compare notes. It would be too bad if we drifted apart now."

"Too bad," sighed Ashenden.

When Ashenden found himself alone in his bedroom for the first time, he sat down and looked about him. It had seemed an age. He had not the energy to start immediately to unpack. How many of these hotel bedrooms had he known since the beginning of the war, grand or shabby, in one place and one land after another! It seemed to him that he had been living in his luggage for as long as he could remember. He was weary. He asked himself how he was going to set about the work that he had been sent to do. He felt lost in the immensity of Russia and very solitary. He had protested when he was chosen for this mission, it looked too large an order, but his protests were ignored. He was chosen not because those in authority thought him particularly suited for the job, but because there was no one to be found who was more suited. There was a knock at the door and Ashenden, pleased to make use of the few words of the language he knew, called out in Russian. The door was opened. He sprang to his feet.

"Come in, come in," he cried. "I'm awfully glad to see you."

Three men entered. He knew them by sight, since they had travelled on the same boat with him from San Francisco to Yokohama, but following their instructions no communications had passed between them and Ashenden. They were Czechs, exiled from their country for their revolutionary activity and long settled in America, who had been sent over to Russia to help Ashenden in his mission and put him in touch with Professor Z. whose authority over the Czechs in Russia was absolute. Their chief was a certain Dr. Egon Orth, a tall thin man, with a little grey head; he was minister to some church in the Middle West and a doctor of divinity; but had abandoned his cure to work for the liberation of his country, and Ashenden had the impression that he was an intelligent fellow who would not put too fine a point on matters of conscience. A parson with a fixed idea has this advantage over common men that he can persuade himself of the Almighty's approval for almost any goings on. Dr. Orth had a merry twinkle in his eye and a dry humour.

Ashenden had had two secret interviews with him in Yokohama and had learnt that Professor Z., though eager to free his country from the Austrian rule and since he knew that this could only come about by the downfall of the Central Powers with the allies body and soul, yet had scruples; he would not do things that outraged his conscience, all must be straightforward and above board, and so some things that it was necessary to do had to be done without his knowledge. His influence was so great that his wishes could not be disregarded, but on occasion it was felt better not to let him know too much of what was going on.

Dr. Orth had arrived in Petrograd a week before Ashenden and now put before him what he had learned of the situation.

It seemed to Ashenden that it was critical and if anything was to be done it must be done quickly. The army was dissatisfied and mutinous, the Government under the weak Kerensky was tottering and held power only because no one else had the courage to seize it, famine was staring the country in the face and already the possibility had to be considered that the Germans would march on Petrograd. The ambassadors of Great Britain and the United States had been apprised of Ashenden's coming, but his mission was secret even from them, and there were particular reasons why he could demand no assistance from them. He arranged with Dr. Orth to make an appointment with Professor Z. so that he could learn his views and explain to him that he had the financial means to support any scheme that seemed likely to prevent the catastrophe that the Allied governments foresaw of Russia's making a separate peace. But he had to get in touch with influential persons in all classes. Mr. Harrington with his business proposition and his letters to Ministers of State would be thrown in contact with members of the Government and Mr. Harrington wanted an interpreter. Dr. Orth spoke Russian almost as well as his own language and it struck Ashenden that he would be admirably suited to the post. He explained the circumstances to him and it was arranged that while Ashenden and Mr. Harrington were at luncheon Dr. Orth should come in, greeting Ashenden as though he had not seen him before, and be introduced to Mr. Harrington; then Ashenden, guiding the conversation, would suggest to Mr. Harrington that the heavens had sent in Dr. Orth the ideal man for his purpose.

But there was another person on whom Ashenden had fixed as possibly useful to him and now he said:

"Have you ever heard of a woman called Anastasia Alexandrovna Leonidov? She's the daughter of Alexander Denisiev."

"I know all about him of course."

"I have reason to believe she's in Petrograd. Will you find out where she lives and what she's doing."

"Certainly."

Dr. Orth spoke in Czech to one of the two men who accompanied him. They were sharp-looking fellows both of them, one was tall and fair and the other was short and dark, but they were younger than Dr. Orth and Ashenden understood that they were there to do as he bade them. The man nodded, got up, shook hands with Ashenden and went out.

"You shall have all the information possible this afternoon."

"Well, I think there's nothing more we can do for the present," said Ashenden. "To tell you the truth I haven't had a bath for eleven days and I badly want one."

Ashenden had never quite made up his mind whether the pleasure of reflection was better pursued in a railway carriage or in a bath. So far as the act of invention was concerned he was inclined to prefer a train that went smoothly and not too fast, and many of his best ideas had come to him when he was thus traversing the plains of France; but for the delight of reminiscence or the entertainment of embroidery upon a theme already in his head he had no doubt that nothing could compare with a hot bath. He considered now, wallowing in soapy water like a water-buffalo in a muddy pond, the grim pleasantry of his relations with Anastasia Alexandrovna Leonidov.

In these stories no more than the barest suggestion has been made that Ashenden was capable on occasions of the passion ironically called tender. The specialists in this matter, those charming creatures who make a business of what philosophers know is but a diversion, assert that writers, painters and musicians, all in short who are connected with the arts, in the relation of love cut no very conspicuous figure. There is much cry but little wool. They rave or sigh, make phrases and strike many a romantic attitude, but in the end, loving art or themselves (which with them is one and the same thing) better than the object of their emotion offer a shadow when the said object, with the practical common sense of the sex, demands a substance. It may be so and this may be the reason (never before suggested) why women in their souls look upon art with such a virulent hatred. Be this as it may Ashenden in the last twenty years had felt his heart go pit-a-pat because of one charming person after another. He had had a good deal of fun and had paid for it with a great deal of misery, but even when suffering most acutely from the pangs of unrequited love he had been able to say to himself, albeit with a wry face, after all, it's grist to the mill.

Anastasia Alexandrovna Leonidov was the daughter of a revolutionary who had escaped from Siberia after being sentenced to penal servitude for life and had settled in England. He was an able man and had supported himself for thirty years by the activity of a restless pen and had even made himself a distinguished position in English letters. When Anastasia Alexandrovna reached a suitable age she married Vladimir Semenovich Leonidov, also an exile from his native country, and it was after she had been married to him for some years that Ashenden made her acquaintance. It was at the time when Europe discovered Russia. Everyone was reading the Russian novelists, the Russian dancers captivated the civilized world, and the Russian composers set shivering the sensibility of persons who were beginning to want a change from Wagner. Russian art seized upon Europe with the virulence of an epidemic of influenza. New phrases became the fashion, new colours, new emotions, and the highbrows described themselves without a moment's hesitation as members of the intelligentsia. It was a difficult word to spell but an easy one to say. Ashenden fell like the rest, changed the cushions of his sitting-room, hung an eikon on the wall, read Chekoff and went to the ballet.

Anastasia Alexandrovna was by birth, circumstances and education very much a member of the intelligentsia. She lived with her husband in a tiny house near Regent's Park and here all the literary folk in London might gaze with humble reverence at pale-faced bearded giants who leaned against the wall like caryatids taking a day off; they were revolutionaries to a man and it was a miracle that they were not in the mines of Siberia. Women of letters tremulously put their lips to a glass of vodka. If you were lucky and greatly favoured you might shake hands there with Diaghileff and now and again, like a peach-blossom wafted by the breeze, Pavlova herself hovered in and out. At this time Ashenden's success had not been so great as to affront the highbrows, he had very distinctly been one of them in his youth, and though some already looked askance, others (optimistic creatures with a faith in human nature) still had hopes of him. Anastasia Alexandrovna told him to his face that he was a member of the intelligentsia. Ashenden was quite ready to believe it. He was in a state when he was ready to believe anything. He was thrilled and excited. It seemed to him that at last he was about to capture that illusive spirit of romance that he had so long been chasing. Anastasia Alexandrovna had fine eyes and a good, though for these days, too voluptuous figure, high cheek bones and a snub nose (this was very Tartar), a wide mouth full of large square teeth and a pale skin. She dressed somewhat flamboyantly. In her dark melancholy eyes Ashenden saw the boundless steppes of Russia, and the Kremlin with its pealing bells, and the solemn ceremonies of Easter at St. Isaac's, and forests of silver beeches and the Nevsky Prospekt; it was astonishing how much he saw in her eyes. They were round and shining and slightly protuberant like those of a Pekinese. They talked together of Alyosha in the *Brothers Karamazov*, of Natasha in *War and Peace*, of Anna Karenina and of *Fathers and Sons*.

Ashenden soon discovered that her husband was quite unworthy of her and presently learned that she shared his opinion. Vladimir Semenovich was a little man with a large, long head that looked as though it had been pulled like a piece of liquorice, and he had a great shock of unruly Russian hair. He was a gentle, unobtrusive creature and it was hard to believe that the Czarist government had really feared his revolutionary activities. He taught Russian and wrote for papers in Moscow. He was amiable and obliging. He needed these qualities for Anastasia Alexandrovna was a woman of character: when she had a toothache Vladimir Semenovich suffered the agonies of the damned and when her heart was wrung by the suffering of her unhappy country Vladimir Semenovich might well have wished he had never been born. Ashenden could not help admitting that he was a poor thing, but he was so harm-less that he conceived quite a liking for him, and when in due course he had disclosed his passion to Anastasia Alex-androvna and to his joy found it was returned he was puz-zled to know what to do about Vladimir Semenovich. Neither Anastasia Alexandrovna nor he felt that they could live an-other minute out of one another's pockets, and Ashenden feared that with her revolutionary views and all that she would never consent to marry him; but somewhat to his sur-prise, and very much to his relief, she accepted the suggestion with alacrity.

"Would Vladimir Semenovich let himself be divorced, do you think?" he asked, as he sat on the sofa, leaning against cushions the colour of which reminded him of raw meat just gone bad, and held her hand.

"Vladimir adores me," she answered. "It'll break his heart."

"He's a nice fellow, I shouldn't like him to be very un-happy. I hope he'll get over it."

"He'll never get over it. That is the Russian spirit. I know that when I leave him he'll feel that he has lost everything that made life worth living for him. I've never known anyone so wrapped up in a woman as he is in me. But of course he wouldn't want to stand in the way of my happiness. He's far too great for that. He'll see that when it's a question of my own self-development I haven't the right to hesitate. Vladimir will give me my freedom without question."

At that time the divorce law in England was even more complicated and absurd than it is now and in case she was not acquainted with its peculiarities Ashenden explained to Anastasia Alexandrovna the difficulties of the case. She put her hand gently on his.

"Vladimir would never expose me to the vulgar notoriety of the divorce court. When I tell him that I have decided to marry you he will commit suicide."

"That would be terrible," said Ashenden.

He was startled, but thrilled. It was really very much like a Russian novel and he saw the moving and terrible pages, pages and pages, in which Dostoievsky would have described

the situation. He knew the lacerations his characters would
have suffered, the broken bottles of champagne, the visits to
the gipsies, the vodka, the swoonings, the catalepsy and the
long, long speeches everyone would have made. It was all
very dreadful and wonderful and shattering.

"It would make us horribly unhappy," said Anastasia Alexandrovna, "but I don't know what else he could do. I couldn't
ask him to live without me. He would be like a ship without
a rudder or a car without a carburettor. I know Vladimir so
well. He will commit suicide."

"How?" asked Ashenden, who had the realist's passion for
the exact detail.

"He will blow his brains out."

Ashenden remembered *Rosmersholm*. In his day he had
been an ardent Ibsenite and had even flirted with the notion
of learning Norwegian so that he might, by reading the
master in the original, get at the secret essence of his thought.
He had once seen Ibsen in the flesh drink a glass of Munich
beer.

"But do you think we could ever pass another easy hour if
we had the death of that man on our conscience?" he asked.
"I have a feeling that he would always be between us."

"I know we shall suffer, we shall suffer dreadfully," said
Anastasia Alexandrovna, "but how can we help it? Life is like
that. We must think of Vladimir. There is his happiness to
be considered too. He will prefer to commit suicide."

She turned her face away and Ashenden saw that the heavy
tears were coursing down her cheeks. He was much moved.
For he had a soft heart and it was dreadful to think of poor
Vladimir lying there with a bullet in his brain.

These Russians, what fun they have!

But when Anastasia Alexandrovna had mastered her emotion she turned to him gravely. She looked at him with her
humid, round and slightly protuberant eyes.

"We must be quite sure that we're doing the right thing,"
she said. "I should never forgive myself if I'd allowed Vladimir to commit suicide and then found I'd made a mistake. I
think we ought to make sure that we really love one another "

"But don't you know?" exclaimed Ashenden in a low, tense voice. "I know."

"Let's go over to Paris for a week and see how we get on. Then we shall know."

Ashenden was a trifle conventional and the suggestion took him by surprise. But only for a moment. Anastasia was wonderful. She was very quick and she saw the hesitation that for an instant troubled him.

"Surely you have no bourgeois prejudices?" she said.

"Of course not," he assured her hurriedly, for he would much sooner have been thought knavish than bourgeois, "I think it's a splendid idea."

"Why should a woman hazard her whole life on a throw? It's impossible to know what a man is really like till you've lived with him. It's only fair to give her the opportunity to change her mind before it's too late."

"Quite so," said Ashenden.

Anastasia Alexandrovna was not a woman to let the grass grow under her feet and so having made their arrangements forthwith on the following Saturday they started for Paris.

"I shall not tell Vladimir that I am going with you," she said. "It would only distress him."

"It would be a pity to do that," said Ashenden.

"And if at the end of the week I come to the conclusion that we've made a mistake he need never know anything about it."

"Quite so," said Ashenden.

They met at Victoria station.

"What class have you got?" she asked him.

"First."

"I'm glad of that. Father and Vladimir travel third on account of their principles, but I always feel sick on a train and I like to be able to lean my head on somebody's shoulder. It's easier in a first-class carriage."

When the train started Anastasia Alexandrovna said she felt dizzy, so she took off her hat and leaned her head on Ashenden's shoulder. He put his arm round her waist.

"Keep quite still, won't you?" she said.

When they got on to the boat she went down to the ladies' cabin and at Calais was able to eat a very hearty meal, but when they got into the train she took off her hat again and rested her head on Ashenden's shoulder. He thought he would like to read and took up a book.

"Do you mind not reading?" she said. "I have to be held and when you turn the pages it makes me feel all funny."

Finally they reached Paris and went to a little hotel on the Left Bank that Anastasia Alexandrovna knew of. She said it had atmosphere. She could not bear those great big grand hotels on the other side; they were hopelessly vulgar and bourgeois.

"I'll go anywhere you like," said Ashenden, "as long as there's a bathroom."

She smiled and pinched his cheek.

"How adorably English you are. Can't you do without a bathroom for a week? My dear, my dear, you have so much to learn."

They talked far into the night about Maxim Gorki and Karl Marx, human destiny, love and the brotherhood of man; and drank innumerable cups of Russian tea, so that in the morning Ashenden would willingly have breakfasted in bed and got up for luncheon; but Anastasia Alexandrovna was an early riser. When life was so short and there was so much to do it was a sinful thing to have breakfast a minute after half-past eight. They sat down in a dingy little dining-room the windows of which showed no signs of having been opened for a month. It was full of atmosphere. Ashenden asked Anastasia Alexandrovna what she would have for breakfast.

"Scrambled eggs," she said.

She ate heartily. Ashenden had already noticed that she had a healthy appetite. He supposed it was a Russian trait: you could not picture Anna Karenina making her midday meal off a bath-bun and a cup of coffee, could you?

After breakfast they went to the Louvre and in the after-noon they went to the Luxembourg. They dined early in order to go to the Comédie Française; then they went to a Russian cabaret where they danced. When next morning at eight-thirty they took their places in the dining-room and Ashenden asked Anastasia Alexandrovna what she fancied, her reply was:

"Scrambled eggs."

"But we had scrambled eggs yesterday," he expostulated.

"Let's have them again to-day," she smiled.

"All right."

They spent the day in the same manner except that they went to the Carnavalet instead of the Louvre and the Musée Guimet instead of the Luxembourg. But when the morning after in answer to Ashenden's enquiry Anastasia Alexandrovna again asked for scrambled eggs, his heart sank.

"But we had scrambled eggs yesterday and the day before," he said.

"Don't you think that's a very good reason to have them again to-day?"

"No, I don't."

"Is it possible that your sense of humour is a little deficient this morning?" she asked. "I eat scrambled eggs every day. It's the only way I like them."

"Oh, very well. In that case of course we'll have scrambled eggs."

But the following morning he could not face them.

"Will you have scrambled eggs as usual?" he asked her.

"Of course," she smiled affectionately, showing him two rows of large square teeth.

"All right, I'll order them for you, I shall have mine fried."

The smile vanished from her lips.

"Oh?" She paused a moment. "Don't you think that's rather inconsiderate? Do you think it's fair to give the cook unnecessary work? You English, you're all the same, you look upon servants as machines. Does it occur to you that they have hearts like yours, the same feelings and the same emotions? How can you be surprised that the proletariat are seething with discontent when the bourgeoisie like you are so monstrously selfish?"

"Do you really think that there'll be a revolution in England if I have my eggs in Paris fried rather than scrambled?"

She tossed her pretty head in indignation.

"You don't understand. It's the principle of the thing. You think it's a jest, of course I know you're being funny, I can laugh at a joke as well as anyone, Chekoff was well-known in Russia as a humorist; but don't you see what is involved? Your whole attitude is wrong. It's a lack of feeling. You wouldn't talk like that if you had been through the events of 1905 in Petersburg. When I think of the crowds in front of the Winter Palace kneeling in the snow while the Cossacks charged them, women and children! No, no, no."

Her eyes filled with tears and her face was all twisted with pain. She took Ashenden's hand.

"I know you have a good heart. It was just thoughtless on your part and we won't say anything more about it. You have imagination. You're very sensitive. I know. You'll have your eggs done in the same way as mine, won't you?"

"Of course," said Ashenden.

He ate scrambled eggs for breakfast every morning after that. The waiter said: *"Monsieur aime les œufs brouillés."* At the end of the week they returned to London. He held Anastasia Alexandrovna in his arms, her head resting on his shoulder, from Paris to Calais and again from Dover to London. He reflected that the journey from New York to San Francisco took five days. When they arrived at Victoria and stood on the platform waiting for a cab she looked at him with her round, shining and slightly protuberant eyes.

"We've had a wonderful time, haven't we?" she said.

"Wonderful."

"I've quite made up my mind. The experiment has justified itself. I'm willing to marry you whenever you like."

But Ashenden saw himself eating scrambled eggs every morning for the rest of his life. When he had put her in a cab, he called another for himself, went to the Cunard office and took a berth on the first ship that was going to America. No immigrant, eager for freedom and a new life, ever looked upon the Statue of Liberty with more heartfelt thankfulness than did Ashenden, when on that bright and sunny morning his ship steamed into the harbour of New York.

Some years had passed since then and Ashenden had not seen Anastasia Alexandrovna again. He knew that on the outbreak of the revolution in March she and Vladimir Semenovich had gone to Russia. It might be that they would be able to help him, in a way Vladimir Semenovich owed him his life, and he made up his mind to write to Anastasia Alexandrovna to ask if he might come to see her.

When Ashenden went down to lunch he felt somewhat rested. Mr. Harrington was waiting for him and they sat down. They ate what was put before them.

"Ask the waiter to bring us some bread," said Mr. Harrington.

"Bread?" replied Ashenden. "There's no bread."

"I can't eat without bread," said Mr. Harrington.

"I'm afraid you'll have to. There's no bread, no butter, no sugar, no eggs, no potatoes. There's fish and meat and green vegetables, and that's all."

Mr. Harrington's jaw dropped.

"But this is war," he said.

"It looks very much like it."

Mr. Harrington was for a moment speechless; then he said: "I'll tell you what I'm going to do, I'm going to get through with my business as quick as I can and then I'm going to get out of this country. I'm sure Mrs. Harrington wouldn't like me to go without sugar or butter. I've got a very delicate stomach. The firm would never have sent me here if they'd thought I wasn't going to have the best of everything."

In a little while Dr. Egon Orth came in and gave Ashenden an envelope. On it was written Anastasia Alexandrovna's address. He introduced him to Mr. Harrington. It was soon clear that he was pleased with Dr. Egon Orth and so without further to-do he suggested that here was the perfect interpreter for him.

"He talks Russian like a Russian. But he's an American citizen so that he won't do you down. I've known him a considerable time and I can assure you that he's absolutely trustworthy."

Mr. Harrington was pleased with the notion and after

luncheon Ashenden left them to settle the matter by themselves. He wrote a note to Anastasia Alexandrovna and presently received an answer to say that she was going to a meeting, but would look in at his hotel about seven. He awaited
her with apprehension. Of course he knew now that he had
not loved her, but Tolstoi and Dostoievsky, Rimsky-Korsakoff,
Stravinsky and Bakst; but he was not quite sure if the point
had occurred to her. When between eight and half-past she
arrived he suggested that she should join Mr. Harrington and
him at dinner. The presence of a third party, he thought, would
prevent any awkwardness their meeting might have; but he
need not have had any anxiety, for five minutes after they had
sat down to a plate of soup it was borne in upon him that
the feelings of Anastasia Alexandrovna towards him were as
cool as were his towards her. It gave him a momentary shock.
It is very hard for a man, however modest, to grasp the possibility that a woman who has once loved him may love him no
longer, and though of course he did not imagine that Anastasia
Alexandrovna had languished for five years with a hopeless
passion for him, he did think that by a heightening of colour,
a flutter of the eyelashes, or a quiver of the lips she would
betray the fact that she had still a soft place in her heart for
him. Not at all. She talked to him as though he were a friend
she was very glad to see again after an absence of a few
days, but whose intimacy with her was purely social. He asked
after Vladimir Semenovich.

"He has been a disappointment to me," she said. "I never
thought he was a clever man, but I thought he was an honest
one. He's going to have a baby."

Mr. Harrington who was about to put a piece of fish into
his mouth, stopped, his fork in the air, and stared at Anastasia
Alexandrovna with astonishment. In extenuation it must be
explained that he had never read a Russian novel in his life.
Ashenden, slightly perplexed too, gave her a questioning
look.

"I'm not the mother," she said with a laugh. "I am not interested in that sort of thing. The mother is a friend of mine
and a well-known writer on Political Economy. I do not think

her views are sound, but I should be the last to deny that they deserve consideration. She has a good brain, quite a good brain." She turned to Mr. Harrington. "Are you interested in Political Economy?"

For once in his life Mr. Harrington was speechless. Anastasia Alexandrovna gave them her views on the subject and they began to speak on the situation in Russia. She seemed to be on intimate terms with the leaders of the various political parties and Ashenden made up his mind to sound her on the possibility of her working with him. His infatuation had not blinded him to the fact that she was an extremely intelligent woman. After dinner he told Mr. Harrington that he wished to talk business with Anastasia Alexandrovna and took her to a retired corner of the lounge. He told her all he thought necessary and found her interested and anxious to help. She had a passion for intrigue and a desire for power. When he hinted that he had command of large sums of money she saw at once that through him she might acquire an influence in the affairs of Russia. It tickled her vanity. She was immensely patriotic, but like many patriots she had an impression that her own aggrandisement tended to the good of her country. When they parted they had come to a working agreement.

"That was a very remarkable woman," said Mr. Harrington next morning when they met at breakfast.

"Don't fall in love with her," smiled Ashenden.

This, however, was not a matter on which Mr. Harrington was prepared to jest.

"I have never looked at a woman since I married Mrs. Harrington," he said. "That husband of hers must be a bad man."

"I could do with a plate of scrambled eggs," said Ashenden, irrelevantly, for their breakfast consisted of a cup of tea without milk and a little jam instead of sugar.

With Anastasia Alexandrovna to help him and Dr. Orth in the background, Ashenden set to work. Things in Russia were going from bad to worse. Kerensky, the head of the Provisional Government, was devoured by vanity and dismissed any minister who gave evidence of a capacity that might endanger his own position. He made speeches. He made endless speeches. At one moment there was a possibility that the Germans would make a dash for Petrograd. Kerensky made speeches. The food shortage grew more serious, the winter was approaching and there was no fuel. Kerensky made speeches. In the background the Bolsheviks were active, Lenin was hiding in Petrograd, it was said that Kerensky knew where he was, but dared not arrest him. He made speeches.

It amused Ashenden to see the unconcern with which Mr. Harrington wandered through this turmoil. History was in the making and Mr. Harrington minded his own business. It was uphill work. He was made to pay bribes to secretaries and underlings under the pretence that the ear of great men would be granted to him. He was kept waiting for hours in antechambers and then sent away without ceremony. When at last he saw the great men he found they had nothing to give him but idle words. They made him promises and in a day or two he discovered that the promises meant nothing. Ashenden advised him to throw in his hand and return to America; but Mr. Harrington would not hear of it; his firm had sent him to do a particular job, and by gum, he was going to do it or perish in the attempt. Then Anastasia Alexandrovna took him in hand. A singular friendship had arisen between the pair. Mr. Harrington thought her a very remarkable and deeply wronged woman; he told her all about his wife and his two sons, he told her all about the Constitution of the United States; she on her side told him all about Vladimir Semeno-vich, and she told him about Tolstoi, Turgenieff and Dostoievsky. They had great times together. He said he couldn't man-age to call her Anastasia Alexandrovna, it was too much of a mouthful; so he called her Delilah. And now she placed her inexhaustible energy at his service and they went together to the persons who might be useful to him. But things were coming to a head. Riots broke out and the streets were growing dangerous. Now and then armoured cars filled with discontented reservists careened wildly along the Nevsky Prospekt and in order to show that they were not happy took pot-shots at the passers-by. On one occasion when Mr. Harrington and

Anastasia Alexandrovna were in a tram together shots peppered the windows and they had to lie down on the floor for safety. Mr. Harrington was highly indignant.

"An old fat woman was lying right on top of me and when I wriggled to get out Delilah caught me a clip on the side of the head and said, stop still, you fool. I don't like your Russian ways, Delilah."

"Anyhow you stopped still," she giggled.

"What you want in this country is a little less art and a little more civilization."

"You are bourgeoisie, Mr. Harrington, you are not a member of the intelligentsia."

"You are the first person who's ever said that, Delilah. If I'm not a member of the intelligentsia I don't know who is," retorted Mr. Harrington with dignity.

Then one day when Ashenden was working in his room there was a knock at the door and Anastasia Alexandrovna stalked in followed, somewhat sheepishly, by Mr. Harrington. Ashenden saw that she was excited.

"What's the matter?" he asked.

"Unless this man goes back to America he'll get killed. You really must talk to him. If I hadn't been there something very unpleasant might have happened to him."

"Not at all, Delilah," said Mr. Harrington, with asperity. "I'm perfectly capable of taking care of myself and I wasn't in the smallest danger."

"What is it all about?" asked Ashenden.

"I'd taken Mr. Harrington to the Lavra of Alexander Nevsky to see Dostoievsky's grave," said Anastasia Alexandrovna, "and on our way back we saw a soldier being rather rough with an old woman."

"Rather rough!" cried Mr. Harrington. "There was an old woman walking along the side-walk with a basket of provisions on her arm. Two soldiers came up behind her and one of them snatched the basket from her and walked off with it. She burst out screaming and crying, I don't know what she was saying, but I can guess, and the other soldier took his gun and with the butt-end of it hit her over the head. Isn't that right, Delilah?"

"Yes," she answered, unable to help smiling. "And before I could prevent it Mr. Harrington jumped out of the cab and ran up to the soldier who had the basket, wrenched it from him and began to abuse the pair of them like pickpockets. At first they were so taken aback they didn't know what to do and then they got in a rage. I ran after Mr. Harrington and explained to them that he was a foreigner and drunk."

"Drunk?" cried Mr. Harrington.

"Yes, drunk. Of course a crowd collected. It looked as though it wasn't going to be very nice."

Mr. Harrington smiled with those large, pale-blue eyes of his.

"It sounded to me as though you were giving them a piece of your mind, Delilah. It was as good as a play to watch you."

"Don't be stupid, Mr. Harrington," cried Anastasia, in a sudden fury, stamping her foot. "Don't you know that those soldiers might very easily have killed you and me too, and not one of the bystanders would have raised a finger to help us?"

"Me? I'm an American citizen, Delilah. They wouldn't dare touch a hair of my head."

"They'd have difficulty in finding one," said Anastasia Alexandrovna, who when she was in a temper had no manners. "But if you think Russian soldiers are going to hesitate to kill you because you're an American citizen you'll get a big surprise one of these days."

"Well, what happened to the old woman?" asked Ashenden.

"The soldiers went off after a little and we went back to her."

"Still with the basket?"

"Yes. Mr. Harrington clung on to that like grim death. She was lying on the ground with the blood pouring from her head. We got her into the cab and when she could speak enough to tell us where she lived we drove her home. She was bleeding dreadfully and we had some difficulty in staunching the blood."

Anastasia Alexandrovna gave Mr. Harrington an odd look and to his surprise Ashenden saw him turn scarlet.

"What's the matter now?"

"You see, we had nothing to bind her up with. Mr. Harrington's handkerchief was soaked. There was only one thing about me that I could get off quickly and so I took off my . . ."

But before she could finish Mr. Harrington interrupted her.

"You need not tell Mr. Ashenden what you took off. I'm a married man and I know ladies wear them, but I see no need to refer to them in general society."

Anastasia Alexandrovna giggled.

"Then you must kiss me, Mr. Harrington. If you don't I shall say."

Mr. Harrington hesitated a moment, considering evidently the pros and cons of the matter, but he saw that Anastasia Alexandrovna was determined.

"Go on then, you may kiss me, Delilah, though I'm bound to say I don't see what pleasure it can be to you."

She put her arms round his neck and kissed him on both cheeks, then without a word of warning burst into a flood of tears.

"You're a brave little man, Mr. Harrington. You're absurd but magnificent," she sobbed.

Mr. Harrington was less surprised than Ashenden would have expected him to be. He looked at Anastasia with a thin, quizzical smile and gently patted her.

"Come, come, Delilah, pull yourself together. It gave you a nasty turn, didn't it? You're quite upset. I shall have terrible rheumatism in my shoulder if you go on weeping all over it."

The scene was ridiculous and touching, Ashenden laughed, but he had the beginnings of a lump in his throat.

When Anastasia Alexandrovna had left them Mr. Harrington sat in a brown study.

"They're very queer, these Russians. Do you know what Delilah did?" he said, suddenly. "She stood up in the cab, in the middle of the street, with people passing on both sides, and took her pants off. She tore them in two and gave me one to hold while she made a bandage of the other. I was never so embarrassed in my life."

"Tell me what gave you the idea of calling her Delilah?" smiled Ashenden.

Mr. Harrington reddened a little.

"She's a very fascinating woman, Mr. Ashenden. She's been deeply wronged by her husband and I naturally felt a great deal of sympathy for her. These Russians are very emotional people and I did not want her to mistake my sympathy for anything else. I told her I was very much attached to Mrs. Harrington."

"You're not under the impression that Delilah was Potiphar's wife?" asked Ashenden.

"I don't know what you mean by that, Mr. Ashenden," replied Mr. Harrington. "Mrs. Harrington has always given me to understand that I'm very fascinating to women, and I thought if I called our little friend Delilah it would make my position quite clear."

"I don't think Russia's any place for you, Mr. Harrington," said Ashenden smiling. "If I were you I'd get out of it as quick as I could."

"I can't go now. I've got them to agree to my terms at last and we're going to sign next week. Then I shall pack my grip and go."

"I wonder if your signatures will be worth the paper they're written on," said Ashenden.

He had at length devised a plan of campaign. It took him twenty-four hours' hard work to code a telegram in which he put his scheme before the persons who had sent him to Petrograd. It was accepted and he was promised all the money he needed. Ashenden knew he could do nothing unless the Provisional Government remained in power for another three months; but winter was at hand and food was getting scarcer every day. The army was mutinous. The people clamoured for peace. Every evening at the Europe Ashenden drank a cup of chocolate with Professor Z. and discussed with him how best to make use of his devoted Czechs. Anastasia Alexandrovna had a flat in a retired spot and here he had meetings with all manner of persons. Plans were drawn up. Measures were taken. Ashenden argued, persuaded, promised. He had to overcome the vacillation of one and wrestle with the fatalism of another. He had to judge who was resolute and who was self-sufficient, who was honest and who was infirm of purpose. He had to curb his impatience with the Russian verbosity; he had to be good-tempered with people who were willing to talk of everything but the matter in hand; he had to listen sympathetically to ranting and rhodomontade. He had to beware of treachery. He had to humour the vanity of fools and elude the greed of the ambitious. Time was pressing. The rumours grew hot and many of the activities of the Bolsheviks. Kerensky ran hither and thither like a frightened hen.

Then the blow fell. On the night of November 7th, 1917, the Bolsheviks rose, Kerensky's ministers were arrested and the Winter Palace was sacked by the mob; the reins of power were seized by Lenin and Trotsky.

Anastasia Alexandrovna came to Ashenden's room at the hotel early in the morning. Ashenden was coding a telegram. He had been up all night, first at the Smolny, and then at the Winter Palace. He was tired out. Her face was white and her shining brown eyes were tragic.

"Have you heard?" she asked Ashenden.

He nodded.

"It's all over then. They say Kerensky has fled. They never even showed fight." Rage seized her. "The buffoon!" she screamed.

At that moment there was a knock at the door and Anastasia Alexandrovna looked at it with sudden apprehension.

"You know the Bolsheviks have got a list of people they've decided to execute. My name is on it, and it may be that yours is too."

"If it's they and they want to come in they only have to turn the handle," said Ashenden, smiling, but with ever so slightly odd a feeling at the pit of his stomach. "Come in."

The door was opened and Mr. Harrington stepped into the room. He was as dapper as ever, in his short black coat and striped trousers, his shoes neatly polished and a derby on his bald head. He took it off when he saw Anastasia Alexandrovna.

"Oh, fancy finding you here so early. I looked in on my way out, I wanted to tell you my news. I tried to find you yesterday evening, but couldn't. You didn't come in to dinner."

"No, I was at a meeting," said Ashenden.

"You must both congratulate me, I got my signatures yesterday, and my business is done."

Mr. Harrington beamed on them, the picture of self-satisfaction, and he arched himself like a bantam-cock who has chased away all rivals. Anastasia Alexandrovna burst into a sudden shriek of hysterical laughter. He stared at her in perplexity.

"Why, Delilah, what is the matter?" he said.

Anastasia laughed till the tears ran from her eyes and then began to sob in earnest. Ashenden explained.

"The Bolsheviks have overthrown the Government. Kerensky's ministers are in prison. The Bolsheviks are out to kill. Delilah says her name is on the list. Your minister signed your documents yesterday because he knew it did not matter what he did then. Your contracts are worth nothing. The Bolsheviks are going to make peace with Germany as soon as they can."

Anastasia Alexandrovna had recovered her self-control as quickly as she had lost it.

"You had better get out of Russia as soon as you can, Mr. Harrington. It's no place for a foreigner now and it may be that in a few days you won't be able to."

Mr. Harrington looked from one to the other.

"O my," he said. "O my!" It seemed inadequate. "Are you going to tell me that that Russian minister was just making a fool of me?"

Ashenden shrugged his shoulders.

"How can one tell what he was thinking of? He may have a keen sense of humour and perhaps he thought it funny to sign a fifty million dollar contract yesterday when there was every chance of his being stood against the wall and shot to-day. Anastasia Alexandrovna's right, Mr. Harrington, you'd better take the first train that'll get you to Sweden."

"And what about you?"

"There's nothing for me to do here any more. I'm cabling for instructions and I shall go as soon as I get leave. The Bolsheviks have got in ahead of us and the people I was working with will have their work cut out to save their lives."

"Boris Petrovich was shot this morning," said Anastasia Alexandrovna with a frown.

They both looked at Mr. Harrington and he stared at the floor. His pride in this achievement of his was shattered and he sagged like a pricked balloon. But in a minute he looked up. He gave Anastasia Alexandrovna a little smile and for the first time Ashenden noticed how attractive and kindly his smile was. There was something peculiarly disarming about it.

"If the Bolsheviks are after you, Delilah, don't you think you'd better come with me? I'll take care of you and if you'd like to come to America I'm sure Mrs. Harrington would be glad to do anything she could for you."

"I can see Mrs. Harrington's face if you arrived in Philadelphia with a Russian refugee," laughed Anastasia Alexandrovna. "I'm afraid it would need more explaining than you could ever manage. No, I shall stay here."

"But if you're in danger?"

"I'm a Russian. My place is here. I will not leave my country when most my country needs me."

"That is the bunk, Delilah," said Mr. Harrington very quietly.

Anastasia Alexandrovna had spoken with deep emotion, but now with a little start she shot a sudden quizzical look at him.

"I know it is, Samson," she answered. "To tell you the truth I think we're all going to have a hell of a time, God knows what's going to happen, but I want to see; I wouldn't miss a minute of it for the world."

Mr. Harrington shook his head.

"Curiosity is the bane of your sex, Delilah," he said.

"Go along and do your packing, Mr Harrington," said Ashenden, smiling, "and then we'll take you to the station. The train will be besieged."

"Very well, I'll go. And I shan't be sorry either. I haven't had a decent meal since I came here and I've done a thing I never thought I should have to do in my life, I've drunk my coffee without sugar and when I've been lucky enough to get a little piece of black bread I've had to eat it without butter. Mrs. Harrington will never believe me when I tell her what I've gone through. What this country wants is organization."

When he left them Ashenden and Anastasia Alexandrovna talked over the situation. Ashenden was depressed because all his careful schemes had come to nothing, but Anastasia Alexandrovna was excited and she hazarded every sort of guess about the outcome of this new revolution. She pretended to be very serious, but in her heart she looked upon it all very much as a thrilling play. She wanted more and more things to happen. Then there was another knock at the door and before Ashenden could answer Mr. Harrington burst in.

"Really the service at this hotel is a scandal," he cried heatedly, "I've been ringing my bell for fifteen minutes and I can't get anyone to pay the smallest attention to me."

"Service?" exclaimed Anastasia Alexandrovna. "There is not a servant left in the hotel."

"But I want my washing. They promised to let me have it back last night."

"I'm afraid you haven't got much chance of getting it now," said Ashenden.

"I'm not going to leave without my washing. Four shirts, two union suits, a pair of pyjamas, and four collars. I wash my handkerchiefs and socks in my room. I want my washing and I'm not going to leave this hotel without it."

"Don't be a fool," cried Ashenden. "What you've got to do is to get out of here while the going's good. If there are no servants to get it you'll just have to leave your washing behind you."

"Pardon me, sir, I shall do nothing of the kind. I'll go and fetch it myself. I've suffered enough at the hands of this country and I'm not going to leave four perfectly good shirts to be worn by a lot of dirty Bolsheviks. No, sir. I do not leave Russia till I have my washing."

Anastasia Alexandrovna stared at the floor for a moment; then with a little smile looked up. It seemed to Ashenden that there was something in her that responded to Mr. Harrington's futile obstinacy. In her Russian way she understood that Mr. Harrington could not leave Petrograd without his washing. His insistence had given it the value of a symbol.

"I'll go downstairs and see if I can find anybody about who knows where the laundry is and if I can, I'll go with you and you can bring your washing away with you."

Mr. Harrington unbent. He answered with that sweet and disarming smile of his.

"That's terribly kind of you, Delilah. I don't mind if it's ready or not, I'll take it just as it is."

Anastasia Alexandrovna left them.

"Well, what do you think of Russia and the Russians now?" Mr. Harrington asked Ashenden.

"I'm fed up with them. I'm fed up with Tolstoi, I'm fed up with Turgeniev and Dostoievski, I'm fed up with Chekov. I'm fed up with the Intelligentsia. I hanker after people who know their mind from one minute to another, who mean what they say an hour after they've said it, whose word you can rely on; I'm sick of fine phrases, and oratory and attitudinizing."

Ashenden, bitten by the prevailing ill, was about to make a speech when he was interrupted by a rattle as of peas on a drum. In the city, so strangely silent, it sounded abrupt and odd.

"What's that?" asked Mr. Harrington.

"Rifle firing. On the other side of the river I should think."

Mr. Harrington gave a funny little look. He laughed, but his face was a trifle pale; he did not like it, and Ashenden did not blame him.

"I think it's high time I got out. I shouldn't so much mind for myself, but I've got a wife and children to think of. I haven't had a letter from Mrs. Harrington for so long I'm a bit worried." He paused an instant. "I'd like you to know Mrs. Harrington, she's a very wonderful woman. She's the best wife a man ever had. Until I came here I'd not been separated from her for more than three days since we were married."

Anastasia Alexandrovna came back and told them that she had found the address.

"It's about forty minutes' walk from here and if you'll come now I'll go with you," she said.

"I'm ready."

"You'd better look out," said Ashenden. "I don't believe the streets are very healthy to-day."

Anastasia Alexandrovna looked at Mr. Harrington.

"I must have my washing, Delilah," he said. "I should never rest in peace if I left it behind me and Mrs. Harrington would never let me hear the last of it."

"Come on then."

They set out and Ashenden went on with the dreary business of translating into a very complicated code the shattering news he had to give. It was a long message, and then he had to ask for instructions upon his own movements. It was a mechanical job and yet it was one in which you could not allow your attention to wander. The mistake of a single figure might make a whole sentence incomprehensible.

Suddenly his door was burst open and Anastasia Alexandrovna flung into the room. She had lost her hat and was dishevelled. She was panting. Her eyes were starting out of her head and she was obviously in a state of great excitement.

"Where's Mr. Harrington?" she cried. "Isn't he here?"

"No."

"Is he in his bedroom?"

"I don't know. Why, what's the matter? We'll go and look if you like. Why didn't you bring him along with you?"

They walked down the passage and knocked at Mr. Harrington's door; there was no answer; they tried the handle; the door was locked.

"He's not there."

They went back to Ashenden's room. Anastasia Alexandrovna sank into a chair.

"Give me a glass of water, will you. I'm out of breath. I've been running."

She drank the water Ashenden poured out for her. She gave a sudden sob.

"I hope he's all right. I should never forgive myself if he was hurt. I was hoping he would have got here before me. He got his washing all right. We found the place. There was only an old woman there and they didn't want to let us take it, but we insisted. Mr. Harrington was furious because it hadn't been touched. It was exactly as he had sent it. They'd promised it last night and it was still in the bundle that Mr. Harrington had made himself. I said that was Russia and Mr. Harrington said he preferred coloured people. I'd led him by side streets because I thought it was better, and we started to come back again. We passed at the top of a street and at the bottom of it I saw a little crowd. There was a man addressing them.

" 'Let's go and hear what he's saying,' I said.

"I could see they were arguing. It looked exciting. I wanted to know what was happening.

" 'Come along, Delilah,' he said. 'Let us mind our own business.'

" 'You go back to the hotel and do your packing. I'm going to see the fun,' I said.

"I ran down the street and he followed me. There were about two or three hundred people there and a student was addressing them. There were some working men and they were shouting at him. I love a row and I edged my way into the crowd. Suddenly we heard the sound of shots and before you could realize what was happening two armoured cars came dashing down the street. There were soldiers in them and they were firing as they went. I don't know why. For fun, I suppose, or because they were drunk. We all scattered like a lot of rabbits. We just ran for our lives. I lost Mr. Harrington. I can't make out why he isn't here. Do you think something has happened to him?"

Ashenden was silent for a while.

"We'd better go out and look for him,' he said. "I don't know why the devil he couldn't leave his washing."

"I understand, I understand so well."

"That's a comfort," said Ashenden irritably. "Let's go."

He put on his hat and coat, and they walked downstairs. The hotel seemed strangely empty. They went out into the street. There was hardly anyone to be seen. They walked along. The trams were not running and the silence in the great city was uncanny. The shops were closed. It was quite startling when a motor car dashed by at breakneck speed. The people they passed looked frightened and downcast. When they had to go through a main thoroughfare they hastened their steps. A lot of people were there and they stood about irresolutely as though they did not know what to do next. Reservists in their shabby grey were walking down the middle of the roadway in little bunches. They did not speak. They looked like sheep looking for their shepherd. Then they came to the street down which Anastasia Alexandrovna had run, but they entered it from the opposite end. A number of windows had been broken by the wild shooting. It was quite empty. You could see where the people had scattered, for strewn about were articles they had dropped in their haste, books, a man's hat, a lady's bag and a basket. Anastasia Alexandrovna touched Ashenden's arm to draw his attention: sitting on the pavement, her head bent right down to her lap, was a woman and she was dead. A little way on two men had fallen together. They were dead too. The wounded, one supposed, had managed to drag themselves away or their friends had carried them. Then they found Mr. Harrington. His derby had rolled in the gutter. He lay on his face, in a pool of blood, his bald head, with its prominent bones, very white; his neat black coat smeared and muddy. But his hand was clenched tight on the parcel that contained four shirts, two union suits, a pair of pyjamas and four collars. Mr. Harrington had not let his washing go.

Red

The skipper thrust his hand into one of his trouser pockets and with difficulty, for they were not at the sides but in front and he was a portly man, pulled out a large silver watch. He looked at it and then looked again at the declining sun. The Kanaka at the wheel gave him a glance, but did not speak. The skipper's eyes rested on the island they were approaching. A white line of foam marked the reef. He knew there was an opening large enough to get his ship through, and when they came a little nearer he counted on seeing it. They had nearly an hour of daylight still before them. In the lagoon the water was deep and they could anchor comfortably. The chief of the village which he could already see among the coconut trees was a friend of the mate's, and it would be pleasant to go ashore for the night. The mate came forward at that minute and the skipper turned to him.

"We'll take a bottle of booze along with us and get some girls in to dance," he said.

"I don't see the opening," said the mate.

He was a Kanaka, a handsome, swarthy fellow, with somewhat the look of a later Roman emperor, inclined to stoutness; but his face was fine and clean-cut.

"I'm dead sure there's one right here," said the captain, looking through his glasses. "I can't understand why I can't pick it up. Send one of the boys up the mast to have a look."

The mate called one of the crew and gave him the order. The captain watched the Kanaka climb and waited for him to speak. But the Kanaka shouted down that he could see

nothing but the unbroken line of foam. The captain spoke
Samoan like a native, and he cursed him freely.

"Shall he stay up there?" asked the mate.

"What the hell good does that do?" answered the captain.
"The blame fool can't see worth a cent. You bet your sweet
life I'd find the opening if I was up there."

He looked at the slender mast with anger. It was all very
well for a native who had been used to climbing up coconut
trees all his life. He was fat and heavy.

"Come down," he shouted. "You're no more use than a dead
dog. We'll just have to go along the reef till we find the
opening."

It was a seventy-ton schooner with paraffin auxiliary, and
it ran, when there was no head wind, between four and five
knots an hour. It was a bedraggled object; it had been painted
white a very long time ago, but it was now dirty, dingy, and
mottled. It smelt strongly of paraffin and of the copra which
was its usual cargo. They were within a hundred feet of the
reef now and the captain told the steersman to run along it
till they came to the opening. But when they had gone a
couple of miles he realized that they had missed it. He went
about and slowly worked back again. The white foam of the
reef continued without interruption and now the sun was setting. With a curse at the stupidity of the crew the skipper
resigned himself to waiting till next morning.

"Put her about," he said. "I can't anchor here."

They went out to sea a little and presently it was quite
dark. They anchored. When the sail was furled the ship began
to roll a good deal. They said in Apia that one day she would
roll right over; and the owner, a German-American who managed one of the largest stores, said that no money was big
enough to induce him to go out in her. The cook, a Chinese in
white trousers, very dirty and ragged, and a thin white tunic,
came to say that supper was ready, and when the skipper went
into the cabin he found the engineer already seated at table.
The engineer was a long, lean man with a scraggy neck. He
was dressed in blue overalls and a sleeveless jersey which
showed his thin arms tattooed from elbow to wrist.

"Hell, having to spend the night outside," said the skipper.

The engineer did not answer, and they ate their supper in silence. The cabin was lit by a dim oil lamp. When they had eaten the canned apricots with which the meal finished the Chink brought them a cup of tea. The skipper lit a cigar and went on the upper deck. The island now was only a darker mass against the night. The stars were very bright. The only sound was the ceaseless breaking of the surf. The skipper sank into a deck-chair and smoked idly. Presently three or four members of the crew came up and sat down. One of them had a banjo and another a concertina. They began to play, and one of them sang. The native song sounded strange on these instruments. Then to the singing a couple began to dance. It was a barbaric dance, savage and primeval, rapid, with quick movements of the hands and feet and contortions of the body; it was sensual, sexual even, but sexual without passion. It was very animal, direct, weird without mystery, natural in short, and one might almost say childlike. At last they grew tired. They stretched themselves on the deck and slept, and all was silent. The skipper lifted himself heavily out of his chair and clambered down the companion. He went into his cabin and got out of his clothes. He climbed into his bunk and lay there. He panted a little in the heat of the night.

But next morning, when the dawn crept over the tranquil sea, the opening in the reef which had eluded them the night before was seen a little to the east of where they lay. The schooner entered the lagoon. There was not a ripple on the surface of the water. Deep down among the coral rocks you saw little coloured fish swim. When he had anchored his ship the skipper ate his breakfast and went on deck. The sun shone from an unclouded sky, but in the early morning the air was grateful and cool. It was Sunday, and there was a feeling of quietness, a silence as though nature were at rest, which gave him a peculiar sense of comfort. He sat, looking at the wooded coast, and felt lazy and well at ease. Presently a slow smile moved his lips and he threw the stump of his cigar into the water.

"I guess I'll go ashore," he said. "Get the boat out."

He climbed stiffly down the ladder and was rowed to a little cove. The coconut trees came down to the water's edge, not
in rows, but spaced out with an ordered formality. They were
like a ballet of spinsters, elderly but flippant, standing in
affected attitudes with the simpering graces of a bygone age.
He sauntered idly through them, along a path that could be
just seen winding its tortuous way, and it led him presently to
a broad creek. There was a bridge across it, but a bridge con-
structed of single trunks of coconut trees, a dozen of them,
placed end to end and supported where they met by a forked
branch driven into the bed of the creek. You walked on a
smooth, round surface, narrow and slippery, and there was no
support for the hand. To cross such a bridge required sure feet
and a stout heart. The skipper hesitated. But he saw on the
other side, nestling among the trees, a white man's house; he
made up his mind and, rather gingerly, began to walk. He
watched his feet carefully, and where one trunk joined on to
the next and there was a difference of level, he tottered a little. It was with a gasp of relief that he reached the last tree
and finally set his feet on the firm ground of the other side.
He had been so intent on the difficult crossing that he never
noticed anyone was watching him, and it was with surprise
that he heard himself spoken to.

"It takes a bit of nerve to cross these bridges when you're
not used to them."

He looked up and saw a man standing in front of him. He
had evidently come out of the house which he had seen.

"I saw you hesitate," the man continued, with a smile on his
lips, "and I was watching to see you fall in."

"Not on your life," said the captain, who had now recovered
his confidence.

"I've fallen in myself before now. I remember, one evening I came back from shooting, and I fell in, gun and all.
Now I get a boy to carry my gun for me."

He was a man no longer young, with a small beard, now
somewhat grey, and a thin face. He was dressed in a singlet,
without arms, and a pair of duck trousers. He wore neither
shoes nor socks. He spoke English with a slight accent.

"Are you Neilson?" asked the skipper.

"I am."

"I've heard about you. I thought you lived somewheres round here."

The skipper followed his host into the little bungalow and sat down heavily in the chair which the other motioned him to take. While Neilson went out to fetch whisky and glasses he took a look round the room. It filled him with amazement. He had never seen so many books. The shelves reached from floor to ceiling on all four walls, and they were closely packed. There was a grand piano littered with music, and a large table on which books and magazines lay in disorder. The room made him feel embarrassed. He remembered that Neilson was a queer fellow. No one knew very much about him, although he had been in the islands for so many years, but those who knew him agreed that he was queer. He was a Swede.

"You've got one big heap of books here," he said, when Neilson returned.

"They do no harm," answered Neilson with a smile.

"Have you read them all?" asked the skipper.

"Most of them."

"I'm a bit of a reader myself. I have the *Saturday Evening Post* sent me regler."

Neilson poured his visitor a good stiff glass of whisky and gave him a cigar. The skipper volunteered a little information.

"I got in last night, but I couldn't find the opening, so I had to anchor outside. I never been this run before, but my people had some stuff they wanted to bring over here. Gray, d'you know him?"

"Yes, he's got a store a little way along."

"Well, there was a lot of canned stuff that he wanted over, an' he's got some copra. They thought I might just as well come over as lie idle at Apia. I run between Apia and Pago-Pago mostly, but they've got smallpox there just now, and there's nothing stirring."

He took a drink of his whisky and lit a cigar. He was a taciturn man, but there was something in Neilson that made him nervous, and his nervousness made him talk. The Swede was looking at him with large dark eyes in which there was an expression of faint amusement.

"This is a tidy little place you've got here."

"I've done my best with it."

"You must do pretty well with your trees. They look fine. With copra at the price it is now. I had a bit of a plantation myself once, in Upolu it was, but I had to sell it."

He looked round the room again, where all those books gave him a feeling of something incomprehensible and hostile.

"I guess you must find it a bit lonesome here though," he said.

"I've got used to it. I've been here for twenty-five years."

Now the captain could think of nothing more to say, and he smoked in silence. Neilson had apparently no wish to break it. He looked at his guest with a meditative eye. He was a tall man, more than six feet high, and very stout. His face was red and blotchy, with a network of little purple veins on the cheeks, and his features were sunk into its fatness. His eyes were bloodshot. His neck was buried in rolls of fat. But for a fringe of long curly hair, nearly white, at the back of his head, he was quite bald; and that immense, shiny surface of forehead, which might have given him a false look of intelligence, on the contrary gave him one of peculiar imbecility. He wore a blue flannel shirt, open at the neck and showing his fat chest covered with a mat of reddish hair, and a very old pair of blue serge trousers. He sat in his chair in a heavy ungainly attitude, his great belly thrust forward and his fat legs uncrossed. All elasticity had gone from his limbs. Neilson wondered idly what sort of man he had been in his youth. It was almost impossible to imagine that this creature of vast bulk had ever been a boy who ran about. The skipper finished his whisky, and Neilson pushed the bottle towards him.

"Help yourself."

The skipper leaned forward and with his great hand seized it.

"And how come you in these parts anyways?" he said.

"Oh, I came out to the islands for my health. My lungs were bad and they said I hadn't a year to live. You see they were wrong."

"I meant, how come you to settle down right here?"

"I am a sentimentalist."

"Oh!"

Neilson knew that the skipper had not an idea what he meant, and he looked at him with an ironical twinkle in his dark eyes. Perhaps just because the skipper was so gross and dull a man the whim seized him to talk further.

"You were too busy keeping your balance to notice, when you crossed the bridge, but this spot is generally considered rather pretty."

"It's a cute little house you've got here."

"Ah, that wasn't here when I first came. There was a native hut, with its beehive roof and its pillars, overshadowed by a great tree with red flowers; and the croton bushes, their leaves yellow and red and golden, made a pied fence around it. And then all about were the coconut trees, as fanciful as women, and as vain. They stood at the water's edge and spent all day looking at their reflections. I was a young man then—Good Heavens, it's a quarter of a century ago—and I wanted to enjoy all the loveliness of the world in the short time allotted to me before I passed into the darkness. I thought it was the most beautiful spot I had ever seen. The first time I saw it I had a catch at my heart, and I was afraid I was going to cry. I wasn't more than twenty-five, and though I put the best face I could on it, I didn't want to die. And somehow it seemed to me that the very beauty of this place made it easier for me to accept my fate. I felt when I came here that all my past life had fallen away, Stockholm and its University, and then Bonn: it all seemed the life of somebody else, as though now at last I had achieved the reality which our doctors of philosophy—I am one myself, you know—had discussed so much. 'A year,' I cried to myself. 'I have a year. I will spend it here and then I am content to die.'

"We are foolish and sentimental and melodramatic at

twenty-five, but if we weren't perhaps we should be less wise at fifty.

"Now drink, my friend. Don't let the nonsense I talk interfere with you."

He waved his thin hand towards the bottle, and the skipper finished what remained in his glass.

"You ain't drinking nothin'," he said, reaching for the whisky.

"I am of a sober habit," smiled the Swede. "I intoxicate myself in ways which I fancy are more subtle. But perhaps that is only vanity. Anyhow, the effects are more lasting and the results less deleterious."

"They say there's a deal of cocaine taken in the States now," said the captain.

Neilson chuckled.

"But I do not see a white man often," he continued, "and for once I don't think a drop of whisky can do me any harm."

He poured himself out a little, added some soda, and took a sip.

"And presently I found out why the spot had such an unearthly loveliness. Here love had tarried for a moment like a migrant bird that happens on a ship in mid-ocean and for a little while folds its tired wings. The fragrance of a beautiful passion hovered over it like the fragrance of hawthorn in May in the meadows of my home. It seems to me that the places where men have loved or suffered keep about them always some faint aroma of something that has not wholly died. It is as though they had acquired a spiritual significance which mysteriously affects those who pass. I wish I could make myself clear." He smiled a little. "Though I cannot imagine that if I did you would understand."

He paused.

"I think this place was beautiful because here had been loved beautifully." And now he shrugged his shoulders. "But perhaps it is only that my æsthetic sense is gratified by the happy conjunction of young love and a suitable setting."

Even a man less thick-witted than the skipper might have

been forgiven if he were bewildered by Neilson's words. For he seemed faintly to laugh at what he said. It was as though he spoke from emotion which his intellect found ridiculous. He had said himself that he was a sentimentalist, and when sentimentality is joined with scepticism there is often the devil to pay.

He was silent for an instant and looked at the captain with eyes in which there was a sudden perplexity.

"You know, I can't help thinking that I've seen you before somewhere or other," he said.

"I couldn't say as I remember you," returned the skipper.

"I have a curious feeling as though your face were familiar to me. It's been puzzling me for some time. But I can't situate my recollection in any place or at any time."

The skipper massively shrugged his heavy shoulders.

"It's thirty years since I first come to the islands. A man can't figure on remembering all the folk he meets in a while like that."

The Swede shook his head.

"You know how one sometimes has the feeling that a place one has never been to before is strangely familiar. That's how I seem to see you." He gave a whimsical smile. "Perhaps I knew you in some past existence. Perhaps, perhaps you were the master of a galley in ancient Rome and I was a slave at the oar. Thirty years have you been here?"

"Every bit of thirty years."

"I wonder if you knew a man called Red?"

"Red?"

"That is the only name I've ever known him by. I never knew him personally. I never even set eyes on him. And yet I seem to see him more clearly than many men, my brothers, for instance, with whom I passed my daily life for many years. He lives in my imagination with the distinctness of a Paolo Malatesta or a Romeo. But I daresay you have never read Dante or Shakespeare?"

"I can't say as I have," said the captain.

Neilson, smoking a cigar, leaned back in his chair and looked vacantly at the ring of smoke which floated in the still

air. A smile played on his lips, but his eyes were grave. Then
he looked at the captain. There was in his gross obesity something extraordinarily repellent. He had the plethoric self-
satisfaction of the very fat. It was an outrage. It set Neilson's
nerves on edge. But the contrast between the man before him
and the man he had in mind was pleasant.

"It appears that Red was the most comely thing you ever
saw. I've talked to quite a number of people who knew him in
those days, white men, and they all agree that the first time
you saw him his beauty just took your breath away. They
called him Red on account of his flaming hair. It had a natural wave and he wore it long. It must have been of that wonderful colour that the pre-Raphaelites raved over. I don't
think he was vain of it, he was much too ingenuous for that,
but no one could have blamed him if he had been. He was
tall, six feet and an inch or two—in the native house that used
to stand here was the mark of his height cut with a knife on
the central trunk that supported the roof—and he was made
like a Greek god, broad in the shoulders and thin in the
flanks; he was like Apollo, with just that soft roundness which
Praxiteles gave him, and that suave, feminine grace which has
in it something troubling and mysterious. His skin was dazzling white, milky, like satin; his skin was like a woman's."

"I had kind of a white skin myself when I was a kiddie,"
said the skipper, with a twinkle in his bloodshot eyes.

But Neilson paid no attention to him. He was telling his
story now and interruption made him impatient.

"And his face was just as beautiful as his body. He had
large blue eyes, very dark, so that some say they were black,
and unlike most red-haired people he had dark eyebrows and
long dark lashes. His features were perfectly regular and his
mouth was like a scarlet wound. He was twenty."

On these words the Swede stopped with a certain sense of
the dramatic. He took a sip of whisky.

"He was unique. There never was anyone more beautiful.
There was no more reason for him than for a wonderful blos-
som to flower on a wild plant. He was a happy accident of
nature.

"One day he landed at that cove into which you must have put this morning. He was an American sailor, and he had deserted from a man-of-war in Apia. He had induced some good-humoured native to give him a passage on a cutter that happened to be sailing from Apia to Safoto, and he had been put ashore here in a dugout. I do not know why he deserted. Perhaps life on a man-of-war with its restrictions irked him, perhaps he was in trouble, and perhaps it was the South Seas and these romantic islands that got into his bones. Every now and then they take a man strangely, and he finds himself like a fly in a spider's web. It may be that there was a softness of fibre in him, and these green hills with their soft airs, this blue sea, took the northern strength from him as Delilah took the Nazarite's. Anyhow, he wanted to hide himself, and he thought he would be safe in this secluded nook till his ship had sailed from Samoa.

"There was a native hut at the cove and as he stood there, wondering where exactly he should turn his steps, a young girl came out and invited him to enter. He knew scarcely two words of the native tongue and she as little English. But he understood well enough what her smiles meant, and her pretty gestures, and he followed her. He sat down on a mat and she gave him slices of pineapple to eat. I can speak of Red only from hearsay, but I saw the girl three years after he first met her, and she was scarcely nineteen then. You cannot imagine how exquisite she was. She had the passionate grace of the hibiscus and the rich colour. She was rather tall, slim, with the delicate features of her race, and large eyes like pools of still water under the palm trees; her hair, black and curling, fell down her back, and she wore a wreath of scented flowers. Her hands were lovely. They were so small, so exquisitely formed, they gave your heart-strings a wrench. And in those days she laughed easily. Her smile was so delightful that it made your knees shake. Her skin was like a field of ripe corn on a summer day. Good Heavens, how can I describe her? She was too beautiful to be real.

"And these two young things, she was sixteen and he was twenty, fell in love with one another at first sight. That is the

real love, not the love that comes from sympathy, common
interests, or intellectual community, but love pure and simple.
That is the love that Adam felt for Eve when he awoke and
found her in the garden gazing at him with dewy eyes. That
is the love that draws the beasts to one another, and the Gods.
That is the love that makes the world a miracle. That is the
love which gives life its pregnant meaning. You have never
heard of the wise, cynical French duke who said that with two
lovers there is always one who loves and one who lets himself be loved; it is a bitter truth to which most of us have to
resign ourselves; but now and then there are two who love
and two who let themselves be loved. Then one might fancy
that the sun stands still as it stood when Joshua prayed to the
God of Israel.

"And even now after all these years, when I think of these
two, so young, so fair, so simple, and of their love, I feel a
pang. It tears my heart just as my heart is torn when on certain nights I watch the full moon shining on the lagoon from
an unclouded sky. There is always pain in the contemplation
of perfect beauty.

"They were children. She was good and sweet and kind. I
know nothing of him, and I like to think that then at all
events he was ingenuous and frank. I like to think that his
soul was as comely as his body. But I daresay he had no more
soul than the creatures of the woods and forests who made
pipes from reeds and bathed in the mountain streams when
the world was young, and you might catch sight of little fawns
galloping through the glade on the back of a bearded centaur.
A soul is a troublesome possession and when man developed
it he lost the Garden of Eden.

"Well, when Red came to the island it had recently been
visited by one of those epidemics which the white man has
brought to the South Seas, and one third of the inhabitants had
died. It seems that the girl had lost all her near kin and she
lived now in the house of distant cousins. The household
consisted of two ancient crones, bowed and wrinkled, two
younger women, and a man and a boy. For a few days he
stayed there. But perhaps he felt himself too near the shore,

with the possibility that he might fall in with white men who
would reveal his hiding-place; perhaps the lovers could not
bear that the company of others should rob them for an instant of the delight of being together. One morning they set
out, the pair of them, with the few things that belonged to the
girl, and walked along a grassy path under the coconuts, till
they came to the creek you see. They had to cross the bridge
you crossed, and the girl laughed gleefully because he was
afraid. She held his hand till they came to the end of the first
tree, and then his courage failed him and he had to go back.
He was obliged to take off all his clothes before he could risk
it, and she carried them over for him on her head. They settled
down in the empty hut that stood here. Whether she had any
rights over it (land tenure is a complicated business in the islands), or whether the owner had died during the epidemic, I
do not know, but anyhow no one questioned them, and they
took possession. Their furniture consisted of a couple of grass
mats on which they slept, a fragment of looking-glass, and a
bowl or two. In this pleasant land that is enough to start
housekeeping on.

"They say that happy people have no history, and certainly a
happy love has none. They did nothing all day long and yet
the days seemed all too short. The girl had a native name, but
Red called her Sally. He picked up the easy language very
quickly, and he used to lie on the mat for hours while she
chattered gaily to him. He was a silent fellow, and perhaps
his mind was lethargic. He smoked incessantly the cigarettes
which she made him out of the native tobacco and pandanus
leaf, and he watched her while with deft fingers she made
grass mats. Often natives would come in and tell long stories
of the old days when the island was disturbed by tribal wars.
Sometimes he would go fishing on the reef, and bring home a
basket full of coloured fish. Sometimes at night he would go
out with a lantern to catch lobster. There were plantains
round the hut and Sally would roast them for their frugal
meal. She knew how to make delicious messes from coconuts,
and the breadfruit tree by the side of the creek gave them its
fruit. On feast-days they killed a little pig and cooked it on

hot stones. They bathed together in the creek; and in the evening they went down to the lagoon and paddled about in a dugout, with its great outrigger. The sea was deep blue, wine-coloured at sundown, like the sea of Homeric Greece; but in the lagoon the colour had an infinite variety, aquamarine and amethyst and emerald; and the setting sun turned it for a short moment to liquid gold. Then there was the colour of the coral, brown, white, pink, red, purple; and the shapes it took were marvellous. It was like a magic garden, and the hurrying fish were like butterflies. It strangely lacked reality. Among the coral were pools with a floor of white sand and here, where the water was dazzling clear, it was very good to bathe. Then, cool and happy, they wandered back in the gloaming over the soft grass road to the creek, walking hand in hand, and now the mynah birds filled the coconut trees with their clamour. And then the night, with that great sky shining with gold, that seemed to stretch more widely than the skies of Europe, and the soft airs that blew gently through the open hut, the long night again was all too short. She was sixteen and he was barely twenty. The dawn crept in among the wooden pillars of the hut and looked at those lovely children sleeping in one another's arms. The sun hid behind the great tattered leaves of the plantains so that it might not disturb them, and then, with playful malice, shot a golden ray, like the outstretched paw of a Persian cat, on their faces. They opened their sleepy eyes and they smiled to welcome another day. The weeks lengthened into months, and a year passed. They seemed to love one another as—I hesitate to say passionately, for passion has in it always a shade of sadness, a touch of bitterness or anguish, but as wholeheartedly, as simply and naturally as on that first day on which, meeting, they had recognized that a god was in them.

"If you had asked them I have no doubt that they would have thought it impossible to suppose their love could ever cease. Do we not know that the essential element of love is a belief in its own eternity? And yet perhaps in Red there was already a very little seed, unknown to himself and unsuspected by the girl, which would in time have grown to weari-

ness. For one day one of the natives from the cove told them
that some way down the coast at the anchorage was a British
whalingship.

" 'Gee,' he said, 'I wonder if I could make a trade of some
nuts and plantains for a pound or two of tobacco.'

"The pandanus cigarettes that Sally made him with untir-
ing hands were strong and pleasant enough to smoke, but
they left him unsatisfied; and he yearned on a sudden for real
tobacco, hard, rank, and pungent. He had not smoked a pipe
for many months. His mouth watered at the thought of it.
One would have thought some premonition of harm would
have made Sally seek to dissuade him, but love possessed her
so completely that it never occurred to her any power on earth
could take him from her. They went up into the hills together
and gathered a great basket of wild oranges, green, but sweet
and juicy; and they picked plantains from around the hut, and
coconuts from their trees, and breadfruit and mangoes; and
they carried them down to the cove. They loaded the un-
stable canoe with them, and Red and the native boy who had
brought them the news of the ship paddled along outside the
reef.

"It was the last time she ever saw him.

"Next day the boy came back alone. He was all in tears.
This is the story he told. When after their long paddle they
reached the ship and Red hailed it, a white man looked over
the side and told them to come on board. They took the fruit
they had brought with them and Red piled it up on the deck.
The white man and he began to talk, and they seemed to
come to some agreement. One of them went below and
brought up tobacco. Red took some at once and lit a pipe.
The boy imitated the zest with which he blew a great cloud of
smoke from his mouth. Then they said something to him and
he went into the cabin. Through the open door the boy,
watching curiously, saw a bottle brought out and glasses. Red
drank and smoked. They seemed to ask him something, for he
shook his head and laughed. The man, the first man who had
spoken to them, laughed too, and he filled Red's glass once
more. They went on talking and drinking, and presently,

growing tired of watching a sight that meant nothing to him, the boy curled himself up on the deck and slept. He was awakened by a kick; and, jumping to his feet, he saw that the ship was slowly sailing out of the lagoon. He caught sight of Red seated at the table, with his head resting heavily on his arms, fast asleep. He made a movement towards him, intending to wake him, but a rough hand seized his arm, and a man, with a scowl and words which he did not understand, pointed to the side. He shouted to Red, but in a moment he was seized and flung overboard. Helpless, he swam round to his canoe which was drifting a little way off, and pushed it on to the reef. He climbed in and, sobbing all the way, paddled back to shore.

"What had happened was obvious enough. The whaler, by desertion or sickness, was short of hands, and the captain when Red came aboard had asked him to sign on; on his refusal he had made him drunk and kidnapped him.

"Sally was beside herself with grief. For three days she screamed and cried. The natives did what they could to comfort her, but she would not be comforted. She would not eat. And then, exhausted, she sank into a sullen apathy. She spent long days at the cove, watching the lagoon, in the vain hope that Red somehow or other would manage to escape. She sat on the white sand, hour after hour, with the tears running down her cheeks, and at night dragged herself wearily back across the creek to the little hut where she had been happy. The people with whom she had lived before Red came to the island wished her to return to them, but she would not; she was convinced that Red would come back, and she wanted him to find her where he had left her. Four months later she was delivered of a still-born child, and the old woman who had come to help her through her confinement remained with her in the hut. All joy was taken from her life. If her anguish with time became less intolerable it was replaced by a settled melancholy. You would not have thought that among these people, whose emotions, though so violent, are very transient, a woman could be found capable of so enduring a passion. She never lost the profound conviction that sooner or later

Red would come back. She watched for him, and every time someone crossed this slender little bridge of coconut trees she looked. It might at last be he."

Neilson stopped talking and gave a faint sigh.

"And what happened to her in the end?" asked the skipper.

Neilson smiled bitterly.

"Oh, three years afterwards she took up with another white man."

The skipper gave a fat, cynical chuckle.

"That's generally what happens to them," he said.

The Swede shot him a look of hatred. He did not know why that gross, obese man excited in him so violent a repulsion. But his thoughts wandered and he found his mind filled with memories of the past. He went back five and twenty years. It was when he first came to the island, weary of Apia, with its heavy drinking, its gambling and coarse sensuality, a sick man, trying to resign himself to the loss of the career which had fired his imagination with ambitious thoughts. He set behind him resolutely all his hopes of making a great name for himself and strove to content himself with the few poor months of careful life which was all that he could count on. He was boarding with a half-caste trader who had a store a couple of miles along the coast at the edge of a native village; and one day, wandering aimlessly along the grassy paths of the coconut groves, he had come upon the hut in which Sally lived. The beauty of the spot had filled him with a rapture so great that it was almost painful, and then he had seen Sally. She was the loveliest creature he had ever seen, and the sadness in those dark, magnificent eyes of hers affected him strangely. The Kanakas were a handsome race, and beauty was not rare among them, but it was the beauty of shapely animals. It was empty. But those tragic eyes were dark with mystery, and you felt in them the bitter complexity of the groping, human soul. The trader told him the story and it moved him.

"Do you think he'll ever come back?" asked Neilson.

"No fear. Why, it'll be a couple of years before the ship is paid off, and by then he'll have forgotten all about her. I bet he was pretty mad when he woke up and found he'd been shanghaied, and I shouldn't wonder but he wanted to fight somebody. But he'd got to grin and bear it, and I guess in a month he was thinking it the best thing that had ever happened to him that he got away from the island."

But Neilson could not get the story out of his head. Perhaps because he was sick and weakly, the radiant health of Red appealed to his imagination. Himself an ugly man, insignificant of appearance, he prized very highly comeliness in others. He had never been passionately in love, and certainly he had never been passionately loved. The mutual attraction of those two young things gave him a singular delight. It had the ineffable beauty of the Absolute. He went again to the little hut by the creek. He had a gift for languages and an energetic mind, accustomed to work, and he had already given much time to the study of the local tongue. Old habit was strong in him and he was gathering together material for a paper on the Samoan speech. The old crone who shared the hut with Sally invited him to come in and sit down. She gave him *kava* to drink and cigarettes to smoke. She was glad to have someone to chat with and while she talked he looked at Sally. She reminded him of the Psyche in the museum at Naples. Her features had the same clear purity of line, and though she had borne a child she had still a virginal aspect.

It was not till he had seen her two or three times that he induced her to speak. Then it was only to ask him if he had seen in Apia a man called Red. Two years had passed since his disappearance, but it was plain that she still thought of him incessantly.

It did not take Neilson long to discover that he was in love with her. It was only by an effort of will now that he prevented himself from going every day to the creek, and when he was not with Sally his thoughts were. At first, looking upon himself as a dying man, he asked only to look at her, and occasionally hear her speak, and his love gave him a wonderful happiness. He exulted in its purity. He wanted nothing from her but the opportunity to weave around her graceful person a web of beautiful fancies. But the open air, the equable tem-

perature, the rest, the simple fare, began to have an unexpected effect on his health. His temperature did not soar at
night to such alarming heights, he coughed less and began to
put on weight; six months passed without his having a
hæmorrhage; and of a sudden he saw the possibility that he
might live. He had studied his disease carefully, and the hope
dawned upon him that with great care he might arrest its
course. It exhilarated him to look forward once more to the
future. He made plans. It was evident that any active life was
out of the question, but he could live on the islands, and the
small income he had, insufficient elsewhere, would be ample
to keep him. He could grow coconuts; that would give him an
occupation; and he would send for his books and a piano; but
his quick mind saw that in all this he was merely trying to
conceal from himself the desire which obsessed him.

He wanted Sally. He loved not only her beauty, but that
dim soul which he divined behind her suffering eyes. He
would intoxicate her with his passion. In the end he would
make her forget. And in an ecstasy of surrender he fancied
himself giving her too the happiness which he had thought
never to know again, but had now so miraculously achieved.

He asked her to live with him. She refused. He had expected that and did not let it depress him, for he was sure that
sooner or later she would yield. His love was irresistible. He
told the old woman of his wishes, and found somewhat to his
surprise that she and the neighbours, long aware of them,
were strongly urging Sally to accept his offer. After all, every
native was glad to keep house for a white man, and Neilson
according to the standards of the island was a rich one. The
trader with whom he boarded went to her and told her not to
be a fool; such an opportunity would not come again, and
after so long she could not still believe that Red would ever
return. The girl's resistance only increased Neilson's desire,
and what had been a very pure love now became an agonizing
passion. He was determined that nothing should stand in his
way. He gave Sally no peace. At last, worn out by his persistence and the persuasions, by turns pleading and angry, of
everyone around her, she consented. But the day after when,

exultant, he went to see her he found that in the night she had burnt down the hut in which she and Red had lived together. The old crone ran towards him full of angry abuse of Sally, but he waved her aside; it did not matter; they would build a bungalow on the place where the hut had stood. A European house would really be more convenient if he wanted to bring out a piano and a vast number of books.

And so the little wooden house was built in which he had now lived for many years, and Sally became his wife. But after the first few weeks of rapture, during which he was satisfied with what she gave him, he had known little happiness. She had yielded to him, through weariness, but she had only yielded what she set no store on. The soul which he had dimly glimpsed escaped him. He knew that she cared nothing for him. She still loved Red, and all the time she was waiting for his return. At a sign from him, Neilson knew that, notwithstanding his love, his tenderness, his sympathy, his generosity, she would leave him without a moment's hesitation. She would never give a thought to his distress. Anguish seized him and he battered at that impenetrable self of hers which sullenly resisted him. His love became bitter. He tried to melt her heart with kindness, but it remained as hard as before; he feigned indifference, but she did not notice it. Sometimes he lost his temper and abused her, and then she wept silently. Sometimes he thought she was nothing but a fraud, and that soul simply an invention of his own, and that he could not get into the sanctuary of her heart because there was no sanctuary there. His love became a prison from which he longed to escape, but he had not the strength merely to open the door —that was all it needed—and walk out into the open air. It was torture and at last he became numb and hopeless. In the end the fire burnt itself out and, when he saw her eyes rest for an instant on the slender bridge, it was no longer rage that filled his heart but impatience. For many years now they had lived together bound by the ties of habit and convenience, and it was with a smile that he looked back on his old passion. She was an old woman, for the women on the islands age quickly, and if he had no love for her any more he had toler-

ance. She left him alone. He was contented with his piano
and his books.

His thoughts led him to a desire for words.

"When I look back now and reflect on that brief passionate
love of Red and Sally, I think that perhaps they should thank
the ruthless fate that separated them when their love seemed
still to be at its height. They suffered, but they suffered in
beauty. They were spared the real tragedy of love."

"I don't know exactly as I get you," said the skipper.

"The tragedy of love is not death or separation. How long
do you think it would have been before one or other of them
ceased to care? Oh, it is dreadfully bitter to look at a woman
whom you have loved with all your heart and soul, so that you
felt you could not bear to let her out of your sight, and realize that you would not mind if you never saw her again. The
tragedy of love is indifference."

But while he was speaking a very extraordinary thing happened. Though he had been addressing the skipper he had not
been talking to him, he had been putting his thoughts into
words for himself, and with his eyes fixed on the man in front
of him he had not seen him. But now an image presented itself to them, an image not of the man he saw, but of another
man. It was as though he were looking into one of those dis-
torting mirrors that make you extraordinarily squat or out-
rageously elongate, but here exactly the opposite took place,
and in the obese, ugly old man he caught the shadowy
glimpse of a stripling. He gave him now a quick, searching
scrutiny. Why had a haphazard stroll brought him just to this
place? A sudden tremor of his heart made him slightly breathless. An absurd suspicion seized him. What had occurred to
him was impossible, and yet it might be a fact.

"What is your name?" he asked abruptly.

The skipper's face puckered and he gave a cunning
chuckle. He looked then malicious and horribly vulgar.

"It's such a damned long time since I heard it that I almost
forget it myself. But for thirty years now in the islands they've
always called me Red."

His huge form shook as he gave a low, almost silent laugh. It was obscene. Neilson shuddered. Red was hugely amused, and from his bloodshot eyes tears ran down his cheeks.

Neilson gave a gasp, for at that moment a woman came in. She was a native, a woman of somewhat commanding presence, stout without being corpulent, dark, for the natives grow darker with age, with very grey hair. She wore a black Mother Hubbard, and its thinness showed her heavy breasts. The moment had come.

She made an observation to Neilson about some household matter and he answered. He wondered if his voice sounded as unnatural to her as it did to himself. She gave the man who was sitting in the chair by the window an indifferent glance, and went out of the room. The moment had come and gone.

Neilson for a moment could not speak. He was strangely shaken. Then he said:

"I'd be very glad if you'd stay and have a bit of dinner with me. Pot luck."

"I don't think I will," said Red. "I must go after this fellow Gray. I'll give him his stuff and then I'll get away. I want to be back in Apia to-morrow."

"I'll send a boy along with you to show you the way."

"That'll be fine."

Red heaved himself out of his chair, while the Swede called one of the boys who worked on the plantation. He told him where the skipper wanted to go, and the boy stepped along the bridge. Red prepared to follow him.

"Don't fall in," said Neilson.

"Not on your life."

Neilson watched him make his way across and when he had disappeared among the coconuts he looked still. Then he sank heavily in his chair. Was that the man who had prevented him from being happy? Was that the man whom Sally had loved all these years and for whom she had waited so desperately? It was grotesque. A sudden fury seized him so that he had an instinct to spring up and smash everything around him. He had been cheated. They had seen each other at last and had not known it. He began to laugh, mirthlessly, and his laughter grew till it became hysterical. The Gods had played him a cruel trick. And he was old now.

At last Sally came in to tell him dinner was ready. He sat down in front of her and tried to eat. He wondered what she would say if he told her now that the fat old man sitting in the chair was the lover whom she remembered still with the passionate abandonment of her youth. Years ago, when he hated her because she made him so unhappy, he would have been glad to tell her. He wanted to hurt her then as she hurt him, because his hatred was only love. But now he did not care. He shrugged his shoulders listlessly.

"What did that man want?" she asked presently.

He did not answer at once. She was old too, a fat old native woman. He wondered why he had ever loved her so madly. He had laid at her feet all the treasures of his soul, and she had cared nothing for them. Waste, what waste! And now, when he looked at her, he felt only contempt. His patience was at last exhausted. He answered her question.

"He's the captain of a schooner. He's come from Apia."

"Yes."

"He brought me news from home. My eldest brother is very ill and I must go back."

"Will you be gone long?"

He shrugged his shoulders.

Mr. Know-All

I WAS PREPARED to dislike Max Kelada even before I knew him. The war had just finished and the passenger traffic in the ocean-going liners was heavy. Accommodation was very hard to get and you had to put up with whatever the agents chose to offer you. You could not hope for a cabin to yourself and I was thankful to be given one in which there were only two berths. But when I was told the name of my companion my heart sank. It suggested closed port-holes and the night air rigidly excluded. It was bad enough to share a cabin for fourteen days with anyone (I was going from San Francisco to Yokohama), but I should have looked upon it with less dismay if my fellow-passenger's name had been Smith or Brown.

When I went on board I found Mr. Kelada's luggage already below. I did not like the look of it; there were too many labels on the suitcases, and the wardrobe trunk was too big. He had unpacked his toilet things, and I observed that he was a patron of the excellent Monsieur Coty; for I saw on the washing-stand his scent, his hair-wash and his brilliantine. Mr. Kelada's brushes, ebony with his monogram in gold, would have been all the better for a scrub. I did not at all like Mr. Kelada. I made my way into the smoking-room. I called for a pack of cards and began to play patience. I had scarcely started before a man came up to me and asked me if he was right in thinking my name was so-and-so.

"I am Mr. Kelada," he added, with a smile that showed a row of flashing teeth, and sat down.

"Oh, yes, we're sharing a cabin, I think."

"Bit of luck, I call it. You never know who you're going to

be put in with. I was jolly glad when I heard you were English. I'm all for us English sticking together when we're abroad, if you understand what I mean."

I blinked.

"Are you English?" I asked, perhaps tactlessly.

"Rather. You don't think I look like an American, do you? British to the backbone, that's what I am."

To prove it, Mr. Kelada took out of his pocket a passport and airily waved it under my nose.

King George has many strange subjects. Mr. Kelada was short and of a sturdy build, clean-shaven and dark-skinned, with a fleshy, hooked nose and very large, lustrous and liquid eyes. His long black hair was sleek and curly. He spoke with a fluency in which there was nothing English and his gestures were exuberant. I felt pretty sure that a closer inspection of that British passport would have betrayed the fact that Mr. Kelada was born under a bluer sky than is generally seen in England.

"What will you have?" he asked me.

I looked at him doubtfully. Prohibition was in force and to all appearances the ship was bone-dry. When I am not thirsty I do not know which I dislike more, ginger-ale or lemon-squash. But Mr. Kelada flashed an oriental smile at me.

"Whisky and soda or a dry Martini, you have only to say the word."

From each of his hip-pockets he fished a flask and laid them on the table before me. I chose the Martini, and calling the steward he ordered a tumbler of ice and a couple of glasses.

"A very good cocktail," I said.

"Well, there are plenty more where that came from, and if you've got any friends on board, you tell them you've got a pal who's got all the liquor in the world."

Mr. Kelada was chatty. He talked of New York and San Francisco. He discussed plays, pictures, and politics. He was patriotic. The Union Jack is an impressive piece of drapery, but when it is flourished by a gentleman from Alexandria or Beirut, I cannot but feel that it loses somewhat in dignity. Mr. Kelada was familiar. I do not wish to put on airs, but I cannot help feeling that it is seemly in a total stranger to put mister before my name when he addresses me. Mr. Kelada, doubtless to set me at my ease, used no such formality. I did not like Mr. Kelada. I had put aside the cards when he sat down, but now, thinking that for this first occasion our conversation had lasted long enough, I went on with my game.

"The three on the four," said Mr. Kelada.

There is nothing more exasperating when you are playing patience than to be told where to put the card you have turned up before you have had a chance to look for yourself.

"It's coming out, it's coming out," he cried. "The ten on the knave."

With rage and hatred in my heart I finished. Then he seized the pack.

"Do you like card tricks?"

"No, I hate card tricks," I answered.

"Well, I'll just show you this one."

He showed me three. Then I said I would go down to the dining-room and get my seat at table.

"Oh, that's all right," he said. "I've already taken a seat for you. I thought that as we were in the same state-room we might just as well sit at the same table."

I did not like Mr. Kelada.

I not only shared a cabin with him and ate three meals a day at the same table, but I could not walk round the deck without his joining me. It was impossible to snub him. It never occurred to him that he was not wanted. He was certain that you were as glad to see him as he was to see you. In your own house you might have kicked him downstairs and slammed the door in his face without the suspicion dawning on him that he was not a welcome visitor. He was a good mixer, and in three days knew everyone on board. He ran everything. He managed the sweeps, conducted the auctions, collected money for prizes at the sports, got up quoit and golf matches, organised the concert and arranged the fancy dress ball. He was everywhere and always. He was certainly the best-hated man in the ship. We called him Mr. Know-All, even to his face. He took it as a compliment. But it was at meal times that he was most intolerable. For the better part of an hour then he had us at his mercy. He was hearty, jovial, loquacious and argumentative. He knew everything better than anybody else, and it was an affront to his overweening vanity that you should disagree with him. He would not drop a subject, however unimportant, till he had brought you round to his way of thinking. The possibility that he could be mistaken never occurred to him. He was the chap who knew. We sat at the doctor's table. Mr. Kelada would certainly have had it all his own way, for the doctor was lazy and I was frigidly indifferent, except for a man called Ramsay who sat there also. He was as dogmatic as Mr. Kelada and resented bitterly the Levantine's cocksureness. The discussions they had were acrimonious and interminable.

Ramsay was in the American Consular Service, and was stationed at Kobe. He was a great heavy fellow from the Middle West, with loose fat under a tight skin, and he bulged out of his ready-made clothes. He was on his way back to resume his post, having been on a flying visit to New York to fetch his wife, who had been spending a year at home. Mrs. Ramsay was a very pretty little thing, with pleasant manners and a sense of humour. The Consular Service is ill paid, and she was dressed always very simply; but she knew how to wear her clothes. She achieved an effect of quiet distinction. I should not have paid any particular attention to her but that she possessed a quality that may be common enough in women, but nowadays is not obvious in their demeanour. You could not look at her without being struck by her modesty. It shone in her like a flower on a coat.

One evening at dinner the conversation by chance drifted to the subject of pearls. There had been in the papers a good deal of talk about the culture pearls which the cunning Japanese were making, and the doctor remarked that they must inevitably diminish the value of real ones. They were very good already; they would soon be perfect. Mr. Kelada, as was his habit, rushed the new topic. He told us all that was to be known about pearls. I do not believe Ramsay knew anything

about them at all, but he could not resist the opportunity to
have a fling at the Levantine, and in five minutes we were in
the middle of a heated argument. I had seen Mr. Kelada vehement and voluble before, but never so voluble and vehement
as now. At last something that Ramsay said stung him, for he
thumped the table and shouted:

"Well, I ought to know what I am talking about. I'm going to Japan just to look into this Japanese pearl business.
I'm in the trade and there's not a man in it who won't tell you
that what I say about pearls goes. I know all the best pearls in
the world, and what I don't know about pearls isn't worth
knowing."

Here was news for us, for Mr. Kelada, with all his loquac-
ity, had never told anyone what his business was. We only
knew vaguely that he was going to Japan on some commercial errand. He looked round the table triumphantly.

"They'll never be able to get a culture pearl that an expert
like me can't tell with half an eye." He pointed to a chain that
Mrs. Ramsay wore. "You take my word for it, Mrs. Ramsay,
that chain you're wearing will never be worth a cent less than
it is now."

Mrs. Ramsay in her modest way flushed a little and slipped
the chain inside her dress. Ramsay leaned forward. He gave
us all a look and a smile flickered in his eyes.

"That's a pretty chain of Mrs. Ramsay's, isn't it?"

"I noticed it at once," answered Mr. Kelada. "Gee, I said to
myself, those are pearls, all right."

"I didn't buy it myself, of course. I'd be interested to know
how much you think it cost."

"Oh, in the trade somewhere round fifteen thousand dollars. But if it was bought on Fifth Avenue I shouldn't be surprised to hear that anything up to thirty thousand was paid
for it."

Ramsay smiled grimly.

"You'll be surprised to hear that Mrs. Ramsay bought
that string at a department store the day before we left New
York, for eighteen dollars."

Mr. Kelada flushed.

"Rot. It's not only real, but it's as fine a string for its size as I've ever seen."

"Will you bet on it? I'll bet you a hundred dollars it's imitation."

"Done."

"Oh, Elmer, you can't bet on a certainty," said Mrs. Ramsay.

She had a little smile on her lips and her tone was gently deprecating.

"Can't I? If I get a chance of easy money like that I should be all sorts of a fool not to take it."

"But how can it be proved?" she continued. "It's only my word against Mr. Kelada's."

"Let me look at the chain, and if it's imitation I'll tell you quickly enough. I can afford to lose a hundred dollars," said Mr. Kelada.

"Take it off, dear. Let the gentleman look at it as much as he wants."

Mrs. Ramsay hesitated a moment. She put her hands to the clasp.

"I can't undo it," she said. "Mr. Kelada will just have to take my word for it."

I had a sudden suspicion that something unfortunate was about to occur, but I could think of nothing to say.

Ramsay jumped up.

"I'll undo it."

He handed the chain to Mr. Kelada. The Levantine took a magnifying glass from his pocket and closely examined it. A smile of triumph spread over his smooth and swarthy face. He handed back the chain. He was about to speak. Suddenly he caught sight of Mrs. Ramsay's face. It was so white that she looked as though she were about to faint. She was staring at him with wide and terrified eyes. They held a desperate appeal; it was so clear that I wondered why her husband did not see it.

Mr. Kelada stopped with his mouth open. He flushed deeply. You could almost *see* the effort he was making over himself.

"I was mistaken," he said. "It's a very good imitation, but of course as soon as I looked through my glass I saw that it wasn't real. I think eighteen dollars is just about as much as the damned thing's worth."

He took out his pocket-book and from it a hundred-dollar note. He handed it to Ramsay without a word.

"Perhaps that'll teach you not to be so cocksure another time, my young friend," said Ramsay as he took the note.

I noticed that Mr. Kelada's hands were trembling.

The story spread over the ship as stories do, and he had to put up with a good deal of chaff that evening. It was a fine joke that Mr. Know-All had been caught out. But Mrs. Ramsay retired to her state-room with a headache.

Next morning I got up and began to shave. Mr. Kelada lay on his bed smoking a cigarette. Suddenly there was a small scraping sound and I saw a letter pushed under the door. I opened the door and looked out. There was nobody there. I picked up the letter and saw that it was addressed to Max Kelada. The name was written in block letters. I handed it to him.

"Who's this from?" He opened it. "Oh!"

He took out of the envelope, not a letter, but a hundred-dollar note. He looked at me and again he reddened. He tore the envelope into little bits and gave them to me.

"Do you mind just throwing them out of the port-hole?"

I did as he asked, and then I looked at him with a smile.

"No one likes being made to look a perfect damned fool," he said.

"Were the pearls real?"

"If I had a pretty little wife I shouldn't let her spend a year in New York while I stayed at Kobe," said he.

At that moment I did not entirely dislike Mr. Kelada. He reached out for his pocket-book and carefully put in it the hundred-dollar note.

The Alien Corn

I HAD known the Blands a long time before I discovered that they had any connection with Ferdy Rabenstein. Ferdy must have been nearly fifty when I first knew him, and at the time of which I write he was well over seventy. He had altered little. His hair, coarse but abundant and curly, was white, but he had kept his figure and held himself as gallantly as ever. It was not hard to believe that in youth he had been as beautiful as people said. He had still his fine Semitic profile and the lustrous black eyes that had caused havoc in so many a Gentile breast. He was very tall, lean, with an oval face and a clear skin. He wore his clothes very well, and in evening dress, even now, he was one of the handsomest men I had ever seen. He wore then large black pearls in his shirt front and platinum and sapphire rings on his fingers. Perhaps he was rather flashy, but you felt it was so much in character that it would have ill become him to be anything else.

"After all, I am an Oriental," he said. "I can carry a certain barbaric magnificence."

I have often thought that Ferdy Rabenstein would make an admirable subject for a biography. He was not a great man, but within the limits he set himself he made of his life a work of art. It was a masterpiece in little, like a Persian miniature, and derived its interest from its perfection. Unfortunately the materials are scanty. They would consist of letters that may very well have been destroyed and the recollections of people who are old now and will soon be dead. His memory is extraordinary, but he would never write his memoirs, for he looks upon his past as a source of purely pri-

vate entertainment; and he is a man of the most perfect discretion. Nor do I know anyone who could do justice to the
subject but Max Beerbohm. There is no one else in this
hard world of to-day who can look upon the trivial with such
tender sympathy and wring such a delicate pathos from futil-
ity. I wonder that Max, who must have known Ferdy much
better than I, and long before, was never tempted to exercise
his exquisite fancy on such a theme. He was born for Max to
write about. And who should have illustrated the elegant
book that I see in my mind's eye but Aubrey Beardsley? Thus
would have been erected a monument of triple brass and the
ephemera imprisoned to succeeding ages in the amber's exquisite translucency.

Ferdy's conquests were social and his venue was the great
world. He was born in South Africa and did not come to England till he was twenty. For some time he was on the Stock
Exchange, but on the death of his father he inherited a considerable fortune, and retiring from business devoted himself
to the life of a man about town. At that period English society
was still a closed body and it was not easy for a Jew to force
its barriers, but to Ferdy they fell like the walls of Jericho. He
was handsome, he was rich, he was a sportsman and he was
good company. He had a house in Curzon Street, furnished
with the most beautiful French furniture, and a French chef,
and a brougham. It would be interesting to know the first
steps in his wonderful career: they are lost in the dark abysm
of time. When I first met him he had been long established as
one of the smartest men in London: this was at a very grand
house in Norfolk to which I had been asked as a promising
young novelist by the hostess who took an interest in letters,
but the company was very distinguished and I was overawed.
We were sixteen, and I felt shy and alone among these cabinet ministers, great ladies and peers of the realm who talked
of people and things of which I knew nothing. They were
civil to me, but indifferent, and I was conscious that I was
somewhat of a burden to my hostess. Ferdy saved me. He sat
with me, walked with me and talked with me. He discovered
that I was a writer and we discussed the drama and the novel;

he learnt that I had lived much on the continent and he talked to me pleasantly of France, Germany and Spain. He seemed really to seek my society. He gave me the flattering impression that he and I stood apart from the other members of the company and by our conversation upon affairs of the spirit made that of the rest of them, the political situation, the scandal of somebody's divorce and the growing disinclination of pheasants to be killed, seem a little ridiculous. But if Ferdy had at the bottom of his heart a feeling of ever so faint a contempt for the hearty British gentry that surrounded us I am sure that it was only to me that he allowed an inkling of it to appear, and looking back I cannot but wonder whether it was not after all a suave and very delicate compliment that he paid me. I think of course that he liked to exercise his charm, and I daresay the obvious pleasure his conversation gave me gratified him, but he could have had no motive for taking so much trouble over an obscure novelist other than his real interest in art and letters. I felt that he and I at bottom were equally alien in that company, I because I was a writer and he because he was a Jew, but I envied the ease with which he bore himself. He was completely at home. Everyone called him Ferdy. He seemed to be always in good spirits. He was never at a loss for a quip, a jest or a repartee. They liked him in that house because he made them laugh but never made them uncomfortable by talking above their heads. He brought a faint savour of Oriental romance into their lives, but so cleverly that they only felt more English. You could never be dull when he was by and with him present you were safe from the fear of the devastating silences that sometimes overwhelm a British company. A pause looked inevitable and Ferdy Rabenstein had broken into a topic that interested everyone. An invaluable asset to any party. He had an inexhaustible fund of Jewish stories. He was a very good mimic and he assumed the Yiddish accent and reproduced the Jewish gestures to perfection; his head sank into his body, his face grew cunning, his voice oily, and he was a rabbi or an old-clothes merchant or a smart commercial traveller or a fat procuress in Frankfort. It was as good as a play. Because he was himself a Jew and insisted on it you laughed without reserve, but for my own part not without an undercurrent of discomfort. I was not quite sure of a sense of humour that made such cruel fun of his own race. I discovered afterwards that Jewish stories were his speciality, and I seldom met him anywhere without hearing him tell sooner or later the last he had heard.

But the best story he told me on this occasion was not a Jewish one. It struck me so that I have never forgotten it, but for one reason or another I have never had occasion to tell it again. I give it here because it is a curious little incident concerning persons whose names at least will live in the social history of the Victorian Era and I think it would be a pity if it were lost. He told me then that once when quite a young man he was staying in the country in a house where Mrs. Langtry, at that time at the height of her beauty and astounding reputation, was also a guest. It happened to be within driving distance of that in which lived the Duchess of Somerset, who had been Queen of Beauty at the Eglinton Tournament, and knowing her slightly, it occurred to him that it would be interesting to bring the two women together. He suggested it to Mrs. Langtry, who was willing, and forthwith wrote to the Duchess asking if he might bring the celebrated beauty to call on her. It was fitting, he said, that the loveliest woman of this generation (this was in the eighties) should pay her respects to the loveliest woman of the last. 'Bring her by all means,' answered the Duchess, 'but I warn you that it will be a shock to her.' They drove over in a carriage and pair, Mrs. Langtry in a close-fitting blue bonnet with long satin strings, which showed the exquisite shape of her head and made her blue eyes even bluer, and were received by a little ugly old hag who looked with irony out of her beady eyes at the radiant beauty who had come to see her. They had tea, they talked and they drove home again. Mrs. Langtry was very silent and when Ferdy looked at her he saw that she was quietly weeping. When they got back to the

house she went to her room and would not come down to
dinner that night. For the first time she had realized that
beauty dies.

Ferdy asked me for my address and a few days after I got
back to London invited me to dinner. There were only six of
us, an American woman married to an English peer, a
Swedish painter, an actress and a well-known critic. We ate
very good food and drank excellent wine. The conversation
was easy and intelligent. After dinner Ferdy was persuaded
to play the piano. He only played Viennese waltzes—I discovered later that they were his speciality—and the light,
tuneful and sensual music seemed to accord well with his
discreet flamboyance. He played without affectation, with a lilt,
and he had a graceful touch. This was the first of a good many
dinners I had with him; he would ask me two or three times
a year, and as time passed I met him more and more frequently at other people's houses. I rose in the world and
perhaps he came down a little. Of late years I had sometimes
found him at parties where other Jews were, and I fancied
that I read in his shining liquid eyes, resting for a moment
on these members of his race, a certain good-natured amusement at the thought of what the world was coming to. There
were people who said he was a snob, but I do not think he
was; it just happened that in his early days he had never met
any but the great. He had a real passion for art, and in his
commerce with those that produced it was at his best. With
them he had never that faint air of persiflage which when he
was with very grand persons made you suspect that he was
never quite the dupe of their grandeur. His taste was exquisite and many of his friends were glad to avail themselves of
his knowledge. He was one of the first to value old furniture,
and he rescued many an exquisite piece from the attics of
ancestral mansions and gave it an honourable place in the
drawing-room. It amused him to saunter round the auction
rooms, and he was always willing to give his advice to great
ladies who desired at once to acquire a beautiful thing and
make a profitable investment. He was rich and good-natured.

He liked to patronize the arts and would take a great deal of trouble to get commissions for some young painter whose talent he admired or an engagement to play at a rich man's house for a violinist who could in no other way get a hearing. But he never let his rich man down. His taste was too good to deceive, and civil though he might be to the mediocre he would not lift a finger to help him. His own musical parties, very small and carefully chosen, were a treat.

He never married.

"I am a man of the world," he said, "and I flatter myself that I have no prejudices, *tous les goûts sont dans la nature,* but I do not think I could bring myself to marry a Gentile. There's no harm in going to the opera in a dinner-jacket, but it just would never occur to me to do so."

"Then why didn't you marry a Jewess?"

(I did not hear this conversation, but the lively and audacious creature who thus tackled him told me of it.)

"Oh, my dear, our women are so prolific. I could not bear the thought of peopling the world with a little Ikey and a little Jacob and a little Rebecca and a little Leah and a little Rachel."

But he had had affairs of note and the glamour of past romance still clung to him. He was in his youth of an amorous complexion. I have met old ladies who told me that he was irresistible, and when in reminiscent mood they talked to me of this woman and that who had completely lost her head over him, I divined that, such was his beauty, they could not find it in their hearts to blame them. It was interesting to hear of great ladies that I had read of in the memoirs of the day or had met as respectable dowagers garrulous over their grandsons at Eton or making a mess of a hand at bridge and bethink myself that they had been consumed with sinful passion for the handsome Jew. Ferdy's most notorious amour was with the Duchess of Hereford, the loveliest, the most gallant and dashing of the beauties of the end of Queen Victoria's reign. It lasted for twenty years. He had doubtless flirtations meanwhile, but their relations were stable and recognized. It was proof of his marvellous tact that when at last they ended he exchanged an aging mistress for a loyal friend. I remember meeting the pair not so very long ago at luncheon. She was an old woman, tall and of a commanding presence, but with a mask of paint on a ravaged face. We were lunching at the Carlton and Ferdy, our host, came a few minutes late. He offered us a cocktail and the Duchess told him we had already had one.

"Ah, I wondered why your eyes were so doubly bright," he said.

The old raddled woman flushed with pleasure.

My youth passed, I grew middle-aged, I wondered how soon I must begin to describe myself as elderly; I wrote books and plays, I travelled, I underwent experiences, I fell in love and out of it; and still I kept meeting Ferdy at parties. War broke out and was waged, millions of men were killed and the face of the world was changed. Ferdy did not like the war. He was too old to take part in it, and his German name was awkward, but he was discreet and took care not to expose himself to humiliation. His old friends were faithful to him, and he lived in a dignified but not too strict seclusion. But then peace came and with courage he set himself to making the best of changed conditions. Society was mixed now, parties were rowdy, but Ferdy fitted himself to the new life. He still told his funny Jewish stories, he still played charmingly the waltzes of Strauss, he still went round auction rooms and told the new rich what they ought to buy. I went to live abroad, but whenever I was in London I saw Ferdy, and now there was something a little uncanny in him. He did not give in. He had never known a day's illness. He seemed never to grow tired. He still dressed beautifully. He was interested in everybody. His mind was alert and people asked him to dinner, not for old times' sake, but because he was worth his salt. He still gave charming little concerts at his house in Curzon Street.

It was when he invited me to one of these that I made the discovery that started the recollections of him I have here set down. We were dining at a house in Hill Street, a large party, and the women having gone upstairs Ferdy and I found ourselves side by side. He told me that Lea Makart was coming to play for him on the following Friday evening and he would be glad if I would come.

"I'm awfully sorry," I said, "but I'm going down to the Blands."

"What Blands?"

"They live in Sussex at a place called Tilby."

"I didn't know you knew them."

He looked at me rather strangely. He smiled. I didn't know what amused him.

"Oh, yes, I've known them for years. It's a very nice house to stay at."

"Adolph is my nephew."

"Sir Adolphus?"

"It suggests one of the bucks of the Regency, doesn't it? But I will not conceal from you that he was named Adolph."

"Everyone I know calls him Freddy."

"I know, and I understand that Miriam, his wife, only answers to the name of Muriel."

"How does he happen to be your nephew?"

"Because Hannah Rabenstein, my sister, married Alphonse Bleikgel, who ended life as Sir Alfred Bland, first baronet and Adolph, their only son, in due course became Sir Adolphus Bland, second baronet."

"Then Freddy Bland's mother, the Lady Bland who lives in Portland Place, is your sister?"

"Yes, my sister Hannah. She was the eldest of the family. She's eighty, but in full possession of her faculties and a remarkable woman."

"I've never met her."

"I think your friends the Blands would just as soon you didn't. She has never lost her German accent."

"Do you never see them?" I asked.

"I haven't spoken to them for twenty years. I am such a Jew and they are so English." He smiled. "I could never remember that their names were Freddy and Muriel. I used to come out with an Adolph or a Miriam at awkward moments. And they didn't like my stories. It was better that we should not meet. When the war broke out and I would not change my name it was the last straw. It was too late. I could never have accustomed my friends to think of me as anything but Ferdy Rabenstein. I was quite content. I was not ambitious to be a Smith, a Brown, or a Robinson."

Though he spoke facetiously, there was in his tone the faintest possible derision and I felt, hardly felt even, the sensation was so shadowy, that, as it had often vaguely seemed to me before, there was in the depth of his impenetrable heart a cynical contempt for the Gentiles he had conquered.

"Then you don't know the two boys?" I said.

"No."

"The eldest is called George, you know. I don't think he's so clever as Harry, the other one, but he's an engaging youth. I think you'd like him."

"Where is he now?"

"Well, he's just been sent down from Oxford. I suppose he's at home. Harry's still at Eton."

"Why don't you bring George to lunch with me?"

"I'll ask him. I should think he'd love to come."

"It has reached my ears that he's been a little troublesome."

"Oh, I don't know. He wouldn't go into the army, which is what they wanted. They rather fancied the Guards. And so he went to Oxford instead. He didn't work and he spent a great deal of money and he painted the town red. It was all quite normal."

"What was he sent down for?"

"I don't know. Nothing of any consequence."

At that moment our host rose and we went upstairs. When Ferdy bade me good-night he asked me not to forget about his great-nephew.

"Ring me up," he said. "Wednesday would suit me. Or Friday."

Next day I went down to Tilby. It was an Elizabethan mansion standing in a spacious park, in which roamed fallow deer, and from its windows you had wide views of rolling downs. It seemed to me that as far as the eye could reach the land belonged to the Blands. His tenants must have found Sir Adolphus a wonderful landlord, for I never saw farms kept in such order, the barns and cow-sheds were spick and span and the pigsties were a picture; the public-houses looked like old English water-colours and the cottages he had built on the estate combined admirably picturesqueness and convenience. It must have cost him a pot of money to run the place on these lines. Fortunately he had it. The park with its grand old trees (and its nine-hole golf course) was tended like a garden, and the wide-stretching gardens were the pride of the neighbourhood. The magnificent house, with its steep roofs and mullioned windows, had been restored by the most celebrated architect in England and furnished by Lady Bland, with taste and knowledge, in a style that perfectly fitted it.

"Of course it's very simple," she said. "Just an English house in the country."

The dining-room was adorned with old English sporting pictures, and the Chippendale chairs were of incredible value. In the drawing-room were portraits by Reynolds and Gainsborough and landscapes by Old Crome and Richard Wilson. Even in my bedroom with its four-post bed were water-colours by Birket Foster. It was very beautiful and a treat to stay there, but though it would have distressed Muriel Bland beyond anything to know it, it missed oddly enough entirely the effect she had sought. It did not give you for a moment the impression of an English house. You had the feeling that every object had been bought with a careful eye to the general scheme. You missed the dull Academy portraits that hung in the dining-room beside a Carlo Dolci that an ancestor had brought back from the grand tour, and the water-colours painted by a great-aunt that cluttered up the drawing-room so engagingly. There was no ugly Victorian sofa that had always been there and that it never occurred to anybody to take away, and no needlework chairs that an unmarried daughter had so painstakingly worked at about the time of the Great Exhibition. There was beauty but no sentiment.

And yet how comfortable it was and how well looked after you were! And what a cordial greeting the Blands gave you!

They seemed really to like people. They were generous and
kindly. They were never happier than when they were entertaining the county, and though they had not owned the prop-
erty for more than twenty years they had established themselves firmly in the favour of their neighbours. Except perhaps
in their splendour and the competent way in which the estate
was run there was nothing to suggest that they had not been
settled there for centuries.

Freddy had been at Eton and Oxford. He was now in the
early fifties. He was quiet in manner, courtly, very clever, I
imagine, but a trifle reserved. He had great elegance, but it
was not an English elegance; he had grey hair and a short
pointed grey beard, fine dark eyes and an aquiline nose. He
was just above middle height; I don't think you would have
taken him for a Jew, but rather for a foreign diplomat of
some distinction. He was a man of character, but gave you,
strangely enough, notwithstanding the success he had had in
life, an impression of faint melancholy. His successes had
been financial and political; in the world of sport, for all his
perseverance, he had never shone. For many years he had
followed hounds, but he was a bad rider and I think it must
have been a relief to him when he could persuade himself
that middle-age and pressure of business forced him to give
up hunting. He had excellent shooting and gave grand parties
for it, but he was a poor shot; and despite the course in his
park he never succeeded in being more than an indifferent
golfer. He knew only too well how much these things meant
in England, and his incapacity was a bitter disappointment
to him. However, George would make up for it.

George was scratch at golf, and though tennis was not his
game he played much better than the average; the Blands had
had him taught to shoot as soon as he was old enough to hold
a gun, and he was a fine shot; they had put him on a pony
when he was two, and Freddy, watching him mount his horse,
knew that out hunting when the boy came to a fence he felt
exhilaration and not that sickening feeling in the pit of his
stomach which, though he had chased the fox with such grim
determination, had always made the sport a torture to him.

George was so tall and slim, his curly hair, of a palish brown, was so fine, his eyes were so blue, he was the perfect type of the young Englishman. He had the engaging candour of the breed. His nose was straight, though perhaps a trifle fleshy, and his lips were perhaps a little full and sensual, but he had beautiful teeth, and his smooth skin was like ivory. George was the apple of his father's eye. He did not like Harry, his second son, so well. He was rather stocky, broad-shouldered and strong for his age, but his black eyes, shining with cleverness, his coarse dark hair and his big nose revealed his race. Freddy was severe with him, and often impatient, but with George he was all indulgence. Harry would go into the business, he had brains and push, but George was the heir. George would be an English gentleman.

George had offered to motor me down in the roadster his father had given him as a birthday present. He drove very fast and we arrived before the rest of the guests. The Blands were sitting on the lawn and tea was laid out under a magnificent cedar.

"By the way," I said presently, "I saw Ferdy Rabenstein the other day and he wants me to bring George to lunch with him."

I had not mentioned the invitation to George on the way because I thought that if there had been a family coldness I had better address his parents as well.

"Who in God's name is Ferdy Rabenstein?" said George.

How brief is human glory! A generation back such a question would have seemed grotesque.

"He's by way of being your great-uncle," I replied.

A glance had passed from father to mother when I first spoke. "He's a horrid old man," said Muriel.

"I don't think it's in the least necessary for George to resume relationships that were definitely severed before he was born," said Freddy with decision.

"Anyhow I've delivered the message," said I, feeling somewhat snubbed.

"I don't want to see the old blighter," said George.

The conversation was broken off by the arrival of other

guests, and in a little while George went off to play golf with one of his Oxford friends.

It was not till next day that the matter was referred to again. I had played an indifferent round with Freddy Bland in the morning, and several sets of what is known as country-house tennis in the afternoon, and was sitting alone with Muriel on the terrace. In England we have so much bad weather that it is only fair that a beautiful day should be more beautiful than anywhere in the world, and this June evening was perfect. The blue sky was cloudless and the air was balmy; before us stretched green rolling downs, and woods, and in the distance you saw red roofs of a little village and the grey tower of the village church. It was a day when to be alive was sufficient happiness. Detached lines of poetry hovered vaguely in my memory. Muriel and I had been chatting desultorily.

"I hope you didn't think it rather horrid of us to refuse to let George lunch with Ferdy," she said suddenly. "He's such a fearful snob, isn't he?"

"D'you think so? He's always been very nice to me."

"We haven't been on speaking terms for twenty years. Freddy never forgave him for his behaviour during the war. So unpatriotic, I thought, and one really must draw the line somewhere. You know, he absolutely refused to drop his horrible German name. With Freddy in Parliament and running munitions and all that sort of thing it was quite impossible. I don't know why he should want to see George. He can't mean anything to him."

"He's an old man. George and Harry are his great-nephews. He must leave his money to some one."

"We'd rather not have his money," said Muriel coldly.

Of course I didn't care a row of pins whether George went to lunch with Ferdy Rabenstein, and I was quite willing to let the matter drop, but evidently the Blands had talked it over and Muriel felt that some explanation was due to me.

"Of course you know that Freddy has Jewish blood in him," she said.

She looked at me sharply. Muriel was rather a big blonde woman and she spent a great deal of time trying to keep down the corpulence to which she was predisposed. She had been very pretty when young and even now was a comely person; but her round blue eyes, slightly prominent, her fleshy nose, the shape of her face and the back of her neck, her exuberant manner, betrayed her race. No Englishwoman, however fair-haired, ever looked like that. And yet her observation was designed to make me take it for granted that she was a Gentile. I answered discreetly.

"So many people have nowadays."

"I know. But there's no reason to dwell on it, is there? After all, we're absolutely English; no one could be more English than George, in appearance and manner and everything; I mean, he's such a fine sportsman and all that sort of thing. I can't see any object in his knowing Jews just because they happen to be distant connections of his."

"It's very difficult in England now not to know Jews, isn't it?"

"Oh, I know, in London one does meet a good many, and I think some of them are very nice. They're so artistic. I don't go so far as to say that Freddy and I deliberately avoid them—of course I wouldn't do that—but it just happens that we don't really know any of them very well. And down here, there simply aren't any to know."

I could not but admire the convincing manner in which she spoke. It would not have surprised me to be told that she really believed every word she said.

"You say that Ferdy might leave George his money. Well, I don't believe it's so very much anyway; it was quite a comfortable fortune before the war, but that's nothing nowadays. Besides, we're hoping that George will go in for politics when he's a little older, and I don't think it would do him any good in the constituency to inherit money from a Mr. Rabenstein."

"Is George interested in politics?" I asked, to change the conversation.

"Oh, I hope so. After all, there's the family constituency waiting for him. It's a safe Conservative seat and one can't expect Freddy to go on with the grind of the House of Commons indefinitely."

Muriel was grand. She talked already of the constituency as though twenty generations of Blands had sat for it. Her remark, however, was my first intimation that Freddy's ambition was not satisfied.

"I suppose Freddy would go to the House of Lords when George was old enough to stand."

"We've done a good deal for the party," said Muriel.

Muriel was a Catholic and she often told you that she had been educated in a convent—"Such sweet women, those nuns. I always said that if I had a daughter I should have sent her to a convent too"—but she liked her servants to be Church of England, and on Sunday evenings we had what was called supper because the fish was cold and there was ice cream, so that they could go to church, and we were waited on by two footmen instead of four. It was still light when we finished, and Freddy and I, smoking our cigars, walked up and down the terrace in the gloaming. I suppose Muriel had told him of her conversation with me, and it may be that his refusal to let George see his great-uncle still troubled him, but being subtler than she he attacked the question more indirectly. He told me that he had been very much worried about George. It had been a great disappointment that he had refused to go into the army.

"I should have thought he'd have loved the life," he said.

"And he would certainly have looked marvellous in his Guards' uniform."

"He would, wouldn't he?" returned Freddy, ingenuously. "I wonder he could resist that."

He had been completely idle at Oxford; although his father had given him a very large allowance, he had got monstrously into debt; and now he had been sent down. But though he spoke so tartly I could see that he was not a little proud of his scapegrace son, he loved him with, oh, such an un-English love, and in his heart it flattered him that George had cut such a dash.

"Why should you worry?" I said. "You don't really care if George has a degree or not."

Freddy chuckled.

"No, I don't suppose I do really. I always think the only important thing about Oxford is that people know you were there, and I daresay that George isn't any wilder than the other young men in his set. It's the future I'm thinking of. He's so damned idle. He doesn't seem to want to do anything but have a good time."

"He's young, you know."

"He's not interested in politics, and though he's so good at games he's not even very keen on sport. He seems to spend most of his time strumming the piano."

"That's a harmless amusement."

"Oh, yes, I don't mind that, but he can't go on loafing indefinitely. You see, all this will be his one day." Freddy gave a sweeping gesture that seemed to embrace the whole country, but I knew that he did not own it all yet. "I'm very anxious that he should be fit to assume his responsibilities. His mother is very ambitious for him, but I only want him to be an English gentleman."

Freddy gave me a sidelong glance as though he wanted to say something but hesitated in case I thought it ridiculous; but there is one advantage in being a writer, that, since people look upon you as of no account, they will often say things to you that they would not to their equals. He thought he would risk it.

"You know, I've got an idea that nowhere in the world now is the Greek ideal of life so perfectly cultivated as by the English country gentleman living on his estates. I think his life has the beauty of a work of art."

I could not but smile when I reflected that it was impossible for the English country gentleman in these days to do anything of the sort without a packet of money safely invested in American bonds, but I smiled with sympathy. I thought it rather touching that this Jewish financier should cherish so romantic a dream.

"I want him to be a good landlord. I want him to take his part in the affairs of the country. I want him to be a thorough sportsman."

"Poor mutt," I thought, but said: "Well, what are your plans for George now?"

"I think he has a fancy for the diplomatic service. He's suggested going to Germany to learn the language."

"A very good idea, I should have thought."

"For some reason he's got it into his head that he wants to go to Munich."

"A nice place."

Next day I went back to London and shortly after my arrival rang up Ferdy.

"I'm sorry, but George isn't able to come to lunch on Wednesday."

"What about Friday?"

"Friday's no good either." I thought it useless to beat about the bush. "The fact is, his people aren't keen on his lunching with you."

There was a moment's silence. Then:

"I see. Well, will you come on Wednesday anyway?"

"Yes, I'd like to," I answered.

So on Wednesday at half-past one I strolled round to Curzon Street. Ferdy received me with the somewhat elaborate graciousness that he cultivated. He made no reference to the Blands. We sat in the drawing-room and I could not help reflecting what an eye for beautiful objects that family had. The room was more crowded than the fashion of to-day approves and the gold snuff-boxes in vitrines, the French china, appealed to a taste that was not mine; but they were no doubt choice pieces; and the Louis XV suite, with its beautiful *petit point,* must have been worth an enormous lot of money. The pictures on the walls by Lancret, Pater and Watteau did not greatly interest me, but I recognized their intrinsic excellence. It was a proper setting for this aged man of the world. It fitted his period. Suddenly the door opened and George was announced. Ferdy saw my surprise and gave me a little smile of triumph.

"I'm very glad you were able to come after all," he said as he shook George's hand.

I saw him in a glance take in his great-nephew whom he saw to-day for the first time. George was very elegantly dressed. He wore a short black coat, striped trousers and the grey double-breasted waistcoat which at that time was the mode. You could only wear it with elegance if you were tall and thin and your belly was slightly concave. I felt sure that Ferdy knew exactly who George's tailor was and what haberdasher he went to, and approved of them. George, so smart and trim, wearing his clothes so beautifully, certainly looked very handsome. We went down to luncheon. Ferdy had the social graces at his fingers' ends and he put the boy at his ease, but I saw that he was carefully appraising him; then, I do not know why, he began to tell some of his Jewish stories. He told them with gusto and with his wonderful mimicry. I saw George flush, and though he laughed at them, I could see that it was with embarrassment. I wondered what on earth had induced Ferdy to be so tactless. But he was watching George and he told story after story. It looked as though he would never stop. I wondered if for some reason I could not grasp he was taking a malicious pleasure in the boy's obvious discomfiture. At last we went upstairs, and to make things easier I asked Ferdy to play the piano. He played us three or four little waltzes. He had lost none of his exquisite lightness nor his sense of their lilting rhythm. Then he turned to George.

"Do you play?" he asked him.

"A little."

"Won't you play something?"

"I'm afraid I only play classical music. I don't think it would interest you."

Ferdy smiled slightly, but did not insist. I said it was time for me to go and George accompanied me.

"What a filthy old Jew," he said as soon as we were in the street. "I hated those stories of his."

"They're his great stunt. He always tells them."

"Would you if you were a Jew?"

I shrugged my shoulders.

"How is it you came to lunch after all?" I asked George.

He chuckled. He was a light-hearted creature, with a sense of humour, and he shook off the slight irritation his great-uncle had caused him.

"He went to see Granny. You don't know Granny, do you?"

"No."

"She treats Daddy like a kid in Etons. Granny said I was to go to lunch with Great-uncle Ferdy, and what Granny says goes."

"I see."

A week or two later George went to Munich to learn German. I happened then to go on a journey, and it was not till the following spring that I was again in London. Soon after my arrival I found myself sitting next to Muriel Bland at dinner. I asked after George.

"He's still in Germany," she said.

"I see in the papers that you're going to have a great beano at Tilby for his coming of age."

"We're going to entertain the tenants and they're making George a presentation."

She was less exuberant than usual, but I did not pay much attention to the fact. She led a strenuous life and it might be that she was tired. I knew she liked to talk of her son, so I continued.

"I suppose George has been having a grand time in Germany," I said.

She did not answer for a moment and I gave her a glance. I was surprised to see that her eyes were filled with tears.

"I'm afraid George has gone mad," she said.

"What *do* you mean?"

"We've been so frightfully worried. Freddy's so angry, he won't even discuss it. I don't know what we're going to do."

Of course it immediately occurred to me that George, who,

I supposed, like most young Englishmen sent to learn the language, had been put with a German family, had fallen in love with the daughter of the house and wanted to marry her. I had a pretty strong suspicion that the Blands were intent on his making a very grand marriage.

"Why, what's happened?" I asked.

"He wants to become a pianist."

"A what?"

"A professional pianist."

"What on earth put that idea in his head?"

"Heaven knows. We didn't know anything about it. We thought he was working for his exam. I went out to see him. I thought I'd like to know that he was getting on all right. Oh, my dear. He looks like nothing on earth. And he used to be so smart; I could have cried. He told me he wasn't going in for the exam and had never had any intention of doing so; he'd only suggested the diplomatic service so that we'd let him go to Germany and he'd be able to study music."

"But has he any talent?"

"Oh, that's neither here nor there. Even if he had the genius of Paderewski we couldn't have George traipsing around the country playing at concerts. No one can deny that I'm very artistic, and so is Freddy—we love music and we've always known a lot of artists—but George will have a very great position; it's out of the question. We've set our hearts on his going into Parliament. He'll be very rich one day. There's nothing he can't aspire to."

"Did you point all that out to him?"

"Of course I did. He laughed at me. I told him he'd break his father's heart. He said his father could always fall back on Harry. Of course I'm devoted to Harry, and he's as clever as a monkey, but it was always understood that he was to go into the business; even though I am his mother I can see that he hasn't got the advantages that George has. Do you know what he said to me? He said that if his father would settle five pounds a week on him he would resign everything in Harry's favour and Harry could be his father's heir and succeed to the baronetcy and everything. It's too ridiculous. He said that if the Crown Prince of Roumania could abdicate a throne he didn't see why he couldn't abdicate a baronetcy. But you can't do that. Nothing can prevent him from being third baronet and, if Freddy should be granted a peerage, from succeeding to it at Freddy's death. Do you know, he even wants to drop the name of Bland and take some horrible German name."

I could not help asking what.

"Bleikogel or something like that," she answered.

That was a name I recognized. I remembered Ferdy telling me that Hannah Rabenstein had married Alphonse Bleikogel, who became eventually Sir Alfred Bland, first baronet. It was all very strange. I wondered what had happened to the charming and so typically English boy whom I had seen only a few months before.

"Of course when I came home and told Freddy he was furious. I've never seen him so angry. He foamed at the mouth. He wired to George to come back immediately, and George wired back to say he couldn't on account of his work."

"Is he working?"

"From morning till night. That's the maddening part of it. He never did a stroke of work in his life. Freddy used to say he was born idle."

"H'm."

"Then Freddy wired to say that if he didn't come he'd stop his allowance, and George wired back: 'Stop it.' That put the lid on. You don't know what Freddy can be when his back is up."

I knew that Freddy had inherited a large fortune, but I knew also that he had immensely increased it, and I could well imagine that behind the courteous and amiable Squire of Tilby there was a ruthless man of affairs. He had been used to having his own way, and I could believe that when crossed he would be hard and cruel.

"We'd been making George a very handsome allowance, but you know how frightfully extravagant he was. We didn't think he'd be able to hold out long, and in point of fact within a month he wrote to Ferdy and asked him to lend him a hundred pounds. Ferdy went to my mother-in-law—she's his sister, you know—and asked her what it meant. Though they hadn't spoken for twenty years Freddy went to see him and begged him not to send George a penny, and he promised he wouldn't. I don't know how George has been making both ends meet. I'm sure Freddy's right, but I can't help being rather worried. If I hadn't given Freddy my word of honour that I wouldn't send him anything I think I'd have slipped a few notes in a letter in case of accident. I mean, it's awful to think that perhaps he hasn't got enough to eat."

"It'll do him no harm to go short for a bit."

"We were in an awful hole, you know. We'd made all sorts of preparations for his coming of age, and I'd issued hundreds of invitations. Suddenly George said he wouldn't come. I was simply frantic. I wrote and wired. I would have gone over to Germany, only Freddy wouldn't let me. I practically went down on my bended knees to George. I begged him not to put us in such a humiliating position. I mean, it's the sort of thing it's so difficult to explain. Then my mother-in-law stepped in. You don't know her, do you? She's an extraordinary old woman. You'd never think she was Freddy's mother. She was German originally but of very good family."

"Oh?"

"To tell you the truth I'm rather frightened of her. She tackled Freddy and then she wrote to George herself. She said that if he'd come home for his twenty-first birthday she'd pay any debts he had in Munich and we'd all give a patient hearing to anything he had to say. He agreed to that and we're expecting him one day next week. But I'm not looking forward to it I can tell you."

She gave a deep sigh. When we were walking upstairs after dinner Freddy addressed me.

"I see Muriel has been telling you about George. The damned fool! I have no patience with him. Fancy wanting to be a pianist! It's so ungentlemanly."

"He's very young, you know," I said soothingly.

"He's had things too easy for him. I've been much too indulgent. There's never been a thing he wanted that I haven't given him. I'll learn him."

The Blands had a discreet apprehension of the uses of advertisement, and I gathered from the papers that the celebrations at Tilby of George's twenty-first birthday were conducted in accordance with the usage of English county families. There were a dinner party and ball for the gentry and a collation and a dance in marquees on the lawn for the tenants. Expensive bands were brought down from London. In the illustrated papers were pictures of George, surrounded by his family being presented with a solid silver tea set by the tenantry. They had subscribed to have his portrait painted, but since his absence from the country had made it impossible for him to sit, the tea service had been substituted. I read in the columns of the gossip writers that his father had given him a hunter, his mother a gramophone that changed its own records, his grandmother the dowager Lady Bland an Encyclopædia Britannica and his great-uncle Ferdinand Rabenstein a Virgin and Child by Pellegrino da Modena. I could not help observing that these gifts were bulky and not readily convertible into cash. From Ferdy's presence at the festivities I concluded that George's unaccountable vagary had effected a reconciliation between uncle and nephew. I was right. Ferdy did not at all like the notion of his great-nephew becoming a professional pianist. At the first hint of danger to its prestige the family drew together and a united front was presented to oppose George's designs. Since I was not there I only know from hearsay what happened when the birthday celebrations were over. Ferdy told me something and so did Muriel, and later George gave me his version. The Blands had very much the impression that when George came home and found himself occupying the centre of the stage, when, surrounded by splendour, he saw for himself once more how much it meant to be the heir of a great estate, he would weaken. They surrounded him with love. They flattered him. They hung on his words. They counted on the goodness of his heart and thought that if they were very kind to him he would not have the courage to cause them pain. They seemed to take it for granted that he had no intention of going back to Germany, and in conversation included him in all their plans.

George did not say very much. He seemed to be enjoying himself. He did not open a piano. Things looked as though they were going very well. Peace descended on the troubled house. Then one day at luncheon when they were discussing a garden party to which they had all been asked for one day of the following week, George said pleasantly:

"Don't count on me. I shan't be here."

"Oh, George, why not?" asked his mother.

"I must get back to my work. I'm leaving for Munich on Monday."

There was an awful pause. Everyone looked for something to say, but was afraid of saying the wrong thing, and at last it seemed impossible to break it. Luncheon was finished in silence. Then George went into the garden and the others, old Lady Bland and Ferdy, Muriel and Sir Adolphus, into the morning-room. There was a family council. Muriel wept. Freddy flew into a temper. Presently from the drawing-room they heard the sound of someone playing a nocturne of Chopin. It was George. It was as though, now he had announced his decision, he had gone for comfort, rest and strength to the instrument he loved. Freddy sprang to his feet.

"Stop that noise," he cried. "I won't have him play the piano in my house."

Muriel rang for a servant and gave him a message.

"Will you tell Mr. Bland that her ladyship has a bad headache and would he mind not playing the piano."

Ferdy, the man of the world, was deputed to have a talk with George. He was authorized to make him certain promises if he would give up the idea of becoming a pianist. If he did not wish to go into the diplomatic service his father would not insist, but if he would stand for Parliament he was prepared to pay his election expenses, give him a flat in London and make him an allowance of five thousand a year. I must say it was a handsome offer. I do not know what Ferdy said to the boy. I suppose he painted to him the life that a young man could lead in London on such an income. I am sure he made it very alluring. It availed nothing. All George asked was five pounds a week to be able to continue his studies and to be left alone. He was indifferent to the position that he might some day enjoy. He didn't want to hunt. He didn't want to shoot. He didn't want to be a Member of Parliament. He didn't want to be a millionaire. He didn't want to be a baronet. He didn't want to be a peer. Ferdy left him, defeated and in a state of considerable exasperation.

After dinner that evening there was a battle royal. Freddy was a quick-tempered man, unused to opposition, and he gave George the rough side of his tongue. I gather that it was very rough indeed. The women who sought to restrain his violence were sternly silenced. Perhaps for the first time in his life Freddy would not listen to his mother. George was obstinate and sullen. He had made up his mind and if his father didn't like it he could lump it. Freddy was peremptory. He forbade George to go back to Germany. George answered that he was twenty-one and his own master. He would go where he chose. Freddy swore he would not give him a penny.

"All right, I'll earn money."

"You! You've never done a stroke of work in your life. What do you expect to do to earn money?"

"Sell old clothes," grinned George.

There was a gasp from all of them. Muriel was so taken aback that she said a stupid thing.

"Like a Jew?"

"Well, aren't I a Jew? And aren't you a Jewess and isn't Daddy a Jew? We're all Jews, the whole gang of us, and everyone knows it and what the hell's the good of pretending we're not?"

Then a very dreadful thing happened. Freddy burst sud-denly into tears. I'm afraid he didn't behave very much like Sir Adolphus Bland, Bart., M.P., and the good old English gentleman he so much wanted to be, but like an emotional Adolph Bleikogel who loved his son and wept with mortifi-cation because the great hopes he had set on him were brought to nothing and the ambition of his life was frustrated. He cried noisily with great loud sobs and pulled his beard and beat his breast and rocked to and fro. Then they all began to cry, old Lady Bland and Muriel, and Ferdy, who sniffed and blew his nose and wiped the tears streaming down his face, and even George cried. Of course it was very painful, but to our rough Anglo-Saxon temperament I am afraid it must seem also a trifle ridiculous. No one tried to console anybody else. They just sobbed and sobbed. It broke up the party.

But it had no result on the situation. George remained obdurate. His father would not speak to him. There were more scenes. Muriel sought to excite his pity; he was deaf to her piteous entreaties, he did not seem to mind if he broke her heart, he did not care two hoots if he killed his father. Ferdy appealed to him as a sportsman and a man of the world. George was flippant and indeed personally offensive. Old Lady Bland with her guttural German accent and strong common sense argued with him, but he would not listen to reason. It was she, however, who at last found a way out. She made George acknowledge that it was no use to throw away all the beautiful things the world laid at his feet unless he had talent. Of course he thought he had, but he might be mistaken. It was not worth while to be a second-rate pianist. His only excuse, his only justification, was genius. If he had genius his family had no right to stand in his way.

"You can't expect me to show genius already," said George. "I shall have to work for years."

"Are you sure you are prepared for that?"

"It's my only wish in the world. I'll work like a dog. I only want to be given my chance."

This was the proposition she made. His father was determined to give him nothing, and obviously they could not let the boy starve. He had mentioned five pounds a week. Well, she was willing to give him that herself. He could go back to Germany and study for two years. At the end of that time he must come back and they would get some competent and disinterested person to hear him play, and if then that person said he showed promise of becoming a first-rate pianist no further obstacles would be placed in his way. He would be given every advantage, help and encouragement. If on the other hand that person decided that his natural gifts were not such as to ensure ultimate success he must promise faithfully to give up all thoughts of making music his profession and in every way accede to his father's wishes. George could hardly believe his ears.

"Do you mean that, Granny?"

"I do."

"But will Daddy agree?"

"I vill see dat he does," she answered.

George seized her in his arms and impetuously kissed her on both cheeks.

"Darling," he cried.

"Ah, but de promise?"

He gave her his solemn word of honour that he would faithfully abide by the terms of the arrangement. Two days later he went back to Germany. Though his father consented unwillingly to his going, and indeed could not help doing so, he would not be reconciled to him and when he left refused to say good-bye to him. I imagine that in no other manner could he have caused himself such pain. I permit myself a trite remark. It is strange that men, inhabitants for so short a while of an alien and inhuman world, should go out of their way to cause themselves so much unhappiness.

George had stipulated that during his two years of study his family should not visit him, so that when Muriel heard some months before he was due to come home that I was passing through Munich on my way to Vienna, whither business called me, it was not unnatural that she should ask me to look him up. She was anxious to have first-hand information about him. She gave me George's address and I wrote ahead, telling him I was spending a day in Munich, and asked him to lunch with me. His answer awaited me at the hotel. He said he worked all day and could not spare the time to lunch with me, but if I would come to his studio about six he would like to show me that and if I had nothing better to do would love to spend the evening with me. So soon after six I went to the address he gave me. He lived on the second floor of a large block of flats and when I came to his door I heard the sound of piano-playing. It stopped when I rang and George opened the door for me. I hardly recognized him. He had grown very fat. His hair was extremely long, it curled all over his head in pictur-esque confusion; and he had certainly not shaved for three days. He wore a grimy pair of Oxford bags, a tennis shirt and slippers. He was not very clean and his fingernails were rimmed with black. It was a startling change from the spruce, slim youth so elegantly dressed in such beautiful clothes that I had last seen. I could not but think it would be a shock to Ferdy to see him now. The studio was large and bare; on the walls were three or four unframed canvases of a highly cubist nature; there were several armchairs much the worse for wear, and a grand piano. Books were littered about and old news-papers and art magazines. It was dirty and untidy and there was a frousty smell of stale beer and stale smoke.

"Do you live here alone?" I asked.

"Yes, I have a woman who comes in twice a week and cleans up. But I make my own breakfast and lunch."

"Can you cook?"

"Oh, I only have bread and cheese and a bottle of beer for lunch. I dine at a *bier stube*."

It was pleasant to discover that he was very glad to see me. He seemed in great spirits and extremely happy. He asked after his relations and we talked of one thing and another. He had a lesson twice a week and for the rest of the time practised. He told me that he worked ten hours a day.

"That's a change," I said.

He laughed.

"Daddy said I was born tired. I wasn't really lazy. I didn't see the use of working at things that bored me."

I asked him how he was getting on with the piano. He seemed to be satisfied with his progress and I begged him to play to me.

"Oh, not now. I'm all in, I've been at it all day. Let's go out and dine and come back here later and then I'll play. I generally go to the same place; there are several students I know there, and it's rather fun."

Presently we set out. He put on socks and shoes and a very old golf coat, and we walked together through the wide quiet streets. It was a brisk cold day. His step was buoyant. He looked round him with a sigh of delight.

"I love Munich," he said. "It's the only city in the world where there's art in the very air you breathe. After all, art is the only thing that matters, isn't it? I loathe the idea of going home."

"All the same I'm afraid you'll have to."

"I know. I'll go all right, but I'm not going to think about it till the time comes."

"When you do, you might do worse than get a haircut. If you don't mind my saying so you look almost too artistic to be convincing."

"You English, you're such Philistines," he said.

He took me to a rather large restaurant in a side street, crowded even at that early hour with people dining and furnished heavily in the German medieval style. A table covered with a red cloth, well away from the air, was reserved for George and his friends, and when we went to it four or five youths were at it. There was a Pole studying Oriental languages, a student of philosophy, a painter—I suppose the author of George's cubist picture—a Swede, and a young man who introduced himself to me, clicking his heels, as Hans Reiting, *dichter,* namely Hans Reiting, poet. Not one of them was more than twenty-two and I felt a trifle out of it. They all addressed George as *du* and I noticed that his German was extremely fluent. I had not spoken it for some time and mine was rusty, so that I could not take much part in the lively conversation. But nevertheless I thoroughly enjoyed myself. They ate sparingly, but drank a good deal of beer. They talked of art and literature and life and ethics and motor-cars and women. They were very revolutionary, and though gay very much in earnest. They were contemptuous of everyone you had ever heard of, and the only point on which they all agreed was that in this topsy-turvy world only the vulgar could hope for success. They argued points of technique with animation, and contradicted one another, and shouted and were obscene. They had a grand time.

At about eleven George and I walked back to his studio. Munich is a city that frolics demurely, and except about the Marienplatz the streets were still and empty. When we got in he took off his coat and said:

"Now I'll play to you."

I sat in one of the dilapidated armchairs, and a broken spring stuck into my behind, but I made myself as comfortable as I could. George played Chopin. I know very little of music, and that is one of the reasons for which I have found this story difficult to write. When I go to a concert at the Queen's Hall and in the intervals read the programme it is all Greek to me. I know nothing of harmony and counterpoint. I shall never forget how humiliated I felt once when, having come to Munich for a Wagner Festival, I went to a wonderful performance of *Tristan und Isolde* and never heard a note of it. The first few bars sent me off and I began to think of what I was writing, my characters leapt into life and I heard their long conversations, I suffered their pains and was a party to their joy; the years swept by and all sorts of things happened to me, the spring brought me its rapture and in the winter I was cold and hungry; and I loved and I hated and I died. I suppose there were intervals in which I walked round and round the garden and probably ate *schinken brödchen* and drank beer, but I have no recollection of them. The only thing I know is that when the curtain for the last time fell I woke with a start. I had had a wonderful time, but I could not help thinking it was very stupid of me to come such a long way and spend so much money if I couldn't pay attention to what I heard and saw.

I knew most of the things George played. They were the familiar pieces of concert programmes. He played with a great deal of dash. Then he played Beethoven's *Appassionata*. I used to play it myself when I played the piano (very badly) in my far distant youth and I still knew every note of it. Of course it is a classic and a great work, it would be foolish to deny it, but I confess that at this time of day it leaves me cold. It is like *Paradise Lost,* splendid, but a trifle stolid. This too George played with vigour. He sweated profusely. At first I could not make out what was the matter with his playing, something did not seem to me quite right, and then it struck me that the two hands did not exactly synchronize, so that there was ever so slight an interval between the bass and the treble; but I repeat, I am ignorant of these things; what disconcerted me might have been merely the effect of his having drunk a good deal of beer that evening, or indeed only my fancy. I said all I could think of to praise him.

"Of course I know I need a lot more work. I'm only a beginner, but I know I can do it. I feel it in my bones. It'll take me ten years, but then I shall be a pianist."

He was tired and came away from the piano. It was after midnight and I suggested going, but he would not hear of it. He opened a couple of bottles of beer and lit his pipe. He wanted to talk.

"Are you happy here?" I asked him.

"Very," he answered gravely. "I'd like to stay for ever. I've never had such fun in my life. This evening for instance. Wasn't it grand?"

"It was very jolly. But one can't go on leading the student's life. Your friends here will grow older and go away."

"Others'll come. There are always students here and people like that."

"Yes, but you'll grow older too. Is there anything more lamentable than the middle-aged man who tries to go on living the undergraduate's life? The old fellow who wants to be a boy among boys, and tries to persuade himself that they'll accept him as one of themselves—how ridiculous he is. It can't be done."

"I feel so at home here. My poor father wants me to be an English gentleman. It gives me gooseflesh. I'm not a sportsman. I don't care a damn for hunting and shooting and playing cricket. I was only acting."

"You gave a very natural performance."

"It wasn't till I came here that I knew it wasn't real. I

loved Eton and Oxford was a riot, but all the same I knew I didn't belong. I played the part all right, because acting's in my blood, but there was always something in me that wasn't satisfied. The house in Grosvenor Square is a freehold, and Daddy paid a hundred and eighty thousand pounds for Tilby; I don't know if you understand what I mean, I felt they were just furnished houses we'd taken for the season and one of these days we'd pack up and the real owners would come back."

I listened to him attentively, but I wondered how much he was describing what he had obscurely felt and how much he imagined now in his changed circumstances that he had felt.

"I used to hate hearing Great-uncle Ferdy tell his Jewish stories. I thought it so damned mean. I understand now; it was a safety valve. My God, the strain of being a man about town. It's easier for Daddy, he can play the old English squire at Tilby, but in the city he can be himself. He's all right. I've taken the make-up off and my stage clothes and at last I can be my real self too. What a relief! You know, I don't like English people. I never really know where I am with you. You're so dull and conventional. You never let yourselves go. There's no freedom in you, freedom of the soul, and you're such funks. There's nothing in the world you're so frightened of as doing the wrong thing."

"Don't forget that you're English yourself, George," I murmured.

He laughed.

"I? I'm not English. I haven't got a drop of English blood in me. I'm a Jew and you know it, and a German Jew into the bargain. I don't want to be English. I want to be a Jew. My friends are Jews. You don't know how much more easy I feel with them. I can be myself. We did everything we could to avoid Jews at home; Mummy because she was blonde thought she could get away with it and pretended she was a Gentile. What rot! D'you know, I have a lot of fun wandering about the Jewish parts of Munich and looking at the people. I went to Frankfort once—there are a lot of them there—and I walked about and looked at the frowsy old men with their hooked noses and the fat women with their false hair. I felt such a sympathy for them, I felt I belonged to them, I could have kissed them. When they looked at me I wondered if they knew that I was one of them. I wish to God I knew Yiddish. I'd like to become friends with them, and go into their houses and eat Kosher food and all that sort of thing. I wanted to go to a synagogue, but I was afraid I'd do the wrong thing and be kicked out. I like the smell of the Ghetto and the sense of life, and the mystery and the dust and the squalor and the romance. I shall never get the longing for it out of my head now. That's the real thing. All the rest is only pretence."

"You'll break your father's heart," I said.

"It's his or mine. Why can't he let me go? There's Harry. Harry would love to be squire of Tilby. He'd be an English gentleman all right. You know, Mummy's set her heart on my marrying a Christian. Harry would love to. He'll found the good old English family all right. After all, I ask so little. I only want five pounds a week, and they can keep the title and the park and the Gainsboroughs and the whole bag of tricks."

"Well, the fact remains that you gave your solemn word of honour to go back after two years."

"I'll go back all right," he said sullenly. "Lea Makart has promised to come and hear me play."

"What'll you do if she says you're no good?"

"Shoot myself," he said gaily.

"What nonsense," I answered in the same tone.

"Do *you* feel at home in England?"

"No," I said, "but then I don't feel at home anywhere else."

But he was quite naturally not interested in me.

"I loathe the idea of going back. Now that I know what life has to offer I wouldn't be an English country gentleman for anything in the world. My God, the boredom of it!"

"Money's a very nice thing and I've always understood it's very pleasant to be an English peer."

"Money means nothing to me. I want none of the things it can buy, and I don't happen to be a snob."

It was growing very late and I had to get up early next day. It seemed unnecessary for me to pay too much attention to what George said. It was the sort of nonsense a young man might very well indulge in when thrown suddenly among painters and poets. Art is strong wine and needs a strong head to carry. The divine fire burns most efficiently in those who temper its fury with horse sense. After all, George was not twenty-three yet. Time teaches. And when all was said and done his future was no concern of mine. I bade him good-night and walked back to my hotel. The stars were shining in the indifferent sky. I left Munich in the morning.

I did not tell Muriel on my return to London what George had said to me, or what he looked like, but contented myself with assuring her that he was well and happy, working very hard, and seemed to be leading a virtuous and sober life. Six months later he came home. Muriel asked me to go down to Tilby for the week-end: Ferdy was bringing Lea Makart to hear George play and he particularly wished me to be there. I accepted. Muriel met me at the station.

"How did you find George?" I asked.

"He's very fat, but he seems in great spirits. I think he's pleased to be back again. He's been very sweet to his father."

"I'm glad of that."

"Oh, my dear, I do hope Lea Makart will say he's no good. It'll be such a relief to all of us."

"I'm afraid it'll be a terrible disappointment to him."

"Life is full of disappointments," said Muriel crisply. "But one learns to put up with them."

I gave her a smile of amusement. We were sitting in a Rolls, and there was a footman as well as a chauffeur on the box. She wore a string of pearls that had probably cost forty thousand pounds. I recollected that in the birthday honours Sir Adolphus Bland had not been one of the three gentlemen on whom the King had been pleased to confer a peerage.

Lea Makart was able to make only a flying visit. She was playing that evening at Brighton and would motor over to Tilby on the Sunday morning for luncheon. She was returning to London the same day because she had a concert in Manchester on the Monday. George was to play in the course of the afternoon.

"He's practising very hard," his mother told me. "That's why he didn't come with me to meet you."

We turned in at the park gates and drove up the imposing avenue of elms that led to the house. I found that there was no party.

I met the dowager Lady Bland for the first time. I had always been curious to see her. I had had in my mind's eye a somewhat sensational picture of an old, old Jewish woman who lived alone in her grand house in Portland Place and, with a finger in every pie, ruled her family with a despotic hand. She did not disappoint me. She was of a commanding presence, rather tall, and stout without being corpulent. Her countenance was markedly Hebraic. She wore a rather heavy moustache and a wig of a peculiarly metallic brown. Her dress was very grand, of black brocade, and she had a row of large diamond stars on her breast and round her neck a chain of diamonds. Diamond rings gleamed on her wrinkled hands. She spoke in a rather loud harsh voice and with a strong German accent. When I was introduced to her she fixed me with shining eyes. She summed me up with despatch and to my fancy at all events made no attempt to conceal from me that the judgment she formed was unfavourable.

"You have known my brother Ferdinand for many years, is it not so?" she said, rolling a guttural r. "My brother Ferdinand has always moved in very good society. Where is Sir Adolphus, Muriel? Does he know your guest is arrived? And will you not send for George? If he does not know his pieces by now he will not know them by to-morrow."

Muriel explained that Freddy was finishing a round of golf with his secretary and that she had had George told I was there. Lady Bland looked as though she thought Muriel's replies highly unsatisfactory and turned again to me.

"My daughter tells me you have been in Italy?"

"Yes, I've only just come back."

"It is a beautiful country. How is the King?"

I said I did not know.

"I used to know him when he was a little boy. He was not very strong then. His mother, Queen Margarita, was a great friend of mine. They thought he would never marry. The Duchess of Aosta was very angry when he fell in love with that Princess of Montenegro."

She seemed to belong to some long past period of history, but she was very alert and I imagine that little escaped her beady eyes. Freddy, very spruce in plus fours, presently came in. It was amusing and yet a little touching to see this grey-bearded man, as a rule somewhat domineering, so obviously on his best behaviour with the old lady. He called her Mamma. Then George came in. He was as fat as ever, but he had taken my advice and had his hair cut; he was losing his boyish looks, but he was a powerful and well-set-up young man. It was good to see the pleasure he took in his tea. He ate quantities of sandwiches and great hunks of cake. He had still a boy's appetite. His father watched him with a tender smile, and as I looked at him I could not be surprised at the attachment which they all so obviously felt for him. He had an ingenuousness, a charm and an enthusiasm which were certainly very pleasant. There was about him a generosity of demeanour, a frankness and a natural cordiality which could not but make people take to him. I do not know whether it was owing to a hint from his grandmother or merely of his own good nature, but it was plain that he was going out of his way to be nice to his father; and in his father's soft eyes, in the way he hung upon the boy's words, in his pleased, proud and happy look, you felt how bitterly the estrangement of the last two years had weighed on him. He adored George.

We played golf in the morning, a three-ball match, since Muriel, having to go to Mass, could not join us, and at one Ferdy arrived in Lea Makart's car. We sat down to luncheon. Of course Lea Makart's reputation was well-known to me. She was acknowledged to be the greatest woman pianist in Europe. She was a very old friend of Ferdy's, who with his

interest and patronage had greatly helped her at the beginning of her career, and it was he who had arranged for her
to come and give her opinion of George's chances. At one
time I went as often as I could to hear her play. She had no
affectations; she played as a bird sings, without any appearance of effort, very naturally, and the silvery notes
dripped from her light fingers in a curiously spontaneous
manner, so that it gave you the impression that she was
improvising those complicated rhythms. They used to tell
me that her technique was wonderful. I could never make
up my mind how much the delight her playing gave me was
due to her person. In those days she was the most ethereal
thing you could imagine, and it was surprising that a creature
so sylphlike should be capable of so much power. She was
very slight, pale, with enormous eyes and magnificent black
hair, and at the piano she had a childlike wistfulness that
was most appealing. She was very beautiful in a hardly human way, and when she played, a little smile on her closed
lips, she seemed to be remembering things she had heard in
another world. Now, however, a woman in the early forties,
she was sylphlike no more; she was stout and her face had
broadened; she had no longer that lovely remoteness, but
the authority of her long succession of triumphs. She was
brisk, businesslike and somewhat overwhelming. Her vitality
lit her with a natural spotlight as his sanctity surrounds the
saint with a halo. She was not interested in anything very
much but her own affairs, but since she had humour and
knew the world she was able to invest them with gaiety. She
held the conversation, but did not absorb it. George talked
little. Every now and then she gave him a glance, but did not
try to draw him in. I was the only Gentile at the table. All
but old Lady Bland spoke perfect English, yet I could not
help feeling that they did not speak like English people; I
think they rounded their vowels more than we do, they certainly spoke louder, and the words seemed not to fall, but to
gush from their lips. I think if I had been in another room
where I could hear the tone but not the words of their speech

I should have thought it was in a foreign language that they were conversing. The effect was slightly disconcerting.

Lea Makart wished to set out for London at about six, so it was arranged that George should play at four. Whatever the result of the audition, I felt that I, a stranger in the circle which her departure must render exclusively domestic, would be in the way and so, pretexting an early engagement in town next morning, I asked her if she would take me with her in her car.

At a little before four we all wandered into the drawing-room. Old Lady Bland sat on a sofa with Ferdy; Freddy, Muriel and I made ourselves comfortable in armchairs; and Lea Makart sat by herself. She chose instinctively a high-backed Jacobean chair that had somewhat the air of a throne, and in a yellow dress, with her olive skin, she looked very handsome. She had magnificent eyes. She was very much made up and her mouth was scarlet.

George gave no sign of nervousness. He was already seated at the piano when I went in with his father and mother, and he watched us quietly settling ourselves down. He gave me the shadow of a smile. When he saw that we were all at our ease he began to play. He played Chopin. He played two waltzes that were familiar to me, a polonaise and an *étude*. He played with a great deal of *brio*. I wish I knew music well enough to give an exact description of his playing. It had strength and a youthful exuberance, but I felt that he missed what to me is the peculiar charm of Chopin, the tenderness, the nervous melancholy, the wistful gaiety and the slightly faded romance that reminds me always of an early Victorian keepsake. And again I had the vague sensation, so slight that it almost escaped me, that the two hands did not quite synchronize. I looked at Ferdy and saw him give his sister a look of faint surprise. Muriel's eyes were fixed on the pianist, but presently she dropped them and for the rest of the time stared at the floor. His father looked at him too, and his eyes were steadfast, but unless I was much mistaken he went pale and his face betrayed something like dismay. Music was in the blood of all of them, all their lives they had heard the greatest pianists in the world, and they judged with instinctive precision. The only person whose face betrayed no emotion was Lea Makart. She listened very attentively. She was as still as an image in a niche.

At last he stopped and turning round on his seat faced her. He did not speak.

"What is it you want me to tell you?" she asked.

They looked into one another's eyes.

"I want you to tell me whether I have any chance of becoming in time a pianist in the first rank."

"Not in a thousand years."

For a moment there was a dead silence. Freddy's head sank and he looked down at the carpet at his feet. His wife put out her hand and took his. But George continued to look steadily at Lea Makart.

"Ferdy has told me the circumstances," she said at last. "Don't think I'm influenced by them. Nothing of this is very important." She made a great sweeping gesture that took in the magnificent room with the beautiful things it contained and all of us. "If I thought you had in you the makings of an artist I shouldn't hesitate to beseech you to give up everything for art's sake. Art is the only thing that matters. In comparison with art, wealth and rank and power are not worth a row of pins." She gave us a look so sincere that it was void of insolence. "We are the only people who count. We give the world significance. You are only our raw material."

I was not too pleased to be included with the rest under that heading, but that is neither here nor there.

"Of course I can see that you've worked very hard. Don't think it's been wasted. It will always be a pleasure to you to be able to play the piano, and it will enable you to appreciate great playing as no ordinary person can hope to do. Look at your hands. They're not a pianist's hands."

Involuntarily I glanced at George's hands. I had never noticed them before. I was astounded to see how podgy they were and how short and stumpy the fingers.

"Your ear is not quite perfect. I don't think you can ever

hope to be more than a very competent amateur. In art the
difference between the amateur and the professional is im-
measurable."

George did not reply. Except for his pallor no one would
have known that he was listening to the blasting of all his
hopes. The silence that fell was quite awful. Lea Makart's
eyes suddenly filled with tears.

"But don't take my opinion alone," she said. "After all,
I'm not infallible. Ask somebody else. You know how good
and generous Paderewski is. I'll write to him about you and
you can go down and play to him. I'm sure he'll hear you."

George now gave a little smile. He had very good manners
and, whatever he was feeling, did not want to make the situation too difficult for others.

"I don't think that's necessary. I am content to accept
your verdict. To tell you the truth it's not so very different
from my master's in Munich."

He got up from the piano and lit a cigarette. It eased
the strain. The others moved a little in their chairs. Lea
Makart smiled at George.

"Shall I play to you?" she said.

"Yes, do."

She got up and went to the piano. She took off the rings
with which her fingers were laden. She played Bach. I do not
know the names of the pieces, but I recognized the stiff
ceremonial of the frenchified little German courts and the sober, thrifty comfort of the burghers, and the dancing on the
village green, the green trees that looked like Christmas trees,
and the sunlight on the wide German country, and a tender
coziness; and in my nostrils there was a warm scent of the
soil and I was conscious of a sturdy strength that seemed
to have its roots deep in mother earth, and of an elemental
power that was timeless and had no home in space. She
played exquisitely, with a soft brilliance that made you think
of the full moon shining at dusk in the summer sky. With
another part of me I watched the others and I saw how intensely they were conscious of the experience. They were rapt.
I wished with all my heart that I could get from music the

wonderful exaltation that possessed them. She stopped, a smile
hovered on her lips, and she put on her rings. George gave a
little chuckle.

"That clinches it, I fancy," he said.

The servants brought in tea, and after tea Lea Makart and
I bade the company farewell and got into the car. We drove
up to London. She talked all the way, if not brilliantly at all
events with immense gusto, she told me of her early years in
Manchester and of the struggle of her beginnings. She was
very interesting. She never even mentioned George; the epi-
sode was of no consequence; it was finished and she thought
of it no more.

We little knew what was happening at Tilby. When we left,
George went out on the terrace and presently his father
joined him. Freddy had won the day, but he was not happy.
With his more than feminine sensitiveness he felt all that
George was feeling, and George's anguish simply broke his
heart. He had never loved his son more than then. When he
appeared George greeted him with a little smile. Freddy's
voice broke. In a sudden and overwhelming emotion he
found it in him to surrender the fruits of his victory.

"Look here, old boy," he said, "I can't bear to think that
you've had such a disappointment. Would you like to go back
to Munich for another year and then see?"

George shook his head.

"No, it wouldn't be any good. I've had my chance. Let's
call it a day."

"Try not to take it too hard."

"You see, the only thing in the world I want is to be a
pianist. And there's nothing doing. It's a bit thick if you come
to think of it."

George, trying so hard to be brave, smiled wanly.

"Would you like to go round the world? You can get one
of your Oxford pals to go with you and I'll pay all the expenses. You've been working very hard for a long time."

"Thanks awfully, Daddy, we'll talk about it. I'm just going
for a stroll now."

"Shall I come with you?"

"I'd rather go alone."

Then George did a strange thing. He put his arm round his father's neck and kissed him on the lips. He gave a funny little moved laugh and walked away. Freddy went back to the drawing-room. His mother, Ferdy and Muriel were sitting there.

"Freddy, why don't you marry the boy?" said the old lady. "He is twenty-three. It would take his mind off his troubles and when he is married and has a baby he will soon settle down like everybody else."

"Who is he to marry, Mamma?" asked Sir Adolphus, smiling.

"That's not so difficult. Lady Frielinghausen came to see me the other day with her daughter Violet. She is a very nice maiden and she will have money of her own. Lady Frieling-hausen gave me to understand that her Sir Jacob would come down very handsome if Violet made a good match."

Muriel flushed.

"I hate Lady Frielinghausen. George is much too young to marry. He can afford to marry anyone he likes."

Old Lady Bland gave her daughter a strange look.

"You are a very foolish girl, Miriam," she said, using the name Muriel had long discarded. "As long as I am here I shall not allow you to commit a foolishness."

She knew as well as if Muriel had said it in so many words that she wanted George to marry a Gentile, but she knew also that so long as she was alive neither Freddy nor his wife would dare to suggest it.

But George did not go for a walk. Perhaps because the shooting season was about to open he took it into his head to go into the gun-room. He began to clean the gun that his mother had given him on his twentieth birthday. No one had used it since he went to Germany. Suddenly the servants were startled by a report. When they went into the gun-room they found George lying on the floor shot through the heart. Apparently the gun had been loaded and George while play-ing about with it had accidentally shot himself. One reads of such accidents in the paper often.

The Book-Bag

Some people read for instruction, which is praiseworthy, and some for pleasure, which is innocent, but not a few read from habit, and I suppose that this is neither innocent nor praiseworthy. Of that lamentable company am I. Conversation after a time bores me, games tire me and my own thoughts, which we are told are the unfailing resource of a sensible man, have a tendency to run dry. Then I fly to my book as the opium-smoker to his pipe. I would sooner read the catalogue of the Army and Navy Stores or Bradshaw's Guide than nothing at all, and indeed I have spent many delightful hours over both these works. At one time I never went out without a second-hand bookseller's list in my pocket. I know no reading more fruity. Of course to read in this way is as reprehensible as doping, and I never cease to wonder at the impertinence of great readers who, because they are such, look down on the illiterate. From the standpoint of what eternity is it better to have read a thousand books than to have ploughed a million furrows? Let us admit that reading with us is just a drug that we cannot do without—who of this band does not know the restlessness that attacks him when he has been severed from reading too long, the apprehension and irritability, and the sigh of relief which the sight of a printed page extracts from him?—and so let us be no more vainglorious than the poor slaves of the hypodermic needle or the pint-pot.

And like the dope-fiend who cannot move from place to place without taking with him a plentiful supply of his deadly balm I never venture far without a sufficiency of reading matter. Books are so necessary to me that when in a

railway train I have become aware that fellow-travellers have
come away without a single one I have been seized with a
veritable dismay. But when I am starting on a long journey
the problem is formidable. I have learnt my lesson. Once, imprisoned by illness for three months in a hill-town in Java, I
came to the end of all the books I had brought with me, and
knowing no Dutch was obliged to buy the school-books from
which intelligent Javanese, I suppose, acquired knowledge
of French and German. So I read again after five and twenty
years the frigid plays of Goethe, the fables of La Fontaine
and the tragedies of the tender and exact Racine. I have
the greatest admiration for Racine, but I admit that to read
his plays one after the other requires a certain effort in a
person who is suffering from colitis. Since then I have made a
point of travelling with the largest sack made for carrying
soiled linen and filling it to the brim with books to suit every
possible occasion and every mood. It weighs a ton and
strong porters reel under its weight. Custom-house officials
look at it askance, but recoil from it with consternation when
I give them my word that it contains nothing but books. Its
inconvenience is that the particular work I suddenly hanker
to read is always at the bottom and it is impossible for me to
get it without emptying the book-bag's entire contents upon
the floor. Except for this, however, I should perhaps never
have heard the singular history of Olive Hardy.

I was wandering about Malaya, staying here and there, a
week or two if there was a rest-house or a hotel, and a day or
so if I was obliged to inflict myself on a planter or a District
Officer whose hospitality I had no wish to abuse; and at the
moment I happened to be at Penang. It is a pleasant little
town, with a hotel that has always seemed to me very agreeable, but the stranger finds little to do there and time hung a
trifle heavily on my hands. One morning I received a letter
from a man I knew only by name. This was Mark Featherstone. He was Acting Resident, in the absence on leave of the
Resident, at a place called Tenggarah. There was a sultan
there and it appeared that a water festival of some sort was
to take place which Featherstone thought would interest me.

He said that he would be glad if I would come and stay with him for a few days. I wired to tell him that I should be delighted and next day took the train to Tenggarah. Featherstone met me at the station. He was a man of about thirty-five, I should think, tall and handsome, with fine eyes and a strong, stern face. He had a wiry black moustache and bushy eyebrows. He looked more like a soldier than a government official. He was very smart in white ducks, with a white topi, and he wore his clothes with elegance. He was a little shy, which seemed odd in a strapping fellow of resolute mien, but I surmised that this was only because he was unused to the society of that strange fish, a writer, and I hoped in a little to put him at his ease.

"My boys'll look after your barang," he said. "We'll go down to the club. Give them your keys and they'll unpack before we get back."

I told him that I had a good deal of luggage and thought it better to leave everything at the station but what I particularly wanted. He would not hear of it.

"It doesn't matter a bit. It'll be safer at my house. It's always better to have one's barang with one."

"All right."

I gave my keys and the ticket for my trunk and my book-bag to a Chinese boy who stood at my host's elbow. Outside the station a car was waiting for us and we stepped in.

"Do you play bridge?" asked Featherstone.

"I do."

"I thought most writers didn't."

"They don't," I said. "It's generally considered among authors a sign of deficient intelligence to play cards."

The club was a bungalow, pleasing but unpretentious; it had a large reading-room, a billiard-room with one table, and a small card-room. When we arrived it was empty but for one or two persons reading the English weeklies, and we walked through to the tennis courts where a couple of sets were being played. A number of people were sitting on the verandah, looking on, smoking and sipping long drinks. I was introduced to one or two of them. But the light was failing and soon the players could hardly see the ball. Featherstone asked one of the men I had been introduced to if he would like a rubber. He said he would. Featherstone looked about for a fourth. He caught sight of a man sitting a little by himself, paused for a second, and went up to him. The two exchanged a few words and then came towards us. We strolled in to the card-room. We had a very nice game. I did not pay much attention to the two men who made up the four. They stood me drinks, and I, a temporary member of the club, returned the compliment. The drinks were very small, quarter whiskies, and in the two hours we played each of us was able to show his open-handedness without an excessive consumption of alcohol. When the advancing hour suggested that the next rubber must be the last we changed from whisky to gin pahits. The rubber came to an end. Featherstone called for the book and the winnings and losings of each one of us were set down. One of the men got up.

"Well, I must be going," he said.

"Going back to the Estate?" asked Featherstone.

"Yes," he nodded. He turned to me. "Shall you be here to-morrow?"

"I hope so."

He went out of the room.

"I'll collect my mem and get along home to dinner," said the other.

"We might be going too," said Featherstone.

"I'm ready whenever you are," I replied.

We got into the car and drove to his house. It was a longish drive. In the darkness I could see nothing much, but presently I realized that we were going up a rather steep hill. We reached the Residency.

It had been an evening like any other, pleasant, but not at all exciting, and I had spent I don't know how many just like it. I did not expect it to leave any sort of impression on me.

Featherstone led me into his sitting-room. It looked comfortable, but it was a trifle ordinary. It had large basket armchairs covered with cretonne and on the walls were a great

many framed photographs; the tables were littered with papers, magazines and official reports, with pipes, yellow tins of
straight-cut cigarettes and pink tins of tobacco. In a row of
shelves were untidily stacked a good many books, their bind-
ings stained with damp and the ravages of white ants.
Featherstone showed me my room and left me with the
words:

"Shall you be ready for a gin pahit in ten minutes?"

"Easily," I said.

I had a bath and changed and went downstairs. Featherstone, ready before me, mixed our drink as he heard me
clatter down the wooden staircase. We dined. We talked. The
festival which I had been invited to see was the next day but
one, but Featherstone told me he had arranged for me before
that to be received by the Sultan.

"He's a jolly old boy," he said. "And the palace is a sight
for sore eyes."

After dinner we talked a little more, Featherstone put on
the gramophone, and we looked at the latest illustrated papers that had arrived from England. Then we went to bed.
Featherstone came to my room to see that I had everything
I wanted.

"I suppose you haven't any books with you," he said. "I
haven't got a thing to read."

"Books?" I cried.

I pointed to my book-bag. It stood upright, bulging oddly,
so that it looked like a humpbacked gnome somewhat the
worse for liquor.

"Have you got books in there? I thought that was your
dirty linen or a camp-bed or something. Is there anything you
can lend me?"

"Look for yourself."

Featherstone's boys had unlocked the bag, but quailing before the sight that then discovered itself had done no more. I
knew from long experience how to unpack it. I threw it over
on its side, seized its leather bottom and, walking backwards, dragged the sack away from its contents. A river of

books poured on to the floor. A look of stupefaction came upon Featherstone's face.

"You don't mean to say you travel with as many books as that? By George, what a snip."

He bent down and turning them over rapidly looked at the titles. There were books of all kinds. Volumes of verse, novels, philosophical works, critical studies (they say books about books are profitless, but they certainly make very pleasant reading), biographies, history; there were books to read when you were ill and books to read when your brain, all alert, craved for something to grapple with, there were books that you had always wanted to read, but in the hurry of life at home had never found time to, there were books to read at sea when you were meandering through narrow waters on a tramp steamer, and there were books for bad weather when your whole cabin creaked and you had to wedge yourself in your bunk in order not to fall out; there were books chosen solely for their length, which you took with you when on some expedition you had to travel light, and there were the books you could read when you could read nothing else. Finally Featherstone picked out a life of Byron that had recently appeared.

"Hullo, what's this?" he said. "I read a review of it some time ago."

"I believe it's very good," I replied. "I haven't read it yet."

"May I take it? It'll do me for to-night at all events."

"Of course. Take anything you like."

"No, that's enough. Well, good-night. Breakfast at eight-thirty."

When I came down next morning the head boy told me that Featherstone, who had been at work since six, would be in shortly. While I waited for him I glanced at his shelves.

"I see you've got a grand library of books on bridge," I remarked as we sat down to breakfast.

"Yes, I get every one that comes out. I'm very keen on it."

"That fellow we were playing with yesterday plays a good game."

"Which? Hardy?"

"I don't know. Not the one who said he was going to collect his wife. The other."

"Yes, that was Hardy. That was why I asked him to play. He doesn't come to the club very often."

"I hope he will to-night."

"I wouldn't bank on it. He has an estate about thirty miles away. It's a longish ride to come just for a rubber of bridge."

"Is he married?"

"No. Well, yes. But his wife is in England."

"It must be awfully lonely for those men who live by themselves on those estates," I said.

"Oh, he's not so badly off as some. I don't think he much cares about seeing people. I think he'd be just as lonely in London."

There was something in the way Featherstone spoke that struck me as a little strange. His voice had what I can only describe as a shuttered tone. He seemed suddenly to have moved away from me. It was as though one were passing along a street at night and paused for a second to look in at a lighted window that showed a comfortable room and suddenly an invisible hand pulled down the blind. His eyes, which habitually met those of the person he was talking to with frankness, now avoided mine and I had a notion that it was not only my fancy that read in his face an expression of pain. It was drawn for a moment as it might be by a twinge of neuralgia. I could not think of anything to say and Featherstone did not speak. I was conscious that his thoughts, withdrawn from me and what we were about, were turned upon a subject unknown to me. Presently he gave a little sigh, very slight, but unmistakable, and seemed with a deliberate effort to pull himself together.

"I'm going down to the office immediately after breakfast," he said. "What are you going to do with yourself?"

"Oh, don't bother about me. I shall slack around. I'll stroll down and look at the town."

"There's not much to see."

"All the better. I'm fed up with sights."

I found that Featherstone's verandah gave me sufficient

entertainment for the morning. It had one of the most enchanting views I had seen in the F.M.S. The Residency was
built on the top of a hill and the garden was large and
well-cared for. Great trees gave it almost the look of an
English park. It had vast lawns and there Tamils, black and
emaciated, were scything with deliberate and beautiful gestures. Beyond and below, the jungle grew thickly to the
bank of a broad, winding and swiftly flowing river, and on
the other side of this, as far as the eye could reach, stretched
the wooded hills of Tenggarah. The contrast between the
trim lawns, so strangely English, and the savage growth of
the jungle beyond pleasantly titillated the fancy. I sat and read
and smoked. It is my business to be curious about people
and I asked myself how the peace of this scene, charged
nevertheless with a tremulous and dark significance, affected
Featherstone who lived with it. He knew it under every
aspect: at dawn when the mist rising from the river
shrouded it with a ghostly pall; in the splendour of noon;
and at last when the shadowy gloaming crept softly out of
the jungle, like an army making its way with caution in
unknown country, and presently enveloped the green lawns
and the great flowering trees and the flaunting cassias in the
silent night. I wondered whether, unbeknownst to him, the
tender and yet strangely sinister aspect of the scene, acting on
his nerves and his loneliness, imbued him with some mysti-
cal quality so that the life he led, the life of the capable
administrator, the sportsman and the good fellow, on occasion
seemed to him not quite real. I smiled at my own fancies,
for certainly the conversation we had had the night before
had not indicated in him any stirrings of the soul. I had
thought him quite nice. He had been at Oxford and was a
member of a good London club. He seemed to attach a good
deal of importance to social things. He was a gentleman and
slightly conscious of the fact that he belonged to a better
class than most of the Englishmen his life brought him in contact with. I gathered from the various silver pots that adorned
his dining-room that he excelled in games. He played tennis
and billiards. When he went on leave he hunted and, anxious

to keep his weight down, he dieted carefully. He talked a good deal of what he would do when he retired. He hankered after the life of a country gentleman. A little house in Leicestershire, a couple of hunters and neighbours to play bridge with. He would have his pension and he had a little money of his own. But meanwhile he worked hard and did his work, if not brilliantly, certainly with competence. I have no doubt that he was looked upon by his superiors as a reliable officer. He was cut upon a pattern that I knew too well to find very interesting. He was like a novel that is careful, honest and efficient, yet a little ordinary, so that you seem to have read it all before, and you turn the pages listlessly knowing that it will never afford you a surprise or move you to excitement.

But human beings are incalculable and he is a fool who tells himself that he knows what a man is capable of.

In the afternoon Featherstone took me to see the Sultan. We were received by one of his sons, a shy, smiling youth who acted as his A.D.C. He was dressed in a neat blue suit, but round his waist he wore a sarong, white flowers on a yellow ground, on his head a red fez, and on his feet knobby American shoes. The palace, built in the Moorish style, was like a very big doll's house and it was painted bright yellow, which is the royal colour. We were led into a spacious room, furnished with the sort of furniture you would find in an English lodging-house at the seaside, but the chairs were covered with yellow silk. On the floor was a Brussels carpet and on the walls photographs in very grand gilt frames of the Sultan at various state functions. In a cabinet was a large collection of all kinds of fruit done entirely in crochet work. The Sultan came in with several attendants. He was a man of fifty, perhaps, short and stout, dressed in trousers and tunic of a large white and yellow check; round his middle he wore a very beautiful yellow sarong and on his head a white fez. He had large, handsome, friendly eyes. He gave us coffee to drink, sweet cakes to eat and cheroots to smoke. Conversation was not difficult, for he was affable, and he told me that he had never been to a theatre or played cards, for he was very religious, and he had four wives and twenty-four children. The only bar to the happiness of his life seemed to be that common decency obliged him to divide his time equally between his four wives. He said that an hour with one was a month and with another five minutes. I remarked that Professor Einstein —or was it Bergson?—had made similar observations upon time and indeed on this question had given the world much to ponder over. Presently we took our leave and the Sultan presented me with some beautiful white Malaccas.

In the evening we went to the club. One of the men we had played with the day before got up from his chair as we entered.

"Ready for a rubber?" he said.

"Where's our fourth?" I asked.

"Oh, there are several fellows here who'll be glad to play."

"What about that man we played with yesterday?" I had forgotten his name.

"Hardy? He's not here."

"It's not worth while waiting for him," said Featherstone.

"He very seldom comes to the club. I was surprised to see him last night."

I did not know why I had the impression that behind the very ordinary words of these two men there was an odd sense of embarrassment. Hardy had made no impression on me and I did not even remember what he looked like. He was just a fourth at the bridge table. I had a feeling that they had something against him. It was no business of mine and I was quite content to play with a man who at that moment joined us. We certainly had a more cheerful game than before. A good deal of chaff passed from one side of the table to the other. We played less serious bridge. We laughed. I wondered if it was only that they were less shy of the stranger who had happened in upon them or if the presence of Hardy had caused in the other two a certain constraint. At half-past eight we broke up and Featherstone and I went back to dine at his house.

After dinner we lounged in arm-chairs and smoked cheroots. For some reason our conversation did not flow easily. I tried topic after topic, but could not get Featherstone to interest himself in any of them. I began to think that in the last twenty-four hours he had said all he had to say. I fell somewhat discouraged into silence. It prolonged itself and again, I did not know why, I had a faint sensation that it was charged with a significance that escaped me. I felt slightly uncomfortable. I had that queer feeling that one sometimes has when sitting in an empty room that one is not by oneself. Presently I was conscious that Featherstone was steadily looking at me. I was sitting by a lamp, but he was in shadow so that the play of his features was hidden from me. But he had very large brilliant eyes and in the half darkness they seemed to shine dimly. They were like new boot-buttons that caught a reflected light. I wondered why he looked at me like that. I gave him a glance and catching his eyes insistently fixed upon me faintly smiled.

"Interesting book that one you lent me last night," he said suddenly, and I could not help thinking his voice did not sound quite natural. The words issued from his lips as though they were pushed from behind.

"Oh, the Life of Byron?" I said breezily. "Have you read it already?"

"A good deal of it. I read till three."

"I've heard it's very well done. I'm not sure that Byron interests me so much as all that. There was so much in him that was so frightfully second-rate. It makes one rather uncomfortable."

"What do you think is the real truth of that story about him and his sister?"

"Augusta Leigh? I don't know very much about it. I've never read Astarte."

"Do you think they were really in love with one another?"

"I suppose so. Isn't it generally believed that she was the only woman he ever genuinely loved?"

"Can you understand it?"

"I can't really. It doesn't particularly shock me. It just seems to me very unnatural. Perhaps 'unnatural' isn't the right word. It's incomprehensible to me. I can't throw myself into the state of feeling in which such a thing seems possible. You know, that's how a writer gets to know the people he writes about, by standing himself in their shoes and feeling with their hearts."

I knew I did not make myself very clear, but I was trying to describe a sensation, an action of the subconscious, which from experience was perfectly familiar to me, but which no words I knew could precisely indicate. I went on.

"Of course she was only his half-sister, but just as habit kills love I should have thought habit would prevent its arising. When two persons have known one another all their lives and lived together in close contact I can't imagine how or why that sudden spark should flash that results in love. The probabilities are that they would be joined by mutual affection and I don't know anything that is more contrary to love than affection."

I could just see in the dimness the outline of a smile flicker for a moment on my host's heavy, and it seemed to me then, somewhat saturnine face.

"You only believe in love at first sight?"

"Well, I suppose I do, but with the proviso that people may have met twenty times before seeing one another. 'Seeing' has an active side and a passive one. Most people we run across mean so little to us that we never bestir ourselves to look at them. We just suffer the impression they make on us."

"Oh, but one's often heard of couples who've known one another for years and it's never occurred to one they cared two straws for each other and suddenly they go and get married. How do you explain that?"

"Well, if you're going to bully me into being logical and consistent, I should suggest that their love is of a different kind. After all, passion isn't the only reason for marriage. It may not even be the best one. Two people may marry because they're lonely or because they're good friends or for convenience' sake. Though I said that affection was the greatest enemy of love, I would never deny that it's a very good substitute. I'm not sure that a marriage founded on it isn't the happiest."

"What did you think of Tim Hardy?"

I was a little surprised at the sudden question, which

seemed to have nothing to do with the subject of our conversation.

"I didn't think of him very much. He seemed quite nice.
Why?"

"Did he seem to you just like everybody else?"

"Yes. Is there anything peculiar about him? If you'd told
me that I'd have paid more attention to him."

"He's very quiet, isn't he? I suppose no one who knew nothing about him would give him a second thought."

I tried to remember what he looked like. The only thing
that had struck me when we were playing cards was that he
had fine hands. It passed idly through my mind that they were
not the sort of hands I should have expected a planter to have.
But why a planter should have different hands from anybody
else I did not trouble to ask myself. His were somewhat large,
but very well formed, with peculiarly long fingers, and the
nails were of an admirable shape. They were virile and yet
oddly sensitive hands. I noticed this and thought no more
about it. But if you are a writer, instinct and the habit of
years enable you to store up impressions that you are not
aware of. Sometimes of course they do not correspond with
the facts and a woman for example may remain in your
subconsciousness as a dark, massive and ox-eyed creature
when she is indeed rather small and of a nondescript colour-
ing. But that is of no consequence. The impression may very
well be more exact than the sober truth. And now, seeking to
call up from the depths of me a picture of this man I had a
feeling of some ambiguity. He was clean-shaven and his face,
oval but not thin, seemed strangely pale under the tan of
long exposure to the tropical sun. His features were vague. I
did not know whether I remembered it or only imagined
now that his rounded chin gave one the impression of a
certain weakness. He had thick brown hair, just turning grey,
and a long wisp fell down constantly over his forehead. He
pushed it back with a gesture that had become habitual. His
brown eyes were rather large and gentle, but perhaps a little
sad; they had a melting softness which, I could imagine,
might be very appealing.

After a pause Featherstone continued:

"It's rather strange that I should run across Tim Hardy here after all these years. But that's the way of the F.M.S. People move about and you find yourself in the same place as a man you'd known years before in another part of the country. I first knew Tim when he had an estate near Sibuku. Have you ever been there?"

"No. Where is it?"

"Oh, it's up north. Towards Siam. It wouldn't be worth your while to go. It's just like every other place in the F.M.S. But it was rather nice. It had a very jolly little club and there were some quite decent people. There was the schoolmaster and the head of the police, the doctor, the padre and the government engineer. The usual lot, you know. A few plant-ers. Three or four women. I was A.D.O. It was one of my first jobs. Tim Hardy had an estate about twenty-five miles away. He lived there with his sister. They had a bit of money of their own and he'd bought the place. Rubber was pretty good then and he wasn't doing at all badly. We rather cot-toned on to one another. Of course it's a toss-up with plant-ers. Some of them are very good fellows, but they're not ex-actly . . ." he sought for a word or a phrase that did not sound snobbish. "Well, they're not the sort of people you'd be likely to meet at home. Tim and Olive were of one's own class, if you understand what I mean."

"Olive was the sister?"

"Yes. They'd had a rather unfortunate past. Their parents had separated when they were quite small, seven or eight, and the mother had taken Olive and the father had kept Tim. Tim went to Clifton, they were West Country people, and only came home for the holidays. His father was a retired naval man who lived at Fowey. But Olive went with her mother to Italy. She was educated in Florence; she spoke Italian perfectly and French too. For all those years Tim and Olive never saw one another once, but they used to write to one another regularly. They'd been very much attached when they were children. As far as I could understand, life when their people were living together had been rather stormy with all sorts of scenes and upsets, you know the sort of thing that happens when two people who are married don't get on together, and that had thrown them on their own resources. They were left a good deal to themselves. Then Mrs. Hardy died and Olive came home to England and went back to her father. She was eighteen then and Tim was seventeen. A year later the war broke out, Tim joined up and his father, who was over fifty, got some job at Portsmouth. I take it he had been a hard liver and a heavy drinker. He broke down before the end of the war and died after a lingering illness. They don't seem to have had any relations. They were the last of a rather old family; they had a fine old house in Dorsetshire that had belonged to them for a good many generations, but they had never been able to afford to live in it and it was always let. I remember seeing photographs of it. It was very much a gentleman's house, of grey stone and rather stately, with a coat of arms carved over the front door and mullioned windows. Their great ambition was to make enough money to be able to live in it. They used to talk about it a lot. They never spoke as though either of them would marry, but always as though it were a settled thing that they would remain together. It was rather funny considering how young they were."

"How old were they then?" I asked.

"Well, I suppose he was twenty-five or twenty-six and she was a year older. They were awfully kind to me when I first went up to Sibuku. They took a fancy to me at once. You see, we had more in common than most of the people there. I think they were glad of my company. They weren't particularly popular."

"Why not?" I asked.

"They were rather reserved and you couldn't help seeing that they liked their own society better than other people's. I don't know if you've noticed it, but that always seems to put people's backs up. They resent it somehow if they have a feeling that you can get along very well without them."

"It's tiresome, isn't it?" I said.

"It was rather a grievance to the other planters that Tim

was his own master and had private means. They had to put
up with an old Ford to get about in, but Tim had a real car.
Tim and Olive were very nice when they came to the club
and they played in the tennis tournaments and all that sort
of thing, but you had an impression that they were always
glad to get away again. They'd dine out with people and
make themselves very pleasant, but it was pretty obvious that
they'd just as soon have stayed at home. If you had any sense
you couldn't blame them. I don't know if you've been much to
planters' houses. They're a bit dreary. A lot of gimcrack
furniture and silver ornaments and tiger skins. And the food's
uneatable. But the Hardys had made their bungalow rather
nice. There was nothing very grand in it; it was just easy
and homelike and comfortable. Their living-room was like a
drawing-room in an English country house. You felt that
their things meant something to them and that they had had
them a long time. It was a very jolly house to stay at. The
bungalow was in the middle of the estate, but it was on the
brow of a little hill and you looked right over the rubber
trees to the sea in the distance. Olive took a lot of trouble
with her garden and it was really topping. I never saw such a
show of cannas. I used to go there for week-ends. It was only
about half an hour's drive to the sea and we'd take our lunch
with us and bathe and sail. Tim kept a small boat there. Those
days were grand. I never knew one could enjoy oneself so
much. It's a beautiful bit of coast and it was really extraordinarily romantic. Then in the evenings we'd play patience and
chess or turn on the gramophone. The cooking was damned
good too. It was a change from what one generally got.
Olive had taught their cook to make all sorts of Italian dishes
and we used to have great wallops of macaroni and risotto
and gnocchi and things like that. I couldn't help envying
them their life, it was so jolly and peaceful, and when they
talked of what they'd do when they went back to England
for good I used to tell them they'd always regret what they'd
left.

" 'We've been very happy here,' said Olive.

"She had a way of looking at Tim, with a slow, sidelong

glance from under her long eyelashes, that was rather engaging.

"In their own house they were quite different from what they were when they went out. They were so easy and cordial. Everybody admitted that and I'm bound to say that people enjoyed going there. They often asked people over. They had the gift of making you feel at home. It was a very happy house, if you know what I mean. Of course no one could help seeing how attached they were to one another. And whatever people said about their being standoffish and self-centred, they were bound to be rather touched by the affection they had for one another. People said they couldn't have been more united if they were married, and when you saw how some couples got on you couldn't help thinking they made most marriages look rather like a washout. They seemed to think the same things at the same time. They had little private jokes that made them laugh like children. They were so charming with one another, so gay and happy, that really to stay with them was, well, a spiritual refreshment. I don't know what else you could call it. When you left them, after a couple of days at the bungalow, you felt that you'd absorbed some of their peace and their sober gaiety. It was as though your soul had been sluiced with cool clear water. You felt strangely purified."

It was singular to hear Featherstone talking in this exalted strain. He looked so spruce in his smart white coat, technically known as a bum-freezer, his moustache was so trim, his thick curly hair so carefully brushed, that his high-flown language made me a trifle uncomfortable. But I realized that he was trying to express in his clumsy way a very sincerely felt emotion.

"What was Olive Hardy like?" I asked.

"I'll show you. I've got quite a lot of snapshots."

He got up from his chair and going to a shelf brought me a large album. It was the usual thing, indifferent photographs of people in groups and unflattering likenesses of single figures. They were in bathing dress or in shorts or tennis things, generally with their faces all screwed up because the sun blinded them, or puckered by the distortion of laughter. I recognized Hardy, not much changed after ten years, with his wisp of hair hanging across his forehead. I remembered him better now that I saw the snapshots. In them he looked nice and fresh and young. He had an alertness of expression that was attractive and that I certainly had not noticed when I saw him. In his eyes was a sort of eagerness for life that danced and sparkled through the fading print. I glanced at the photographs of his sister. Her bathing dress showed that she had a good figure, well-developed, but slender; and her legs were long and slim.

"They look rather alike," I said.

"Yes, although she was a year older they might have been twins, they were so much alike. They both had the same oval face and that pale skin without any colour in the cheeks, and they both had those soft brown eyes, very liquid and appealing, so that you felt whatever they did you could never be angry with them. And they both had a sort of careless elegance that made them look charming whatever they wore and however untidy they were. He's lost that now, I suppose, but he certainly had it when I first knew him. They always rather reminded me of the brother and sister in Twelfth Night. You know whom I mean."

"Viola and Sebastian."

"They never seemed to belong quite to the present. There was something Elizabethan about them. I don't think it was only because I was very young then that I couldn't help feeling they were strangely romantic somehow. I could see them living in Illyria."

I gave one of the snapshots another glance.

"The girl looks as though she had a good deal more character than her brother," I remarked.

"She had. I don't know if you'd have called Olive beautiful, but she was awfully attractive. There was something poetic in her, a sort of lyrical quality as it were, that coloured her movements, her acts and everything about her. It seemed to exalt her above common cares. There was something so candid in her expression, so courageous and independent in her bearing, that—oh, I don't know, it made mere beauty just flat and dull."

"You speak as if you'd been in love with her," I interrupted.

"Of course I was. I should have thought you'd guessed that at once. I was frightfully in love with her."

"Was it love at first sight?" I smiled.

"Yes, I think it was, but I didn't know it for a month or so. When it suddenly struck me that what I felt for her—I don't know how to explain it, it was a sort of shattering turmoil that affected every bit of me—that that was love, I knew I'd felt it all along. It was not only her looks, though they were awfully alluring, the smoothness of her pale skin and the way her hair fell over her forehead and the grave sweetness of her brown eyes, it was more than that; you had a sensation of well-being when you were with her, as though you could relax and be quite natural and needn't pretend to be anything you weren't. You felt she was incapable of meanness. It was impossible to think of her as envious of other people or catty. She seemed to have a natural generosity of soul. One could be silent with her for an hour at a time and yet feel that one had had a good time."

"A rare gift," I said.

"She was a wonderful companion. If you made a suggestion to do something she was always glad to fall in with it. She was the least exacting girl I ever knew. You could throw her over at the last minute and however disappointed she was it made no difference. Next time you saw her she was just as cordial and serene as ever."

"Why didn't you marry her?"

Featherstone's cheroot had gone out. He threw the stub away and deliberately lit another. He did not answer for a while. It may seem strange to persons who live in a highly civilized state that he should confide these intimate things to a stranger; it did not seem strange to me. I was used to it. People who lived so desperately alone, in the remote places of the earth, find it a relief to tell someone whom in all probability they will never meet again the story that has burdened perhaps for years their waking thoughts and their dreams at night. And I have an inkling that the fact of your being a writer attracts their confidence. They feel that what they tell you will excite your interest in an impersonal way that makes it easier for them to discharge their souls. Besides, as we all know from our own experience, it is never unpleasant to talk about oneself.

"Why didn't you marry her?" I had asked him.

"I wanted to badly enough," Featherstone answered at length. "But I hesitated to ask her. Although she was always so nice to me and so easy to get on with, and we were such good friends, I always felt that there was something a little mysterious in her. Although she was so simple, so frank and natural, you never quite got over the feeling of an inner kernel of aloofness, as if deep in her heart she guarded, not a secret, but a sort of privacy of the soul that not a living person would ever be allowed to know. I don't know if I make myself clear."

"I think so."

"I put it down to her upbringing. They never talked of their mother, but somehow I got the impression that she was one of those neurotic, emotional women who wreck their own happiness and are a pest to everyone connected with them. I had a suspicion that she'd led rather a hectic life in Florence and it struck me that Olive owed her beautiful serenity to a disciplined effort of her own will and that her aloofness was a sort of citadel she'd built to protect herself from the knowledge of all sorts of shameful things. But of course that aloofness was awfully captivating. It was strangely exciting to think that if she loved you, and you were married to her, you would at last pierce right into the hidden heart of that mystery; and you felt that if you could share that with her it would be as it were a consummation of all you'd ever desired in your life. Heaven wouldn't be in it. You know, I felt about it just like Bluebeard's wife about the forbidden chamber in the castle. Every room was open to me, but I should never rest till I had gone into that last one that was locked against me."

My eye was caught by a chik-chak, a little brown house lizard with a large head, high up on the wall. It is a friendly little beast and it is good to see it in a house. It watched a fly. It was quite still. On a sudden it made a dart and then as the fly flew away fell back with a sort of jerk into a strange immobility.

"And there was another thing that made me hesitate. I couldn't bear the thought that if I proposed to her and she refused me she wouldn't let me come to the bungalow in the same old way. I should have hated that, I enjoyed going there so awfully. It made me so happy to be with her. But you know, sometimes one can't help oneself. I did ask her at last, but it was almost by accident. One evening, after dinner, when we were sitting on the verandah by ourselves, I took her hand. She withdrew it at once.

" 'Why did you do that?' I asked her.

" 'I don't very much like being touched,' she said. She turned her head a little and smiled. 'Are you hurt? You mustn't mind, it's just a funny feeling I have. I can't help it.'

" 'I wonder if it's ever occurred to you that I'm frightfully fond of you,' I said.

"I expect I was terribly awkward about it, but I'd never proposed to anyone before." Featherstone gave a little sound that was not quite a chuckle and not quite a sigh. "For the matter of that, I've never proposed to anyone since. She didn't say anything for a minute. Then she said:

" 'I'm very glad, but I don't think I want you to be anything more than that.'

" 'Why not?' I asked.

" 'I could never leave Tim.'

" 'But supposing he marries?'

" 'He never will.'

"I'd gone so far then that I thought I'd better go on. But my throat was so dry that I could hardly speak. I was shaking with nervousness.

" 'I'm frightfully in love with you, Olive. I want to marry you more than anything in the world.'

"She put her hand very gently on my arm. It was like a flower falling to the ground.

" 'No, dear, I can't,' she said.

"I was silent. It was difficult for me to say what I wanted to. I'm naturally rather shy. She was a girl. I couldn't very well tell her that it wasn't quite the same thing living with a husband and living with a brother. She was normal and healthy; she must want to have babies; it wasn't reasonable to starve her natural instincts. It was such a waste of her youth. But it was she who spoke first.

" 'Don't let's talk about this any more,' she said. 'D'you mind? It did strike me once or twice that perhaps you cared for me. Tim noticed it. I was sorry because I was afraid it would break up our friendship. I don't want it to do that, Mark. We do get on so well together, the three of us, and we have such jolly times. I don't know what we should do without you now.'

" 'I thought of that too,' I said.

" 'D'you think it need?' she asked me.

" 'My dear, I don't want it to,' I said. 'You must know how much I love coming here. I've never been so happy anywhere before!'

" 'You're not angry with me?'

" 'Why should I be? It's not your fault. It only means that you're not in love with me. If you were you wouldn't care a hang about Tim.'

" 'You are rather sweet,' she said.

"She put her arm round my neck and kissed me lightly on the cheek. I had a notion that in her mind it settled our relation. She adopted me as a second brother.

"A few weeks later Tim went back to England. The tenant of their house in Dorset was leaving and though there was another in the offing, he thought he ought to be on the spot to conduct negotiations. And he wanted some new machinery for the estate. He thought he'd get it at the same time. He didn't expect to be gone more than three months and Olive made up her mind not to go. She knew hardly anyone in England, and it was practically a foreign country to her, she didn't mind being left alone, and she wanted to look after the estate. Of course they could have put a manager in charge, but that wasn't the same thing. Rubber was falling and in case of accidents it was just as well that one or other of them should be there. I promised Tim I'd look after her and if she wanted me she could always call me up. My proposal hadn't changed anything. We carried on as though nothing had happened. I don't know whether she'd told Tim. He made no sign that he knew. Of course I loved her as much as ever, but I kept it to myself. I have a good deal of self-control, you know. I had a sort of feeling I hadn't a chance. I hoped eventually my love would change into something else and we could just be wonderful friends. It's funny, it never has, you know. I suppose I was hit too badly ever to get quite over it.

"She went down to Penang to see Tim off and when she came back I met her at the station and drove her home. I couldn't very well stay at the bungalow while Tim was away, but I went over every Sunday and had tiffin and we'd go down to the sea and have a bathe. People tried to be kind to her and asked her to stay with them, but she wouldn't. She seldom left the estate. She had plenty to do. She read a lot. She was never bored. She seemed quite happy in her own company, and when she had visitors it was only from a sense of duty. She didn't want them to think her ungracious. But it was an effort and she told me she heaved a sigh of relief when she saw the last of them and could again enjoy without disturbance the peaceful loneliness of the bungalow. She was a very curious girl. It was strange that at her age she should be so indifferent to parties and the other small gaieties the station afforded. Spiritually, if you know what I mean, she was entirely self-supporting. I don't know how people found out that I was in love with her; I thought I'd never given myself away in anything, but I had hints here and there that they knew. I gathered they thought Olive hadn't gone home with her brother on my account. One woman, a Mrs. Sergison, the policeman's wife, actually asked me when they were going to be able to congratulate me. Of course I pretended I didn't know what she was talking about, but it didn't go down very well. I couldn't help being amused. I meant so little to Olive in that way that I really believe she'd entirely forgotten that I'd asked her to marry me. I can't say she was unkind to me, I don't think she could have been unkind to anyone; but she treated me with just the casualness with which a sister might treat a younger brother. She was two or three years older than I. She was always terribly glad to see me, but it never occurred to her to put herself out for me, she was almost amazingly intimate with me; but unconsciously, you know, as you might be with a person you'd known so well all your life that you never thought of putting on frills with him, I might not have been a man at all, but an old coat that she wore all the time because it was easy and comfortable and she didn't mind what she did in it. I should have been crazy not to see that she was a thousand miles away from loving me.

"Then one day, three of four weeks before Tim was due back, when I went to the bungalow I saw she'd been crying. I was startled. She was always so composed. I'd never seen her upset over anything.

" 'Hullo, what's the matter?' I said.

" 'Nothing.'

" 'Come off it, darling,' I said. 'What have you been crying about?'

"She tried to smile.

" 'I wish you hadn't got such sharp eyes,' she said. 'I think I'm being silly. I've just had a cable from Tim to say he's postponed his sailing.'

" 'Oh, my dear, I am sorry,' I said. 'You must be awfully disappointed.'

" 'I've been counting the days. I want him back so badly.'

" 'Does he say why he's postponing?' I asked.

" 'No, he says he's writing. I'll show you the cable.'

"I saw that she was very nervous. Her slow quiet eyes were filled with apprehension and there was a little frown of anxiety between her brows. She went into her bedroom and in a moment came back with the cable. I felt that she was watching me anxiously as I read. So far as I remember it ran: *Darling, I cannot sail on the seventh after all. Please forgive me. Am writing fully. Fondest love. Tim.*

"'Well, perhaps the machinery he wanted isn't ready and he can't bring himself to sail without it,' I said.

"'What could it matter if it came by a later ship? Anyhow, it'll be hung up at Penang.'

"'It may be something about the house.'

"'If it is why doesn't he say so? He must know how frightfully anxious I am.'

"'It wouldn't occur to him,' I said. 'After all, when you're away you don't realize that the people you've left behind don't know something that you take as a matter of course.'

"She smiled again, but now more happily.

"'I daresay you're right. In point of fact Tim is a little like that. He's always been rather slack and casual. I daresay I've been making a mountain out of a molehill. I must just wait patiently for his letter.'

"Olive was a girl with a lot of self-control and I saw her by an effort of will pull herself together. The little line between her eyebrows vanished and she was once more her serene, smiling and kindly self. She was always gentle: that day she had a mildness so heavenly that it was shattering. But for the rest of the time I could see that she kept her restlessness in check only by the deliberate exercise of her common sense. It was as though she had a foreboding of ill. I was with her the day before the mail was due. Her anxiety was all the more pitiful to see because she took such pains to hide it. I was always busy on mail day, but I promised to go up to the estate later on and hear the news. I was just thinking of starting when Hardy's seis came along in the car with a message from the amah asking me to go at once to her mistress. The amah was a decent, elderly woman to whom I had given a dollar or two and said that if anything went wrong on the estate she was to let me know at once. I jumped into my car. When I arrived I found the amah waiting for me on the steps.

"'A letter came this morning,' she said.

"I interrupted her. I ran up the steps. The sitting-room was empty.

" 'Olive,' I called.

"I went into the passage and suddenly I heard a sound that froze my heart. The amah had followed me and now she opened the door of Olive's room. The sound I had heard was the sound of Olive crying. I went in. She was lying on her bed, on her face, and her sobs shook her from head to foot. I put my hand on her shoulder.

" 'Olive, what is it?' I asked.

" 'Who's that?' she cried. She sprang to her feet suddenly, as though she were scared out of her wits. And then: 'Oh, it's you,' she said. She stood in front of me, with her head thrown back and her eyes closed, and the tears streamed from them. It was dreadful. 'Tim's married,' she gasped, and her face screwed up in a sort of grimace of pain.

"I must admit that for one moment I had a thrill of exultation, it was like a little electric shock tingling through my heart; it struck me that now I had a chance, she might be willing to marry me; I know it was terribly selfish of me; you see, the news had taken me by surprise; but it was only for a moment, after that I was melted by her awful distress and the only thing I felt was deep sorrow because she was unhappy. I put my arm round her waist.

" 'Oh, my dear, I'm so sorry,' I said. 'Don't stay here. Come into the sitting-room and sit down and we'll talk about it. Let me give you something to drink.'

"She let me lead her into the next room and we sat down on the sofa. I told the amah to fetch the whisky and syphon and I mixed her a good strong stengah and made her drink a little. I took her in my arms and rested her head on my shoulder. She let me do what I liked with her. The great tears streamed down her poor face.

" 'How could he?' she moaned. 'How could he?'

" 'My darling,' I said, 'it was bound to happen sooner or later. He's a young man. How could you expect him never to marry? It's only natural.'

" 'No, no, no,' she gasped.

"Tight-clenched in her hand I saw that she had a letter and I guessed that it was Tim's.

" 'What does he say?' I asked.

"She gave a frightened movement and clutched the letter to her heart as though she thought I would take it from her.

" 'He says he couldn't help himself. He says he had to. What does it mean?'

" 'Well, you know, in his way he's just as attractive as you are. He has so much charm. I suppose he just fell madly in love with some girl and she with him.'

" 'He's so weak,' she moaned.

" 'Are they coming out?' I asked.

" 'They sailed yesterday. He says it won't make any difference. He's insane. How *can* I stay here?'

"She began to cry hysterically. It was torture to see that girl, usually so calm, utterly shattered by her emotion. I had always felt that her lovely serenity masked a capacity for deep feeling. But the abandon of her distress simply broke me up. I held her in my arms and kissed her, her eyes and her wet cheek and her hair. I don't think she knew what I was doing. I was hardly conscious of it myself. I was so deeply moved.

" 'What shall I do?' she wailed.

" 'Why won't you marry me?' I said.

"She tried to withdraw herself from me, but I wouldn't let her go.

" 'After all, it would be a way out,' I said.

" 'How can I marry you?' she moaned. 'I'm years older than you are.'

" 'Oh, what nonsense, two or three. What do I care?'

" 'No, no.'

" 'Why not?' I said.

" 'I don't love you,' she said.

" 'What does that matter? I love you.'

"I don't know what I said. I told her that I'd try to make her happy. I said I'd never ask anything from her but what she was prepared to give me. I talked and talked. I tried to make her see reason. I felt that she didn't want to stay there, in the same place as Tim, and I told her that I'd be moved soon to some other district. I thought that might tempt her. She couldn't deny that we'd always got on awfully well together. After a time she did seem to grow a little quieter. I had a feeling that she was listening to me. I had even a sort of feeling that she knew that she was lying in my arms and that it comforted her. I made her drink a drop more whisky. I gave her a cigarette. At last I thought I might be just mildly facetious.

" You know, I'm not a bad sort really,' I said. 'You might do worse.'

" 'You don't know me,' she said. 'You know nothing whatever about me.'

" 'I'm capable of learning,' I said.

"She smiled a little.

" 'You're awfully kind, Mark,' she said.

" 'Say yes, Olive,' I begged.

"She gave a deep sigh. For a long time she stared at the ground. But she did not move and I felt the softness of her body in my arms. I waited. I was frightfully nervous and the minutes seemed endless.

" 'All right,' she said at last, as though she were not conscious that any time had passed between my prayer and her answer.

"I was so moved that I had nothing to say. But when I wanted to kiss her lips, she turned her face away, and wouldn't let me. I wanted us to be married at once, but she was quite firm that she wouldn't. She insisted on waiting till Tim came back. You know how sometimes you see so clearly in people's thoughts that you're more certain of them than if they'd spoken them; I saw that she couldn't quite believe that what Tim had written was true and that she had a sort of miserable hope that it was all a mistake and he wasn't married after all. It gave me a pang, but I loved her so much, I just bore it. I was willing to bear anything. I adored her. She wouldn't even let me tell anyone that we were engaged. She made me promise not to say a word till Tim's return. She said she couldn't bear the thought of the congratulations and all that. She wouldn't even let me make any announcement of Tim's marriage. She

was obstinate about it. I had a notion that she felt if the fact
were spread about it gave it a certainty that she didn't want it
to have.

"But the matter was taken out of her hands. News travels
mysteriously in the East. I don't know what Olive had said
in the amah's hearing when first she received the news of
Tim's marriage; anyhow, the Hardys' seis told the Sergisons'
and Mrs. Sergison attacked me the next time I went into the
club.

" 'I hear Tim Hardy's married,' she said.

" 'Oh?' I answered, unwilling to commit myself.

"She smiled at my blank face, and told me that her amah
having told her the rumour she had rung up Olive and asked
her if it was true. Olive's answer had been rather odd. She had
not exactly confirmed it, but said that she had received a letter
from Tim telling her he was married.

" 'She's a strange girl,' said Mrs. Sergison. 'When I asked
her for details she said she had none to give and when I said:
"Aren't you thrilled?" she didn't answer.'

" 'Olive's devoted to Tim, Mrs. Sergison,' I said. 'His marriage has naturally been a shock to her. She knows nothing
about Tim's wife. She's nervous about her.'

" 'And when are you two going to be married?' she asked
me abruptly.

" 'What an embarrassing question!' I said, trying to laugh it
off.

"She looked at me shrewdly.

" 'Will you give me your word of honour that you're not engaged to her?'

"I didn't like to tell her a deliberate lie, nor to ask her to
mind her own business, and I'd promised Olive faithfully that
I would say nothing till Tim got back. I hedged.

" 'Mrs. Sergison,' I said, 'when there's anything to tell I
promise that you'll be the first person to hear it. All I can say
to you now is that I do want to marry Olive more than anything in the world.'

" 'I'm very glad that Tim's married,' she answered. 'And I
hope she'll marry you very soon. It was a morbid and un-

healthy life that they led up there, those two, they kept far too much to themselves and they were far too much absorbed in one another.'

"I saw Olive practically every day. I felt that she didn't want me to make love to her, and I contented myself with kissing her when I came and when I went. She was very nice to me, kindly and thoughtful; I knew she was glad to see me and sorry when it was time for me to go. Ordinarily, she was apt to fall into silence, but during this time she talked more than I had ever heard her talk before. But never of the future and never of Tim and his wife. She told me a lot about her life in Florence with her mother. She had led a strange lonely life, mostly with servants and governesses, while her mother, I suspected, engaged in one affair after another with vague Italian counts and Russian princes. I guessed that by the time she was fourteen there wasn't much she didn't know. It was natural for her to be quite unconventional: in the only world she knew till she was eighteen conventions weren't mentioned because they didn't exist. Gradually, Olive seemed to regain her serenity and I should have thought that she was beginning to accustom herself to the thought of Tim's marriage if it hadn't been that I couldn't but notice how pale and tired she looked. I made up my mind that the moment he arrived I'd press her to marry me at once. I could get short leave whenever I asked for it, and by the time that was up I thought I could manage a transfer to some other post. What she wanted was change of air and fresh scenes.

"We knew, of course, within a day when Tim's ship would reach Penang, but it was a question whether she'd get in soon enough for him to catch the train and I wrote to the P. & O. agent asking him to telegraph as soon as he had definite news. When I got the wire and took it up to Olive I found that she'd just received one from Tim. The ship had docked early and he was arriving next day. The train was supposed to get in at eight o'clock in the morning, but it was liable to be anything from one to six hours late, and I bore with me an invitation from Mrs. Sergison asking Olive to come back with me to stay the night with her so that she would be on the spot and

need not go to the station till the news came through that the
train was coming.

"I was immensely relieved. I thought that when the blow
at last fell Olive wouldn't feel it so much. She had worked herself up into such a state that I couldn't help thinking that she
must have a reaction now. She might take a fancy to her
sister-in-law. There was no reason why they shouldn't all three
get on very well together. To my surprise Olive said she
wasn't coming down to the station to meet them.

" 'They'll be awfully disappointed,' I said.

" 'I'd rather wait here,' she answered. She smiled a little.
'Don't argue with me, Mark, I've quite made up my mind.'

" 'I've ordered breakfast in my house,' I said.

" 'That's all right. You meet them and take them to your
house and give them breakfast, and then they can come along
here afterwards. Of course I'll send the car down.'

" 'I don't suppose they'll want to breakfast if you're not
there,' I said.

" 'Oh, I'm sure they will. If the train gets in on time they
wouldn't have thought of breakfasting before it arrived and
they'll be hungry. They won't want to take this long drive
without anything to eat.'

"I was puzzled. She had been looking forward so intensely
to Tim's coming, it seemed strange that she should want to
wait all by herself while the rest of us were having a jolly
breakfast. I supposed she was nervous and wanted to delay as
long as possible meeting the strange woman who had come to
take her place. It seemed unreasonable. I couldn't see that an
hour sooner or an hour later could make any difference, but I
knew women were funny, and anyhow I felt Olive wasn't in
the mood for me to press it.

" 'Telephone when you're starting so that I shall know
when to expect you,' she said.

" 'All right,' I said, 'but you know I shan't be able to come
with them. It's my day for going to Lahad.'

"This was a town that I had to go to once a week to take
cases. It was a good way off and one had to ferry across a
river, which took some time, so that I never got back till late.

There were a few Europeans there and a club. I generally had to go on there for a bit to be sociable and see that things were getting along all right.

" 'Besides,' I added, 'with Tim bringing his wife home for the first time I don't suppose he'll want me about. But if you'd like to ask me to dinner I'll be glad to come to that.'

"Olive smiled.

" 'I don't think it'll be my place to issue any more invitations, will it?' she said. 'You must ask the bride.'

"She said this so lightly that my heart leaped. I had a feeling that at last she had made up her mind to accept the altered circumstances and, what was more, was accepting them with cheerfulness. She asked me to stay to dinner. Generally I left about eight and dined at home. She was very sweet, almost tender, and I was happier than I'd been for weeks, I had never been more desperately in love with her. I had a couple of gin pahits and I think I was in rather good form at dinner. I know I made her laugh. I felt that at last she was casting away the load of misery that had oppressed her. That was why I didn't let myself be very much disturbed by what happened at the end.

" 'Don't you think it's about time you were leaving a presumably maiden lady?' she said.

"She spoke in a manner that was so quietly gay that I answered without hesitation:

" 'Oh, my dear, if you think you've got a shred of reputation left you deceive yourself. You're surely not under the impression that the ladies of Sibuku don't know that I've been coming to see you every day for a month. The general feeling is that if we're not married it's high time we were. Don't you think it would be just as well if I broke it to them that we're engaged?'

" 'Oh, Mark, you mustn't take our engagement very seriously,' she said.

"I laughed.

" 'How else do you expect me to take it? It is serious.'

"She shook her head a little.

" 'No. I was upset and hysterical that day. You were being

very sweet to me. I said yes because I was too miserable to say no. But now I've had time to collect myself. Don't think me unkind. I made a mistake. I've been very much to blame. You must forgive me.'

" 'Oh, darling, you're talking nonsense. You've got nothing against me.'

"She looked at me steadily. She was quite calm. She had even a little smile at the back of her eyes.

" 'I can't marry you. I can't marry anyone. It was absurd of me ever to think I could.'

"I didn't answer at once. She was in a queer state and I thought it better not to insist.

" 'I suppose I can't drag you to the altar by main force,' I said.

"I held out my hand and she gave me hers. I put my arm round her, and she made no attempt to withdraw. She suffered me to kiss her as usual on her cheek.

"Next morning I met the train. For once in a way it was punctual. Tim waved to me as his carriage passed the place where I was standing, and by the time I had walked up he had already jumped out and was handing down his wife. He grasped my hand warmly.

" 'Where's Olive?' he said, with a glance along the platform. 'This is Sally.'

"I shook hands with her and at the same time explained why Olive was not there.

" 'It was frightfully early, wasn't it?' said Mrs. Hardy.

"I told them that the plan was for them to come and have a bit of breakfast at my house and then drive home.

" 'I'd love a bath,' said Mrs. Hardy.

" 'You shall have one,' I said.

"She was really an extremely pretty little thing, very fair, with enormous blue eyes and a lovely little straight nose. Her skin, all milk and roses, was exquisite. A little of the chorus girl type, of course, and you may happen to think that rather namby-pamby, but in that style she was enchanting. We drove to my house, they both had a bath and Tim a shave; I just had two minutes alone with him. He asked me how Olive had taken his marriage. I told him she'd been upset.

" 'I was afraid so,' he said, frowning a little. He gave a short sigh. 'I couldn't do anything else.'

"I didn't understand what he meant. At that moment Mrs. Hardy joined us and slipped her arm through her husband's. He took her hand in his and gently pressed it. He gave her a look that had in it something pleased and humorously affectionate, as though he didn't take her quite seriously, but enjoyed his sense of proprietorship and was proud of her beauty. She really was lovely. She was not at all shy, she asked me to call her Sally before we'd known one another ten minutes, and she was quick on the uptake. Of course, just then she was excited at arriving. She'd never been East and everything thrilled her. It was quite obvious that she was head over heels in love with Tim. Her eyes never left him and she hung on his words. We had a jolly breakfast and then we parted. They got into their car to go home and I into mine to go to Lahad. I promised to go straight to the estate from there and in point of fact it was out of my way to pass by my house. I took a change with me. I didn't see why Olive shouldn't like Sally very much, she was frank and gay, and ingenuous; she was extremely young, she couldn't have been more than nineteen, and her wonderful prettiness couldn't fail to appeal to Olive. I was just as glad to have had a reasonable excuse to leave the three of them by themselves for the day, but as I started out from Lahad I had a notion that by the time I arrived they would all be pleased to see me. I drove up to the bungalow and blew my horn two or three times, expecting someone to appear. Not a soul. The place was in total darkness. I was surprised. It was absolutely silent. I couldn't make it out. They must be in. Very odd, I thought. I waited a moment, then got out of the car and walked up the steps. At the top of them I stumbled over something. I swore and bent down to see what it was; it had felt like a body. There was a cry and I saw it was the amah. She shrank back cowering as I touched her and broke into loud wails.

" 'What the hell's the matter?' I cried, and then I felt a hand on my arm and heard a voice. 'Tuan, Tuan.' I turned and in the darkness recognized Tim's head boy. He began to speak in little frightened gasps. I listened to him with horror. What he told me was unspeakable. I pushed him aside and rushed into the house. The sitting-room was dark. I turned on the light. The first thing I saw was Sally huddled up in an armchair. She was startled by my sudden appearance and cried out. I could hardly speak. I asked her if it was true. When she told me it was I felt the room suddenly going round and round me. I had to sit down. As the car that bore Tim and Sally drove up the road that led to the house and Tim sounded the claxon to announce their arrival and the boys and the amah ran out to greet them there was the sound of a shot. They ran to Olive's room and found her lying in front of the looking-glass in a pool of blood. She had shot herself with Tim's revolver.

" 'Is she dead?' I said.

" 'No, they sent for the doctor, and he took her to the hospital.'

"I hardly knew what I was doing. I didn't even trouble to tell Sally where I was going. I got up and staggered to the door. I got into the car and told my seis to drive like hell to the hospital. I rushed in. I asked where she was. They tried to bar my way, but I pushed them aside. I knew where the private rooms were. Someone clung to my arm, but I shook him off. I vaguely understood that the doctor had given instructions that no one was to go into the room. I didn't care about that. There was an orderly at the door; he put out his arm to prevent me from passing. I swore at him and told him to get out of my way. I suppose I made a row, I was beside myself; the door was opened and the doctor came out.

" 'Who's making all this noise?' he said. 'Oh, it's you. What do you want?'

" 'Is she dead?' I asked.

" 'No. But she's unconscious. She never regained consciousness. It's only a matter of an hour or two.'

" 'I want to see her.'

" 'You can't.'

" 'I'm engaged to her.'

" 'You?' he cried, and even at that moment I was aware that he looked at me strangely. 'That's all the more reason.'

"I didn't know what he meant. I was stupid with horror.

" 'Surely you can do something to save her,' I cried.

"He shook his head.

" 'If you saw her you wouldn't wish it,' he said.

"I stared at him aghast. In the silence I heard a man's convulsive sobbing.

" 'Who's that?' I asked.

" 'Her brother.'

"Then I felt a hand on my arm. I looked round and saw it was Mrs. Sergison.

" 'My poor boy,' she said, 'I'm so sorry for you.'

" 'What on earth made her do it?' I groaned.

" 'Come away, my dear,' said Mrs. Sergison. 'You can do no good here.'

" 'No, I must stay,' I said.

" 'Well, go and sit in my room,' said the doctor.

"I was so broken that I let Mrs. Sergison take me by the arm and lead me into the doctor's private room. She made me sit down. I couldn't bring myself to realize that it was true. I thought it was a horrible nightmare from which I must awake. I don't know how long we sat there. Three hours. Four hours. At last the doctor came in.

" 'It's all over,' he said.

"Then I couldn't help myself, I began to cry. I didn't care what they thought of me. I was so frightfully unhappy.

"We buried her next day.

"Mrs. Sergison came back to my house and sat with me for a while. She wanted me to go to the club with her. I hadn't the heart. She was very kind, but I was glad when she left me by myself. I tried to read, but the words meant nothing to me. I felt dead inside. My boy came in and turned on the lights. My head was aching like mad. Then he came back and said that a lady wished to see me. I asked who it was. He wasn't quite sure, but he thought it must be the new wife of the tuan at Putatan. I couldn't imagine what she wanted. I

got up and went to the door. He was right. It was Sally. I
asked her to come in. I noticed that she was deathly white. I
felt sorry for her. It was a frightful experience for a girl of
that age and for a bride a miserable home-coming. She sat
down. She was very nervous. I tried to put her at her ease by
saying conventional things. She made me very uncomfortable
because she stared at me with those enormous blue eyes of
hers, and they were simply ghastly with horror. She interrupted me suddenly.

" 'You're the only person here I know,' she said. 'I had to
come to you. I want you to get me away from here.'

"I was dumbfounded.

" 'What *do* you mean?' I said.

" 'I don't want you to ask me any questions. I just want you
to get me away. At once. I want to go back to England!'

" 'But you can't leave Tim like that just now,' I said. 'My
dear, you must pull yourself together. I know it's been awful
for you. But think of Tim. I mean, he'll be miserable. If you
have any love for him the least you can do is to try and make
him a little less unhappy.'

" 'Oh, you don't know,' she cried. 'I can't tell you. It's too
horrible. I beseech you to help me. If there's a train to-night
let me get on it. If I can only get to Penang I can get a ship.
I can't stay in this place another night. I shall go mad.'

"I was absolutely bewildered.

" 'Does Tim know?' I asked her.

" 'I haven't seen Tim since last night. I'll never see him
again. I'd rather die.'

"I wanted to gain a little time.

" 'But how can you go without your things? Have you got
any luggage?'

" 'What does that matter?' she cried impatiently. 'I've got
what I want for the journey.'

" 'Have you any money?'

" 'Enough. Is there a train to-night?'

" 'Yes,' I said. 'It's due just after midnight.'

" 'Thank God. Will you arrange everything? Can I stay
here till then?'

" 'You're putting me in a frightful position,' I said. 'I don't know what to do for the best. You know, it's an awfully serious step you're taking.'

" 'If you knew everything you'd know it was the only possible thing to do.'

" 'It'll create an awful scandal here. I don't know what people'll say. Have you thought of the effect on Tim?' I was worried and unhappy. 'God knows I don't want to interfere in what isn't my business. But if you want me to help you I ought to know enough to feel justified in doing so. You must tell me what's happened.'

" 'I can't. I can only tell you that I know everything.'

"She hid her face with her hands and shuddered. Then she gave herself a shake as though she were recoiling from some frightful sight.

" 'He had no right to marry me. It was monstrous.'

"And as she spoke her voice rose shrill and piercing. I was afraid she was going to have an attack of hysterics. Her pretty doll-like face was terrified and her eyes stared as though she could never close them again.

" 'Don't you love him any more?' I asked.

" 'After that?'

" 'What will you do if I refuse to help you?' I said.

" 'I suppose there's a clergyman here or a doctor. You can't refuse to take me to one of them.'

" 'How did you get here?'

" 'The head boy drove me. He got a car from somewhere.'

" 'Does Tim know you've gone?'

" 'I left a letter for him.'

" 'He'll know you're here.'

" 'He won't try to stop me. I promise you that. He daren't. For God's sake don't you try either. I tell you I shall go mad if I stay here another night.'

"I sighed. After all she was of an age to decide for herself."

I, the writer of this, hadn't spoken for a long time.

"Did you know what she meant?" I asked Featherstone.

He gave me a long, haggard look.

"There was only one thing she could mean. It was unspeakable. Yes, I knew all right. It explained everything. Poor Olive. Poor sweet. I suppose it was unreasonable of me, at that moment I only felt a horror of that little pretty fair-haired thing with her terrified eyes. I hated her. I didn't say anything for a while. Then I told her I'd do as she wished. She didn't even say thank you. I think she knew what I felt about her. When it was dinner time I made her eat something and then she asked me if there was a room she could go and lie down in till it was time to go to the station. I showed her into my spare room and left her. I sat in the sitting-room and waited. My God, I don't think the time has ever passed so slowly for me. I thought twelve would never strike. I rang up the station and was told the train wouldn't be in till nearly two. At midnight she came back to the sitting-room and we sat there for an hour and a half. We had nothing to say to one another and we didn't speak. Then I took her to the station and put her on the train."

"Was there an awful scandal?"

Featherstone frowned.

"I don't know. I applied for short leave. After that I was moved to another post. I heard that Tim had sold his estate and bought another. But I didn't know where. It was a shock to me at first when I found him here."

Featherstone, getting up, went over to a table and mixed himself a whiskey and soda. In the silence that fell now I heard the monotonous chorus of the croaking frogs. And suddenly the bird that is known as the fever-bird, perched in a tree close to the house, began to call. First, three notes in a descending, chromatic scale, then five, then four. The varying notes of the scale succeeded one another with maddening persistence. One was compelled to listen and to count them, and because one did not know how many there would be it tortured one's nerves.

"Blast that bird," said Featherstone. "That means no sleep for me to-night."

The Round Dozen

I LIKE Elsom. It is a seaside resort in the south of England, not very far from Brighton, and it has something of the late Georgian charm of that agreeable town. But it is neither bustling nor garish. Ten years ago, when I used to go there not infrequently, you might still see here and there an old house, solid and pretentious in no unpleasing fashion (like a decayed gentlewoman of good family whose discreet pride in her ancestry amuses rather than offends you) which was built in the reign of the First Gentleman in Europe and where a courtier of fallen fortunes may well have passed his declining years. The main street had a lackadaisical air and the doctor's motor seemed a trifle out of place. The housewives did their housekeeping in a leisurely manner. They gossiped with the butcher as they watched him cut from his great joint of South Down a piece of the best end of the neck, and they asked amiably after the grocer's wife as he put half a pound of tea and a packet of salt into their string bag. I do not know whether Elsom was ever fashionable: it certainly was not so then; but it was respectable and cheap. Elderly ladies, maiden and widowed, lived there. Indian civilians and retired soldiers: they looked forward with little shudders of dismay to August and September which would bring holiday-makers; but did not disdain to let them their houses and on the proceeds spend a few worldly weeks in a Swiss pension. I never knew Elsom at that hectic time when the lodging-houses were full and young men in blazers sauntered along the front, when Pierrots performed on the beach and in the billiard-room at the Dolphin you heard the click of balls till eleven at night. I only knew it in winter.

Then in every house on the sea-front, stucco houses with bow-windows built a hundred years ago, there was a sign to inform you that apartments were to let; and the guests of the Dolphin were waited on by a single waiter and the boots. At ten o'clock the porter came into the smoking-room and looked at you in so marked a manner that you got up and went to bed. Then Elsom was a restful place and the Dolphin a very comfortable inn. It was pleasing to think that the Prince Regent drove over with Mrs. Fitzherbert more than once to drink a dish of tea in its coffee-room. In the hall was a framed letter from Mr. Thackeray ordering a sitting-room and two bedrooms overlooking the sea and giving instructions that a fly should be sent to the station to meet him.

One November, two or three years after the war, having had a bad attack of influenza, I went down to Elsom to regain my strength. I arrived in the afternoon and when I had unpacked my things went for a stroll on the front. The sky was overcast and the calm sea grey and cold. A few seagulls flew close to the shore. Sailing boats, their masts taken down for the winter, were drawn up high on the shingly beach and the bathing huts stood side by side in a long, grey and tattered row. No one was sitting on the benches that the town council had put here and there, but a few people were trudging up and down for exercise. I passed an old colonel with a red nose who stamped along in plus fours followed by a terrier, two elderly women in short skirts and stout shoes and a plain girl in a Tam o' Shanter. I had never seen the front so deserted. The lodging-houses looked like bedraggled old maids waiting for lovers who would never return, and even the friendly Dolphin seemed wan and desolate. My heart sank. Life on a sudden seemed very drab. I returned to the hotel, drew the curtains of my sitting-room, poked the fire and with a book sought to dispel my melancholy. But I was glad enough when it was time to dress for dinner. I went into the coffee-room and found the guests of the hotel already seated. I gave them a casual glance. There was one lady of middle age by herself and there were two elderly gentlemen, golfers probably, with red faces and baldish heads, who ate their food in moody silence. The only other persons in the room were a group of three who sat in the bow-window, and they immediately attracted my surprised attention. The party consisted of an old gentleman and two ladies, one of whom was old and probably his wife, while the other was younger and possibly his daughter. It was the old lady who first excited my interest. She wore a voluminous dress of black silk and a black lace cap; on her wrists were heavy gold bangles and round her neck a substantial gold chain from which hung a large gold locket; at her neck was a large gold brooch. I did not know that anyone still wore jewelry of that sort. Often, passing second-hand jewellers and pawnbrokers, I had lingered for a moment to look at these strangely old-fashioned articles, so solid, costly and hideous, and thought, with a smile in which there was a tinge of sadness, of the women long since dead who had worn them. They suggested the period when the bustle and the flounce were taking the place of the crinoline and the porkpie hat was ousting the poke-bonnet. The British people liked things solid and good in those days. They went to church on Sunday morning and after church walked in the Park. They gave dinner parties of twelve courses where the master of the house carved the beef and the chickens, and after dinner the ladies who could play favoured the company with Mendelssohn's Songs Without Words and the gentleman with the fine baritone voice sang an old English ballad.

The younger woman had her back turned to me and at first I could see only that she had a slim and youthful figure. She had a great deal of brown hair which seemed to be elaborately arranged. She wore a grey dress. The three of them were chatting in low tones and presently she turned her head so that I saw her profile. It was astonishingly beautiful. The nose was straight and delicate, the line of the cheek exquisitely modelled; I saw then that she wore her hair after the manner of Queen Alexandra. The dinner proceeded to its close and the party got up. The old lady sailed out of the room, looking neither to the right nor to the left, and the young one followed her. Then I saw with a shock that she was old. Her frock was simple enough. The skirt was longer than was at

that time worn, and there was something slightly old-fashioned in the cut. I daresay the waist was more clearly indicated than was then usual, but it was a girl's frock. She was
tall, like a heroine of Tennyson's, slight, with long legs and a
graceful carriage. I had seen the nose before: it was the nose
of a Greek goddess; her mouth was beautiful, and her eyes
were large and blue. Her skin was of course a little tight on
the bones, and there were wrinkles on her forehead and about
her eyes, but in youth it must have been lovely. She reminded
you of those Roman ladies with features of an exquisite
regularity whom Alma-Tadema used to paint, but who, notwithstanding their antique dress, were so stubbornly English.
It was a type of cold perfection that one had not seen for five-
and-twenty years. Now it is as dead as the epigram. I was like
an archæologist who finds some long-buried statue and I was
thrilled in so unexpected a manner to hit upon this survival
of a past era. For no day is so dead as the day before yesterday.

The gentleman rose to his feet when the two ladies left, and
then resumed his chair. A waiter brought him a glass of heavy
port. He smelt it, sipped it, and rolled it round his tongue. I
observed him. He was a little man, much shorter than his
imposing wife, well-covered without being stout, with a fine
head of curling grey hair. His face was much wrinkled and it
bore a faintly humorous expression. His lips were tight and his
chin was square. He was, according to our present notions,
somewhat extravagantly dressed. He wore a black velvet
jacket, a frilled shirt with a low collar and a large black tie,
and very wide evening trousers. It gave you vaguely the effect
of costume. Having drunk his port with deliberation, he got
up and sauntered out of the room.

When I passed through the hall, curious to know who these
singular people were, I glanced at the visitors' book. I saw,
written in an angular feminine hand, the writing that was
taught to young ladies in modish schools forty years or so
ago, the names: Mr. and Mrs. Edwin St. Clair and Miss Porchester. Their address was given as 68, Leinster Square, Bays-
water, London. These must be the names and this the address

of the persons who had so much interested me. I asked the manageress who Mr. St. Clair was and she told me that she believed he was something in the City. I went into the billiard-room and knocked the balls about for a little while and then on my way upstairs passed through the lounge. The two red-faced gentlemen were reading the evening paper and the middle-aged lady was dozing over a novel. The party of three sat in a corner. Mrs. St. Clair was knitting, Miss Porchester was busy with embroidery, and Mr. St. Clair was reading aloud in a discreet but resonant tone. As I passed I discovered that he was reading *Bleak House*.

I read and wrote most of the next day, but in the afternoon I went for a walk and on my way home I sat down for a little on one of those convenient benches on the sea-front. It was not quite so cold as the day before and the air was pleasant. For want of anything better to do I watched a figure advancing towards me from a distance. It was a man and as he came nearer I saw that it was rather a shabby little man. He wore a thin black greatcoat and a somewhat battered bowler. He walked with his hands in his pockets and looked cold. He gave me a glance as he passed by, went on a few steps, hesitated, stopped and turned back. When he came up once more to the bench on which I sat he took a hand out of his pocket and touched his hat. I noticed that he wore shabby black gloves, and surmised that he was a widower in straitened circumstances. Or he might have been a mute recovering, like myself, from influenza.

"Excuse me, sir," he said, "but could you oblige me with a match?"

"Certainly."

He sat down beside me and while I put my hand in my pocket for matches he hunted in his for cigarettes. He took out a small packet of Goldflakes and his face fell.

"Dear, dear, how very annoying! I haven't got a cigarette left."

"Let me offer you one," I replied, smiling.

I took out my case and he helped himself.

"Gold?" he asked, giving the case a tap as I closed it.

"Gold? That's a thing I never could keep. I've had three. All stolen."

His eyes rested in a melancholy way on his boots, which were sadly in need of repair. He was a wizened little man with a long thin nose and pale blue eyes. His skin was sallow and he was much lined. I could not tell what his age was; he might have been five-and-thirty or he might have been sixty. There was nothing remarkable about him except his insignificance. But though evidently poor he was neat and clean. He was respectable and he clung to respectability. No, I did not think he was a mute, I thought he was a solicitor's clerk who had lately buried his wife and been sent to Elsom by an indulgent employer to get over the first shock of his grief.

"Are you making a long stay, sir?" he asked me.

"Ten days or a fortnight."

"Is this your first visit to Elsom, sir?"

"I have been here before."

"I know it well, sir. I flatter myself there are very few sea-side resorts that I have not been to at one time or another. Elsom is hard to beat, sir. You get a very nice class of people here. There's nothing noisy or vulgar about Elsom if you understand what I mean. Elsom has very pleasant recollec-tions for me, sir. I knew Elsom well in bygone days. I was married in St. Martin's Church, sir."

"Really," I said feebly.

"It was a very happy marriage, sir."

"I'm very glad to hear it," I returned.

"Nine months, that one lasted," he said reflectively.

Surely the remark was a trifle singular. I had not looked forward with any enthusiasm to the probability which I so clearly foresaw that he would favour me with an account of his matrimonial experiences, but now I waited if not with eagerness at least with curiosity for a further observation. He made none. He sighed a little. At last I broke the silence.

"There don't seem to be very many people about," I re-marked.

"I like it so. I'm not one for crowds. As I was saying just now I reckon I've spent a good many years at one seaside resort after the other, but I never came in the season. It's the winter I like."

"Don't you find it a little melancholy?"

He turned towards me and placed his black-gloved hand for an instant on my arm.

"It is melancholy. And because it's melancholy a little ray of sunshine is very welcome."

The remark seemed to me perfectly idiotic and I did not answer. He withdrew his hand from my arm and got up.

"Well, I mustn't keep you, sir. Pleased to have made your acquaintance."

He took off his dingy hat very politely and strolled away. It was beginning now to grow chilly and I thought I would return to the Dolphin. As I reached its broad steps a landau drove up, drawn by two scraggy horses, and from it stepped Mr. St. Clair. He wore a hat that looked like the unhappy result of a union between a bowler and a top-hat. He gave his hand to his wife and then to his niece. The porter carried in after them rugs and cushions. As Mr. St. Clair paid the driver I heard him tell him to come at the usual time next day, and I understood that the St. Clairs took a drive every afternoon in a landau. It would not have surprised me to learn that none of them had ever been in a motor-car.

The manageress told me that they kept very much to themselves and sought no acquaintance among the other persons staying at the hotel. I rode my imagination on a loose rein. I watched them eat three meals a day. I watched Mr. and Mrs. St. Clair sit at the top of the hotel steps in the morning. He read *The Times* and she knitted. I supposed Mrs. St. Clair had never read a paper in her life, for they never took anything but *The Times* and Mr. St. Clair of course took it with him every day to the City. At about twelve Miss Porchester joined them.

"Have you enjoyed your walk, Eleanor?" asked Mrs. St. Clair.

"It was very nice, Aunt Gertrude," answered Miss Porchester.

And I understood that just as Mrs. St. Clair took "her

drive" every afternoon Miss Porchester took "her walk" every morning.

"When you have come to the end of your row, my dear," said Mr. St. Clair, with a glance at his wife's knitting, "we might go for a constitutional before luncheon."

"That will be very nice," answered Mrs. St. Clair. She folded up her work and gave it to Miss Porchester. "If you're going upstairs, Eleanor, will you take my work?"

"Certainly, Aunt Gertrude."

"I daresay you're a little tired after your walk, my dear."

"I shall have a little rest before luncheon."

Miss Porchester went into the hotel and Mr. and Mrs. St. Clair walked slowly along the sea-front, side by side, to a certain point, and then walked slowly back.

When I met one of them on the stairs I bowed and received an unsmiling, polite bow in return, and in the morning I ventured upon a good-day, but there the matter ended. It looked as though I should never have a chance to speak to any of them. But presently I thought that Mr. St. Clair gave me now and then a glance, and thinking he had heard my name I imagined, perhaps vainly, that he looked at me with curiosity. And a day or two after that I was sitting in my room when the porter came in with a message.

"Mr. St. Clair presents his compliments and could you oblige him with the loan of Whitaker's Almanack."

I was astonished.

"Why on earth should he think that I have a Whitaker's Almanack?"

"Well, sir, the manageress told him you wrote."

I could not see the connection.

"Tell Mr. St. Clair that I'm very sorry that I haven't got a Whitaker's Almanack, but if I had I would very gladly lend it to him."

Here was my opportunity. I was by now filled with eagerness to know these fantastic persons more closely. Now and then in the heart of Asia I have come upon a lonely tribe living in a little village among an alien population. No one knows how they came there or why they settled in that spot. They live their own lives, speak their own language, and have no communication with their neighbours. No one knows whether they are the descendants of a band that was left behind when their nation swept in a vast horde across the continent or whether they are the dying remnant of some great people that in that country once held empire. They are a mystery. They have no future and no history. This odd little family seemed to me to have something of the same character. They were of an era that is dead and gone. They reminded me of persons in one of those leisurely, old-fashioned novels that one's father read. They belonged to the eighties and they had not moved since then. How extraordinary it was that they could have lived through the last forty years as though the world stood still! They took me back to my childhood and I recollected people who are long since dead. I wonder if it is only distance that gives me the impression that they were more peculiar than anyone is now. When a person was describing then as "quite a character," by heaven, it meant something.

So that evening after dinner I went into the lounge and boldly addressed Mr. St. Clair.

"I'm so sorry I haven't got a Whitaker's Almanack," I said, "but if I have any other book that can be of service to you I shall be delighted to lend it to you."

Mr. St. Clair was obviously startled. The two ladies kept their eyes on their work. There was an embarrassed hush.

"It does not matter at all, but I was given to understand by the manageress that you were a novelist."

I racked my brain. There was evidently some connection between my profession and Whitaker's Almanack that escaped me.

"In days gone by Mr. Trollope used often to dine with us in Leinster Square and I remember him saying that the two most useful books to a novelist were the Bible and Whitaker's Almanack."

"I see that Thackeray once stayed in this hotel," I remarked, anxious not to let the conversation drop.

"I never very much cared for Mr. Thackeray, though he

dined more than once with my wife's father, the late Mr. Sargeant Saunders. He was too cynical for me. My niece has not read *Vanity Fair* to this day."

Miss Porchester blushed slightly at this reference to herself. A waiter brought in the coffee and Mrs. St. Clair turned to her husband.

"Perhaps, my dear, this gentleman would do us the pleasure to have his coffee with us."

Although not directly addressed, I answered promptly.

"Thank you very much."

I sat down.

"Mr. Trollope was always my favourite novelist," said Mr. St. Clair. "He was so essentially a gentleman. I admire Charles Dickens. But Charles Dickens could never draw a gentleman. I am given to understand that young people nowadays find Mr. Trollope a little slow. My niece, Miss Porchester, prefers the novels of Mr. William Black."

"I'm afraid I've never read any," I said.

"Ah, I see that you are like me; you are not up-to-date. My niece once persuaded me to read a novel by a Miss Rhoda Broughton, but I could not manage more than a hundred pages of it."

"I did not say I liked it, Uncle Edwin," said Miss Porchester, defending herself, with another blush. "I told you it was rather fast, but everybody was talking about it."

"I'm quite sure it is not the sort of book your Aunt Gertrude would have wished you to read, Eleanor."

"I remember Miss Broughton telling me once that when she was young people said her books were fast and when she was old they said they were slow, and it was very hard, since she had written exactly the same sort of book for forty years."

"Oh, did you know Miss Broughton?" asked Miss Porchester, addressing me for the first time. "How very interesting! And did you know Ouida?"

"My dear Eleanor, what will you say next! I'm quite sure you've never read anything by Ouida."

"Indeed, I have, Uncle Edwin. I've read *Under Two Flags* and I liked it very much."

"You amaze and shock me. I don't know what girls are coming to nowadays."

"You always said that when I was thirty you gave me complete liberty to read anything I liked."

"There is a difference, my dear Eleanor, between liberty and license," said Mr. St. Clair, smiling a little in order not to make his reproof offensive, but with a certain gravity.

I do not know if in recounting this conversation I have managed to convey the impression it gave me of a charming and old-fashioned air. I could have listened all night to them discussing the depravity of an age that was young in the eighteen-eighties. I would have given a good deal for a glimpse of their large and roomy house in Leinster Square. I should have recognized the suite covered in red brocade that stood stiffly about the drawing-room, each piece in its appointed place; and the cabinets filled with Dresden china would have brought me back my childhood. In the dining-room, where they habitually sat, for the drawing-room was used only for parties, there was a Turkey carpet and a vast mahogany sideboard "groaning" with silver. On the walls were the pictures that had excited the admiration of Mrs. Humphry Ward and her uncle Matthew in the Academy of eighteen-eighty.

Next morning, strolling through a pretty lane at the back of Elsom, I met Miss Porchester, who was taking "her walk." I should have liked to go a little way with her, but felt certain that it would embarrass this maiden of fifty to saunter alone with a man even of my respectable years. She bowed as I passed her, and blushed. Oddly enough, a few yards behind her I came upon the funny shabby little man in black gloves with whom I had spoken for a few minutes on the front. He touched his old bowler hat.

"Excuse me, sir, but could you oblige me with a match?" he said.

"Certainly," I retorted, "but I'm afraid I have no cigarettes on me."

"Allow me to offer you one of mine," he said, taking out

the paper case. It was empty. "Dear, dear, I haven't got one either. What a curious coincidence!"

He went on and I had a notion that he a little hastened his steps. I was beginning to have my doubts about him. I hoped he was not going to bother Miss Porchester. For a moment I thought of walking back, but I did not. He was a civil little man and I did not believe he would make a nuisance of himself to a single lady.

I saw him again that very afternoon. I was sitting on the front. He walked towards me with little, halting steps. There was something of a wind and he looked like a dried leaf being driven before it. This time he did not hesitate, but sat down beside me.

"We meet again, sir. The world is a small place. If it will not inconvenience you perhaps you will allow me to rest a few minutes. I am a wee bit tired."

"This is a public bench, and you have just as much right to sit on it as I."

I did not wait for him to ask me for a match, but at once offered him a cigarette.

"How very kind of you, sir! I have to limit myself to so many cigarettes a day, but I enjoy those I smoke. As one grows older the pleasures of life diminish, but my experience is that one enjoys more those that remain."

"That is a very consoling thought."

"Excuse me, sir, but am I right in thinking that you are the well-known author?"

"I am an author," I replied. "But what made you think it?"

"I have seen your portrait in the illustrated papers. I suppose you don't recognize me?"

I looked at him again, a weedy little man in neat but shabby black clothes, with a long nose and watery blue eyes.

"I'm afraid I don't."

"I daresay I've changed," he sighed. "There was a time when my photograph was in every paper in the United Kingdom. Of course, those press photographs never do you justice. I give you my word, sir, that if I hadn't seen my name underneath I should never have guessed that some of them were meant for me."

He was silent for a while. The tide was out, and beyond the shingle of the beach was a strip of yellow mud. The breakwaters were half buried in it like the backbones of prehistoric beasts.

"It must be a wonderfully interesting thing to be an author, sir. I've often thought I had quite a turn for writing myself. At one time and another I've done a rare lot of reading. I haven't kept up with it much lately. For one thing my eyes are not so good as they used to be. I believe I could write a book if I tried."

"They say anybody can write one," I answered.

"Not a novel, you know. I'm not much of a one for novels; I prefer histories and that like. But memoirs. If anybody was to make it worth my while I wouldn't mind writing my memoirs."

"It's very fashionable just now."

"There are not many people who've had the experiences I've had in one way and another. I did write to one of the Sunday papers about it some little while back, but they never answered my letter."

He gave me a long, appraising look. He had too respectable an air to be about to ask me for half a crown.

"Of course you don't know who I am, sir, do you?"

"I honestly don't."

He seemed to ponder for a moment, then he smoothed down his black gloves on his fingers, looked for a moment at a hole in one of them, and then turned to me not without self-consciousness.

"I am the celebrated Mortimer Ellis," he said.

"Oh?"

I did not know what other ejaculation to make, for to the best of my belief I had never heard the name before. I saw a look of disappointment come over his face, and I was a trifle embarrassed.

"Mortimer Ellis," he repeated. "You're not going to tell me you don't know."

"I'm afraid I must. I'm very often out of England."

I wondered to what he owed his celebrity. I passed over in my mind various possibilities. He could never have been an athlete, which alone in England gives a man real fame, but he might have been a faith-healer or a champion billiard-player. There is of course no one so obscure as a cabinet minister out of office and he might have been the President of the Board of Trade in a defunct administration. But he had none of the look of a politician.

"That's fame for you," he said bitterly. "Why, for weeks I was the most talked-about man in England. Look at me. You must have seen my photograph in the papers. Mortimer Ellis."

"I'm sorry," I said, shaking my head.

He paused a moment to give his disclosure effectiveness.

"I am the well-known bigamist."

Now what are you to reply when a person who is practically a stranger to you informs you that he is a well-known bigamist? I will confess that I have sometimes had the vanity to think that I am not as a rule at a loss for a retort, but here I found myself speechless.

"I've had eleven wives, sir," he went on.

"Most people find one about as much as they can manage."

"Ah, that's want of practice. When you've had eleven there's very little you don't know about women."

"But why did you stop at eleven?"

"There now, I knew you'd say that. The moment I set eyes on you I said to myself, he's got a clever face. You know, sir, that's the thing that always grizzles me. Eleven does seem a funny number, doesn't it? There's something unfinished about it. Now three anyone might have, and seven's all right, they say nine's lucky, and there's nothing wrong with ten. But eleven! That's the one thing I regret. I shouldn't have minded anything if I could have brought it up to the Round Dozen."

He unbuttoned his coat and from an inside pocket produced a bulging and very greasy pocketbook. From this he took a large bundle of newspaper cuttings; they were worn and creased and dirty. But he spread out two or three.

"Now just you look at those photographs, I ask you, are they like me? It's an outrage. Why, you'd think I was a criminal to look at them."

The cuttings were of imposing length. In the opinion of sub-editors Mortimer Ellis had obviously been a news item of value. One was headed, A Much Married Man; another, Heartless Ruffian Brought to Book; a third, Contemptible Scoundrel Meets His Waterloo.

"Not what you would call a good press," I murmured.

"I never pay any attention to what the newspapers say," he answered, with a shrug of his thin shoulders. "I've known too many journalists myself for that. No, it's the judge I blame. He treated me shocking and it did him no good, mind you; he died within the year."

I ran my eyes down the report I held.

"I see he gave you five years."

"Disgraceful, I call it, and see what it says." He pointed to a place with his forefinger. " 'Three of his victims pleaded for mercy to be shown to him.' That shows what they thought of me. And after that he gave me five years. And just look what he called me, a heartless scoundrel—me, the best-hearted man that ever lived—a pest of society and a danger to the public. Said he wished he had the power to give me the cat. I don't so much mind his giving me five years, though you'll never get me to say it wasn't excessive, but I ask you, had he the right to talk to me like that? No, he hadn't, and I'll never forgive him, not if I live to be a hundred."

The bigamist's cheeks flushed and his watery eyes were filled for a moment with fire. It was a sore subject with him.

"May I read them?" I asked him.

"That's what I gave them you for. I want you to read them, sir. And if you can read them without saying that I'm a much wronged man, well, you're not the man I took you for."

As I glanced through one cutting after another I saw why Mortimer Ellis had so wide an acquaintance with the sea-side resorts of England. They were his hunting-ground. His method was to go to some place when the season was over and take apartments in one of the empty lodging-houses. Apparently it did not take him long to make acquaintance with some woman or other, widow or spinster, and I noticed that their ages at the time were between thirty-five and fifty. They stated in the witness-box that they had met him first on the sea-front. He generally proposed marriage to them within a fortnight of this and they were married shortly after. He induced them in one way or another to entrust him with their savings and in a few months, on the pretext that he had to go to London on business, he left them, never to return. Only one had ever seen him again till, obliged to give evidence, they saw him in the dock. They were women of a certain respectability; one was the daughter of a doctor and another of a clergyman; there was a lodging-house keeper, there was the widow of a commercial traveller, and there was a retired dressmaker. For the most part, their fortunes ranged from five hundred to a thousand pounds, but whatever the sum the misguided women were stripped of every penny. Some of them told really pitiful stories of the destitution to which they had been reduced. But they all acknowledged that he had been a good husband to them. Not only had three actually pleaded for mercy to be shown him; but one said in the witness-box that, if he was willing to come, she was ready to take him back. He noticed that I was reading this.

"And she'd have worked for me," he said, "there's no doubt about that. But I said, better let bygones be bygones. No one likes a cut off the best end of the neck better than I do, but I'm not much of a one for cold roast mutton, I will confess."

It was only by an accident that Mortimer Ellis did not marry his twelfth wife and so achieve the Round Dozen which I understand appealed to his love of symmetry. For he was engaged to be married to a Miss Hubbard—"two thousand pounds she had, if she had a penny, in war-loan," he confided to me—and the banns had been read, when one of his former wives saw him, made enquiries, and communicated with the police. He was arrested on the very day before his twelfth wedding.

"She was a bad one, she was," he told me. "She deceived me something cruel."

"How did she do that?"

"Well, I met her at Eastbourne, one December it was, on the pier, and she told me in course of conversation that she'd been in the millinery business and had retired. She said she'd made a tidy bit of money. She wouldn't say exactly how much it was, but she gave me to understand it was something like fifteen hundred pounds. And when I married her —would you believe it?—she hadn't got three hundred. And that's the one who gave me away. And mind you, I'd never blamed her. Many a man would have cut up rough when he found out he'd been made a fool of. I never showed her that I was disappointed even, I just went away without a word."

"But not without the three hundred pounds, I take it."

"Oh come, sir, you must be reasonable," he returned in an injured tone. "You can't expect three hundred pounds to last for ever, and I'd been married to her four months before she confessed the truth."

"Forgive my asking," I said, "and pray don't think my question suggests a disparaging view of your personal attractions, but—why did they marry you?"

"Because I asked them," he answered, evidently very much surprised at my enquiry.

"But did you never have any refusals?"

"Very seldom. Not more than four or five in the whole course of my career. Of course I didn't propose till I was pretty sure of my ground and I don't say I didn't draw a blank sometimes. You can't expect to click every time, if you know what I mean, and I've often wasted several weeks making up to a woman before I saw there was nothing doing."

I surrendered myself for a time to my reflections. But I noticed presently that a broad smile spread over the mobile features of my friend.

"I understand what you mean," he said. "It's my appearance that puzzles you. You don't know what it is they see in me. That's what comes of reading novels and going to the pictures. You think what women want is the cowboy type, or the romance-of-old-Spain touch, flashing eyes, an olive skin, and a beautiful dancer. You make me laugh."

"I'm glad," I said.

"Are you a married man, sir?"

"I am. But I only have one wife."

"You can't judge by that. You can't generalize from a single instance, if you know what I mean. Now, I ask you, what would you know about dogs if you'd never had anything but one bull-terrier?"

The question was rhetorical and I felt sure did not require an answer. He paused for an effective moment and went on.

"You're wrong, sir. You're quite wrong. They may take a fancy to a good-looking young fellow, but they don't want to marry him. They don't really care about looks."

"Douglas Jerrold, who was as ugly as he was witty, used to say that if he was given ten minutes' start with a woman he could cut out the handsomest man in the room."

"They don't want wit. They don't want a man to be funny; they think he's not serious. They don't want a man who's too handsome; they think he's not serious either. That's what they want, they want a man who's serious. Safety first. And then—attention. I may not be handsome and I may not be amusing, but believe me, I've got what every woman wants. Poise. And the proof is, I've made every one of my wives happy."

"It certainly is much to your credit that three of them pleaded for mercy to be shown to you and that one was willing to take you back."

"You don't know what an anxiety that was to me all the time I was in prison. I thought she'd be waiting for me at the gate when I was released, and I said to the Governor,

'For God's sake, sir, smuggle me out so as no one can see me.' "

He smoothed his gloves again over his hands and his eye once more fell upon the hole in the first finger.

"That's what comes of living in lodgings, sir. How's a man to keep himself neat and tidy without a woman to look after him? I've been married too often to be able to get along without a wife. There are men who don't like being married. I can't understand them. The fact is, you can't do a thing really well unless you've got your heart in it, and I like being a married man. It's no difficulty to me to do the little things that women like and that some men can't be bothered with. As I was saying just now, it's attention a woman wants. I never went out of the house without giving my wife a kiss and I never came in without giving her another. And it was very seldom I came in without bringing her some chocolates or a few flowers. I never grudged the expense."

"After all, it was her money you were spending," I interposed.

"And what if it was? It's not the money that you've paid for a present that signifies, it's the spirit you give it in. That's what counts with women. No, I'm not one to boast, but I will say this for myself, I am a good husband."

I looked desultorily at the reports of the trial which I still held.

"I'll tell you what surprises me," I said. "All these women were very respectable, of a certain age, quiet, decent persons. And yet they married you without any enquiry after the shortest possible acquaintance."

He put his hand impressively on my arm.

"Ah, that's what you don't understand, sir. Women have got a craving to be married. It doesn't matter how young they are or how old they are, if they're short or tall, dark or fair, they've all got one thing in common: they want to be married. And mind you, I married them in church. No woman feels really safe unless she's married in church. You say I'm no beauty. Well, I never thought I was, but if I had one leg and a hump on my back I could find any number of women who'd jump at the chance of marrying me. It's not the man they care about, it's marriage. It's a mania with them. It's a disease. Why, there's hardly one of them who wouldn't have accepted me the second time I saw her only I like to make sure of my ground before I commit myself. When it all came out there was a rare to-do because I'd married eleven times. Eleven times? Why, it's nothing, it's not even a Round Dozen. I could have married thirty times if I'd wanted to. I give you my word, sir, when I consider my opportunities, I'm astounded at my moderation."

"You told me you were very fond of reading history."

"Yes, Warren Hastings said that, didn't he? It struck me at the time I read it. It seemed to fit me like a glove."

"And you never found these constant courtships a trifle monotonous?"

"Well, sir, I think I've got a logical mind, and it always gave me a rare lot of pleasure to see how the same effects followed on the same causes, if you know what I mean. Now, for instance, with a woman who'd never been married before I always passed myself off as a widower. It worked like a charm. You see, a spinster likes a man who knows a thing or two. But with a widow I always said I was a bachelor: a widow's afraid a man who's been married before knows too much."

I gave him back his cuttings; he folded them up neatly and replaced them in his greasy pocketbook.

"You know, sir, I always think I've been misjudged. Just see what they say about me: a pest of society, unscrupulous villain, contemptible scoundrel. Now just look at me. I ask you, do I look that sort of man? You know me, you're a judge of character, I've told you all about myself; do you think me a bad man?"

"My acquaintance with you is very slight," I answered with what I thought considerable tact.

"I wonder if the judge, I wonder if the jury, I wonder if the public ever thought about my side of the question. The public booed me when I was taken into court and the police had to protect me from their violence. Did any of them think what I'd done for these women?"

"You took their money."

"Of course I took their money. I had to live the same as anybody has to live. But what did I give them in exchange for their money?"

This was another rhetorical question, and though he looked at me as though he expected an answer I held my tongue. Indeed I did not know the answer. His voice was raised and he spoke with emphasis. I could see that he was serious.

"I'll tell you what I gave them in exchange for their money. Romance. Look at this place." He made a wide, circular gesture that embraced the sea and the horizon. "There are a hundred places in England like this. Look at that sea and that sky; look at these lodging-houses; look at that pier and the front. Doesn't it make your heart sink? It's dead as mutton. It's all very well for you who come down here for a week or two because you're run down. But think of all those women who live here from one year's end to another. They haven't a chance. They hardly know anyone. They've just got enough money to live on and that's all. I wonder if you know how terrible their lives are. Their lives are just like the front, a long, straight, cemented walk that goes on and on from one seaside resort to another. Even in the season there's nothing for them. They're out of it. They might as well be dead. And then I come along. Mind you, I never made advances to a woman who wouldn't have gladly acknowledged to thirty-five. And I give them love. Why, many of them had never known what it was to have a man do them up behind. Many of them had never known what it was to sit on a bench in the dark with a man's arm round their waist. I bring them change and excitement. I give them a new pride in themselves. They were on the shelf and I come along quite quietly and I deliberately take them down. A little ray of sunshine in those drab lives, that's what I was. No wonder they jumped at me, no wonder they wanted me to go back to them. The only one who gave me away was the milliner. She said she was a widow. My private opinion is that she'd never been married at all. You say I did the dirty on them; why, I brought happiness and glamour

into eleven lives that never thought they had even a dog's
chance of it again. You say I'm a villain and a scoundrel.
You're wrong. I'm a philanthropist. Five years, they gave
me; they should have given me the medal of the Royal
Humane Society."

He took out his empty packet of Goldflakes and looked at
it with a melancholy shake of the head. When I handed him
my cigarette case he helped himself without a word. I
watched the spectacle of a good man struggling with his
emotion.

"And what did I get out of it, I ask you?" he continued
presently. "Board and lodging and enough to buy cigarettes.
But I never was able to save, and the proof is that now,
when I'm not so young as I was, I haven't got half a crown
in my pocket." He gave me a sidelong glance. "It's a great
comedown for me to find myself in this position. I've always
paid my way and I've never asked a friend for a loan in all
my life. I was wondering, sir, if you could oblige me with a
trifle. It's humiliating to me to have to suggest it, but the
fact is, if you could oblige me with a pound it would mean
a great deal to me."

Well, I had certainly had a pound's worth of entertainment
out of the bigamist and I dived for my pocketbook.

"I shall be very glad," I said.

He looked at the notes I took out.

"I suppose you couldn't make it two, sir?"

"I think I could."

I handed him a couple of pound notes and he gave a little
sigh as he took them.

"You don't know what it means to a man who's used to
the comforts of home life not to know where to turn for a
night's lodging."

"But there is one thing I should like you to tell me," I said.
"I shouldn't like you to think me cynical, but I had a notion
that women on the whole take the maxim, it is more blessed
to give than to receive, as applicable exclusively to our sex.
How did you persuade these respectable, and no doubt

thrifty, women to entrust you so confidently with all their savings?"

An amused smile spread over his undistinguished features.

"Well, sir, you know what Shakespeare said about ambition o'erleaping itself. That's the explanation. Tell a woman you'll double her capital in six months if she'll give it you to handle and she won't be able to give you the money quick enough. Greed, that's what it is. Just greed."

It was a sharp sensation, stimulating to the appetite (like hot sauce with ice cream) to go from this diverting ruffian to the respectability, all lavender bags and crinolines, of the St. Clairs and Miss Porchester. I spent every evening with them now. No sooner had the ladies left him than Mr. St. Clair sent his compliments to my table and asked me to drink a glass of port with him. When we had finished it we went into the lounge and drank coffee. Mr. St. Clair enjoyed his glass of old brandy. The hour I thus spent with them was so exquisitely boring that it had for me a singular fascination. They were told by the manageress that I had written plays.

"We used often to go to the theatre when Sir Henry Irving was at the Lyceum," said Mr. St. Clair. "I once had the pleasure of meeting him. I was taken to supper at the Garrick Club by Sir Everard Millais and I was introduced to Mr. Irving as he then was."

"Tell him what he said to you, Edwin," said Mrs. St. Clair.

Mr. St. Clair struck a dramatic attitude and gave not at all a bad imitation of Henry Irving.

" 'You have the actor's face, Mr. St. Clair,' he said to me. 'If you ever think of going on the stage, come to me and I will give you a part.' " Mr. St. Clair resumed his natural manner. "It was enough to turn a young man's head."

"But it didn't turn yours," I said.

"I will not deny that if I had been otherwise situated I might have allowed myself to be tempted. But I had my family to think of. It would have broken my father's heart if I had not gone into the business."

"What is that?" I asked.

"I am a tea-merchant, sir. My firm is the oldest in the City of London. I have spent forty years of my life in combating to the best of my ability the desire of my fellow-countrymen to drink Ceylon tea instead of the China tea which was universally drunk in my youth."

I thought it charmingly characteristic of him to spend a lifetime in persuading the public to buy something they didn't want rather than something they did.

"But in his younger days my husband did a lot of amateur acting and he was thought very clever," said Mrs. St. Clair.

"Shakespeare, you know, and sometimes *The School for Scandal*. I would never consent to act trash. But that is a thing of the past. I had a gift. Perhaps it was a pity to waste it, but it's too late now. When we have a dinner-party I sometimes let the ladies persuade me to recite the great soliloquies of Hamlet. But that is all I do."

Oh! Oh! Oh! I thought with shuddering fascination of those dinner-parties and wondered whether I should ever be asked to one of them. Mrs. St. Clair gave me a little smile, half shocked, half prim.

"My husband was very bohemian as a young man," she said.

"I sowed my wild oats. I knew quite a lot of painters and writers, Wilkie Collins, for instance, and even men who wrote for the papers. Watts painted a portrait of my wife, and I bought a picture of Millais. I knew a number of the pre-Raphaelites."

"Have you a Rossetti?" I asked.

"No. I admired Rossetti's talent, but I could not approve of his private life. I would never buy a picture by an artist whom I should not care to ask to dinner at my house."

My brain was reeling when Miss Porchester, looking at her watch, said: "Are you not going to read to us to-night, Uncle Edwin?"

I withdrew.

It was while I was drinking a glass of port with Mr. St. Clair one evening that he told me the sad story of Miss Porchester. She was engaged to be married to a nephew of

Mrs. St. Clair, a barrister, when it was discovered that he had had an intrigue with the daughter of his laundress.

"It was a terrible thing," said Mr. St. Clair. "A terrible thing. But of course my niece took the only possible course. She returned him his ring, his letters and his photograph, and said that she could never marry him. She implored him to marry the young person he had wronged and said she would be a sister to her. It broke her heart. She has never cared for anyone since."

"And did he marry the young person?"

Mr. St. Clair shook his head and sighed.

"No, we were greatly mistaken in him. It has been a sore grief to my dear wife to think that a nephew of hers should behave in such a dishonourable manner. Some time later we heard that he was engaged to a young lady in a very good position with ten thousand pounds of her own. I considered it my duty to write to her father and put the facts before him. He answered my letter in a most insolent fashion. He said he would much rather his son-in-law had a mistress before marriage than after."

"What happened then?"

"They were married and now my wife's nephew is one of His Majesty's Judges of the High Court, and his wife is My Lady. But we've never consented to receive them. When my wife's nephew was knighted Eleanor suggested that we should ask them to dinner, but my wife said that he should never darken our doors and I upheld her."

"And the laundress's daughter?"

"She married in her own class of life and has a public-house at Canterbury. My niece, who has a little money of her own, did everything for her and is godmother to her eldest child."

Poor Miss Porchester. She had sacrificed herself on the altar of Victorian morality, and I am afraid the consciousness that she had behaved beautifully was the only benefit she had got from it.

"Miss Porchester is a woman of striking appearance," I said. "When she was younger she must have been perfectly lovely. I wonder she never married somebody else."

"Miss Porchester was considered a great beauty. Alma-Tadema admired her so much that he asked her to sit as a model for one of his pictures, but of course we couldn't very well allow that." Mr. St. Clair's tone conveyed that the suggestion had deeply outraged his sense of decency. "No, Miss Porchester never cared for anyone but her cousin. She never speaks of him and it is now thirty years since they parted, but I am convinced that she loves him still. She is a true woman, my dear sir, one life, one love, and though perhaps I regret that she has been deprived of the joys of marriage and motherhood I am bound to admire her fidelity."

But the heart of woman is incalculable, and rash is the man who thinks she will remain in one stay. Rash, Uncle Edwin. You have known Eleanor for many years, for when, her mother having fallen into a decline and died, you brought the orphan to your comfortable and even luxurious house in Leinster Square, she was but a child; but what, when it comes down to brass tacks, Uncle Edwin, do you really know of Eleanor?

It was but two days after Mr. St. Clair had confided to me the touching story which explained why Miss Porchester had remained a spinster that, coming back to the hotel in the afternoon after a round of golf, the manageress came up to me in an agitated manner.

"Mr. St. Clair's compliments and will you go up to number twenty-seven the moment you come in."

"Certainly. But why?"

"Oh, there's a rare upset. They'll tell you."

I knocked at the door. I heard a "come in, come in," which reminded me that Mr. St. Clair had played Shakespearean parts in probably the most refined amateur dramatic company in London. I entered and found Mrs. St. Clair lying on the sofa with a handkerchief soaked in eau-de-Cologne on her brow and a bottle of smelling salts in her hand. Mr. St. Clair was standing in front of the fire in such a manner as to prevent anyone else in the room from obtaining any benefit from it.

"I must apologize for asking you to come up in this un-ceremonious fashion, but we are in great distress, and we thought you might be able to throw some light on what has happened."

His perturbation was obvious.

"What *has* happened?"

"Our niece, Miss Porchester, has eloped. This morning she sent in a message to my wife that she had one of her sick headaches. When she has one of her sick headaches she likes to be left absolutely alone, and it wasn't till this afternoon that my wife went to see if there was anything she could do for her. The room was empty. Her trunk was packed. Her dress-ing-case with silver fittings was gone. And on the pillow was a letter telling us of her rash act."

"I'm very sorry," I said. "I don't know exactly what I can do."

"We were under the impression that you were the only gentleman at Elsom with whom she had any acquaintance."

His meaning flashed across me.

"I see you haven't eloped with her. At the first moment we thought perhaps . . . but if it isn't you, who is it?"

"I'm sure I don't know."

"Show him the letter, Edwin," said Mrs. St. Clair from the sofa.

"Don't move, Gertrude. It will bring on your lumbago."

Miss Porchester had "her" sick headaches and Mrs. St. Clair had "her" lumbago. What had Mr. St. Clair? I was willing to bet a fiver that Mr. St. Clair had "his" gout. He gave me the letter and I read it with an air of decent commiseration.

Dearest Uncle Edwin and Aunt Gertrude:

When you receive this I shall be far away. I am going to be married this morning to a gentleman who is very dear to me. I know I am doing wrong in running away like this, but I was afraid you would endeavour to set obstacles in the way of my marriage, and since nothing would induce me to change my mind I thought it would save us all much unhappiness if I did it without telling you anything about it. My fiancé is a

*very retiring man, owing to his long residence in tropical
countries not in the best of health, and he thought it much
better that we should be married quite privately. When you
know how radiantly happy I am I hope you will forgive me.
Please send my box to the luggage office at Victoria Station,*

Your loving niece,

Eleanor.

"I will never forgive her," said Mr. St. Clair as I returned
him the letter. "She shall never darken my doors again. Gertrude, I forbid you ever to mention Eleanor's name in my
hearing."

Mrs. St. Clair began to sob quietly.

"Aren't you rather hard?" I said. "Is there any reason why
Miss Porchester shouldn't marry?"

"At her age?" he answered angrily. "It's ridiculous. We
shall be the laughing-stock of everyone in Leinster Square.
Do you know how old she is? She's fifty-one."

"Fifty-four," said Mrs. St. Clair through her sobs.

"She's been the apple of my eye. She's been like a daughter
to us. She's been an old maid for years. I think it's positively
improper for her to think of marriage."

"She was always a girl to us, Edwin," pleaded Mrs. St. Clair.

"And who is this man she's married? It's the deception that
rankles. She must have been carrying on with him under our
very noses. She does not even tell us his name. I fear the very
worst."

Suddenly I had an inspiration. That morning after breakfast I had gone out to buy myself some cigarettes and at the
tobacconist's I ran across Mortimer Ellis. I had not seen him
for some days.

"You're looking very spruce," I said.

His boots had been repaired and were neatly blacked, his
hat was brushed, he was wearing a clean collar and new
gloves. I thought he had laid out my two pounds to advantage.

"I have to go to London this morning on business," he said.

I nodded and left the shop.

I remembered that a fortnight before, walking in the cou*r*-

try, I had met Miss Porchester and, a few yards behind, Mortimer Ellis. Was it possible that they had been walking together and he had fallen back as they caught sight of me? By heaven, I saw it all.

"I think you said that Miss Porchester had money of her own," I said.

"A trifle. She has three thousand pounds."

Now I was certain. I looked at them blankly. Suddenly Mrs. St. Clair, with a cry, sprang to her feet.

"Edwin, Edwin, supposing he doesn't marry her?"

Mr. St. Clair at this put his hand to his head and in a state of collapse sank into a chair.

"The disgrace would kill me," he groaned.

"Don't be alarmed," I said. "He'll marry her all right. He always does. He'll marry her in church."

They paid no attention to what I said. I suppose they thought I'd suddenly taken leave of my senses. I was quite sure now. Mortimer Ellis had achieved his ambition after all. Miss Porchester completed the Round Dozen.

The Voice of The Turtle

For SOME TIME I could not make up my mind if I liked Peter Melrose or not. He had had a novel published that had caused some stir among the rather dreary but worthy people who are always on the lookout for new talent. Elderly gentlemen with nothing much to do but go to luncheon parties praised it with girlish enthusiasm, and wiry little women who didn't get on with their husbands thought it showed promise. I read a few reviews. They contradicted one another freely. Some of the critics claimed that with this first novel the author had sprung into the front rank of English novelists: others reviled it. I did not read it. I have learnt by experience that when a book makes a sensation it is just as well to wait a year before you read it. It is astonishing how many books then you need not read at all. But it chanced that one day I met Peter Melrose. With some misgiving I had accepted an invitation to a sherry party. It was in the top flat of a converted house in Bloomsbury, and I was a trifle out of breath when I had climbed four flights of stairs. My hostesses were two women, much over life-size, in early middle life, the sort of women who know all about the insides of motorcars and like a good tramp in the rain, but very feminine for all that, fond of eating out of paper bags. The drawing-room, which they called "our work-shop," though being of independent means neither had ever done a stroke of work in her life, was large and bare, furnished with rustless-steel chairs, which looked as though they could with difficulty support the very substantial weight of their owners, glass-topped tables and a vast divan covered with zebra-skin. On the walls were book-shelves, and pictures by the better-known English

imitators of Cézanne, Braque and Picasso. In the shelves, besides a number of "curious" books of the eighteenth century
(for pornography is ageless) there were only the works of
living authors, mostly first editions, and it was indeed to sign
some of my own that I had been asked to the party.

It was quite small. There was but one other woman, who
might have been a younger sister of my hostesses, for, though
stout, she was not quite so stout, though tall, not quite so tall,
and though hearty, not quite so hearty. I did not catch her
name, but she answered to that of Boofuls. The only man besides myself was Peter Melrose. He was quite young, twenty-
two or twenty-three, of the middle height, but with an ungainly figure that made him look squat. He had a reddish skin
that seemed to fit over the bones of his face too tightly, a
rather large Semitic nose, though he was not a Jew, and alert
green eyes under bushy eyebrows. His brown hair, cut very
short, was scurfy. He was dressed in the brown Norfolk jacket
and grey flannel trousers that are worn by the art students
who wander hatless along King's Road, Chelsea. An uncouth
young man. Nor was there much to attract in his manner. He
was self-assertive, disputatious and intolerant. He had a hearty
contempt for his fellow-writers which he expressed with zest.
The satisfaction he gave me by his breezy attacks on reputa-
tions which for my part I considered exaggerated, but pru-
dently held my tongue about, was only lessened by the conviction that no sooner was my back turned than he would tear my
own to shreds. He talked well. He was amusing and sometimes witty. I should have laughed at his sallies more easily if
those three ladies had not been so unreasonably convulsed by
them. They roared with laughter at what he said, whether it
was funny or whether it was inept. He said many silly things,
for he talked without stopping, but he also said some very
clever ones. He had a point of view, crude and not so original
as he thought, but sincere. But the most striking thing about
him was his eager, impetuous vitality; it was like a hot flame
that burnt him with an unendurable fury. It even shed a glow
on those about him. He had something, if only that, and when
I left it was with a slight sense of curiosity at what would come

of him. I did not know if he had talent; so many young things can write a clever novel—that means nothing; but it seemed to me that as a man he was not quite like everybody else. He was the sort of person who at thirty, when time had softened his asperity and experience had taught him that he was not quite so intelligent as he thought, would turn into an interesting and agreeable fellow. But I never expected to see him again.

It was with surprise that I received two or three days later a copy of his novel with a very flattering dedication. I read it. It was obviously autobiographical. The scene was a small town in Sussex, and the characters of the upper middle class that strives to keep up appearances on an inadequate income. The humour was rather brutal and rather vulgar. It grated on me, for it consisted chiefly of mockery at people because they were old and poor. Peter Melrose did not know how hard those misfortunes are to bear, and that the efforts made to cope with them are more deserving of sympathy than of derision. But there were descriptions of places, little pictures of a room or impressions of the countryside, which were excellently done. They showed tenderness and a sense of the spiritual beauty of material things. The book was written easily, without affectation, and with a pleasant feeling for the sound of words. But what made it indeed somewhat remarkable, so that I understood why it had attracted attention, was the passion that quivered in the love story of which the plot, such as it was, consisted. It was, as is the modern fashion, more than a trifle coarse and, again in the modern fashion, it trailed off vaguely, without any particular result, so that everything was left in the end pretty much as it had been in the beginning; but you did get the impression of young love, idealistic and yet vehemently sexual; it was so vivid and so deeply felt that it took your breath away. It seemed to throb on the printed page like the pulse of life. It had no reticence. It was absurd, scandalous and beautiful. It was like a force of nature. That was passion all right. There is nothing, anywhere, so moving and so awe-inspiring.

I wrote to Peter Melrose and told him what I thought of his

THE VOICE OF THE TURTLE

book, then suggested that we might lunch together. He rang me up next day and we made a date.

I found him unaccountably shy when we sat down opposite one another at a table in a restaurant. I gave him a cocktail. He talked glibly enough, but I could not help seeing that he was ill at ease. I gained the impression that his self-assurance was a pose assumed to conceal, from himself, maybe, a diffidence that tortured him. His manners were brusque and awkward. He would say a rude thing and then laugh nervously to cover his own embarrassment. Though he pretended to be so sure of himself he wanted all the time to be reassured by you. By irritating you, by saying the things he thought would annoy, he tried to force from you some admission, tacit it might be, that he was as wonderful as he longed to think himself. He wanted to despise the opinion of his fellows, and nothing was more important to him. I thought him rather an odious young man, but I did not mind that. It is very natural that clever young men should be rather odious. They are conscious of gifts that they do not know how to use. They are exasperated with the world that will not recognize their merit. They have something to give, and no hand is stretched out to receive it. They are impatient for the fame they regard as their due. No, I do not mind odious young men; it is when they are charming that I button up the pockets of my sympathy.

Peter Melrose was extremely modest about his book. He blushed through his reddish skin when I praised what I liked in it, and accepted my strictures with a humility that was almost embarrassing. He had made very little money out of it, and his publishers were giving him a small monthly allowance in advance of royalties on the next one. This he had just started, but he wanted to get away to write it in peace, and knowing I lived on the Riviera he asked me if I could tell him of a quiet place where he could bathe and live cheaply. I suggested that he should come and spend a few days with me so that he could look about till he found something to suit him. His green eyes sparkled when I proposed this and he flushed.

"Shouldn't I be an awful nuisance?"

"No. I shall be working. All I can offer you is three meals a day and a room to sleep in. It'll be very dull, but you can do. exactly what you like."

"It sounds grand. May I let you know if I decide to come?"

"Of course."

We separated, and a week or two later I went home. This was in May. Early in June I received a letter from Peter Melrose asking, if I had really meant what I said when I invited him to spend a few days with me, whether he might arrive on such and such a date. Well, at the time I had meant it, but now, a month later, I remembered that he was an arrogant and ill-bred youth, whom I had seen but twice and wasn't in the least interested in, and I didn't mean it any longer. It seemed to me very likely that he would be bored stiff. I lived a very quiet life and saw few people. And I thought it would be a great strain on my nerves if he were as rude as I knew he could be, and I as his host felt it behooved me to keep my temper. I saw myself driven beyond endurance, and ringing the bell to have his clothes packed and the car brought round to take him away within half an hour. But there was nothing to do about it. It would save him the cost of board and lodging to spend a short period with me, and if he was tired and unhappy as he said in his letter it might be that it would do him good. I sent him a wire and shortly afterwards he arrived.

He looked very hot and grubby in his grey flannel trousers and brown tweed coat when I met him at the station, but after a swim in the pool he changed into white shorts and a Cochet shirt. He looked then quite absurdly young. He had never been out of England before. He was excited. It was touching to see his delight. He seemed, amid those unaccustomed surroundings, to lose his sense of himself, and he was simple, boyish and modest. I was agreeably surprised. In the evening, after dinner, sitting in the garden, with only the croaking of the little green frogs to break the silence, he began talking to me of his novel. It was a romantic story about a young writer and a celebrated prima donna. The theme was reminiscent of Ouida, the last thing I should have expected this hard-boiled youth to write, and I was tickled; it was odd how the fashion completed the circle and returned generation after generation to the same themes. I had no doubt that Peter Melrose would treat it in a very modern way, but there it was, the same old story as had entranced sentimental readers in the three-volume novels of the eighties. He proposed to set it in the beginning of the Edwardian era, which to the young has already acquired the fantastic, far-away feeling of a past age. He talked and talked. He was not unpleasant to listen to. He had no notion that he was putting into fiction his own day-dreams, the comic and touching day-dreams of a rather unattractive, obscure young man who sees himself beloved, to the admiration of the whole world, by an incredibly beautiful, celebrated and magnificent woman. I always enjoyed the novels of Ouida and Peter's idea did not at all displease me. With his charming gift of description, his vivid, ingenuous way of looking at material things, fabrics, pieces of furniture, walls, trees, flowers, and his power of representing the passion of life, the passion of love, that thrilled every fibre of his own uncouth body, I had a notion that he might well produce something exuberant, absurd and poetical. But I asked him a question.

"Have you ever known a prima donna?"

"No, but I've read all the autobiographies and memoirs that I could find. I've gone into it pretty thoroughly. Not only the obvious things, you know, but I've hunted around in all sorts of byways to get the revealing touch or the suggestive anecdote."

"And have you got what you wanted?"

"I think so."

He began to describe his heroine to me. She was young and beautiful, wilful it is true and with a quick temper, but magnanimous. A woman on the grand scale. Music was her passion; there was music not only in her voice, but in her gestures and in her inmost thoughts. She was devoid of envy, and her appreciation of art was such that when another singer had done her an injury she forgave her when she heard her sing a role beautifully. She was of a wonderful generosity, and would give away everything she possessed when a story of misfortune touched her soft heart. She was a great lover, prepared to sacrifice the world for the man she loved. She was intelligent and well-read. She was tender, unselfish and disinterested. In fact she was much too good to be true.

"I think you'd better meet a prima donna," I said at last.

"How can I?"

"Have you ever heard of La Falterona?"

"Of course I have. I've read her memoirs."

"She lives just along the coast. I'll ring her up and ask her to dinner."

"Will you really? It would be wonderful."

"Don't blame me if you don't find her quite what you expect."

"It's the truth I want."

Everyone has heard of La Falterona. Not even Melba had a greater reputation. She had ceased now to sing in opera, but her voice was still lovely, and she could fill a concert hall in any part of the world. She went for long tours every winter, and in summer rested in a villa by the sea. On the Riviera people are neighbours if they live thirty miles from one another, and for some years I had seen a good deal of La Falterona. She was a woman of ardent temperament, and she was celebrated not only for her singing, but for her love affairs: she never minded talking about them, and I had often sat entranced for hours while with the humour which to me was her most astonishing characteristic she regaled me with lurid tales of royal or very opulent adorers. I was satisfied that there was at least a measure of truth in them. She had been married, for short periods, three or four times, and in one of these unions had annexed a Neapolitan prince. Thinking that to be known as La Falterona was grander than any title, she did not use his name (to which indeed she had no right, since after divorcing him she had married somebody else); but her silver, her cutlery and her dinner-service were heavily decorated with a coat of arms and a crown, and her servants invariably addressed her as *madame la princesse*. She claimed to be a Hungarian, but her English was perfect; she spoke it with a slight accent (when she remembered), but with an intonation suggestive, I had been told, of Kansas City. This she explained by saying that her father was a political exile who had fled to America when she was no more than a child; but she did not seem quite sure whether he was a distinguished scientist who had got into trouble for his liberal views, or a Magyar of high rank who had brought down on his head the imperial wrath because he had had a love affair with an Archduchess. It depended on whether she was just an artist among artists, or a great lady among persons of noble birth.

With me she was not natural, for that she could never have been if she had tried, but franker than with anyone else. She had a natural and healthy contempt for the arts. She genuinely looked upon the whole thing as a gigantic bluff, and deep down in her heart was an amused sympathy for all the people who were able to put it over on the public. I will admit that I looked forward to the encounter between Peter Melrose and La Falterona with a good deal of sardonic amusement.

She liked coming to dine with me because she knew the food was good. It was the only meal she ate in the day, for she took great care of her figure, but she liked that one to be succulent and ample. I asked her to come at nine, knowing that was the earliest hour she dreamt of eating, and ordered dinner for half past. She turned up at a quarter to ten. She was dressed in apple-green satin, cut very low in front, with no back at all, and she wore a string of huge pearls, a number of expensive-looking rings, and on her left arm diamond and emerald bracelets from the wrist to the elbow. Two or three of them were certainly real. On her raven-black hair was a thin circlet of diamonds. She could not have looked more splendid if she had been going to a ball at Stafford House in the old days. We were in white ducks.

"How grand you are," I said. "I told you it wasn't a party."

She flashed a look of her magnificent black eyes at Peter.

"Of course it's a party. You told me your friend was a writer of talent. I am only an interpreter." She ran one finger down her flashing bracelets. "This is the homage I pay to the creative artist."

I did not utter the vulgar monosyllable that rose to my lips, but offered her what I knew was her favourite cocktail. I was privileged to call her Maria, and she always called me Master.

This she did, first because she knew it made me feel a perfect fool, and secondly because, though she was in point of fact not more than two or three years younger than I, it made it quite clear that we belonged to different generations. Sometimes, however, she also called me you dirty swine. This evening she certainly might very well have passed for thirty-five. She had those rather large features which somehow do not seem to betray age. On the stage she was a beautiful woman, and even in private life, notwithstanding her big nose, large mouth and fleshy face, a good-looking one. She wore a brown make-up, with dark rouge, and her lips were vividly scarlet. She looked very Spanish and, I suspected, felt it, for her accent at the beginning of dinner was quite Sevillian. I wanted her to talk so that Peter should get his money's worth, and I knew there was but one subject in the world that she could talk about. She was in point of fact a stupid woman who had acquired a line of glib chatter which made people on first meeting her think she was as brilliant as she looked; but it was merely a performance she gave, and you soon discovered that she not only did not know what she was talking about, but was not in the least interested in it. I do not think she had ever read a book in her life. Her knowledge of what was going on in the world was confined to what she was able to gather by looking at the pictures in the illustrated press. Her passion for music was complete bunkum. Once at a concert to which I went with her she slept all through the Fifth Symphony, and I was charmed to hear her during the interval telling people that Beethoven stirred her so much that she hesitated to come and hear him, for with those glorious themes singing through her head, it meant that she wouldn't sleep a wink all night. I could well believe she would lie awake, for she had had so sound a nap during the Symphony that it could not but interfere with her night's rest.

But there was one subject in which her interest never failed. She pursued it with indefatigable energy. No obstacle prevented her from returning to it; no chance word was so remote that she could not use it as a stepping-stone to come back to it, and in effecting this she displayed a cleverness of which one would never have thought her capable. On this subject she could be witty, vivacious, philosophic, tragic and inventive. It enabled her to exhibit all the resources of her ingenuity. There was no end to its ramifications, and no limit to its variety. This subject was herself. I gave her an opening at once and then all I had to do was to make suitable interjections. She was in great form. We were dining on the terrace and a full moon was obligingly shining on the sea in front of us. Nature, as though she knew what was proper to the occasion, had set just the right scene. The view was framed by two tall black cypresses, and all round us on the terrace the orange trees in full flower exhaled their heady perfume. There was no wind, and the candles on the table flamed with a steady softness. It was a light that exactly suited La Falterona. She sat between us, eating heartily and thoroughly appreciating the champagne, and she was enjoying herself. She gave the moon a glance. On the sea was a broad pathway of silver.

"How beautiful nature is," she said. "My God, the scenery one has to play in. How can they expect one to sing? You know, really, the sets at Covent Garden are a disgrace. The last time I sang Juliet I just told them I wouldn't go on unless they did something about the moon."

Peter listened to her in silence. He ate her words. She was better value than I had dared to hope. She got a little tight not only on the champagne but on her own loquaciousness. To listen to her you would have thought she was a meek and docile creature against whom the whole world was in conspiracy. Her life had been one long bitter struggle against desperate odds. Managers treated her vilely, impresarios played foul tricks on her, singers combined to ruin her, critics bought by the money of her enemies wrote scandalous things about her, lovers for whom she had sacrificed everything used her with base ingratitude; and yet, by the miracle of her genius and her quick wits, she had discomfited them all. With joyous glee, her eyes flashing, she told us how she had defeated their machinations and what disaster had befallen the wretches who had stood in her way. I wondered how she had the nerve to tell the disgraceful stories she told. Without the smallest consciousness of what she was doing she showed herself vindictive and envious, hard as nails, incredibly vain, cruel, selfish, scheming and mercenary. I stole a glance now and then at Peter. I was tickled at the confusion he must be experiencing when he compared his ideal picture of the prima donna with the ruthless reality. She was a woman without a heart. When at last she left us I turned to Peter with a smile.

"Well," I said, "at all events you've got some good material."

"I know, and it all fits in so beautifully," he said with enthusiasm.

"Does it?" I exclaimed, taken aback.

"She's exactly like my woman. She'll never believe that I'd sketched out the main lines of the character before I'd ever seen her."

I stared at him in amazement.

"The passion for art. The disinterestedness. She has that same nobility of soul that I saw in my mind's eye. The small-minded, the curious, the vulgar put every obstacle in her way and she sweeps them all aside by the greatness of her purpose and the purity of her ends." He gave a little happy laugh. "Isn't it wonderful how nature copies art? I swear to you, I've got her to the life."

I was about to speak; I held my tongue; though I shrugged a spiritual shoulder I was touched. Peter had seen in her what he was determined to see. There was something very like beauty in his illusion. In his own way he was a poet. We went to bed, and two or three days later, having found a pension to his liking, he left me.

In course of time his book appeared, and like most second novels by young people it had but a very moderate success. The critics had overpraised his first effort and now were unduly censorious. It is of course a very different thing to write a novel about yourself and the people you have known from childhood and to write one about persons of your own invention. Peter's was too long. He had allowed his gift for word-painting to run away with him, the humour was still rather vulgar; but he had reconstructed the period with skill, and the romantic story had that same thrill of real passion which in his first book had so much impressed me.

After dinner at my house I did not see La Falterona for more than a year. She went for a long tour in South America and did not come down to the Riviera till late in the summer. One night she asked me to dine with her. We were alone but for her companion-secretary, an Englishwoman, Miss Glaser by name, whom La Falterona bullied and ill-treated, hit and swore at, but whom she could not do without. Miss Glaser was a haggard person of fifty, with grey hair and a sallow, wrinkled face. She was a queer creature. She knew everything there was to be known about La Falterona. She both adored and hated her. Behind her back she could be extremely funny at her expense, and the imitation she gave in secret of the great singer with her admirers was the most richly comic thing I have ever heard. But she watched over her like a mother. It was she who, sometimes by wheedling, sometimes by sheer plainness of speech, caused La Falterona to behave herself something like a human being. It was she who had written the singer's exceedingly inaccurate memoirs.

La Falterona wore pale-blue satin pyjamas (she liked satin) and, presumably to rest her hair, a green silk wig; except for a few rings, a pearl necklace, a couple of bracelets and a diamond brooch at her waist, she wore no jewellery. She had much to tell me of her triumphs in South America. She talked on and on. She had never been in more superb voice and the ovations she had received were unparalleled. The concert halls were sold out for every performance, and she had made a packet.

"Is it true or is it not true, Glaser?" cried Maria with a strong South American accent.

"Most of it," said Miss Glaser.

La Falterona had the objectionable habit of addressing her companion by her surname. But it must long since have ceased to annoy the poor woman, so there was not much point in it.

"Who was that man we met in Buenos Aires?"

"Which man?"

"You fool, Glaser. You remember perfectly. The man I was married to once."

"Pepe Zapata," Miss Glaser replied without a smile.

"He was broke. He had the impudence to ask me to give him back a diamond necklace he'd given me. He said it had belonged to his mother."

"It wouldn't have hurt you to give it him," said Miss Glaser. "You never wear it."

"Give it him back?" cried La Falterona, and her astonishment was such that she spoke the purest English. "Give it him back? You're crazy."

She looked at Miss Glaser as though she expected her there and then to have an attack of acute mania. She got up from the table, for we had finished our dinner.

"Let us go outside," she said. "If I hadn't the patience of an angel I'd have sacked that woman long ago."

La Falterona and I went out, but Miss Glaser did not come with us. We sat on the verandah. There was a magnificent cedar in the garden, and its dark branches were silhouetted against the starry sky. The sea, almost at our feet, was marvellously still. Suddenly La Falterona gave a start.

"I almost forgot. Glaser, you fool," she shouted, "why didn't you remind me?" And then again to me: "I'm furious with you."

"I'm glad you didn't remember till after dinner," I answered.

"That friend of yours and his book."

I didn't immediately grasp what she was talking about.

"What friend and what book?"

"Don't be so stupid. An ugly little man with a shiny face and a bad figure. He wrote a book about me."

"Oh! Peter Melrose. But it's not about you."

"Of course it is. Do you take me for a fool? He had the impudence to send it me."

"I hope you had the decency to acknowledge it."

"Do you think I have the time to acknowledge all the books twopenny-halfpenny authors send me? I expect Glaser wrote to him. You had no right to ask me to dinner to meet him. I came to oblige you, because I thought you liked me for my-self, I didn't know I was just being made use of. It's awful that one can't trust one's oldest friends to behave like gentlemen. I'll never dine with you again so long as I live. Never, never, never."

She was working herself into one of her tantrums, so I interrupted her before it was too late.

"Come off it, my dear," I said. "In the first place the character of the singer in that book, which I suppose is the one you're referring to . . ."

"You don't suppose I'm referring to the charwoman, do you?"

"Well, the character of the singer was roughed out before he'd even seen you, and besides, it isn't in the least like you."

"How d'you mean, it's not like me? All my friends have recognised me. I mean, it's the most obvious portrait."

"Mary," I expostulated.

"My name is Maria and no one knows it better than you, and if you can't call me Maria you can call me Madame Falterona or Princess."

I paid no attention to this.

"Did you read the book?"

"Of course I read it. When everyone told me it was about me."

"But the boy's heroine, the prima donna, is twenty-five."

"A woman like me is ageless."

"She's musical to her finger-tips, gentle as a dove, and a miracle of unselfishness; she's frank, loyal and disinterested. Is that the opinion you have of yourself?"

"And what is *your* opinion of me?"

"Hard as nails, absolutely ruthless, a born intriguer and as self-centred as they make 'em."

She then called me a name which a lady does not habitually apply to a gentleman who, whatever his faults, has never had his legitimacy called in question. But though her eyes flashed I could see that she was not in the least angry. She accepted my description of her as complimentary.

"And what about the emerald ring? Are you going to deny that I told him that?"

The story of the emerald ring was this: La Falterona was having a passionate love-affair with the Crown Prince of a powerful state and he had made her a present of an emerald of immense value. One night they had a quarrel, high words passed, and some reference being made to the ring she tore it off her finger and flung it in the fire. The Crown Prince, being a man of thrifty habit, with a cry of consternation, threw himself on his knees and began raking out the coals till he recovered the ring. The Falterona watched him scornfully as he grovelled on the floor. She didn't give much away herself, but she could not bear economy in others. She finished the story with these splendid words:

"After that I *couldn't* love him."

The incident was picturesque and had taken Peter's fancy. He had used it very neatly.

"I told you both about that in the greatest confidence and I've never told it to a soul before. It's a scandalous breach of confidence to have put it into a book. There are no excuses either for him or for you."

"But I've heard you tell the story dozens of times. And it was told me by Florence Montgomerie about herself and the Crown Prince Rudolf. It was one of her favourite stories too. Lola Montez used to tell it about herself and the King of Bavaria. I have little doubt that Nell Gwyn told it about herself and Charles II. It's one of the oldest stories in the world."

She was taken aback, but only for an instant.

"I don't see anything strange in its having happened more than once. Everyone knows that women are passionate and that men are as mean as cat's-meat. I could show you the emerald if you liked. I had to have it reset, of course."

"With Lola Montez it was pearls," I said ironically. "I believe they were considerably damaged."

"Pearls?" She gave that brilliant smile of hers. "Have I ever told you about Benjy Riesenbaum and the pearls? You might make a story out of it."

Benjy Riesenbaum was a person of great wealth, and it was common knowledge that for a long time he had been the Falterona's lover. In fact it was he who had bought her the luxurious little villa in which we were now sitting.

"He'd given me a very handsome string in New York. I was singing at the Metropolitan, and at the end of the season we travelled back to Europe together. You never knew him, did you?"

"No."

"Well, he wasn't bad in some ways, but he was insanely jealous. We had a row on the boat because a young Italian officer was paying me a good deal of attention. Heaven knows, I'm the easiest woman in the world to get on with, but I will not be bullied by any man. After all, I have my self-respect to think of. I told him where he got off, if you understand what I mean, and he slapped my face. On deck if you please. I don't mind telling you I was mad. I tore the string of pearls off my neck and flung it in the sea. 'They cost fifty thousand dollars,' he gasped. He went white. I drew myself up to my full height. 'I only valued them because I loved you,' I said. And I turned on my heel."

"You were a fool," I said.

"I wouldn't speak to him for twenty-four hours. At the end of that time I had him eating out of my hand. When we got to Paris the first thing he did was to go to Cartier's and buy me another just as good."

She began to giggle.

"Did you say I was a fool? I'd left the real string in the bank in New York, because I knew I was going back next season. It was an imitation one that I threw in the sea."

She started to laugh, and her laugh was rich and joyous and like a child's. That was the sort of trick that thoroughly appealed to her. She chortled with glee.

"What fools men are," she gasped. "And you, you thought I'd throw a real string into the sea."

She laughed and laughed. At last she stopped. She was excited.

"I want to sing. Glaser, play an accompaniment."

A voice came from the drawing-room.

"You can't sing after all that food you walloped down."

"Shut up, you old cow. Play something, I tell you."

There was no reply, but in a moment Miss Glaser began to play the opening bars of one of Schumann's songs. It was no strain on the voice, and I guessed that Miss Glaser knew what she was doing when she chose it. La Falterona began to sing, in an undertone, but as she heard the sounds come from her lips and found that they were clear and pure she let herself go. The song finished. There was silence. Miss Glaser had heard that La Falterona was in magnificent voice, and she sensed that she wished to sing again. The prima donna was standing in the window, with her back to the lighted room, and she looked out at the darkly shining sea. The cedar made a lovely pattern against the sky. The night was soft and balmy. Miss Glaser played a couple of bars. A cold shiver ran down my spine. La Falterona gave a little start as she recognised the music, and I felt her gather herself together.

"Mild und leise wie er lächelt
Wie das Auge er öffnet."

It was Isolde's death song. She had never sung in Wagner, fearing the strain on her voice, but this, I suppose, she had often sung in concerts. It did not matter now that instead of an orchestral accompaniment she had only the thin tinkle of a piano. The notes of the heavenly melody fell upon the still air and travelled over the water. In that too romantic scene, in that starry night, the effect was shattering. La Falterona's voice, even now, was exquisite in its quality, mellow and crystalline; and she sang with wonderful emotion, so tenderly, with such tragic, beautiful anguish that my heart melted within me. I had a most awkward lump in my throat when she finished, and looking at her I saw that tears were streaming down her face. I did not want to speak. She stood quite still looking out at that ageless sea.

What a strange woman! I thought then that I would sooner

have her as she was, with her monstrous faults, than as Peter Melrose saw her, a pattern of all the virtues. But then people blame me because I rather like people who are a little worse than is reasonable. She was hateful, of course, but she was irresistible.

The Facts of Life

It was Henry Garnet's habit on leaving the city of an afternoon to drop in at his club and play bridge before going home to dinner. He was a pleasant man to play with. He knew the game well and you could be sure that he would make the best of his cards. He was a good loser; and when he won was more inclined to ascribe his success to his luck than to his skill. He was indulgent, and if his partner made a mistake could be trusted to find an excuse for him. It was surprising then on this occasion to hear him telling his partner with unnecessary sharpness that he had never seen a hand worse played; and it was more surprising still to see him not only make a grave error himself, an error of which you would never have thought him capable, but when his partner, not unwilling to get a little of his own back, pointed it out, insist against all reason and with considerable heat that he was perfectly right. But they were all old friends, the men he was playing with, and none of them took his ill-humour very seriously. Henry Garnet was a broker, a partner in a firm of repute, and it occurred to one of them that something had gone wrong with some stock he was interested in.

"How's the market to-day?" he asked.

"Booming. Even the suckers are making money."

It was evident that stocks and shares had nothing to do with Henry Garnet's vexation; but something was the matter; that was evident too. He was a hearty fellow, who enjoyed excellent health; he had plenty of money; he was fond of his wife and devoted to his children. As a rule he had high spirits, and he laughed easily at the nonsense they were apt to talk while they played; but to-day he sat glum and silent. His brows were

crossly puckered and there was a sulky look about his mouth.
Presently, to ease the tension, one of the others mentioned a
subject upon which they all knew Henry Garnet was glad to
speak.

"How's your boy, Henry? I see he's done pretty well in the
tournament."

Henry Garnet's frown grew darker.

"He's done no better than I expected him to."

"When does he come back from Monte?"

"He got back last night."

"Did he enjoy himself?"

"I suppose so; all I know is that he made a damned fool of
himself."

"Oh. How?"

"I'd rather not talk about it if you don't mind."

The three men looked at him with curiosity. Henry Garnet
scowled at the green baize.

"Sorry, old boy. Your call."

The game proceeded in a strained silence. Garnet got his
bid, and when he played his cards so badly that he went three
down not a word was said. Another rubber was begun and in
the second game Garnet denied a suit.

"Having none?" his partner asked him.

Garnet's irritability was such that he did not even reply,
and when at the end of the hand it appeared that he had re-
voked, and that his revoke cost the rubber, it was not to be
expected that his partner should let his carelessness go without remark.

"What the devil's the matter with you, Henry?" he said.
"You're playing like a fool."

Garnet was disconcerted. He did not so much mind losing a
big rubber himself, but he was sore that his inattention should
have made his partner lose too. He pulled himself together.

"I'd better not play any more. I thought a few rubbers
would calm me, but the fact is I can't give my mind to the
game. To tell you the truth I'm in a hell of a temper."

They all burst out laughing.

"You don't have to tell us that, old boy. It's obvious."

Garnet gave them a rueful smile.

"Well, I bet you'd be in a temper if what's happened to me had happened to you. As a matter of fact I'm in a damned awkward situation, and if any of you fellows can give me any advice how to deal with it I'd be grateful."

"Let's have a drink and you tell us all about it. With a K.C., a Home Office official and an eminent surgeon—if we can't tell you how to deal with a situation, nobody can."

The K.C. got up and rang the bell for a waiter.

"It's about that damned boy of mine," said Henry Garnet.

Drinks were ordered and brought. And this is the story that Henry Garnet told them.

The boy of whom he spoke was his only son. His name was Nicholas and of course he was called Nicky. He was eighteen. The Garnets had two daughters besides, one of sixteen and the other of twelve, but however unreasonable it seemed, for a father is generally supposed to like his daughters best, and though he did all he could not to show his preference, there was no doubt that the greater share of Henry Garnet's affection was given to his son. He was kind, in a chaffing, casual way, to his daughters, and gave them handsome presents on their birthdays and at Christmas; but he doted on Nicky. Nothing was too good for him. He thought the world of him. He could hardly take his eyes off him. You could not blame him, for Nicky was a son that any parent might have been proud of. He was six foot two, lithe but muscular, with broad shoulders and a slim waist, and he held himself gallantly erect; he had a charming head, well placed on the shoulders, with pale brown hair that waved slightly, blue eyes with long dark lashes under well-marked eyebrows, a full red mouth and a tanned, clean skin. When he smiled he showed very regular and very white teeth. He was not shy, but there was a modesty in his demeanour that was attractive. In social intercourse he was easy, polite and quietly gay. He was the offspring of nice, healthy, decent parents, he had been well brought up in a good home, he had been sent to a good school, and the general result was as engaging a specimen of young manhood as you were likely to find in a long time. You felt

that he was as honest, open and virtuous as he looked. He had
never given his parents a moment's uneasiness. As a child he
was seldom ill and never naughty. As a boy he did everything that was expected of him. His school reports were excellent. He was wonderfully popular, and he ended his career,
with a creditable number of prizes, as head of the school and
captain of the football team. But this was not all. At the age of
fourteen Nicky had developed an unexpected gift for lawn
tennis. This was a game that his father not only was fond of,
but played very well, and when he discerned in the boy the
promise of a tennis-player he fostered it. During the holidays
he had him taught by the best professionals and by the time
he was sixteen he had won a number of tournaments for boys
of his age. He could beat his father so badly that only parental
affection reconciled the older player to the poor show he put
up. At eighteen Nicky went to Cambridge and Henry Garnet
conceived the ambition that before he was through with the
university he should play for it. Nicky had all the qualifica-
tions for becoming a great tennis-player. He was tall, he had a
long reach, he was quick on his feet and his timing was perfect. He realised instinctively where the ball was coming and,
seemingly without hurry, was there to take it. He had a
powerful serve, with a nasty break that made it difficult to
return, and his forehand drive, low, long and accurate, was
deadly. He was not so good on the backhand and his volleying
was wild, but all through the summer before he went to
Cambridge Henry Garnet made him work on these points under the best teacher in England. At the back of his mind,
though he did not even mention it to Nicky, he cherished a
further ambition, to see his son play at Wimbledon, and who
could tell, perhaps be chosen to represent his country in the
Davis Cup. A great lump came into Henry Garnet's throat as
he saw in fancy his son leap over the net to shake hands with
the American champion whom he had just defeated, and walk
off the court to the deafening plaudits of the multitude.

As an assiduous frequenter of Wimbledon Henry Garnet
had a good many friends in the tennis world, and one evening
he found himself at a City dinner sitting next to one of

them, a Colonel Brabazon, and in due course began talking to
him of Nicky and what chance there might be of his being
chosen to play for his university during the following season.
"Why don't you let him go down to Monte Carlo and play
in the spring tournament there?" said the Colonel suddenly.
"Oh, I don't think he's good enough for that. He's not nineteen yet, he only went up to Cambridge last October; he
wouldn't stand a chance against all those cracks."

"Of course, Austin and von Cramm and so on would knock
spots off him, but he might snatch a game or two; and if he
got up against some of the smaller fry there's no reason why
he shouldn't win two or three matches. He's never been up
against any of the first-rate players and it would be wonderful
practice for him. He'd learn a lot more than he'll ever learn in
the seaside tournaments you enter him for."

"I wouldn't dream of it. I'm not going to let him leave Cambridge in the middle of a term. I've always impressed upon
him that tennis is only a game and it mustn't interfere with
work."

Colonel Brabazon asked Garnet when the term ended.

"That's all right. He'd only have to cut about three days.
Surely that could be arranged. You see, two of the men we
were depending on have let us down, and we're in a hole. We
want to send as good a team as we can. The Germans are
sending their best players and so are the Americans."

"Nothing doing, old boy. In the first place Nicky's not good
enough, and secondly, I don't fancy the idea of sending a kid
like that to Monte Carlo without anyone to look after him. If
I could get away myself I might think of it, but that's out of
the question."

"I shall be there. I'm going as the non-playing captain of
the English team. I'll keep an eye on him."

"You'll be busy, and besides, it's not a responsibility I'd like
to ask you to take. He's never been abroad in his life, and to
tell you the truth, I shouldn't have a moment's peace all the
time he was there."

They left it at that and presently Henry Garnet went home.

He was so flattered by Colonel Brabazon's suggestion that he could not help telling his wife.

"Fancy his thinking Nicky's as good as that. He told me he'd seen him play and his style was fine. He only wants more practice to get into the first flight. We shall see the kid playing in the semi-finals at Wimbledon yet, old girl."

To his surprise Mrs. Garnet was not so much opposed to the notion as he would have expected.

"After all the boy's eighteen. Nicky's never got into mischief yet and there's no reason to suppose he will now."

"There's his work to be considered; don't forget that. I think it would be a very bad precedent to let him cut the end of term."

"But what can three days matter? It seems a shame to rob him of a chance like that. I'm sure he'd jump at it if you asked him."

"Well, I'm not going to. I haven't sent him to Cambridge just to play tennis. I know he's steady, but it's silly to put temptation in his way. He's much too young to go to Monte Carlo by himself."

"You say he won't have a chance against these crack players, but you can't tell."

Henry Garnet sighed a little. On the way home in the car it had struck him that Austin's health was uncertain and that von Cramm had his off-days. Supposing, just for the sake of argument, that Nicky had a bit of luck like that—then there would be no doubt that he would be chosen to play for Cambridge. But of course that was all nonsense.

"Nothing doing, my dear. I've made up my mind and I'm not going to change it."

Mrs. Garnet held her peace. But next day she wrote to Nicky, telling him what had happened, and suggested to him what she would do in his place if, wanting to go, he wished to get his father's consent. A day or two later Henry Garnet received a letter from his son. He was bubbling over with excitement. He had seen his tutor, who was a tennis-player himself, and the Provost of his college, who happened to know Colonel Brabazon, and no objection would be made to his leaving before the end of term; they both thought it an opportunity that shouldn't be missed. He didn't see what harm he could come to, and if only, just this once, his father would stretch a point, well, next term, he promised faithfully, he'd work like blazes. It was a very pretty letter. Mrs. Garnet watched her husband read it at the breakfast table; she was undisturbed by the frown on his face. He threw it over to her.

"I don't know why you thought it necessary to tell Nicky something I told you in confidence. It's too bad of you. Now you've thoroughly unsettled him."

"I'm sorry. I thought it would please him to know that Colonel Brabazon had such a high opinion of him. I don't see why one should only tell people the disagreeable things that are said about them. Of course I made it quite clear that there could be no question of his going."

"You've put me in an odious position. If there's anything I hate it's for the boy to look upon me as a spoil-sport and a tyrant."

"Oh, he'll never do that. He may think you rather silly and unreasonable, but I'm sure he'll understand that it's only for his own good that you're being so unkind."

"Christ," said Henry Garnet.

His wife had a great inclination to laugh. She knew the battle was won. Dear, oh dear, how easy it was to get men to do what you wanted. For appearance' sake Henry Garnet held out for forty-eight hours, but then he yielded, and a fortnight later Nicky came to London. He was to start for Monte Carlo next morning, and after dinner, when Mrs. Garnet and her elder daughter had left them, Henry took the opportunity to give his son some good advice.

"I don't feel quite comfortable about letting you go off to a place like Monte Carlo at your age practically by yourself," he finished, "but there it is and I can only hope you'll be sensible. I don't want to play the heavy father, but there are three things especially that I want to warn you against: one is gambling, don't gamble; the second is money, don't lend anyone money; and the third is women, don't have anything to do with women. If you don't do any of those three things you can't come to much harm, so remember them well."

"All right, father," Nicky smiled.

"That's my last word to you. I know the world pretty well and believe me, my advice is sound."

"I won't forget it. I promise you."

"That's a good chap. Now let's go up and join the ladies."

Nicky beat neither Austin nor von Cramm in the Monte Carlo tournament, but he did not disgrace himself. He snatched an unexpected victory over a Spanish player and gave one of the Austrians a closer match than anyone had thought possible. In the mixed doubles he got into the semi-finals. His charm conquered everyone and he vastly enjoyed himself. It was generally allowed that he showed promise, and Colonel Brabazon told him that when he was a little older and had had more practice with first-class players he would be a credit to his father. The tournament came to an end and the day following he was to fly back to London. Anxious to play his best he had lived very carefully, smoking little and drinking nothing, and going to bed early; but on his last evening he thought he would like to see something of the life in Monte Carlo of which he had heard so much. An official dinner was given to the tennis-players and after dinner with the rest of them he went into the Sporting Club. It was the first time he had been there. Monte Carlo was very full and the rooms were crowded. Nicky had never before seen roulette played except in the pictures; in a maze he stopped at the first table he came to; chips of different sizes were scattered over the green cloth in what looked like a hopeless muddle; the croupier gave the wheel a sharp turn and with a flick threw in the little white ball. After what seemed an endless time the ball stopped and another croupier with a broad, indifferent gesture raked in the chips of those who had lost.

Presently Nicky wandered over to where they were playing *trente et quarante,* but he couldn't understand what it was all about and he thought it dull. He saw a crowd in another room and sauntered in. A big game of baccara was in progress and he was immediately conscious of the tension. The players were protected from the thronging bystanders by a brass rail; they sat round the table, nine on each side, with the dealer in the middle and the croupier facing him. Big money was changing hands. The dealer was a member of the Greek Syndicate. Nicky looked at his impassive face. His eyes were watchful, but his expression never changed whether he won or lost. It was a terrifying, strangely impressive sight. It gave Nicky, who had been thriftily brought up, a peculiar thrill to see someone risk a thousand pounds on the turn of a card and when he lost make a little joke and laugh. It was all terribly exciting. An acquaintance came up to him.

"Been doing any good?" he asked.

"I haven't been playing."

"Wise of you. Rotten game. Come and have a drink."

"All right."

While they were having it Nicky told his friends that this was the first time he had ever been in the rooms.

"Oh, but you must have one little flutter before you go. It's idiotic to leave Monte without having tried your luck. After all it won't hurt you to lose a hundred francs or so."

"I don't suppose it will, but my father wasn't any too keen on my coming at all and one of the three things he particularly advised me not to do was to gamble."

But when Nicky left his companion he strolled back to one of the tables where they were playing roulette. He stood for a while looking at the losers' money being raked-in by the croupier and the money that was won paid out to the winners. It was impossible to deny that it was thrilling. His friend was right, it did seem silly to leave Monte without putting something on the table just once. It would be an experience, and at his age you had to have all the experience you could get. He reflected that he hadn't promised his father not to gamble, he'd promised him not to forget his advice. It wasn't quite the same, was it? He took a hundred-franc note out of his pocket and rather shyly put it on number eighteen. He chose it because that was his age. With a wildly beating heart he watched the wheel turn; the little white ball whizzed about like a small demon of mischief; the wheel went round more slowly, the little white ball hesitated, it seemed about to stop, it went on again; Nicky could hardly believe his eyes when it fell into number eighteen. A lot of chips were passed over to him and his hands trembled as he took them. It seemed to amount to a lot of money. He was so confused that he never thought of putting anything on the following round; in fact he had no intention of playing any more, once was enough; and he was surprised when eighteen again came up. There was only one chip on it.

"By George, you've won again," said a man who was standing near to him.

"Me? I hadn't got anything on."

"Yes, you had. Your original stake. They always leave it on unless you ask for it back. Didn't you know?"

Another packet of chips was handed over to him. Nicky's head reeled. He counted his gains: seven thousand francs. A queer sense of power seized him; he felt wonderfully clever. This was the easiest way of making money that he had ever heard of. His frank, charming face was wreathed in smiles. His bright eyes met those of a woman standing by his side. She smiled.

"You're in luck," she said.

She spoke English, but with a foreign accent.

"I can hardly believe it. It's the first time I've ever played."

"That explains it. Lend me a thousand francs, will you? I've lost everything I've got. I'll give it you back in half an hour."

"All right."

She took a large red chip from his pile and with a word of thanks disappeared. The man who had spoken to him before grunted.

"You'll never see that again."

Nicky was dashed. His father had particularly advised him not to lend anyone money. What a silly thing to do! And to somebody he'd never seen in his life. But the fact was, he felt at that moment such a love for the human race that it had never occurred to him to refuse. And that big red chip, it was almost impossible to realise that it had any value. Oh well, it didn't matter, he still had six thousand francs, he'd just try his luck once or twice more and if he didn't win he'd go home. He put a chip on sixteen, which was his elder sister's age, but it didn't come up; then on twelve, which was his younger sister's, and that didn't come up either; he tried various numbers at random, but without success. It was funny, he seemed to have lost his knack. He thought he would try just once more and then stop; he won. He had made up all his losses and had something over. At the end of an hour, after various ups and downs, having experienced such thrills as he had never known in his life, he found himself with so many chips that they would hardly go in his pockets. He decided to go. He went to the changers' office and he gasped when twenty thousand-franc notes were spread out before him. He had never had so much money in his life. He put it in his pocket and was turning away when the woman to whom he had lent the thousand francs came up to him.

"I've been looking for you everywhere," she said. "I was afraid you'd gone. I was in a fever, I didn't know what you'd think of me. Here's your thousand francs and thank you so much for the loan."

Nicky, blushing scarlet, stared at her with amazement. How he had misjudged her! His father had said, don't gamble; well, he had, and he'd made twenty thousand francs; and his father had said, don't lend anyone money; well, he had, he'd lent quite a lot to a total stranger, and she'd returned it. The fact was that he wasn't nearly such a fool as his father thought: he'd had an instinct that he could lend her the money with safety, and you see, his instinct was right. But he was so obviously taken aback that the little lady was forced to laugh.

"What is the matter with you?" she asked.

"To tell you the truth I never expected to see the money back."

"What did you take me for? Did you think I was a— cocotte?"

Nicky reddened to the roots of his wavy hair.

"No, of course not."

"Do I look like one?"

"Not a bit."

She was dressed very quietly, in black, with a string of gold beads round her neck; her simple frock showed off a neat, slight figure; she had a pretty little face and a trim head. She was made up, but not excessively, and Nicky supposed that she was not more than three or four years older than himself. She gave him a friendly smile.

"My husband is in the administration in Morocco, and I've come to Monte Carlo for a few weeks because he thought I wanted a change."

"I was just going," said Nicky because he couldn't think of anything else to say.

"Already!"

"Well, I've got to get up early to-morrow. I'm going back to London by air."

"Of course. The tournament ended to-day, didn't it? I saw you play, you know, two or three times."

"Did you? I don't know why you should have noticed me."

"You've got a beautiful style. And you looked very sweet in your shorts."

Nicky was not an immodest youth, but it did cross his mind that perhaps she had borrowed that thousand francs in order to scrape acquaintance with him.

"Do you ever go to the Knickerbocker?" she asked.

"No. I never have."

"Oh, but you mustn't leave Monte Carlo without having been there. Why don't you come and dance a little? To tell you the truth, I'm starving with hunger and I should adore some bacon and eggs.".

Nicky remembered his father's advice not to have anything to do with women, but this was different; you had only to look at the pretty little thing to know at once that she was perfectly respectable. Her husband was in what corresponded, he supposed, to the Civil Service. His father and mother had friends who were Civil Servants and they and their wives sometimes came to dinner. It was true that the wives were neither so young nor so pretty as this one, but she was just as ladylike as they were. And after winning twenty thousand francs he thought it wouldn't be a bad idea to have a little fun.

"I'd love to go with you," he said. "But you won't mind if I don't stay very long. I've left instructions at my hotel that I'm to be called at seven."

"We'll leave as soon as ever you like."

Nicky found it very pleasant at the Knickerbocker. He ate his bacon and eggs with appetite. They shared a bottle of champagne. They danced, and the little lady told him he danced beautifully. He knew he danced pretty well, and of course she was easy to dance with. As light as a feather. She laid her cheek against his and when their eyes met there was in hers a smile that made his heart go pit-a-pat. A coloured woman sang in a throaty, sensual voice. The floor was crowded.

"Have you ever been told that you're very good-looking?" she asked.

"I don't think so," he laughed. "Gosh," he thought, "I believe she's fallen for me."

Nicky was not such a fool as to be unaware that women often liked him, and when she made that remark he pressed her to him a little more closely. She closed her eyes and a faint sigh escaped her lips.

"I suppose it wouldn't be quite nice if I kissed you before all these people," he said.

"What do you think they would take me for?"

It began to grow late and Nicky said that really he thought he ought to be going.

"I shall go too," she said. "Will you drop me at my hotel on your way?"

Nicky paid the bill. He was rather surprised at its amount, but with all that money he had in his pocket he could afford not to care, and they got into a taxi. She snuggled up to him and he kissed her. She seemed to like it.

"By Jove," he thought, "I wonder if there's anything doing."

It was true that she was a married woman, but her husband was in Morocco, and it certainly did look as if she'd fallen for him. Good and proper. It was true also that his father had warned him to have nothing to with women, but, he reflected again, he hadn't actually promised he wouldn't, he'd only promised not to forget his advice. Well, he hadn't; he was bearing it in mind that very minute. But circumstances alter cases. She was a sweet little thing; it seemed silly to miss the chance of an adventure when it was handed to you like that on a tray. When they reached the hotel he paid off the taxi.

"I'll walk home," he said. "The air will do me good after the stuffy atmosphere of that place."

"Come up a moment," she said. "I'd like to show you the photo of my little boy."

"Oh, have you got a little boy?" he exclaimed, a trifle dashed.

"Yes, a sweet little boy."

He walked upstairs after her. He didn't in the least want to see the photograph of her little boy, but he thought it only civil to pretend he did. He was afraid he'd made a fool of himself; it occurred to him that she was taking him up to look at the photograph in order to show him in a nice way that he'd made a mistake. He'd told her he was eighteen.

"I suppose she thinks I'm just a kid."

He began to wish he hadn't spent all that money on champagne at the night-club.

But she didn't show him the photograph of her little boy after all. They had no sooner got into her room than she turned to him, flung her arms round his neck, and kissed him full on the lips. He had never in all his life been kissed so passionately.

"Darling," she said.

For a brief moment his father's advice once more crossed Nicky's mind and then he forgot it.

Nicky was a light sleeper and the least sound was apt to wake him. Two or three hours later he woke and for a moment could not imagine where he was. The room was not quite dark, for the door of the bathroom was ajar, and the light in it had been left on. Suddenly he was conscious that someone was moving about the room. Then he remembered. He saw that it was his little friend, and he was on the point of speaking when something in the way she was behaving stopped him. She was walking very cautiously, as though she were afraid of waking him; she stopped once or twice and looked over at the bed. He wondered what she was after. He soon saw. She went over to the chair on which he had placed his clothes and once more looked in his direction. She waited for what seemed to him an interminable time. The silence was so intense that Nicky thought he could hear his own heart beating. Then, very slowly, very quietly, she took up his coat, slipped her hand into the inside pocket and drew out all those beautiful thousand-franc notes that Nicky had been so proud to win. She put the coat back and placed some other clothes on it so that it should look as though it had not been disturbed, then, with the bundle of notes in her hand, for an appreciable time stood once more stock-still. Nicky had repressed an instinctive impulse to jump up and grab her, it was partly surprise that had kept him quiet, partly the notion that he was in a strange hotel, in a foreign country, and if he made a row he didn't know what might happen. She looked at him. His eyes were partly closed and he was sure that she thought he was asleep. In the silence she could hardly fail to hear his regular breathing. When she had reassured herself that her movements had not disturbed him she stepped, with infinite caution, across the room. On a small table in the window a cineraria was growing in a pot. Nicky watched her now with his eyes wide open. The plant was evidently placed quite loosely in the pot, for taking it by the stalks she lifted it out; she put the banknotes in the bottom of the pot and replaced the plant. It was an excellent hiding-place. No one could have guessed that anything was concealed under that richly-flowering plant. She pressed the earth down with her fingers and then, very slowly, taking care not to make the smallest noise, crept across the room, and slipped back into bed.

"Chéri," she said, in a caressing voice.

Nicky breathed steadily, like a man immersed in deep

sleep. The little lady turned over on her side and disposed herself to slumber. But though Nicky lay so still his thoughts worked busily. He was extremely indignant at the scene he had just witnessed, and to himself he spoke his thoughts with vigour.

"She's nothing but a damned tart. She and her dear little boy and her husband in Morocco. My eye! She's a rotten thief, that's what she is. Took me for a mug. If she thinks she's going to get away with anything like that, she's mistaken."

He had already made up his mind what he was going to do with the money had had so cleverly won. He had long wanted a car of his own, and had thought it rather mean of his father not to have given him one. After all, a feller doesn't always want to drive about in the family bus. Well, he'd just teach the old man a lesson and buy one himself. For twenty thousand francs, two hundred pounds roughly, he could get a very decent second-hand car. He meant to get the money back, but just then he didn't quite know how. He didn't like the idea of kicking up a row, he was a stranger, in an hotel he knew nothing of; it might very well be that the beastly woman had friends there, he didn't mind facing anyone in a fair fight, but he'd look pretty foolish if someone pulled a gun on him. He reflected besides, very sensibly, that he had no proof the money was his. If it came to a showdown and she swore it was hers, he might very easily find himself hauled off to a police-station. He really didn't know what to do. Presently by her regular breathing he knew that the little lady was asleep. She must have fallen asleep with an easy mind, for she had done her job without a hitch. It infuriated Nicky that she should rest so peacefully while he lay awake worried to death. Suddenly an idea occurred to him. It was such a good one that it was only by the exercise of all his self-control that he prevented himself from jumping out of bed and carrying it out at once. Two could play at her game. She'd stolen his money; well, he'd steal it back again, and they'd be all square. He made up his mind to wait quite quietly until

he was sure that deceitful woman was sound asleep. He waited
for what seemed to him a very long time. She did not stir. Her
breathing was as regular as a child's.

"Darling," he said at last.

No answer. No movement. She was dead to the world.
Very slowly, pausing after every movement, very silently, he
slipped out of bed. He stood still for a while, looking at her to
see whether he had disturbed her. Her breathing was as
regular as before. During the time he was waiting he had
taken note carefully of the furniture in the room so that in
crossing it he should not knock against a chair or a table and
make a noise. He took a couple of steps and waited, he took
a couple of steps more; he was very light on his feet and made
no sound as he walked; he took fully five minutes to get to
the window, and here he waited again. He started, for the bed
slightly creaked, but it was only because the sleeper turned
in her sleep. He forced himself to wait till he had counted one
hundred. She was sleeping like a log. With infinite care he
seized the cineraria by the stalks and gently pulled it out of
the pot; he put his other hand in, his heart beat nineteen
to the dozen as his fingers touched the notes, his hand closed
on them and he slowly drew them out. He replaced the plant
and in his turn carefully pressed down the earth. While he
was doing all this he had kept one eye on the form lying in
the bed. It remained still. After another pause he crept softly
to the chair on which his clothes were lying. He first put the
bundle of notes in his coat pocket and then proceeded to
dress. It took him a good quarter of an hour, because he
could afford to make no sound. He had been wearing a soft
shirt with his dinner jacket, and he congratulated himself on
this, because it was easier to put on silently than a stiff one.
He had some difficulty in tying his tie without a looking-
glass, but he very wisely reflected that it didn't really matter
if it wasn't tied very well. His spirits were rising. The whole
thing now began to seem rather a lark. At length he was
completely dressed except for his shoes, which he took in his
hand; he thought he would put them on when he got into
the passage. Now he had to cross the room to get to the door.

He reached it so quietly that he could not have disturbed the lightest sleeper. But the door had to be unlocked. He turned the key very slowly; it creaked.

"Who's that?"

The little woman suddenly sat up in bed. Nicky's heart jumped to his mouth. He made a great effort to keep his head

"It's only me. It's six o'clock and I've got to go. I was trying not to wake you."

"Oh, I forgot."

She sank back on to the pillow.

"Now that you're awake I'll put on my shoes."

He sat down on the edge of the bed and did this.

"Don't make a noise when you go out. The hotel people don't like it. Oh, I'm so sleepy."

"You go right off to sleep again."

"Kiss me before you go." He bent down and kissed her. "You're a sweet boy and a wonderful lover. *Bon voyage.*"

Nicky did not feel quite safe till he got out of the hotel. The dawn had broken. The sky was unclouded, and in the harbour the yachts and the fishing-boats lay motionless on the still water. On the quay fishermen were getting ready to start on their day's work. The streets were deserted. Nicky took a long breath of the sweet morning air. He felt alert and well. He also felt as pleased as Punch. With a swinging stride, his shoulders well thrown back, he walked up the hill and along the gardens in front of the Casino—the flowers in that clear light had a dewy brilliance that was delicious—till he came to his hotel. Here the day had already begun. In the hall porters with mufflers round their necks and berets on their heads were busy sweeping. Nicky went up to his room and had a hot bath. He lay in it and thought with satisfaction that he was not such a mug as some people might think. After his bath he did his exercises, dressed, packed and went down to breakfast. He had a grand appetite. No continental breakfast for him! He had grapefruit, porridge, bacon and eggs, rolls fresh from the oven, so crisp and delicious they melted in your mouth, marmalade and three cups of coffee. Though feeling perfectly well before, he felt better after that. He lit the pipe he had recently learnt to smoke, paid his bill and stepped into the car that was waiting to take him to the aerodrome on the other side of Cannes. The road as far as Nice ran over the hills and below him was the blue sea and the coast-line. He couldn't help thinking it damned pretty. They passed through Nice, so gay and friendly in the early morning, and presently they came to a long stretch of straight road that ran by the sea. Nicky had paid his bill, not with the money he had won the night before, but with the money his father had given him; he had changed a thousand francs to pay for supper at the Knickerbocker, but that deceitful little woman had returned him the thousand francs he had lent her, so that he still had twenty thousand-franc notes in his pocket. He thought he would like to have a look at them. He had so nearly lost them that they had a double value for him. He took them out of his hip-pocket into which for safety's sake he had stuffed them when he put on the suit he was travelling in, and counted them one by one. Something very strange had happened to them. Instead of there being twenty notes as there should have been there were twenty-six. He couldn't understand it at all. He counted them twice more. There was no doubt about it; somehow or other he had twenty-six thousand francs instead of the twenty he should have had. He couldn't make it out. He asked himself if it was possible that he had won more at the Sporting Club than he had realised. But no, that was out of the question; he distinctly remembered the man at the desk laying the notes out in four rows of five, and he had counted them himself. Suddenly the explanation occurred to him; when he had put his hand into the flower-pot, after taking out the cineraria, he had grabbed everything he felt there. The flower-pot was the little hussy's money-box and he had taken out not only his own money, but her savings as well. Nicky leant back in the car and burst into a roar of laughter. It was the funniest thing he had ever heard in his life. And when he thought of her going to the flower-pot some time later in the morning when she awoke, expecting to find the money she had so cleverly got away with, and finding, not only that it wasn't there, but that her own had gone too, he laughed more than ever. And so far as he was concerned there was nothing to do about it; he neither knew her name, nor the name of the hotel to which she had taken him. He couldn't return her money even if he wanted to.

"It serves her damned well right," he said.

This then was the story that Henry Garnet told his friends over the bridge-table, for the night before, after dinner when his wife and daughter had left them to their port, Nicky had narrated it in full.

"And you know what infuriated me is that he's so damned pleased with himself. Talk of a cat swallowing a canary. And d'you know what he said to me when he'd finished? He looked at me with those innocent eyes of his and said: 'You know, father, I can't help thinking there was something wrong about the advice you gave me. You said, don't gamble; well, I did, and I made a packet; you said, don't lend money; well, I did, and I got it back; and you said, don't have anything to do with women; well, I did, and I made six thousand francs on the deal.' "

It didn't make it any better for Henry Garnet that his three companions burst out laughing.

"It's all very well for you fellows to laugh, but you know, I'm in a damned awkward position. The boy looked up to me, he respected me, he took whatever I said as gospel truth, and now, I saw it in his eyes, he just looks upon me as a drivelling old fool. It's no good my saying one swallow doesn't make a summer; he doesn't see that it was just a fluke, he thinks the whole thing was due to his own cleverness. It may ruin him."

"You do look a bit of a damned fool, old man," said one of the others. "There's no denying that, is there?"

"I know I do, and I don't like it. It's so dashed unfair. Fate has no right to play one tricks like that. After all, you must admit that my advice was good."

"Very good."

"And the wretched boy ought to have burnt his fingers.
Well, he hasn't. You're all men of the world, you tell me how
I'm to deal with the situation now."

But they none of them could.

"Well, Henry, if I were you I wouldn't worry," said the
lawyer. "My belief is that your boy's born lucky, and in the
long run that's better than to be born clever or rich."

Lord Mountdrago

D~R.~ A~UDLIN~ looked at the clock on his desk. It was twenty minutes to six. He was surprised that his patient was late, for Lord Mountdrago prided himself on his punctuality; he had a sententious way of expressing himself which gave the air of an epigram to a commonplace remark, and he was in the habit of saying that punctuality is a compliment you pay to the intelligent and a rebuke you administer to the stupid. Lord Mountdrago's appointment was for five-thirty.

There was in Dr. Audlin's appearance nothing to attract attention. He was tall and spare, with narrow shoulders and something of a stoop; his hair was grey and thin; his long, sallow face deeply lined. He was not more than fifty, but he looked older. His eyes, pale-blue and rather large, were weary. When you had been with him for a while you noticed that they moved very little; they remained fixed on your face, but so empty of expression were they that it was no discomfort. They seldom lit up. They gave no clue to his thoughts nor changed with the words he spoke. If you were of an observant turn it might have struck you that he blinked much less often than most of us. His hands were on the large side, with long, tapering fingers; they were soft, but firm, cool but not clammy. You could never have said what Dr. Audlin wore unless you had made a point of looking. His clothes were dark. His tie was black. His dress made his sallow lined face paler, and his pale eyes more wan. He gave you the impression of a very sick man.

Dr. Audlin was a psycho-analyst. He had adopted the profession by accident and practised it with misgiving. When the

war broke out he had not been long qualified and was getting
experience at various hospitals; he offered his services to the
authorities, and after a time was sent out to France. It was
then that he discovered his singular gift. He could allay
certain pains by the touch of his cool, firm hands, and by talking to them often induce sleep in men who were suffering
from sleeplessness. He spoke slowly. His voice had no particular colour, and its tone did not alter with the words he
uttered, but it was musical, soft and lulling. He told the men
that they must rest, that they mustn't worry, that they must
sleep; and rest stole into their jaded bones, tranquillity
pushed their anxieties away, like a man finding a place for
himself on a crowded bench, and slumber fell on their tired
eyelids like the light rain of spring upon the fresh-turned
earth. Dr. Audlin found that by speaking to men with that
low, monotonous voice of his, by looking at them with his
pale, quiet eyes, by stroking their weary foreheads with his
long firm hands, he could soothe their perturbations, resolve
the conflicts that distracted them and banish the phobias that
made their lives a torment. Sometimes he effected cures that
seemed miraculous. He restored speech to a man who, after
being buried under the earth by a bursting shell, had been
struck dumb, and he gave back the use of his limbs to
another who had been paralysed after a crash in a plane. He
could not understand his powers; he was of a sceptical turn,
and though they say that in circumstances of this kind the
first thing is to believe in yourself, he never quite succeeded
in doing that; and it was only the outcome of his activities,
patent to the most incredulous observer, that obliged him to
admit that he had some faculty, coming from he knew not
where, obscure and uncertain, that enabled him to do things
for which he could offer no explanation. When the war was
over he went to Vienna and studied there, and afterwards to
Zurich; and then settled down in London to practise the art
he had so strangely acquired. He had been practising now for
fifteen years, and had attained, in the speciality he followed, a
distinguished reputation. People told one another of the
amazing things he had done, and though his fees were high,

he had as many patients as he had time to see. Dr. Audlin knew that he had achieved some very extraordinary results; he had saved men from suicide, others from the lunatic asylum, he had assuaged griefs that embittered useful lives, he had turned unhappy marriages into happy ones, he had eradicated abnormal instincts and thus delivered not a few from a hateful bondage, he had given health to the sick in spirit; he had done all this, and yet at the back of his mind remained the suspicion that he was little more than a quack.

It went against his grain to exercise a power that he could not understand, and it offended his honesty to trade on the faith of the people he treated when he had no faith in himself. He was rich enough now to live without working, and the work exhausted him; a dozen times he had been on the point of giving up practice. He knew all that Freud and Jung and the rest of them had written. He was not satisfied; he had an intimate conviction that all their theory was hocus-pocus, and yet there the results were, incomprehensible, but manifest. And what had he not seen of human nature during the fifteen years that patients had been coming to his dingy back room in Wimpole Street? The revelations that had been poured into his ears, sometimes only too willingly, sometimes with shame, with reservations, with anger, had long ceased to surprise him. Nothing could shock him any longer. He knew by now that men were liars, he knew how extravagant was their vanity; he knew far worse than that about them; but he knew that it was not for him to judge or to condemn. But year by year as these terrible confidences were imparted to him his face grew a little greyer, its lines a little more marked and his pale eyes more weary. He seldom laughed, but now and again when for relaxation he read a novel he smiled. Did their authors really think the men and women they wrote of were like that? If they only knew how much more complicated they were, how much more unexpected, what irreconcilable elements co-existed within their souls and what dark and sinister contentions afflicted them!

It was a quarter to six. Of all the strange cases he had been called upon to deal with Dr. Audlin could remember none stranger than that of Lord Mountdrago. For one thing the personality of his patient made it singular. Lord Mountdrago was an able and a distinguished man. Appointed Secretary for Foreign Affairs when still under forty, now after three years in office he had seen his policy prevail. It was generally acknowledged that he was the ablest politician in the Conservative Party and only the fact that his father was a peer, on whose death he would no longer be able to sit in the House of Commons, made it impossible for him to aim at the premiership. But if in these democratic times it is out of the question for a Prime Minister of England to be in the House of Lords, there was nothing to prevent Lord Mountdrago from continuing to be Secretary for Foreign Affairs in successive Conservative administrations and so for long directing the foreign policy of his country.

Lord Mountdrago had many good qualities. He had intelligence and industry. He was widely travelled, and spoke several languages fluently. From early youth he had specialised in foreign affairs, and had conscientiously made himself acquainted with the political and economic circumstances of other countries. He had courage, insight and determination. He was a good speaker, both on the platform and in the House, clear, precise and often witty. He was a brilliant debater and his gift of repartee was celebrated. He had a fine presence: he was a tall, handsome man, rather bald and somewhat too stout, but this gave him solidity and an air of maturity that were of service to him. As a young man he had been something of an athlete and had rowed in the Oxford boat, and he was known to be one of the best shots in England. At twenty-four he had married a girl of eighteen whose father was a duke and her mother a great American heiress, so that she had both position and wealth, and by her he had had two sons. For several years they had lived privately apart, but in public united, so that appearances were saved, and no other attachment on either side had given the gossips occasion to whisper. Lord Mountdrago indeed was too ambitious, too hard-working, and it must be added too patriotic, to be tempted by any pleasures that might interfere with his career.

He had, in short, a great deal to make him a popular and successful figure. He had unfortunately great defects.

He was a fearful snob. You would not have been surprised at this if his father had been the first holder of the title. That the son of an ennobled lawyer, a manufacturer or a distiller should attach an inordinate importance to his rank is understandable. The earldom held by Lord Mountdrago's father was created by Charles II, and the barony held by the first Earl dated from the Wars of the Roses. For three hundred years the successive holders of the title had allied themselves with the noblest families of England. But Lord Mountdrago was as conscious of his birth as a *nouveau riche* is conscious of his money. He never missed an opportunity of impressing it upon others. He had beautiful manners when he chose to display them, but this he did only with people whom he regarded as his equals. He was coldly insolent to those whom he looked upon as his social inferiors. He was rude to his servants and insulting to his secretaries. The subordinate officials in the government offices to which he had been successively attached feared and hated him. His arrogance was horrible. He knew that he was a great deal cleverer than most of the persons he had to do with, and never hesitated to apprise them of the fact. He had no patience with the infirmities of human nature. He felt himself born to command and was irritated with people who expected him to listen to their arguments or wished to hear the reasons for his decisions. He was immeasurably selfish. He looked upon any service that was rendered him as a right due to his rank and intelligence and therefore deserving of no gratitude. It never entered his head that he was called upon to do anything for others. He had many enemies: he despised them. He knew no one who merited his assistance, his sympathy or his compassion. He had no friends. He was distrusted by his chiefs, because they doubted his loyalty; he was unpopular with his party, because he was over-bearing and discourteous; and yet his merit was so great, his patriotism so evident, his intelligence so solid and his management of affairs so brilliant that they had to put up with him. And what made it possible to do this was that on occasion he could be enchanting: when he was with persons whom he considered his equals, or whom he wished to captivate, in the company of foreign dignitaries or women of distinction, he could be gay, witty and debonair; his manners then reminded you that in his veins ran the same blood as had run in the veins of Lord Chesterfield; he could tell a story with point, he could be natural, sensible and even profound. You were surprised at the extent of his knowledge and the sensitiveness of his taste. You thought him the best company in the world; you forgot that he had insulted you the day before and was quite capable of cutting you dead the next.

Lord Mountdrago almost failed to become Dr. Audlin's patient. A secretary rang up the doctor and told him that his lordship, wishing to consult him, would be glad if he would come to his house at ten o'clock on the following morning. Dr. Audlin answered that he was unable to go to Lord Mountdrago's house, but would be pleased to give him an appointment at his consulting-room at five o'clock on the next day but one. The secretary took the message and presently rang back to say that Lord Mountdrago insisted on seeing Dr. Audlin in his own house and the doctor could fix his own fee. Dr. Audlin replied that he only saw patients in his consulting-room and expressed his regret that unless Lord Mountdrago was prepared to come to him he could not give him his attention. In a quarter of an hour a brief message was delivered to him that his lordship would come not next day but one, but next day, at five.

When Lord Mountdrago was then shown in he did not come forward, but stood at the door and insolently looked the doctor up and down. Dr. Audlin perceived that he was in a rage; he gazed at him, silently, with still eyes. He saw a big heavy man, with greying hair, receding on the forehead so that it gave nobility to his brow, a puffy face with bold regular features and an expression of haughtiness. He had somewhat the look of one of the Bourbon sovereigns of the eighteenth century.

"It seems that it is as difficult to see you as a Prime Minister, Dr. Audlin. I'm an extremely busy man."

"Won't you sit down?" said the doctor.

His face showed no sign that Lord Mountdrago's speech in any way affected him. Dr. Audlin sat in his chair at the desk. Lord Mountdrago still stood and his frown darkened.

"I think I should tell you that I am His Majesty's Secretary for Foreign Affairs," he said acidly.

"Won't you sit down?" the doctor repeated.

Lord Mountdrago made a gesture, which might have suggested that he was about to turn on his heel and stalk out of the room; but if that was his intention he apparently thought better of it. He seated himself. Dr. Audlin opened a large book and took up his pen. He wrote without looking at his patient.

"How old are you?"

"Forty-two."

"Are you married?"

"Yes."

"How long have you been married?"

"Eighteen years."

"Have you any children?"

"I have two sons."

Dr. Audlin noted down the facts as Lord Mountdrago abruptly answered his questions. Then he leaned back in his chair and looked at him. He did not speak; he just looked, gravely, with pale eyes that did not move.

"Why have you come to see me?" he asked at length.

"I've heard about you. Lady Canute is a patient of yours, I understand. She tells me you've done her a certain amount of good."

Dr. Audlin did not reply. His eyes remained fixed on the other's face, but they were so empty of expression that you might have thought he did not even see him.

"I can't do miracles," he said at length. Not a smile, but the shadow of a smile flickered in his eyes. "The Royal College of Physicians would not approve of it if I did."

Lord Mountdrago gave a brief chuckle. It seemed to lessen his hostility. He spoke more amiably.

"You have a very remarkable reputation. People seem to believe in you."

"Why have you come to me?" repeated Dr. Audlin.

Now it was Lord Mountdrago's turn to be silent. It looked as though he found it hard to answer. Dr. Audlin waited. At last Lord Mountdrago seemed to make an effort. He spoke.

"I'm in perfect health. Just as a matter of routine I had myself examined by my own doctor the other day, Sir Augustus Fitzherbert, I daresay you've heard of him, and he tells me I have the physique of a man of thirty. I work hard, but I'm never tired, and I enjoy my work. I smoke very little and I'm an extremely moderate drinker. I take a sufficiency of exercise and I lead a regular life. I am a perfectly sound, normal, healthy man. I quite expect you to think it very silly and childish of me to consult you."

Dr. Audlin saw that he must help him.

"I don't know if I can do anything to help you. I'll try. You're distressed?"

Lord Mountdrago frowned.

"The work that I'm engaged in is important. The decisions I am called upon to make can easily affect the welfare of the country and even the peace of the world. It is essential that my judgment should be balanced and my brain clear. I look upon it as my duty to eliminate any cause of worry that may interfere with my usefulness."

Dr. Audlin had never taken his eyes off him. He saw a great deal. He saw behind his patient's pompous manner and arrogant pride an anxiety that he could not dispel.

"I asked you to be good enough to come here because I know by experience that it's easier for someone to speak openly in the dingy surroundings of a doctor's consulting-room than in his accustomed environment."

"They're certainly dingy," said Lord Mountdrago acidly. He paused. It was evident that this man who had so much self-assurance, so quick and decided a mind that he was never at a loss, at this moment was embarrassed. He smiled in order to show the doctor that he was at his ease, but his eyes betrayed his disquiet. When he spoke again it was with unnatural heartiness.

"The whole thing's so trivial that I can hardly bring myself to bother you with it. I'm afraid you'll just tell me not to be a fool and waste your valuable time."

"Even things that seem very trivial may have their importance. They can be a symptom of a deep-seated derangement. And my time is entirely at your disposal."

Dr. Audlin's voice was low and grave. The monotone in which he spoke was strangely soothing. Lord Mountdrago at length made up his mind to be frank.

"The fact is I've been having some very tiresome dreams lately. I know it's silly to pay any attention to them, but— well, the honest truth is that I'm afraid they've got on my nerves."

"Can you describe any of them to me?"

Lord Mountdrago smiled, but the smile that tried to be careless was only rueful.

"They're so idiotic, I can hardly bring myself to narrate them."

"Never mind."

"Well, the first I had was about a month ago. I dreamt that I was at a party at Connemara House. It was an official party. The King and Queen were to be there and of course decorations were worn. I was wearing my ribbon and my star. I went into a sort of cloakroom they have to take off my coat. There was a little man there called Owen Griffiths, who's a Welsh Member of Parliament, and to tell you the truth, I was surprised to see him. He's very common, and I said to myself: 'Really, Lydia Connemara is going too far, whom will she ask next?' I thought he looked at me rather curiously, but I didn't take any notice of him; in fact I cut the little bounder and walked upstairs. I suppose you've never been there?"

"Never."

"No, it's not the sort of house you'd ever be likely to go to. It's a rather vulgar house, but it's got a very fine marble staircase, and the Connemaras were at the top receiving their guests. Lady Connemara gave me a look of surprise when I shook hands with her, and began to giggle; I didn't pay much attention, she's a very silly, ill-bred woman and her manners are no better than those of her ancestors whom King Charles II made a duchess. I must say the reception rooms at Connemara House are stately. I walked through, nodding to a number of people and shaking hands; then I saw the German Ambassador talking with one of the Austrian Archdukes. I particularly wanted to have a word with him, so I went up and held out my hand. The moment the Archduke saw me he burst into a roar of laughter. I was deeply affronted. I looked him up and down sternly, but he only laughed the more. I was about to speak to him rather sharply, when there was a sudden hush and I realised that the King and Queen had come. Turning my back on the Archduke, I stepped forward, and then, quite suddenly, I noticed that I hadn't got any trousers on. I was in short silk drawers, and I wore scarlet sock-suspenders. No wonder Lady Connemara had giggled; no wonder the Archduke had laughed! I can't tell you what that moment was. An agony of shame. I awoke in a cold sweat. Oh, you don't know the relief I felt to find it was only a dream."

"It's the kind of dream that's not so very uncommon," said Dr. Audlin.

"I dare say not. But an odd thing happened next day. I was in the lobby of the House of Commons, when that fellow Griffiths walked slowly past me. He deliberately looked down at my legs and then he looked me full in the face and I was almost certain he winked. A ridiculous thought came to me. He'd been there the night before and seen me make that ghastly exhibition of myself and was enjoying the joke. But of course I knew that was impossible because it was only a dream. I gave him an icy glare and he walked on. But he was grinning his head off."

Lord Mountdrago took his handkerchief out of his pocket and wiped the palms of his hands. He was making no attempt now to conceal his perturbation. Dr. Audlin never took his eyes off him.

"Tell me another dream."

"It was the night after, and it was even more absurd than the first one. I dreamt that I was in the House. There was a debate on foreign affairs which not only the country, but the world, had been looking forward to with the gravest concern. The government had decided on a change in their policy which vitally affected the future of the Empire. The occasion was historic. Of course the House was crowded. All the ambassadors were there. The galleries were packed. It fell to me to make the important speech of the evening. I had prepared it carefully. A man like me has enemies, there are a lot of people who resent my having achieved the position I have at an age when even the cleverest men are content with situations of relative obscurity, and I was determined that my speech should not only be worthy of the occasion, but should silence my detractors. It excited me to think that the whole world was hanging on my lips. I rose to my feet. If you've ever been in the House you'll know how members chat to one another during a debate, rustle papers and turn over reports. The silence was the silence of the grave when I began to speak. Suddenly I caught sight of that odious little bounder on one of the benches opposite, Griffiths the Welsh member; he put out his tongue at me. I don't know if you've ever heard a vulgar music-hall song called *A Bicycle Made for Two*. It was very popular a great many years ago. To show Griffiths how completely I despised him I began to sing it. I sang the first verse right through. There was a moment's surprise, and when I finished they cried 'Hear, hear,' on the opposite benches. I put up my hand to silence them and sang the second verse. The House listened to me in stony silence and I felt the song wasn't going down very well. I was vexed, for I have a good baritone voice, and I was determined that they should do me justice. When I started the third verse the members began to laugh; in an instant the laughter spread; the ambassadors, the strangers in the Distinguished Strangers' Gallery, the ladies in the Ladies' Gallery, the reporters, they shook, they bellowed, they held their sides, they rolled in their seats; everyone was overcome with laughter except the ministers on the Front Bench immediately behind me. In that

incredible, in that unprecedented uproar, they sat petrified. I
gave them a glance, and suddenly the enormity of what I had
done fell upon me. I had made myself the laughing-stock of
the whole world. With misery I realised that I should have to
resign. I woke and knew it was only a dream."

Lord Mountdrago's grand manner had deserted him as he
narrated this, and now having finished he was pale and trembling. But with an effort he pulled himself together. He
forced a laugh to his shaking lips.

"The whole thing was so fantastic that I couldn't help
being amused. I didn't give it another thought, and when I
went into the House on the following afternoon I was feeling
in very good form. The debate was dull, but I had to be there,
and I read some documents that required my attention. For
some reason I chanced to look up and I saw that Griffiths
was speaking. He has an unpleasant Welsh accent and an
unprepossessing appearance. I couldn't imagine that he had
anything to say that it was worth my while to listen to, and I
was about to return to my papers when he quoted two lines
from *A Bicycle Made for Two*. I couldn't help glancing at
him and I saw that his eyes were fixed on me with a grin
of bitter mockery. I faintly shrugged my shoulders. It was
comic that a scrubby little Welsh member should look at me
like that. It was an odd coincidence that he should quote two
lines from that disastrous song that I'd sung all through in my
dream. I began to read my papers again, but I don't mind
telling you that I found it difficult to concentrate on them. I
was a little puzzled. Owen Griffiths had been in my first
dream, the one at Connemara House, and I'd received a very
definite impression afterwards that he knew the sorry figure
I'd cut. Was it a mere coincidence that he had just quoted
those two lines? I asked myself if it was possible that he was
dreaming the same dreams as I was. But of course the idea
was preposterous and I determined not to give it a second
thought."

There was a silence. Dr. Audlin looked at Lord Mountdrago and Lord Mountdrago looked at Dr. Audlin.

"Other people's dreams are very boring. My wife used to

dream occasionally and insist on telling me her dreams next day with circumstantial detail. I found it maddening."

Dr. Audlin faintly smiled.

"You're not boring me."

"I'll tell you one more dream I had a few days later. I dreamt that I went into a public-house at Limehouse. I've never been to Limehouse in my life and I don't think I've ever been in a public-house since I was at Oxford, and yet I saw the street and the place I went into as exactly as if I were at home there. I went into a room, I don't know whether they call it the saloon bar or the private bar; there was a fireplace and a large leather arm-chair on one side of it, and on the other a small sofa; a bar ran the whole length of the room and over it you could see into the public bar. Near the door was a round marble-topped table and two arm-chairs beside it. It was a Saturday night and the place was packed. It was brightly lit, but the smoke was so thick that it made my eyes smart. I was dressed like a rough, with a cap on my head and a handkerchief round my neck. It seemed to me that most of the people there were drunk. I thought it rather amusing. There was a gramophone going, or the radio, I don't know which, and in front of the fireplace two women were doing a grotesque dance. There was a little crowd round them, laughing, cheering and singing. I went up to have a look and some man said to me: ''Ave a drink, Bill?' There were glasses on the table full of a dark liquid which I understand is called brown ale. He gave me a glass and not wishing to be conspicuous I drank it. One of the women who were dancing broke away from the other and took hold of the glass. ' 'Ere, what's the idea?' she said. 'That's my beer you're putting away.' 'Oh, I'm so sorry,' I said, 'this gentleman offered it me and I very naturally thought it was his to offer.' 'All right, mate,' she said, 'I don't mind. You come an' 'ave a dance with me.' Before I could protest she'd caught hold of me and we were dancing together. And then I found myself sitting in the arm-chair with the woman on my lap and we were sharing a glass of beer. I should tell you that sex has never played any great part in my life. I married young because in my position it was desirable that I should marry, but also in order to settle once for all the question of sex. I had the two sons I had made up my mind to have, and then I put the whole matter on one side. I've always been too busy to give much thought to that kind of thing, and living so much in the public eye as I do it would have been madness to do anything that might give rise to scandal. The greatest asset a politician can have is a blameless record as far as women are concerned. I have no patience with the men who smash up their careers for women. I only despise them. The woman I had on my knees was drunk; she wasn't pretty and she wasn't young: in fact, she was just a blowsy old prostitute. She filled me with disgust, and yet when she put her mouth to mine and kissed me, though her breath stank of beer and her teeth were decayed, though I loathed myself, I wanted her—I wanted her with all my soul. Suddenly I heard a voice. 'That's right, old boy, have a good time.' I looked up and there was Owen Griffiths. I tried to spring out of the chair, but that horrible woman wouldn't let me. 'Don't you pay no attention to 'im,' she said, ' 'e's only one of them nosy-parkers.' 'You go to it,' he said. 'I know Moll. She'll give you your money's worth all right.' You know, I wasn't so much annoyed at his seeing me in that absurd situation as angry that he should address me as 'old boy.' I pushed the woman aside and stood up and faced him. 'I don't know you and I don't want to know you,' I said. 'I know you all right,' he said. 'And my advice to you, Molly, is, see that you get your money, he'll bilk you if he can.' There was a bottle of beer standing on the table close by. Without a word I seized it by the neck and hit him over the head with it as hard as I could. I made such a violent gesture that it woke me up."

"A dream of that sort is not incomprehensible," said Dr. Audlin. "It is the revenge nature takes on persons of unimpeachable character."

"The story's idiotic. I haven't told it you for its own sake. I've told it you for what happened next day. I wanted to look up something in a hurry and I went into the library of the House. I got the book and began reading. I hadn't noticed when I sat down that Griffiths was sitting in a chair close by me. Another of the Labour Members came in and went up to him. 'Hullo, Owen,' he said to him, 'you're looking pretty dicky today.' 'I've got an awful headache,' he answered. 'I feel as if I'd been cracked over the head with a bottle.' "

Now Lord Mountdrago's face was grey with anguish.

"I knew then that the idea I'd had and dismissed as pre-posterous was true. I knew that Griffiths was dreaming my dreams and that he remembered them as well as I did."

"It may also have been a coincidence."

"When he spoke he didn't speak to his friend, he deliber-ately spoke to me. He looked at me with sullen resentment."

"Can you offer any suggestion why this same man should come into your dreams?"

"None."

Dr. Audlin's eyes had not left his patient's face and he saw that he lied. He had a pencil in his hand and he drew a strag-gling line or two on his blotting-paper. It often took a long time to get people to tell the truth, and yet they knew that unless they told it he could do nothing for them.

"The dream you've just described to me took place just over three weeks ago. Have you had any since?"

"Every night."

"And does this man Griffiths come into them all?"

"Yes."

The doctor drew more lines on his blotting-paper. He wanted the silence, the drabness, the dull light of that little room to have its effect on Lord Mountdrago's sensibility. Lord Mountdrago threw himself back in his chair and turned his head away so that he should not see the other's grave eyes.

"Dr. Audlin, you must do something for me. I'm at the end of my tether. I shall go mad if this goes on. I'm afraid to go to sleep. Two or three nights I haven't. I've sat up reading and when I felt drowsy put on my coat and walked till I was ex-hausted. But I must have sleep. With all the work I have to do I must be at concert pitch; I must be in complete control of all my faculties. I need rest; sleep brings me none. I no-

sooner fall asleep than my dreams begin, and he's always
there, that vulgar little cad, grinning at me, mocking me,
despising me. It's a monstrous persecution. I tell you, doctor,
I'm not the man of my dreams; it's not fair to judge me by
them. Ask anyone you like. I'm an honest, upright, decent
man. No one can say anything against my moral character
either private or public. My whole ambition is to serve my
country and maintain its greatness. I have money, I have rank,
I'm not exposed to many of the temptations of lesser men, so
that it's no credit to me to be incorruptible; but this I can
claim, that no honour, no personal advantage, no thought of
self would induce me to swerve by a hair's breadth from my
duty. I've sacrificed everything to become the man I am.
Greatness is my aim. Greatness is within my reach and I'm
losing my nerve. I'm not that mean, despicable, cowardly,
lewd creature that horrible little man sees. I've told you three
of my dreams; they're nothing; that man has seen me do
things that are so beastly, so horrible, so shameful, that even
if my life depended on it I wouldn't tell them. And he
remembers them. I can hardly meet the derision and disgust
I see in his eyes and I even hesitate to speak because I know
my words can seem to him nothing but utter humbug. He's
seen me do things that no man with any self-respect would do,
things for which men are driven out of the society of their
fellows and sentenced to long terms of imprisonment; he's
heard the foulness of my speech; he's seen me not only
ridiculous, but revolting. He despises me and he no longer
pretends to conceal it. I tell you that if you can't do something to help me I shall either kill myself or kill him."

"I wouldn't kill him if I were you," said Dr. Audlin, coolly,
in that soothing voice of his. "In this country the consequences of killing a fellow-creature are awkward."

"I shouldn't be hanged for it, if that's what you mean. Who
would know that I'd killed him? That dream of mine has
shown me how. I told you, the day after I'd hit him over the
head with a beer-bottle he had such a headache that he
couldn't see straight. He said so himself. That shows that he
can feel with his waking body what happens to his body

asleep. It's not with a bottle I shall hit him next time. One night, when I'm dreaming, 1 shall find myself with a knife in my hand or a revolver in my pocket, I must because I want to so intensely, and then I shall seize my opportunity. I'll stick him like a pig; I'll shoot him like a dog. In the heart. And then I shall be free of this fiendish persecution."

Some people might have thought that Lord Mountdrago was mad; after all the years during which Dr. Audlin had been treating the diseased souls of men he knew how thin a line divides those whom we call sane from those whom we call insane. He knew how often in men who to all appearance were healthy and normal, who were seemingly devoid of imagination, and who fulfilled the duties of common life with credit to themselves and with benefit to their fellows, when you gained their confidence, when you tore away the mask they wore to the world, you found not only hideous abnormality, but kinks so strange, mental extravagances so fantastic, that in that respect you could only call them lunatic. If you put them in an asylum not all the asylums in the world would be large enough. Anyhow, a man was not certifiable because he had strange dreams and they had shattered his nerve. The case was singular, but it was only an exaggeration of others that had come under Dr. Audlin's observation; he was doubtful, however, whether the methods of treatment that he had so often found efficacious would here avail.

"Have you consulted any other member of my profession?" he asked.

"Only Sir Augustus. I merely told him that I suffered from nightmares. He said I was overworked and recommended me to go for a cruise. That's absurd. I can't leave the Foreign Office just now when the international situation needs constant attention. I'm indispensable, and I know it. On my conduct at the present juncture my whole future depends. He gave me sedatives. They had no effect. He gave me tonics. They were worse than useless. He's an old fool."

"Can you give any reason why it should be this particular man who persists in coming into your dreams?"

"You asked me that question before. I answered it."

That was true. But Dr. Audlin had not been satisfied with the answer.

"Just now you talked of persecution. Why should Owen Griffiths want to persecute you?"

"I don't know."

Lord Mountdrago's eyes shifted a little. Dr. Audlin was sure that he was not speaking the truth.

"Have you ever done him an injury?"

"Never."

Lord Mountdrago made no movement, but Dr. Audlin had a queer feeling that he shrank into his skin. He saw before him a large, proud man who gave the impression that the questions put to him were an insolence, and yet for all that, behind that façade, was something shifting and startled that made you think of a frightened animal in a trap. Dr. Audlin leaned forward and by the power of his eyes forced Lord Mountdrago to meet them.

"Are you quite sure?"

"Quite sure. You don't seem to understand that our ways lead along different paths. I don't wish to harp on it, but I must remind you that I am a Minister of the Crown and Griffiths is an obscure member of the Labour Party. Naturally there's no social connection between us; he's a man of very humble origin, he's not the sort of person I should be likely to meet at any of the houses I go to; and politically our respective stations are so far separated that we could not possibly have anything in common."

"I can do nothing for you unless you tell me the complete truth."

Lord Mountdrago raised his eyebrows. His voice was rasping.

"I'm not accustomed to having my word doubted, Dr. Audlin. If you're going to do that I think to take up any more of your time can only be a waste of mine. If you will kindly let my secretary know what your fee is he will see that a cheque is sent to you."

For all the expression that was to be seen on Dr. Audlin's face you might have thought that he simply had not heard what Lord Mountdrago said. He continued to look steadily into his eyes and his voice was grave and low.

"Have you done anything to this man that *he* might look upon as an injury?"

Lord Mountdrago hesitated. He looked away, and then, as though there were in Dr. Audlin's eyes a compelling force that he could not resist, looked back. He answered sulkily: "Only if he was a dirty, second-rate little cad."

"But that is exactly what you've described him to be."

Lord Mountdrago sighed. He was beaten. Dr. Audlin knew that the sigh meant he was going at last to say what he had till then held back. Now he had no longer to insist. He dropped his eyes and began again drawing vague geometrical figures on his blotting-paper. The silence lasted two or three minutes.

"I'm anxious to tell you everything that can be of any use to you. If I didn't mention this before, it's only because it was so unimportant that I didn't see how it could possibly have anything to do with the case. Griffiths won a seat at the last election and he began to make a nuisance of himself almost at once. His father's a miner, and he worked in a mine himself when he was a boy; he's been a schoolmaster in the board schools and a journalist. He's that half-baked, conceited intellectual, with inadequate knowledge, ill-considered ideas and impracticable plans, that compulsory education has brought forth from the working-classes. He's a scrawny, grey-faced man, who looks half-starved, and he's always very slovenly in appearance; heaven knows members nowadays don't bother much about their dress, but his clothes are an outrage to the dignity of the House. They're ostentatiously shabby, his collar's never clean and his tie's never tied properly; he looks as if he hadn't had a bath for a month and his hands are filthy. The Labour Party have two or three fellows on the Front Bench who've got a certain ability, but the rest of them don't amount to much. In the kingdom of the blind the one-eyed man is king: because Griffiths is glib and has a lot of superficial information on a number of subjects, the Whips on his side began to put him up to speak whenever there was a chance. It appeared that he fancied himself on foreign affairs, and he was continually asking me silly, tiresome questions. I don't mind telling you that I made a point of snubbing him as soundly as I thought he deserved. From the beginning I hated the way he talked, his whining voice and his vulgar accent; he had nervous mannerisms that intensely irritated me. He talked rather shyly, hesitatingly, as though it were torture to him to speak and yet he was forced to by some inner passion, and often he used to say some very disconcerting things. I'll admit that now and again he had a sort of tub-thumping eloquence. It had a certain influence over the ill-regulated minds of the members of his party. They were impressed by his earnestness and they weren't, as I was, nauseated by his sentimentality. A certain sentimentality is the common coin of political debate. Nations are governed by self-interest, but they prefer to believe that their aims are altruistic, and the politician is justified if with fair words and fine phrases he can persuade the electorate that the hard bargain he is driving for his country's advantage tends to the good of humanity. The mistake people like Griffiths make is to take these fair words and fine phrases at their face value. He's a crank, and a noxious crank. He calls himself an idealist. He has at his tongue's end all the tedious blather that the intelligentsia have been boring us with for years. Non-resistance. The brotherhood of man. You know the hopeless rubbish. The worst of it was that it impressed not only his own party, it even shook some of the sillier, more sloppy-minded members of ours. I heard rumours that Griffiths was likely to get office when a Labour Government came in; I even heard it suggested that he might get the Foreign Office. The notion was grotesque but not impossible. One day I had occasion to wind up a debate on foreign affairs which Griffiths had opened. He'd spoken for an hour. I thought it a very good opportunity to cook his goose, and by God, sir, I cooked it. I tore his speech to pieces. I pointed out the faultiness of his reasoning and emphasised the deficiency of his knowledge. In the House of Commons the most devastating weapon is ridicule: I mocked him; I bantered him; I was in good form that day and the House rocked with laughter. Their laughter excited me and I excelled myself. The Opposition sat glum and silent, but even some of them couldn't help laughing once or twice; it's not intolerable, you know, to see a colleague, perhaps a rival, made a fool of. And if ever a man was made a fool of I made a fool of Griffiths. He shrank down in a seat, I saw his face go white, and presently he buried it in his hands. When I sat down I'd killed him. I'd destroyed his prestige for ever; he had no more chance of getting office when a Labour Government came in than the policeman at the door. I heard afterwards that his father, the old miner, and his mother had come up from Wales, with various supporters of his in the constituency, to watch the triumph they expected him to have. They had seen only his utter humiliation. He'd won the constituency by the narrowest margin. An incident like that might very easily lose him his seat. But that was no business of mine."

"Should I be putting it too strongly if I said you had ruined his career?" asked Dr. Audlin.

"I don't suppose you would."

"That is a very serious injury you've done him."

"He brought it on himself."

"Have you never felt any qualms about it?"

"I think perhaps if I'd known that his father and mother were there I might have let him down a little more gently."

There was nothing further for Dr. Audlin to say, and he set about treating his patient in such a manner as he thought might avail. He sought by suggestion to make him forget his dreams when he awoke; he sought to make him sleep so deeply that he would not dream. He found Lord Mountdrago's resistance impossible to break down. At the end of an hour he dismissed him. Since then he had seen Lord Mountdrago half a dozen times. He had done him no good. The frightful dreams continued every night to harass the unfortunate man, and it was clear that his general condition was growing rapidly worse. He was worn out. His irritability was uncontrollable. Lord Mountdrago was angry because he received no benefit from his treatment, and yet continued it, not only because it seemed his only hope, but because it was a relief to him to have someone with whom he could talk openly. Dr. Audlin came to the conclusion at last that there was only one way in which Lord Mountdrago could achieve deliverance, but he knew him well enough to be assured that of his own free will he would never, never take it. If Lord Mountdrago was to be saved from the breakdown that was threatening he must be induced to take a step that must be abhorrent to his pride of birth and his self-complacency. Dr. Audlin was convinced that to delay was impossible. He was treating his patient by suggestion, and after several visits found him more susceptible to it. At length he managed to get him into a condition of somnolence. With his low, soft, monotonous voice he soothed his tortured nerves. He repeated the same words over and over again. Lord Mountdrago lay quite still, his eyes closed; his breathing was regular, and his limbs were relaxed. Then Dr. Audlin in the same quiet tone spoke the words he had prepared.

"You will go to Owen Griffiths and say that you are sorry that you caused him that great injury. You will say that you will do whatever lies in your power to undo the harm that you have done him."

The words acted on Lord Mountdrago like the blow of a whip across his face. He shook himself out of his hypnotic state and sprang to his feet. His eyes blazed with passion and he poured forth upon Dr. Audlin a stream of angry vituperation such as even he had never heard. He swore at him. He cursed him. He used language of such obscenity that Dr. Audlin, who had heard every sort of foul word, sometimes from the lips of chaste and distinguished women, was surprised that he knew it.

"Apologise to that filthy little Welshman? I'd rather kill myself."

"I believe it to be the only way in which you can regain your balance."

Dr. Audlin had not often seen a man presumably sane in such a condition of uncontrollable fury. He grew red in the face and his eyes bulged out of his head. He did really foam at the mouth. Dr. Audlin watched him coolly, waiting for the storm to wear itself out, and presently he saw that Lord Mountdrago, weakened by the strain to which he had been subjected for so many weeks, was exhausted.

"Sit down," he said then, sharply.

Lord Mountdrago crumpled up into a chair.

"Christ, I feel all in. I must rest a minute and then I'll go."

For five minutes perhaps they sat in complete silence. Lord Mountdrago was a gross, blustering bully, but he was also a gentleman. When he broke the silence he had recovered his self-control.

"I'm afraid I've been very rude to you. I'm ashamed of the things I've said to you and I can only say you'd be justified if you refused to have anything more to do with me. I hope you won't do that. I feel that my visits to you do help me. I think you're my only chance."

"You mustn't give another thought to what you said. It was of no consequence."

"But there's one thing you mustn't ask me to do, and that is to make excuses to Griffiths."

"I've thought a great deal about your case. I don't pretend to understand it, but I believe that your only chance of release is to do what I proposed. I have a notion that we're none of us one self, but many, and one of the selves in you has risen up against the injury you did Griffiths and has taken on the form of Griffiths in your mind and is punishing you for what you cruelly did. If I were a priest I should tell you that it is your conscience that has adopted the shape and lineaments of this man to scourge you to repentance and persuade you to reparation."

"My conscience is clear. It's not my fault if I smashed the man's career. I crushed him like a slug in my garden. I regret nothing."

It was on these words that Lord Mountdrago had left him. Reading through his notes, while he waited, Dr. Audlin considered how best he could bring his patient to the state of mind that, now that his usual methods of treatment had failed, he thought alone could help him. He glanced at his clock. It was six. It was strange that Lord Mountdrago did not come. He knew he had intended to because a secretary had rung up that morning to say that he would be with him at the usual hour. He must have been detained by pressing work. This notion gave Dr. Audlin something else to think of: Lord Mountdrago was quite unfit to work and in no condition to deal with important matters of state. Dr. Audlin wondered whether it behooved him to get in touch with someone in authority, the Prime Minister or the Permanent Under-Secretary for Foreign Affairs, and impart to him his conviction that Lord Mountdrago's mind was so unbalanced that it was dangerous to leave affairs of moment in his hands. It was a ticklish thing to do. He might cause needless trouble and get roundly snubbed for his pains. He shrugged his shoulders.

"After all," he reflected, "the politicians have made such a mess of the world during the last five-and-twenty years, I don't suppose it makes much odds if they're mad or sane."

He rang the bell.

"If Lord Mountdrago comes now will you tell him that I have another appointment at six-fifteen and so I'm afraid I can't see him."

"Very good, sir."

"Has the evening paper come yet?"

"I'll go and see."

In a moment the servant brought it in. A huge headline ran across the front page: Tragic Death of Foreign Minister.

"My God!" cried Dr. Audlin.

For once he was wrenched out of his wonted calm. He was shocked, horribly shocked, and yet he was not altogether surprised. The possibility that Lord Mountdrago might commit suicide had occurred to him several times, for that it was suicide he could not doubt. The paper said that Lord Mountdrago had been waiting in a Tube station, standing on the edge of the platform, and as the train came in was seen to fall on the rail. It was supposed that he had had a sudden attack of faintness. The paper went on to say that Lord Mountdrago had been suffering for some weeks from the effects of overwork, but had felt it impossible to absent himself while the foreign situation demanded his unremitting attention. Lord Mountdrago was another victim of the strain that modern politics placed upon those who played the more important parts in it. There was a neat little piece about the talents and industry, the patriotism and vision, of the deceased statesman, followed by various surmises upon the Prime Minister's choice of his successor. Dr. Audlin read all this. He had not liked Lord Mountdrago. The chief emotion that his death caused in him was dissatisfaction with himself because he had been able to do nothing for him.

Perhaps he had done wrong in not getting into touch with Lord Mountdrago's doctor. He was discouraged, as always when failure frustrated his conscientious efforts, and repulsion seized him for the theory and practice of this empiric doctrine by which he earned his living. He was dealing with dark and mysterious forces that it was perhaps beyond the powers of the human mind to understand. He was like a man blindfold trying to feel his way to he knew not whither. Listlessly he turned the pages of the paper. Suddenly he gave a great start, and an exclamation once more was forced from his lips. His eyes had fallen on a small paragraph near the bottom of a column. Sudden Death of an M.P., he read. Mr. Owen Griffiths, member for so-and-so, had been taken ill in Fleet Street that afternoon and when he was brought to Charing Cross Hospital life was found to be extinct. It was supposed that death was due to natural causes, but an inquest would be held. Dr. Audlin could hardly believe his eyes. Was it possible that the night before Lord Mountdrago had at last in his dream found himself possessed of the weapon, knife or gun, that he had wanted, and had killed his tormentor, and had that ghostly murder, in the same way as the blow with the bottle had given him a racking headache on the following day, taken effect a certain number of hours later on the waking man? Or was it, more mysterious and more frightful, that when Lord Mountdrago sought relief in death, the enemy he had so cruelly wronged, unappeased, escaping from his own mortality, had pursued him to some other sphere there to torment him still? It was strange. The sensible thing was to look upon it merely as an odd coincidence. Dr. Audlin rang the bell.

"Tell Mrs. Milton that I'm sorry I can't see her this evening. I'm not well."

It was true; he shivered as though of an ague. With some kind of spiritual sense he seemed to envisage a bleak, a horrible void. The dark night of the soul engulfed him, and he felt a strange, primeval terror of he knew not what.

The Colonel's Lady

ALL THIS happened two or three years before the outbreak of the war.

The Peregrines were having breakfast. Though they were alone and the table was long they sat at opposite ends of it. From the walls George Peregrine's ancestors, painted by the fashionable painters of the day, looked down upon them. The butler brought in the morning post. There were several letters for the colonel, business letters, *The Times* and a small parcel for his wife Evie. He looked at his letters and then, opening *The Times,* began to read it. They finished breakfast and rose from the table. He noticed that his wife hadn't opened the parcel.

"What's that?" he asked.

"Only some books."

"Shall I open it for you?"

"If you like."

He hated to cut string and so with some difficulty untied the knots.

"But they're all the same," he said when he had unwrapped the parcel. "What on earth d'you want six copies of the same book for?" He opened one of them. "Poetry." Then he looked at the title page. *When Pyramids Decay,* he read, by E. K. Hamilton. Eva Katherine Hamilton: that was his wife's maiden name. He looked at her with smiling surprise. "Have you written a book, Evie? You are a slyboots."

"I didn't think it would interest you very much. Would you like a copy?"

"Well, you know poetry isn't much in my line, but—yes,

I'd like a copy; I'll read it. I'll take it along to my study. I've got a lot to do this morning."

He gathered up *The Times,* his letters and the book, and went out. His study was a large and comfortable room, with a big desk, leather arm-chairs and what he called "trophies of the chase" on the walls. On the bookshelves were works of reference, books on farming, gardening, fishing and shooting, and books on the last war, in which he had won an M.C. and a D.S.O. For before his marriage he had been in the Welsh Guards. At the end of the war he retired and settled down to the life of a country gentleman in the spacious house, some twenty miles from Sheffield, which one of his forebears had built in the reign of George III. George Peregrine had an estate of some fifteen hundred acres which he managed with ability; he was a Justice of the Peace and performed his duties conscientiously. During the season he rode to hounds two days a week. He was a good shot, a golfer and though now a little over fifty could still play a hard game of tennis. He could describe himself with propriety as an all-round sportsman.

He had been putting on weight lately, but was still a fine figure of a man; tall, with grey curly hair, only just beginning to grow thin on the crown, frank blue eyes, good features and a high colour. He was a public-spirited man, chairman of any number of local organisations and, as became his class and station, a loyal member of the Conservative Party. He looked upon it as his duty to see to the welfare of the people on his estate and it was a satisfaction to him to know that Evie could be trusted to tend the sick and succour the poor. He had built a cottage hospital on the outskirts of the village and paid the wages of a nurse out of his own pocket. All he asked of the recipients of his bounty was that at elections, county or general, they should vote for his candidate. He was a friendly man, affable to his inferiors, considerate with his tenants and popular with the neighbouring gentry. He would have been pleased and at the same time slightly embarrassed if someone had told him he was a jolly good fellow. That was what he wanted to be. He desired no higher praise.

It was hard luck that he had no children. He would have been an excellent father, kindly but strict, and would have brought up his sons as gentlemen's sons should be brought up, sent them to Eton, you know, taught them to fish, shoot and ride. As it was, his heir was a nephew, son of his brother killed in a motor accident, not a bad boy, but not a chip off the old block, no, sir, far from it; and would you believe it, his fool of a mother was sending him to a co-educational school. Evie had been a sad disappointment to him. Of course she was a lady, and she had a bit of money of her own; she managed the house uncommonly well and she was a good hostess. The village people adored her. She had been a pretty little thing when he married her, with a creamy skin, light brown hair and a trim figure, healthy too and not a bad tennis player; he couldn't understand why she'd had no children; of course she was faded now, she must be getting on for five and forty; her skin was drab, her hair had lost its sheen and she was as thin as a rail. She was always neat and suitably dressed, but she didn't seem to bother how she looked, she wore no make-up and didn't even use lipstick; sometimes at night when she dolled herself up for a party you could tell that once she'd been quite attractive, but ordinarily she was— well, the sort of woman you simply didn't notice. A nice woman, of course, a good wife, and it wasn't her fault if she was barren, but it was tough on a fellow who wanted an heir of his own loins; she hadn't any vitality, that's what was the matter with her. He supposed he'd been in love with her when he asked her to marry him, as least sufficiently in love for a man who wanted to marry and settle down, but with time he discovered that they had nothing much in common. She didn't care about hunting, and fishing bored her. Naturally they'd drifted apart. He had to do her the justice to admit that she'd never bothered him. There'd been no scenes. They had no quarrels. She seemed to take it for granted that he should go his own way. When he went up to London now and then she never wanted to come with him. He had a girl there, well, she wasn't exactly a girl, she was thirty-five if she was a day, but she was blonde and luscious and he only

had to wire ahead of time and they'd dine, do a show and
spend the night together. Well, a man, a healthy normal
man had to have some fun in his life. The thought crossed
his mind that if Evie hadn't been such a good woman she'd
have been a better wife; but it was not the sort of thought
that he welcomed and he put it away from him.

George Peregrine finished his *Times* and being a considerate fellow rang the bell and told the butler to take it to
Evie. Then he looked at his watch. It was half-past ten and at
eleven he had an appointment with one of his tenants. He
had half an hour to spare.

"I'd better have a look at Evie's book," he said to himself.

He took it up with a smile. Evie had a lot of highbrow
books in her sitting-room, not the sort of books that interested him, but if they amused her he had no objection to her
reading them. He noticed that the volume he now held in his
hand contained no more than ninety pages. That was all to
the good. He shared Edgar Allan Poe's opinion that poems
should be short. But as he turned the pages he noticed that
several of Evie's had long lines of irregular length and didn't
rhyme. He didn't like that. At his first school, when he was a
little boy, he remembered learning a poem that began: *The
boy stood on the burning deck,* and later, at Eton, one that
started: *Ruin seize thee, ruthless king;* and then there was
Henry V; they'd had to take that, one half. He stared at
Evie's pages with consternation.

"That's not what I call poetry," he said.

Fortunately it wasn't all like that. Interspersed with the
pieces that looked so odd, lines of three or four words and
then a line of ten or fifteen, there were little poems, quite
short, that rhymed, thank God, with the lines all the same
length. Several of the pages were just headed with the word
Sonnet, and out of curiosity he counted the lines; there were
fourteen of them. He read them. They seemed all right, but
he didn't quite know what they were all about. He repeated
to himself: *Ruin seize thee, ruthless king.*

"Poor Evie," he sighed.

At that moment the farmer he was expecting was ushered

into the study, and putting the book down he made him welcome. They embarked on their business.

"I read your book, Evie," he said as they sat down to lunch. "Jolly good. Did it cost you a packet to have it printed?"

"No, I was lucky. I sent it to a publisher and he took it."

"Not much money in poetry, my dear," he said in his good-natured, hearty way.

"No, I don't suppose there is. What did Bannock want to see you about this morning?"

Bannock was the tenant who had interrupted his reading of Evie's poems.

"He's asked me to advance the money for a pedigree bull he wants to buy. He's a good man and I've half a mind to do it."

George Peregrine saw that Evie didn't want to talk about her book and he was not sorry to change the subject. He was glad she had used her maiden name on the title page; he didn't suppose anyone would ever hear about the book, but he was proud of his own unusual name and he wouldn't have liked it if some damned penny-a-liner had made fun of Evie's effort in one of the papers.

During the few weeks that followed he thought it tactful not to ask Evie any questions about her venture into verse, and she never referred to it. It might have been a discreditable incident that they had silently agreed not to mention. But then a strange thing happened. He had to go to London on business and he took Daphne out to dinner. That was the name of the girl with whom he was in the habit of passing a few agreeable hours whenever he went to town.

"Oh, George," she said, "is that your wife who's written a book they're all talking about?"

"What on earth d'you mean?"

"Well, there's a fellow I know who's a critic. He took me out to dinner the other night and he had a book with him. 'Got anything for me to read?' I said. 'What's that?' 'Oh, I don't think that's your cup of tea,' he said. 'It's poetry. I've just been reviewing it.' 'No poetry for me,' I said. 'It's about the hottest stuff I ever read,' he said. 'Selling like hot cakes. And it's damned good.'"

"Who's the book by?" asked George.

"A woman called Hamilton. My friend told me that wasn't her real name. He said her real name was Peregrine. 'Funny,' I said, 'I know a fellow called Peregrine.' 'Colonel in the army,' he said. 'Lives near Sheffield.' "

"I'd just as soon you didn't talk about me to your friends," said George with a frown of vexation.

"Keep your shirt on, dearie. Who d'you take me for? I just said: 'It's not the same one.' " Daphne giggled. "My friend said: 'They say he's a regular Colonel Blimp.' "

George had a keen sense of humour.

"You could tell them better than that," he laughed. "If my wife had written a book I'd be the first to know about it, wouldn't I?"

"I suppose you would."

Anyhow the matter didn't interest her and when the colonel began to talk of other things she forgot about it. He put it out of his mind too. There was nothing to it, he decided, and that silly fool of a critic had just been pulling Daphne's leg. He was amused at the thought of her tackling that book because she had been told it was hot stuff and then finding it just a lot of bosh cut up into unequal lines.

He was a member of several clubs and next day he thought he'd lunch at one in St. James's Street. He was catching a train back to Sheffield early in the afternoon. He was sitting in a comfortable arm-chair having a glass of sherry before going into the dining-room when an old friend came up to him.

"Well, old boy, how's life?" he said. "How d'you like being the husband of a celebrity?"

George Peregrine looked at his friend. He thought he saw an amused twinkle in his eyes.

"I don't know what you're talking about," he answered.

"Come off it, George. Everyone knows E. K. Hamilton is your wife. Not often a book of verse has a success like that. Look here, Henry Dashwood is lunching with me. He'd like to meet you."

"Who the devil is Henry Dashwood and why should he want to meet me?"

"Oh, my dear fellow, what do you do with yourself all the time in the country? Henry's about the best critic we've got. He wrote a wonderful review of Evie's book. D'you mean to say she didn't show it you?"

Before George could answer his friend had called a man over. A tall, thin man, with a high forehead, a beard, a long nose and a stoop, just the sort of man whom George was prepared to dislike at first sight. Introductions were effected. Henry Dashwood sat down.

"Is Mrs. Peregrine in London by any chance? I should very much like to meet her," he said.

"No, my wife doesn't like London. She prefers the country," said George stiffly.

"She wrote me a very nice letter about my review. I was pleased. You know, we critics get more kicks than halfpence. I was simply bowled over by her book. It's so fresh and original, very modern without being obscure. She seems to be as much at her ease in free verse as in the classical metres." Then because he was a critic he thought he should criticise. "Sometimes her ear is a trifle at fault, but you can say the same of Emily Dickinson. There are several of those short lyrics of hers that might have been written by Landor."

All this was gibberish to George Peregrine. The man was nothing but a disgusting highbrow. But the colonel had good manners and he answered with proper civility: Henry Dash-wood went on as though he hadn't spoken.

"But what makes the book so outstanding is the passion that throbs in every line. So many of these young poets are so anaemic, cold, bloodless, dully intellectual, but here you have real naked, earthy passion; of course deep, sincere emotion like that is tragic—ah, my dear Colonel, how right Heine was when he said that the poet makes little songs out of his great sorrows. You know, now and then, as I read and re-read those heart-rending pages I thought of Sappho."

This was too much for George Peregrine and he got up.

"Well, it's jolly nice of you to say such nice things about my wife's little book. I'm sure she'll be delighted. But I must bolt, I've got to catch a train and I want to get a bite of lunch."

"Damned fool," he said irritably to himself as he walked upstairs to the dining-room.

He got home in time for dinner and after Evie had gone to bed he went into his study and looked for her book. He thought he'd just glance through it again to see for himself what they were making such a fuss about, but he couldn't find it. Evie must have taken it away.

"Silly," he muttered.

He'd told her he thought it jolly good. What more could a fellow be expected to say? Well, it didn't matter. He lit his pipe and read the *Field* till he felt sleepy. But a week or so later it happened that he had to go into Sheffield for the day. He lunched there at his club. He had nearly finished when the Duke of Haverel came in. This was the great local magnate and of course the colonel knew him, but only to say how d'you do to; and he was surprised when the Duke stopped at his table.

"We're so sorry your wife couldn't come to us for the week-end," he said, with a sort of shy cordiality. "We're expecting rather a nice lot of people."

George was taken aback. He guessed that the Haverels had asked him and Evie over for the week-end and Evie, without saying a word to him about it, had refused. He had the presence of mind to say he was sorry too.

"Better luck next time," said the Duke pleasantly and moved on.

Colonel Peregrine was very angry and when he got home he said to his wife:

"Look here, what's this about our being asked over to Haverel? Why on earth did you say we couldn't go? We've never been asked before and it's the best shooting in the county."

"I didn't think of that. I thought it would only bore you."

"Damn it all, you might at least have asked me if I wanted to go."

"I'm sorry."

He looked at her closely. There was something in her expression that he didn't quite understand. He frowned.

"I suppose *I* was asked?" he barked.

Evie flushed a little.

"Well, in point of fact you weren't."

"I call it damned rude of them to ask you without asking me."

"I suppose they thought it wasn't your sort of party. The Duchess is rather fond of writers and people like that, you know. She's having Henry Dashwood, the critic, and for some reason he wants to meet me."

"It was damned nice of you to refuse, Evie."

"It's the least I could do," she smiled. She hesitated a moment. "George, my publishers want to give a little dinner party for me one day towards the end of the month and of course they want you to come too."

"Oh, I don't think that's quite my mark. I'll come up to London with you if you like. I'll find someone to dine with."

Daphne.

"I expect it'll be very dull, but they're making rather a point of it. And the day after, the American publisher who's taken my book is giving a cocktail party at Claridge's. I'd like you to come to that if you wouldn't mind."

"Sounds like a crashing bore, but if you really want me to come I'll come."

"It would be sweet of you."

George Peregrine was dazed by the cocktail party. There were a lot of people. Some of them didn't look so bad, a few of the women were decently turned out, but the men seemed to him pretty awful. He was introduced to everyone as Colonel Peregrine, E. K. Hamilton's husband, you know. The men didn't seem to have anything to say to him, but the women gushed.

"You *must* be proud of your wife. Isn't it *wonderful?* You know, I read it right through at a sitting, I simply couldn't put it down, and when I'd finished I started again at the beginning and read it right through a second time. I was simply *thrilled.*"

The English publisher said to him:

"We've not had a success like this with a book of verse for twenty years. I've never seen such reviews."

The American publisher said to him:

"It's swell. It'll be a smash hit in America. You wait and see."

The American publisher had sent Evie a great spray of orchids. Damned ridiculous, thought George. As they came in, people were taken up to Evie, and it was evident that they said flattering things to her, which she took with a pleasant smile and a word or two of thanks. She was a trifle flushed with the excitement, but seemed quite at her ease. Though he thought the whole thing a lot of stuff and nonsense George noted with approval that his wife was carrying it off in just the right way.

"Well, there's one thing," he said to himself, "you can see she's a lady and that's a damned sight more than you can say of anyone else here."

He drank a good many cocktails. But there was one thing that bothered him. He had a notion that some of the people he was introduced to looked at him in rather a funny sort of way, he couldn't quite make out what it meant, and once when he strolled by two women who were sitting together on a sofa he had the impression that they were talking about him and after he passed he was almost certain they tittered. He was very glad when the party came to an end.

In the taxi on their way back to their hotel Evie said to him:

"You were wonderful, dear. You made quite a hit. The girls simply raved about you: they thought you so handsome."

"Girls," he said bitterly. "Old hags."

"Were you bored, dear?"

"Stiff."

She pressed his hand in a gesture of sympathy.

"I hope you won't mind if we wait and go down by the afternoon train. I've got some things to do in the morning."

"No, that's all right. Shopping?"

"I do want to buy one or two things, but I've got to go and

be photographed. I hate the idea, but they think I ought to be. For America, you know."

He said nothing. But he thought. He thought it would be a shock to the American public when they saw the portrait of the homely, desiccated little woman who was his wife. He'd always been under the impression that they liked glamour in America.

He went on thinking, and next morning when Evie had gone out he went to his club and up to the library. There he looked up recent numbers of *The Times Literary Supplement*, *The New Statesman* and *The Spectator*. Presently he found reviews of Evie's book. He didn't read them very carefully, but enough to see that they were extremely favourable. Then he went to the bookseller's in Piccadilly where he occasionally bought books. He'd made up his mind that he had to read this damned thing of Evie's properly, but he didn't want to ask her what she'd done with the copy she'd given him. He'd buy one for himself. Before going in he looked in the window and the first thing he saw was a display of *When Pyramids Decay*. Damned silly title! He went in. A young man came forward and asked if he could help him.

"No, I'm just having a look round." It embarrassed him to ask for Evie's book and he thought he'd find it for himself and then take it to the salesman. But he couldn't see it anywhere and at last, finding the young man near him, he said in a carefully casual tone: "By the way, have you got a book called *When Pyramids Decay?*"

"The new edition came in this morning. I'll get a copy."

In a moment the young man returned with it. He was a short, rather stout young man, with a shock of untidy carroty hair and spectacles. George Peregrine, tall, upstanding, very military, towered over him.

"Is this a new edition then?" he asked.

"Yes, sir. The fifth. It might be a novel the way it's selling."

George Peregrine hesitated a moment.

"Why d'you suppose it's such a success? I've always been told no one reads poetry."

"Well, it's good, you know. I've read it meself." The young

man, though obviously cultured, had a slight Cockney accent, and George quite instinctively adopted a patronising attitude. "It's the story they like. Sexy, you know, but tragic."

George frowned a little. He was coming to the conclusion that the young man was rather impertinent. No one had told him anything about there being a story in the damned book and he had not gathered that from reading the reviews. The young man went on:

"Of course it's only a flash in the pan, if you know what I mean. The way I look at it, she was sort of inspired like by a personal experience, like Housman was with *The Shropshire Lad*. She'll never write anything else."

"How much is the book?" said George coldly to stop his chatter. "You needn't wrap it up, I'll just slip it into my pocket."

The November morning was raw and he was wearing a greatcoat.

At the station he bought the evening papers and magazines and he and Evie settled themselves comfortably in opposite corners of a first-class carriage and read. At five o'clock they went along to the restaurant car to have tea and chatted a little. They arrived. They drove home in the car which was waiting for them. They bathed, dressed for dinner, and after dinner Evie, saying she was tired out, went to bed. She kissed him, as was her habit, on the forehead. Then he went into the hall, took Evie's book out of his greatcoat pocket and going into the study began to read it. He didn't read verse very easily and though he read with attention, every word of it, the impression he received was far from clear. Then he began at the beginning again and read it a second time. He read with increasing malaise, but he was not a stupid man and when he had finished he had a distinct understanding of what it was all about. Part of the book was in free verse, part in conventional metres, but the story it related was coherent and plain to the meanest intelligence. It was the story of a passionate love affair between an older woman, married, and a young man. George Peregrine made out the steps of it as easily as if he had been doing a sum in simple addition.

Written in the first person, it began with the tremulous surprise of the woman, past her youth, when it dawned upon her that the young man was in love with her. She hesitated to believe it. She thought she must be deceiving herself. And she was terrified when on a sudden she discovered that she was passionately in love with him. She told herself it was absurd; with the disparity of age between them nothing but unhappiness could come to her if she yielded to her emotion. She tried to prevent him from speaking but the day came when he told her that he loved her and forced her to tell him that she loved him too. He begged her to run away with him. She couldn't leave her husband, her home; and what life could they look forward to, she an ageing woman, he so young? How could she expect his love to last? She begged him to have mercy on her. But his love was impetuous. He wanted her, he wanted her with all his heart, and at last trembling, afraid, desirous, she yielded to him. Then there was a period of ecstatic happiness. The world, the dull, humdrum world of every day, blazed with glory. Love songs flowed from her pen. The woman worshipped the young, virile body of her lover. George flushed darkly when she praised his broad chest and slim flanks, the beauty of his legs and the flatness of his belly.

Hot stuff, Daphne's friend had said. It was that all right. Disgusting.

There were sad little pieces in which she lamented the emptiness of her life when as must happen he left her, but they ended with a cry that all she had to suffer would be worth it for the bliss that for a while had been hers. She wrote of the long, tremulous nights they passed together and the languor that lulled them to sleep in one another's arms. She wrote of the rapture of brief stolen moments when, braving all danger, their passion overwhelmed them and they surrendered to its call.

She thought it would be an affair of a few weeks, but miraculously it lasted. One of the poems referred to three years having gone by without lessening the love that filled their hearts. It looked as though he continued to press her to go away with him, far away, to a hill town in Italy, a Greek island, a walled city in Tunisia, so that they could be together always, for in another of the poems she besought him to let things be as they were. Their happiness was precarious. Perhaps it was owing to the difficulties they had to encounter and the rarity of their meetings that their love had retained for so long its first enchanting ardour. Then on a sudden the young man died. How, when or where George could not discover. There followed a long, heart-broken cry of bitter grief, grief she could not indulge in, grief that had to be hidden. She had to be cheerful, give dinner-parties and go out to dinner, behave as she had always behaved, though the light had gone out of her life and she was bowed down with anguish. The last poem of all was a set of four short stanzas in which the writer, sadly resigned to her loss, thanked the dark powers that rule man's destiny that she had been privileged at least for a while to enjoy the greatest happiness that we poor human beings can ever hope to know.

It was three o'clock in the morning when George Peregrine finally put the book down. It had seemed to him that he heard Evie's voice in every line, over and over again he came upon turns of phrase he had heard her use, there were details that were as familiar to him as to her: there was no doubt about it; it was her own story she had told, and it was as plain as anything could be that she had had a lover and her lover had died. It was not anger so much that he felt, nor horror or dismay, though he was dismayed and he was horrified, but amazement. It was as inconceivable that Evie should have had a love affair, and a wildly passionate one at that, as that the trout in a glass case over the chimney piece in his study, the finest he had ever caught, should suddenly wag its tail. He understood now the meaning of the amused look he had seen in the eyes of that man he had spoken to at the club, he understood why Daphne when she was talking about the book had seemed to be enjoying a private joke, and why those two women at the cocktail party had tittered when he strolled past them.

He broke out into a sweat. Then on a sudden he was seized with fury and he jumped up to go and awake Evie and ask her sternly for an explanation. But he stopped at the door. After all, what proof had he? A book. He remembered that he'd told Evie he thought it jolly good. True, he hadn't read it, but he'd pretended he had. He would look a perfect fool if he had to admit that.

"I must watch my step," he muttered.

He made up his mind to wait for two or three days and think it all over. Then he'd decide what to do. He went to bed, but he couldn't sleep for a long time.

"Evie," he kept on saying to himself. "Evie, of all people."

They met at breakfast next morning as usual. Evie was as she always was, quiet, demure and self-possessed, a middle-aged woman who made no effort to look younger than she was, a woman who had nothing of what he still called It. He looked at her as he hadn't looked at her for years. She had her usual placid serenity. Her pale blue eyes were untroubled. There was no sign of guilt on her candid brow. She made the same little casual remarks she always made.

"It's nice to get back to the country again after those two hectic days in London. What are you going to do this morning?"

It was incomprehensible.

Three days later he went to see his solicitor. Henry Blane was an old friend of George's as well as his lawyer. He had a place not far from Peregrine's and for years they had shot over one another's preserves. For two days a week he was a country gentleman and for the other five a busy lawyer in Sheffield. He was a tall, robust fellow, with a boisterous manner and a jovial laugh, which suggested that he liked to be looked upon essentially as a sportsman and a good fellow and only incidentally as a lawyer. But he was shrewd and worldly-wise.

"Well, George, what's brought you here today?" he boomed as the colonel was showed into his office. "Have a good time in London? I'm taking my missus up for a few days next week. How's Evie?"

"It's about Evie I've come to see you," said Peregrine, giving him a suspicious look. "Have you read her book?"

His sensitivity had been sharpened during those last days of troubled thought and he was conscious of a faint change in the lawyer's expression. It was as though he were suddenly on his guard.

"Yes, I've read it. Great success, isn't it? Fancy Evie breaking out into poetry. Wonders will never cease."

George Peregrine was inclined to lose his temper.

"It's made me look a perfect damned fool."

"Oh, what nonsense, George! There's no harm in Evie's writing a book. You ought to be jolly proud of her."

"Don't talk such rot. It's her own story. You know it and everyone else knows it. I suppose I'm the only one who doesn't know who her lover was."

"There is such a thing as imagination, old boy. There's no reason to suppose the whole thing isn't made up."

"Look here, Henry, we've known one another all our lives. We've had all sorts of good times together. Be honest with me. Can you look me in the face and tell me you believe it's a made-up story?"

Harry Blane moved uneasily in his chair. He was disturbed by the distress in old George's voice.

"You've got no right to ask me a question like that. Ask Evie."

"I daren't," George answered after an anguished pause. "I'm afraid she'd tell me the truth."

There was an uncomfortable silence.

"Who was the chap?"

Harry Blane looked at him straight in the eye.

"I don't know, and if I did I wouldn't tell you."

"You swine. Don't you see what a position I'm in? Do you think it's very pleasant to be made absolutely ridiculous?"

The lawyer lit a cigarette and for some moments silently puffed it.

"I don't see what I can do for you," he said at last.

"You've got private detectives you employ, I suppose. I want you to put them on the job and let them find everything out."

"It's not very pretty to put detectives on one's wife, old

boy; and besides, taking for granted for a moment that Evie had an affair, it was a good many years ago and I don't suppose it would be possible to find out a thing. They seem to have covered their tracks pretty carefully."

"I don't care. You put the detectives on. I want to know the truth."

"I won't, George. If you're determined to do that you'd better consult someone else. And look here, even if you got evidence that Evie had been unfaithful to you what would you do with it? You'd look rather silly divorcing your wife because she'd committed adultery ten years ago."

"At all events I could have it out with her."

"You can do that now, but you know just as well as I do that if you do she'll leave you. D'you want her to do that?"

George gave him an unhappy look.

"I don't know. I always thought she'd been a damned good wife to me. She runs the house perfectly, we never have any servant trouble; she's done wonders with the garden and she's splendid with all the village people. But damn it, I have my self-respect to think of. How can I go on living with her when I know that she was grossly unfaithful to me?"

"Have you always been faithful to her?"

"More or less, you know. After all, we've been married for nearly twenty-four years and Evie was never much for bed."

The solicitor slightly raised his eyebrows, but George was too intent on what he was saying to notice.

"I don't deny that I've had a bit of fun now and then. A man wants it. Women are different."

"We only have men's word for that," said Harry Blane, with a faint smile.

"Evie's absolutely the last woman I'd have suspected of kicking over the traces. I mean, she's a very fastidious, reticent woman. What on earth made her write the damned book?"

"I suppose it was a very poignant experience and perhaps it was a relief to her to get it off her chest like that."

"Well, if she had to write it why the devil didn't she write it under an assumed name?"

"She used her maiden name. I suppose she thought that was

enough, and it would have been if the book hadn't had this amazing boom."

George Peregrine and the lawyer were sitting opposite one another with a desk between them. George, his elbow on the desk, his cheek on his hand, frowned at his thought.

"It's so rotten not to know what sort of a chap he was. One can't even tell if he was by way of being a gentleman. I mean, for all I know he may have been a farm-hand or a clerk in a lawyer's office."

Harry Blane did not permit himself to smile and when he answered there was in his eyes a kindly, tolerant look.

"Knowing Evie so well I think the probabilities are that he was all right. Anyhow I'm sure he wasn't a clerk in my office."

"It's been a shock to me," the colonel sighed. "I thought she was fond of me. She couldn't have written that book unless she hated me."

"Oh, I don't believe that. I don't think she's capable of hatred."

"You're not going to pretend that she loves me."

"No."

"Well, what does she feel for me?"

Harry Blane leaned back in his swivel chair and looked at George reflectively.

"Indifference, I should say."

The colonel gave a little shudder and reddened.

"After all, you're not in love with her, are you?"

George Peregrine did not answer directly.

"It's been a great blow to me not to have any children, but I've never let her see that I think she's let me down. I've always been kind to her. Within reasonable limits I've tried to do my duty by her."

The lawyer passed a large hand over his mouth to conceal the smile that trembled on his lips.

"It's been such an awful shock to me," Peregrine went on. "Damn it all, even ten years ago Evie was no chicken and God knows, she wasn't much to look at. It's so ugly." He sighed deeply. "What would *you* do in my place?"

"Nothing."

George Peregrine drew himself bolt upright in his chair and he looked at Harry with the stern set face that he must have worn when he inspected his regiment.

"I can't overlook a thing like this. I've been made a laughing-stock. I can never hold up my head again."

"Nonsense," said the lawyer sharply, and then in a pleasant, kindly manner, "Listen, old boy: the man's dead; it all happened a long while back. Forget it. Talk to people about Evie's book, rave about it, tell 'em how proud you are of her. Behave as though you had so much confidence in her, you *knew* she could never have been unfaithful to you. The world moves so quickly and people's memories are so short. They'll forget."

"I shan't forget."

"You're both middle-aged people. She probably does a great deal more for you than you think and you'd be awfully lonely without her. I don't think it matters if you don't forget. It'll be all to the good if you can get it into that thick head of yours that there's a lot more in Evie than you ever had the gumption to see."

"Damn it all, you talk as if *I* was to blame."

"No, I don't think you were to blame, but I'm not so sure that Evie was either. I don't suppose she wanted to fall in love with this boy. D'you remember those verses right at the end? The impression they gave me was that though she was shattered by his death, in a strange sort of way she welcomed it. All through she'd been aware of the fragility of the tie that bound them. He died in the full flush of his first love and had never known that love so seldom endures; he'd only known its bliss and beauty. In her own bitter grief she found solace in the thought that he'd been spared all sorrow."

"All that's a bit above my head, old boy. I see more or less what you mean."

George Peregrine stared unhappily at the inkstand on the desk. He was silent and the lawyer looked at him with curious, yet sympathetic, eyes.

"Do you realise what courage she must have had never by a sign to show how dreadfully unhappy she was?" he said gently.

Colonel Peregrine sighed.

"I'm broken. I suppose you're right; it's no good crying over spilt milk and it would only make things worse if I made a fuss."

"Well?"

George Peregrine gave him a pitiful little smile.

"I'll take your advice. I'll do nothing. Let them think me a damned fool and to hell with them. The truth is, I don't know what I'd do without Evie. But I'll tell you what, there's one thing I shall never understand till my dying day: What in the name of heaven did the fellow ever see in her?"

The Treasure

RICHARD HARENGER was a happy man. Notwithstanding what the pessimists, from Ecclesiastes onwards, have said, this is not so rare a thing to find in this unhappy world, but Richard Harenger knew it, and that is a very rare thing indeed. The golden mean which the ancients so highly prized is out of fashion, and those who follow it must put up with polite derision from those who see no merit in self-restraint and no virtue in common-sense. Richard Harenger shrugged a polite and amused shoulder. Let others live dangerously, let others burn with a hard gemlike flame, let others stake their fortunes on the turn of a card, walk the tight-rope that leads to glory or the grave, or hazard their lives for a cause, a passion or an adventure. He neither envied the fame their exploits brought them nor wasted his pity on them when their efforts ended in disaster.

But it must not be inferred from this that Richard Harenger was a selfish or a callous man. He was neither. He was considerate and of a generous disposition. He was always ready to oblige a friend and he was sufficiently well off to be able to indulge himself in the pleasure of helping others. He had some money of his own and he occupied in the Home Office a position that brought him an adequate stipend. The work suited him. It was regular, responsible and pleasant. Every day when he left the office he went to his club to play bridge for a couple of hours, and on Saturdays and Sundays he played golf. He went abroad for his holidays, staying at good hotels, and visited churches, galleries and museums. He was a regular first-nighter. He dined out a good deal. His friends liked him. He was easy to talk to. He was well-read.

knowledgeable and amusing. He was besides of a personable exterior, not remarkably handsome, but tall, slim and erect of carriage, with a lean, intelligent face; his hair was growing thin, for he was now approaching the age of fifty, but his brown eyes retained their smile and his teeth were all his own. He had from nature a good constitution and he had always taken care of himself. There was no reason in the world why he should not be a happy man, and if there had been in him a trace of self-complacency he might have claimed that he deserved to be.

He had the good fortune even to sail safely through those perilous, unquiet straits of marriage in which so many wise and good men have made shipwreck. Married for love in the early twenties, his wife and he, after some years of almost perfect felicity, had drifted gradually apart. Neither of them wished to marry anyone else, so there was no question of divorce (which indeed Richard Harenger's situation in the government service made undesirable), but for convenience' sake, with the help of the family lawyer, they arranged a separation which left them free to lead their lives as each one wished without interference from the other. They parted with mutual expressions of respect and good will.

Richard Harenger sold his house in St. John's Wood and took a flat within convenient walking distance of Whitehall. It had a sitting-room which he lined with his books, a dining-room into which his Chippendale furniture just fitted, a nice-sized bedroom for himself, and beyond the kitchen a couple of maids' rooms. He brought his cook, whom he had had for many years, from St. John's Wood, but needing no longer so large a staff dismissed the rest of the servants and applied at a registry office for a house-parlourmaid. He knew exactly what he wanted and he explained his needs to the superintendent of the agency with precision. He wanted a maid who was not too young, first because young women are flighty and secondly because, though he was of mature age and a man of principle, people would talk, the porter and the tradesmen if nobody else, and both for the sake of his own reputation and that of the young person he considered that the applicant should have reached years of discretion. Besides that he wanted a maid who could clean silver well. He had always had a fancy for old silver, and it was reasonable to demand that the forks and spoons that had been used by a woman of quality under the reign of Queen Anne should be treated with tenderness and respect. He was of a hospitable nature and liked to give at least once a week little dinners of not less than four people and not more than eight. He could trust his cook to send in a meal that his guests would take pleasure in eating and he desired his parlourmaid to wait with neatness and dispatch. Then he needed a perfect valet. He dressed well, in a manner that suited his age and condition, and he liked his clothes to be properly looked after. The parlourmaid he was looking for must be able to press trousers and iron a tie, and he was very particular that his shoes should be well shone. He had small feet and he took a good deal of trouble to have well-cut shoes. He had a large supply and he insisted that they should be treed up the moment he took them off. Finally the flat must be kept clean and tidy. It was of course understood that any applicant for the post must be of irreproachable character, sober, honest, reliable and of a pleasing exterior. In return for this he was prepared to offer good wages, reasonable liberty and ample holidays. The superintendent listened without batting an eyelash and, telling him that she was quite sure she could suit him, sent him a string of candidates which proved that she had not paid the smallest attention to a word he said. He saw them all personally. Some were obviously inefficient, some looked fast, some were too old, others too young, some lacked the presence he thought essential; there was not one to whom he was inclined even to give a trial. He was a kindly, polite man and he declined their services with a smile and a pleasant expression of regret. He did not lose patience. He was prepared to interview house-parlourmaids till he found one who was suitable.

Now it is a funny thing about life, if you refuse to accept anything but the best you very often get it: if you utterly decline to make do with what you can get, then somehow or other you are very likely to get what you want. It is as though fate said, this man's a perfect fool, he's asking for perfection, and then just out of her feminine wilfulness flung it in his lap. One day the porter of the flats said to Richard Harenger out of a blue sky:

"I hear you're lookin' for a house-parlourmaid, sir. There's someone I know lookin' for a situation as might do."

"Can you recommend her personally?"

Richard Harenger had the sound opinion that one servant's recommendation of another was worth much more than that of an employer.

"I can vouch for her respectability. She's been in some very good situations."

"I shall be coming in to dress about seven. If that's convenient to her I could see her then."

"Very good, sir. I'll see that she's told."

He had not been in more than five minutes when the cook, having answered a ring at the front door, came in and told him that the person the porter had spoken to him about had called.

"Show her in," he said.

He turned on some more light so that he could see what the applicant looked like and, getting up, stood with his back to the fireplace. A woman came in and stood just inside the door in a respectful attitude.

"Good-evening," he said. "What is your name?"

"Pritchard, sir."

"How old are you?"

"Thirty-five, sir."

"Well, that's a reasonable age."

He gave his cigarette a puff and looked at her reflectively. She was on the tall side, nearly as tall as he, but he guessed that she wore high heels. Her black dress fitted her station. She held herself well. She had good features and a rather high colour.

"Will you take off your hat?" he asked.

She did so and he saw that she had pale brown hair. It was neatly and becomingly dressed. She looked strong and healthy. She was neither fat nor thin. In a proper uniform she would look very presentable. She was not inconveniently handsome, but she was certainly a comely, in another class of life you might almost have said a handsome, woman. He proceeded to ask her a number of questions. Her answers were satisfactory. She had left her last place for an adequate reason. She had been trained under a butler and appeared to be well acquainted with her duties. In her last place she had been head parlourmaid of three, but she did not mind undertaking the work of the flat singlehanded. She had valeted a gentleman before who had sent her to a tailor's to learn how to press clothes. She was a little shy, but neither timid nor ill-at-ease. Richard asked her his questions in his amiable, leisurely way and she answered them with modest composure. He was considerably impressed. He asked her what references she could give. They seemed extremely satisfactory.

"Now look here," he said, "I'm very much inclined to engage you. But I hate changes, I've had my cook for twelve years: if you suit me and the place suits you I hope you'll stay. I mean, I don't want you to come to me in three or four months and say that you're leaving to get married."

"There's not much fear of that, sir. I'm a widow. I don't believe marriage is much catch for anyone in my position, sir. My husband never did a stroke of work from the day I married him to the day he died, and I had to keep him. What I want now is a good home."

"I'm inclined to agree with you," he smiled. "Marriage is a very good thing, but I think it's a mistake to make a habit of it."

She very properly made no reply to this, but waited for him to announce his decision. She did not seem anxious about it. He reflected that if she was as competent as she appeared she must be well aware that she would have no difficulty in finding a place. He told her what wages he was offering and these seemed to be satisfactory to her. He gave her the necessary information about the place, but she gave him to understand that she was already apprised of this, and he received the impression, which amused rather than disconcerted him, that she had made certain enquiries about him before applying for the situation. It showed prudence on her part and good sense.

"When would you be able to come in if I engaged you? I haven't got anybody at the moment. The cook's managing as best she can with a char, but I should like to get settled as soon as possible."

"Well, sir, I was going to give myself a week's holiday, but if it's a matter of obliging a gentleman I don't mind giving that up. I could come in to-morrow if it was convenient."

Richard Harenger gave her his attractive smile.

"I shouldn't like you to do without a holiday that I dare say you've been looking forward to. I can very well go on like this for another week. Go and have your holiday and come to me when it's over."

"Thank you very much, sir. Would it do if I came in to-morrow week?"

"Quite well."

When she left, Richard Harenger felt he had done a good day's work. It looked as though he had found exactly what he was after. He rang for the cook and told her he had engaged a house-parlourmaid at last.

"I think you'll like her, sir," she said. "She came in and 'ad a talk with me this afternoon. I could see at once she knew her duties. And she's not one of them flighty ones."

"We can but try, Mrs. Jeddy. I hope you gave me a good character."

"Well, I said you was particular, sir. I said you was a gentleman as liked things just so."

"I admit that."

"She said she didn't mind that. She said she liked a gentleman as knew what was what. She said there's no satisfaction in doing things proper if nobody notices. I expect you'll find she'll take a rare lot of pride in her work."

"That's what I want her to do. I think we might go farther and fare worse."

"Well, sir, there is that to it, of course. And the proof of the pudding's the eating. But if you ask my opinion I think she's going to be a real treasure."

And that is precisely what Pritchard turned out. No man

was ever better served. The way she shone shoes was marvellous, and he set out of a fine morning for his walk to the office with a more jaunty step because you could almost see yourself reflected in them. She looked after his clothes with such attention that his colleagues began to chaff him about being the best-dressed man in the Civil Service. One day, coming home unexpectedly, he found a line of socks and handkerchiefs hung up to dry in the bathroom. He called Prichard.

"D'you wash my socks and handkerchiefs yourself, Pritchard? I should have thought you had enough to do without that."

"They do ruin them so at the laundry, sir. I prefer to do them at home if you have no objection."

She knew exactly what he should wear on every occasion, and without asking him was aware whether she should put out a dinner jacket and a black tie in the evening or a dress coat and a white one. When he was going to a party where decorations were to be worn he found his neat little row of medals automatically affixed to the lapel if his coat. He soon ceased to choose every morning from his wardrobe the tie he wanted, for he found that she put out for him without fail the one he would have himself selected. Her taste was perfect. He supposed she read his letters, for she always knew what his movements were, and if he had forgotten at what hour he had an engagement he had no need to look in his book, for Pritchard could tell him. She knew exactly what tone to use with persons with whom she conversed on the telephone. Except with tradesmen, with whom she was apt to be peremptory, she was always polite, but there was a distinct difference in her manner if she was addressing one of Mr. Harenger's literary friends or the wife of a Cabinet Minister. She knew by instinct with whom he wished to speak and with whom he didn't. From his sitting-room he sometimes heard her with placid sincerity assuring a caller that he was out, and then she would come in and tell him that So-and-So had rung up, but she thought he wouldn't wish to be disturbed.

"Quite right, Pritchard," he smiled.

"I knew she only wanted to bother you about that concert," said Pritchard.

His friends made appointments with him through her, and she would tell him what she had done on his return in the evening.

"Mrs. Soames rang up, sir, and asked if you would lunch with her on Thursday, the eighth, but I said you were very sorry but you were lunching with Lady Versinder. Mr. Oakley rang up and asked if you'd go to a cocktail party at the Savoy next Tuesday at six. I said you would if you possibly could, but you might have to go to the dentist's."

"Quite right."

"I thought you could see when the time came, sir."

She kept the flat like a new pin. On one occasion soon after she entered his service, Richard coming back from a holiday took out a book from his shelves and at once noticed that it had been dusted. He rang the bell.

"I forgot to tell you when I went away under no circumstances ever to touch my books. When books are taken out to be dusted they're never put back in the right place. I don't mind my books being dirty, but I hate not being able to find them."

"I'm very sorry, sir," said Pritchard. "I know some gentlemen are very particular and I took care to put back every book exactly where I took it from."

Richard Harenger gave his books a glance. So far as he could see every one was in its accustomed place. He smiled.

"I apologise, Pritchard."

"They were in a muck, sir. I mean, you couldn't open one without getting your hands black with dust."

She certainly kept his silver as he had never had it kept before. He felt called upon to give her a special word of praise.

"Most of it's Queen Anne and George I, you know," he explained.

"Yes, I know, sir. When you've got something good like that to look after it's a pleasure to keep it like it should be."

"You certainly have a knack for it. I never knew a butler who kept his silver as well as you do."

"Men haven't the patience women have," she replied modestly.

As soon as he thought Pritchard had settled down in the place he resumed the little dinners he was fond of giving once a week. He had already discovered that she knew how to wait at table, but it was with a warm sense of complacency that he realised then how competently she could manage a party. She was quick, silent and watchful. A guest had hardly felt the need of something before Pritchard was at his elbow offering him what he wanted. She soon learned the tastes of his more intimate friends and remembered that one liked water instead of soda with his whisky and that another particularly fancied the knuckle end of a leg of lamb. She knew exactly how cold a hock should be not to ruin its taste and how long claret should have stood in the room to bring out its bouquet. It was a pleasure to see her pour out a bottle of burgundy in such a fashion as not to disturb the grounds. On one occasion she did not serve the wine Richard had ordered. He somewhat sharply pointed this out to her.

"I opened the bottle sir, and it was slightly corked. So I got the Chambertin, as I thought it was safer."

"Quite right, Pritchard."

Presently he left this matter entirely in her hands, for he discovered that she knew perfectly what wines his guests would like. Without orders from him she would provide the best in his cellar and his oldest brandy if she thought they were the sort of people who knew what they were drinking. She had no belief in the palate of women, and when they were of the party was apt to serve the champagne which had to be drunk before it went off. She had the English servant's instinctive knowledge of social differences and neither rank nor money blinded her to the fact that someone was not a gentleman, but she had favourites among his friends, and when someone she particularly liked was dining, with the air of a cat that has swallowed a canary she would pour out for him a bottle of a wine that Harenger kept for very special occasions. It amused him.

"You've got on the right side of Pritchard, old boy," he

exclaimed. "There aren't many people she gives this wine to."

Pritchard became an institution. She was known very soon to be the perfect parlourmaid. People envied Harenger the possession of her as they envied nothing else that he had. She was worth her weight in gold. Her price was above rubies. Richard Harenger beamed with self-complacency when they praised her.

"Good masters make good servants," he said gaily.

One evening, when they were sitting over their port and she had left the room, they were talking about her.

"It'll be an awful blow when she leaves you."

"Why should she leave me? One or two people have tried to get her away from me, but she turned them down. She knows where she's well off."

"She'll get married one of these days."

"I don't think she's that sort."

"She's a good-looking woman."

"Yes, she has quite a decent presence."

"What are you talking about? She's a very handsome creature. In another class of life she'd be a well-known society beauty with her photograph in all the papers."

At that moment Pritchard came in with the coffee. Richard Harenger looked at her. After seeing her every day, off and on, for four years it was now—my word, how time flies—he had really forgotten what she looked like. She did not seem to have changed much since he had first seen her. She was no stouter than then, she still had the high colour, and her regular features bore the same expression which was at once intent and vacuous. The black uniform suited her. She left the room.

"She's a paragon and there's no doubt about it."

"I know she is," answered Harenger. "She's perfection. I should be lost without her. And the strange thing is that I don't very much like her."

"Why not?"

"I think she bores me a little. You see, she has no conversation. I've often tried to talk to her. She answers when I speak to her, but that's all. In four years she's never volunteered a remark of her own. I know absolutely nothing about her. I don't know if she likes me or if she's completely indifferent to me. She's an automaton. I respect her, I appreciate her, I trust her. She has every quality in the world and I've often wondered why it is that with all that I'm so completely indifferent to her. I think it must be that she is entirely devoid of charm."

They left it at that.

Two or three days after this, since it was Pritchard's night out and he had no engagement, Richard Harenger dined by himself at his club. A page-boy came to him and told him that they had just rung up from his flat to say that he had gone out without his keys and should they be brought along to him in a taxi? He put his hand to his pocket. It was a fact. By a singular chance he had forgotten to replace them when he had changed into a blue serge suit before coming out to dinner. His intention had been to play bridge, but it was an off-night at the club and there seemed little chance of a decent game; it occurred to him that it would be a good opportunity to see a picture that he had heard talked about, so he sent back the message by the page that he would call for the keys himself in half an hour.

He rang at the door of his flat and it was opened by Pritchard. She had the keys in her hand.

"What are you doing here, Pritchard?" he asked. "It's your night out, isn't it?"

"Yes, sir. But I didn't care about going, so I told Mrs. Jeddy she could go instead."

"You ought to get out when you have the chance," he said, with his usual thoughtfulness. "It's not good for you to be cooped up here all the time."

"I get out now and then on an errand, but I haven't been out in the evening for the last month."

"Why on earth not?"

"Well, it's not very cheerful going out by yourself, and somehow I don't know anyone just now I'm particularly keen on going out with."

"You ought to have a bit of fun now and then. It's good for you."

"I've got out of the habit of it somehow."

"Look here, I'm just going to the cinema. Would you like to come along with me?"

He spoke in kindliness, on the spur of the moment, and the moment he had said the words half regretted them.

"Yes, sir, I'd like to," said Pritchard.

"Run along then and put on a hat."

"I shan't be a minute."

She disappeared and he went into the sitting-room and lit a cigarette. He was a little amused at what he was doing, and pleased too; it was nice to be able to make someone happy with so little trouble to himself. It was characteristic of Pritchard that she had shown neither surprise nor hesitation. She kept him waiting about five minutes, and when she came back he noticed that she had changed her dress. She wore a blue frock in what he supposed was artificial silk, a small black hat with a blue brooch on it, and a silver fox round her neck. He was a trifle relieved to see that she looked neither shabby nor showy. It would never occur to anyone who happened to see them that this was a distinguished official in the Home Office taking his housemaid to the pictures.

"I'm sorry to have kept you waiting, sir."

"It doesn't matter at all," he said graciously.

He opened the front door for her and she went out before him. He remembered the familiar anecdote of Louis XIV and the courtier and appreciated the fact that she had not hesitated to precede him. The cinema for which they were bound was at no great distance from Mr. Harenger's flat and they walked there. He talked about the weather and the state of the roads and Adolf Hitler. Pritchard made suitable replies. They arrived just as Mickey Mouse was starting and this put them in a good humour. During the four years she had been in his service Richard Harenger had hardly ever seen Pritchard even smile, and now it diverted him vastly to hear her peal upon peal of joyous laughter. He enjoyed her pleasure. Then the principal attraction was thrown on the screen. It was a good picture and they both watched it with breathless excitement. Taking his cigarette-case out to help himself he automatically offered it to Pritchard.

"Thank you, sir," she said, taking one.

He lit it for her. Her eyes were on the screen and she was almost unconscious of his action. When the picture was finished they streamed out with the crowd into the street. They walked back towards the flat. It was a fine starry night.

"Did you like it?" he said.

"Like anything, sir. It was a real treat."

A thought occurred to him.

"By the way, did you have any supper to-night?"

"No, sir, I didn't have time."

"Aren't you starving?"

"I'll have a bit of bread and cheese when I get in and I'll make meself a cup of cocoa."

"That sounds rather grim." There was a feeling of gaiety in the air, and the people who poured past them, one way and another, seemed filled with a pleasant elation. In for a penny, in for a pound, he said to himself. "Look here, would you like to come and have a bit of supper with me somewhere?"

"If you'd like to, sir."

"Come on."

He hailed a cab. He was feeling very philanthropic and it was not a feeling that he disliked at all. He told the driver to go to a restaurant in Oxford Street which was gay, but at which he was confident there was no chance of meeting anyone he knew. There was an orchestra and people danced. It would amuse Pritchard to see them. When they sat down a waiter came up to them.

"They've got a set supper here," he said, thinking that was what she would like. "I suggest we have that. What would you like to drink? A little white wine?"

"What I really fancy is a glass of ginger beer," she said.

Richard Harenger ordered himself a whisky and soda. She ate the supper with hearty appetite, and though Harenger was not hungry, to put her at her ease he ate too. The picture they had just seen gave them something to talk about. It was quite true what they had said the other night, Pritchard was not a bad-looking woman, and even if someone had seen them together he would not have minded. It would make rather a good story for his friends when he told them how he had taken the incomparable Pritchard to the cinema and then afterwards to supper. Pritchard was looking at the dancers with a faint smile on her lips.

"Do you like dancing?" he said.

"I used to be a rare one for it when I was a girl. I never danced much after I was married. My husband was a bit shorter than me and somehow I never think it looks well unless the gentleman's taller, if you know what I mean. I suppose I shall be getting too old for it soon."

Richard was certainly taller than his parlourmaid. They would look all right. He was fond of dancing and he danced well. But he hesitated. He did not want to embarrass Pritchard by asking her to dance with him. It was better not to go too far perhaps. And yet what did it matter? It was a drab life she led. She was so sensible, if she thought it a mistake he was pretty sure she would find a decent excuse.

"Would you like to take a turn, Pritchard?" he said, as the band struck up again.

"I'm terribly out of practice, sir."

"What does that matter?"

"If you don't mind, sir," she answered coolly, rising from her seat.

She was not in the least shy. She was only afraid that she would not be able to follow his step. They moved on to the floor. He found she danced very well.

"Why, you dance perfectly, Pritchard," he said.

"It's coming back to me."

Although she was a big woman she was light on her feet and she had a natural sense of rhythm. She was very pleasant to dance with. He gave a glance at the mirrors that lined the walls and he could not help reflecting that they looked very well together. Their eyes met in the mirror; he wondered

whether she was thinking that too. They had two more dances
and then Richard Harenger suggested that they should go. He
paid the bill and they walked out. He noticed that she
threaded her way through the crowd without a trace of self-
consciousness. They got into a taxi and in ten minutes were at
home.

"I'll go up the back way, sir," said Pritchard.

"There's no need to do that. Come up in the lift with me."

He took her up, giving the night-porter an icy glance, so
that he should not think it strange that he came back at that
somewhat late hour with his parlourmaid, and with his latch-
key let her into the flat.

"Well, good-night, sir," she said. "Thank you very much.
It's been a real treat for me."

"Thank *you* Pritchard. I should have had a very dull evening by myself. I hope you've enjoyed your outing."

"That I have, sir, more than I can say."

It had been a success. Richard Harenger was satisfied with
himself. It was a kindly thing for him to have done. It was a
very agreeable sensation to give anyone so much real pleasure.
His benevolence warmed him and for a moment he felt a
great love in his heart for the whole human race.

"Good-night, Pritchard," he said, and because he felt happy
and good he put his arm round her waist and kissed her on
the lips.

Her lips were very soft. They lingered on his and she returned his kiss. It was the warm, hearty embrace of a healthy
woman in the prime of life. He found it very pleasant and he
held her to him a little more closely. She put her arms round
his neck.

As a general rule he did not wake till Pritchard came in
with his letters, but next morning he woke at half-past seven.
He had a curious sensation that he did not recognise. He was
accustomed to sleep with two pillows under his head and he
suddenly grew aware of the fact that he had only one. Then
he remembered and with a start looked round. The other pil-

low was beside his own. Thank God, no sleeping head rested there, but it was plain that one had. His heart sank. He broke out into a cold sweat.

"My God, what a fool I've been!" he cried out loud.

How could he have done anything so stupid? What on earth had come over him? He was the last man to play about with servant girls. What a disgraceful thing to do! At his age and in his position. He had not heard Pritchard slip away. He must have been asleep. It wasn't even as if he'd liked her very much. She wasn't his type. And, as he had said the other night, she rather bored him. Even now he only knew her as Pritchard. He had no notion what her first name was. What madness! And what was to happen now? The position was impossible. It was obvious he couldn't keep her, and yet to send her away for what was his fault as much as hers seemed shockingly unfair. How idiotic to lose the best parlourmaid a man ever had just for an hour's folly!

"It's that damned kindness of heart of mine," he groaned.

He would never find anyone else to look after his clothes so admirably or clean the silver so well. She knew all his friends' telephone numbers and she understood wine. But of course she must go. She must see for herself that after what had happened things could never be the same. He would make her a handsome present and give her an excellent reference. At any minute she would be coming in now. Would she be arch, would she be familiar? Or would she put on airs? Perhaps even she wouldn't trouble to come in with his letters. It would be awful if he had to ring the bell and Mrs. Jeddy came in and said: Pritchard's not up yet, sir, she's having a lie in after last night.

"What a fool I've been! What a contemptible cad!"

There was a knock at the door. He was sick with anxiety.

"Come in."

Richard Harenger was a very unhappy man.

Pritchard came in as the clock struck. She wore the print dress she was in the habit of wearing during the early part of the day.

"Good-morning, sir," she said.

"Good-morning."

She drew the curtains and handed him his letters and the papers. Her face was impassive. She looked exactly as she always looked. Her movements had the same competent deliberation that they always had. She neither avoided Richard's glance nor sought it.

"Will you wear your grey, sir? It came back from the tailor's yesterday."

"Yes."

He pretended to read his letters, but he watched her from under his eyelashes. Her back was turned to him. She took his vest and drawers and folded them over a chair. She took the studs out of the shirt he had worn the day before and studded a clean one. She put out some clean socks for him and placed them on the seat of a chair with the suspenders to match by the side. Then she put out his grey suit and attached the braces to the back buttons of the trousers. She opened his wardrobe and after a moment's reflection chose a tie to go with the suit. She collected on her arm the suit of the day before and picked up the shoes.

"Will you have breakfast now, sir, or will you have your bath first?"

"I'll have breakfast now," he said.

"Very good, sir."

With her slow quiet movements, unruffled, she left the room. Her face bore that rather serious, deferential, vacuous look it always bore. What had happened might have been a dream. Nothing in Pritchard's demeanour suggested that she had the smallest recollection of the night before. He gave a sigh of relief. It was going to be all right. She need not go, she need not go. Pritchard was the perfect parlourmaid. He knew that never by word nor gesture would she ever refer to the fact that for a moment their relations had been other than those of master and servant. Richard Harenger was a very happy man.

Rain

IT WAS nearly bed-time and when they awoke next morning land would be in sight. Dr. Macphail lit his pipe and, leaning over the rail, searched the heavens for the Southern Cross. After two years at the front and a wound that had taken longer to heal than it should, he was glad to settle down quietly at Apia for twelve months at least, and he felt already better for the journey. Since some of the passengers were leaving the ship next day at Pago-Pago they had had a little dance that evening and in his ears hammered still the harsh notes of the mechanical piano. But the deck was quiet at last. A little way off he saw his wife in a long chair talking with the Davidsons, and he strolled over to her. When he sat down under the light and took off his hat you saw that he had very red hair, with a bald patch on the crown, and the red, freckled skin which accompanies red hair; he was a man of forty, thin, with a pinched face, precise and rather pedantic; and he spoke with a Scots accent in a very low, quiet voice.

Between the Macphails and the Davidsons, who were missionaries, there had arisen the intimacy of shipboard, which is due to propinquity rather than to any community of taste. Their chief tie was the disapproval they shared of the men who spent their days and nights in the smoking-room playing poker or bridge and drinking. Mrs. Macphail was not a little flattered to think that she and her husband were the only people on board with whom the Davidsons were willing to associate, and even the doctor, shy but no fool, half unconsciously acknowledged the compliment. It was only because he was of an argumentative mind that in their cabin at night he permitted himself to carp.

"Mrs. Davidson was saying she didn't know how they'd have got through the journey if it hadn't been for us," said Mrs. Macphail, as she neatly brushed out her transformation. "She said we were really the only people on the ship they cared to know."

"I shouldn't have thought a missionary was such a big bug that he could afford to put on frills."

"It's not frills. I quite understand what she means. It wouldn't have been very nice for the Davidsons to have to mix with all that rough lot in the smoking-room."

"The founder of their religion wasn't so exclusive," said Dr. Macphail with a chuckle.

"I've asked you over and over again not to joke about religion," answered his wife. "I shouldn't like to have a nature like yours, Alec. You never look for the best in people."

He gave her a sidelong glance with his pale, blue eyes, but did not reply. After many years of married life he had learned that it was more conducive to peace to leave his wife with the last word. He was undressed before she was, and climbing into the upper bunk he settled down to read himself to sleep.

When he came on deck next morning they were close to land. He looked at it with greedy eyes. There was a thin strip of silver beach rising quickly to hills covered to the top with luxuriant vegetation. The coconut trees, thick and green, came nearly to the water's edge, and among them you saw the grass houses of the Samoans; and here and there, gleaming white, a little church. Mrs. Davidson came and stood beside him. She was dressed in black and wore round her neck a gold chain, from which dangled a small cross. She was a little woman, with brown, dull hair very elaborately arranged, and she had prominent blue eyes behind invisible *pince-nez*. Her face was long, like a sheep's, but she gave no impression of foolishness, rather of extreme alertness; she had the quick movements of a bird. The most remarkable thing about her was her voice, high, metallic, and without inflection; it fell

on the ear with a hard monotony, irritating to the nerves like
the pitiless clamour of the pneumatic drill.

"This must seem like home to you," said Dr. Macphail, with
his thin, difficult smile.

"Ours are low islands, you know, not like these. Coral.
These are volcanic. We've got another ten days' journey to
reach them."

"In these parts that's almost like being in the next street at
home," said Dr. Macphail facetiously.

"Well, that's rather an exaggerated way of putting it, but
one does look at distances differently in the South Seas. So
far you're right."

Dr. Macphail sighed faintly.

"I'm glad we're not stationed here," she went on. "They
say this is a terribly difficult place to work in. The steamers'
touching makes the people unsettled; and then there's the
naval station; that's bad for the natives. In our district we
don't have difficulties like that to contend with. There are one
or two traders, of course, but we take care to make them behave, and if they don't we make the place so hot for them
they're glad to go."

Fixing the glasses on her nose she looked at the green island
with a ruthless stare.

"It's almost a hopeless task for the missionaries here. I can
never be sufficiently thankful to God that we are at least
spared that."

Davidson's district consisted of a group of islands to the
North of Samoa; they were widely separated and he had frequently to go long distances by canoe. At these times his wife
remained at their headquarters and managed the mission. Dr.
Macphail felt his heart sink when he considered the effi-
ciency with which she certainly managed it. She spoke of
the depravity of the natives in a voice which nothing could
hush, but with a vehemently unctuous horror. Her sense of
delicacy was singular. Early in their acquaintance she had said
to him:

"You know, their marriage customs when we first settled in
the islands were so shocking that I couldn't possibly describe

them to you. But I'll tell Mrs. Macphail and she'll tell you."

Then he had seen his wife and Mrs. Davidson, their deck-chairs close together, in earnest conversation for about two hours. As he walked past them backwards and forwards for the sake of exercise, he had heard Mrs. Davidson's agitated whisper, like the distant flow of a mountain torrent, and he saw by his wife's open mouth and pale face that she was enjoying an alarming experience. At night in their cabin she repeated to him with bated breath all she had heard.

"Well, what did I say to you?" cried Mrs. Davidson, exultant, next morning. "Did you ever hear anything more dreadful? You don't wonder that I couldn't tell you myself, do you? Even though you are a doctor."

Mrs. Davidson scanned his face. She had a dramatic eagerness to see that she had achieved the desired effect.

"Can you wonder that when we first went there our hearts sank? You'll hardly believe me when I tell you it was impossible to find a single good girl in any of the villages."

She used the word *good* in a severely technical manner.

"Mr. Davidson and I talked it over, and we made up our minds the first thing to do was to put down the dancing. The natives were crazy about dancing."

"I was not averse to it myself when I was a young man," said Dr. Macphail.

"I guessed as much when I heard you ask Mrs. Macphail to have a turn with you last night. I don't think there's any real harm if a man dances with his wife, but I was relieved that she wouldn't. Under the circumstances I thought it better that we should keep ourselves to ourselves."

"Under what circumstances?"

Mrs. Davidson gave him a quick look through the *pince-nez,* but did not answer his question.

"But among white people it's not quite the same," she went on, "though I must say I agree with Mr. Davidson, who says he can't understand how a husband can stand by and see his wife in another man's arms, and as far as I'm concerned I've never danced a step since I married. But the native dancing is quite another matter. It's not only immoral in itself, but it distinctly leads to immorality. However, I'm thankful to God that we stamped it out, and I don't think I'm wrong in saying that no one has danced in our district for eight years."

But now they came to the mouth of the harbour and Mrs. Macphail joined them. The ship turned sharply and steamed slowly in. It was a great land-locked harbour big enough to hold a fleet of battleships; and all around it rose, high and steep, the green hills. Near the entrance, getting such breeze as blew from the sea, stood the governor's house in a garden. The Stars and Stripes dangled languidly from a flagstaff. They passed two or three trim bungalows, and a tennis court, and then they came to the quay with its warehouses. Mrs. Davidson pointed out the schooner, moored two or three hundred yards from the side, which was to take them to Apia. There was a crowd of eager, noisy, and good-humoured natives come from all parts of the island, some from curiosity, others to barter with the travellers on their way to Sydney; and they brought pineapples and huge bunches of bananas, *tapa* cloths, necklaces of shells or sharks' teeth, *kava*-bowls, and models of war canoes. American sailors, neat and trim, clean-shaven and frank of face, sauntered among them, and there was a little group of officials. While their luggage was being landed the Macphails and Mrs. Davidson watched the crowd. Dr. Macphail looked at the yaws from which most of the children and the young boys seemed to suffer, disfiguring sores like torpid ulcers, and his professional eyes glistened when he saw for the first time in his experience cases of elephantiasis, men going about with a huge, heavy arm or dragging along a grossly disfigured leg. Men and women wore the *lava-lava*.

"It's a very indecent costume," said Mrs. Davidson. "Mr. Davidson thinks it should be prohibited by law. How can you expect people to be moral when they wear nothing but a strip of red cotton round their loins?"

"It's suitable enough to the climate," said the doctor, wiping the sweat off his head.

Now that they were on land the heat, though it was so early in the morning, was already oppressive. Closed in by its hills, not a breath of air came in to Pago-Pago.

"In our islands," Mrs. Davidson went on in her high-pitched tones, "we've practically eradicated the *lava-lava*. A few old men still continue to wear it, but that's all. The women have all taken to the Mother Hubbard, and the men wear trousers and singlets. At the very beginning of our stay Mr. Davidson said in one of his reports: the inhabitants of these islands will never be thoroughly Christianized till every boy of more than ten years is made to wear a pair of trousers."

But Mrs. Davidson had given two or three of her birdlike glances at heavy grey clouds that came floating over the mouth of the harbour. A few drops began to fall.

"We'd better take shelter," she said.

They made their way with all the crowd to a great shed of corrugated iron, and the rain began to fall in torrents. They stood there for some time and then were joined by Mr. Davidson. He had been polite enough to the Macphails during the journey, but he had not his wife's sociability, and had spent much of his time reading. He was a silent, rather sullen man, and you felt that his affability was a duty that he imposed on himself Christianly; he was by nature reserved, even morose. His appearance was singular. He was very tall and thin, with long limbs loosely jointed; hollow cheeks and curiously high cheek-bones; he had so cadaverous an air that it surprised you to notice how full and sensual were his lips. He wore his hair very long. His dark eyes, set deep in their sockets, were large and tragic; and his hands with their big, long fingers, were finely shaped; they gave him a look of great strength. But the most striking thing about him was the feeling he gave you of suppressed fire. It was impressive and vaguely troubling. He was not a man with whom any intimacy was possible.

He brought now unwelcome news. There was an epidemic of measles, a serious and often fatal disease among the Kanakas, on the island, and a case had developed among the crew of the schooner which was to take them on their journey. The sick man had been brought ashore and put in hospital on the quarantine station, but telegraphic instructions had been sent from Apia to say that the schooner would not be allowed to enter the harbour till it was certain no other member of the crew was affected.

"It means we shall have to stay here for ten days at least."

"But I'm urgently needed at Apia," said Dr. Macphail.

"That can't be helped. If no more cases develop on board, the schooner will be allowed to sail with white passengers, but all native traffic is prohibited for three months."

"Is there a hotel here?" asked Mrs. Macphail.

Davidson gave a low chuckle.

"There's not."

"What shall we do then?"

"I've been talking to the governor. There's a trader along the front who has rooms that he rents, and my proposition is that as soon as the rain lets up we should go along there and see what we can do. Don't expect comfort. You've just got to be thankful if we get a bed to sleep on and a roof over our heads."

But the rain showed no sign of stopping, and at length with umbrellas and waterproofs they set out. There was no town, but merely a group of official buildings, a store or two, and at the back, among the coconut trees and plantains, a few native dwellings. The house they sought was about five minutes' walk from the wharf. It was a frame house of two storeys, with broad verandahs on both floors and a roof of corrugated iron. The owner was a half-caste named Horn, with a native wife surrounded by little brown children, and on the ground-floor he had a store where he sold canned goods and cottons. The rooms he showed them were almost bare of furniture. In the Macphails' there was nothing but a poor, worn bed with a ragged mosquito net, a rickety chair, and a washstand. They looked round with dismay. The rain poured down without ceasing.

"I'm not going to unpack more than we actually need," said Mrs. Macphail.

Mrs. Davidson came into the room as she was unlocking a portmanteau. She was very brisk and alert. The cheerless surroundings had no effect on her.

"If you'll take my advice you'll get a needle and cotton and start right in to mend the mosquito net," she said, "or you'll not be able to get a wink of sleep to-night."

"Will they be very bad?" asked Dr. Macphail.

"This is the season for them. When you're asked to a party at Government House at Apia you'll notice that all the ladies are given a pillow-slip to put their—their lower extremities in."

"I wish the rain would stop for a moment," said Mrs. Macphail. "I could try to make the place comfortable with more heart if the sun were shining."

"Oh, if you wait for that, you'll wait a long time. Pago-Pago is about the rainiest place in the Pacific. You see, the hills, and that bay, they attract the water, and one expects rain at this time of year anyway."

She looked from Macphail to his wife, standing helplessly in different parts of the room, like lost souls, and she pursed her lips. She saw that she must take them in hand. Feckless people like that made her impatient, but her hands itched to put everything in order which came so naturally to her.

"Here, you give me a needle and cotton and I'll mend that net of yours, while you go on with your unpacking. Dinner's at one. Dr. Macphail, you'd better go down to the wharf and see that your heavy luggage has been put in a dry place. You know what these natives are, they're quite capable of storing it where the rain will beat in on it all the time."

The doctor put on his waterproof again and went downstairs. At the door Mr. Horn was standing in conversation with the quartermaster of the ship they had just arrived in and a second-class passenger whom Dr. Macphail had seen several times on board. The quartermaster, a little, shrivelled man, extremely dirty, nodded to him as he passed.

"This is a bad job about the measles, doc," he said. "I see you've fixed yourself up already."

Dr. Macphail thought he was rather familiar, but he was a timid man and he did not take offence easily.

"Yes, we've got a room upstairs."

"Miss Thompson was sailing with you to Apia, so I've brought her along here."

The quartermaster pointed with his thumb to the woman standing by his side. She was twenty-seven perhaps, plump, and in a coarse fashion pretty. She wore a white dress and a large white hat. Her fat calves in white cotton stockings bulged over the tops of long white boots in glacé kid. She gave Macphail an ingratiating smile.

"The feller's tryin' to soak me a dollar and a half a day for the meanest sized room," she said in a hoarse voice.

"I tell you she's a friend of mine, Jo," said the quarter-master. "She can't pay more than a dollar, and you've sure got to take her for that."

The trader was fat and smooth and quietly smiling.

"Well, if you put it like that, Mr. Swan, I'll see what I can do about it. I'll talk to Mrs. Horn and if we think we can make a reduction we will."

"Don't try to pull that stuff with me," said Miss Thompson. "We'll settle this right now. You get a dollar a day for the room and not one bean more."

Dr. Macphail smiled. He admired the effrontery with which she bargained. He was the sort of man who always paid what he was asked. He preferred to be over-charged than to hag-gle. The trader sighed.

"Well, to oblige Mr. Swan I'll take it."

"That's the goods," said Miss Thompson. "Come right in and have a shot of hooch. I've got some real good rye in that grip if you'll bring it along, Mr. Swan. You come along too, doctor."

"Oh, I don't think I will, thank you," he answered. "I'm just going down to see that our luggage is all right."

He stepped out into the rain. It swept in from the opening of the harbour in sheets and the opposite shore was all blurred. He passed two or three natives clad in nothing but the *lava-lava*, with huge umbrellas over them. They walked finely, with leisurely movements, very upright; and they smiled and greeted him in a strange tongue as they went by.

It was nearly dinner-time when he got back, and their meal was laid in the trader's parlour. It was a room designed not to live in but for purposes of prestige, and it had a musty, melancholy air. A suite of stamped plush was arranged neatly round the walls, and from the middle of the ceiling, protected from the flies by yellow tissue paper, hung a gilt chandelier. Davidson did not come.

"I know he went to call on the governor," said Mrs. Davidson, "and I guess he's kept him to dinner."

A little native girl brought them a dish of hamburger steak, and after a while the trader came up to see that they had everything they wanted.

"I see we have a fellow lodger, Mr. Horn," said Dr. Macphail.

"She's taken a room, that's all," answered the trader. "She's getting her own board."

He looked at the two ladies with an obsequious air.

"I put her downstairs so she shouldn't be in the way. She won't be any trouble to you."

"Is it someone who was on the boat?" asked Mrs. Macphail.

"Yes, ma'am, she was in the second cabin. She was going to Apia. She has a position as cashier waiting for her."

"Oh!"

When the trader was gone Macphail said:

"I shouldn't think she'd find it exactly cheerful having her meals in her room."

"If she was in the second cabin I guess she'd rather," answered Mrs. Davidson. "I don't exactly know who it can be."

"I happened to be there when the quartermaster brought her along. Her name's Thompson."

"It's not the woman who was dancing with the quartermaster last night?" asked Mrs. Davidson.

"That's who it must be," said Mrs. Macphail. "I wondered at the time what she was. She looked rather fast to me."

"Not good style at all," said Mrs. Davidson.

They began to talk of other things, and after dinner, tired with their early rise, they separated and slept. When they awoke, though the sky was still grey and the clouds hung low, it was not raining and they went for a walk on the high road which the Americans had built along the bay.

On their return they found that Davidson had just come in.

"We may be here for a fortnight," he said irritably. "I've argued it out with the governor, but he says there is nothing to be done."

"Mr. Davidson's just longing to get back to his work," said his wife, with an anxious glance at him.

"We've been away for a year," he said, walking up and down the verandah. "The mission has been in charge of native missionaries and I'm terribly nervous that they've let things slide. They're good men, I'm not saying a word against them, God-fearing, devout, and truly Christian men—their Christianity would put many so-called Christians at home to the blush—but they're pitifully lacking in energy. They can make a stand once, they can make a stand twice, but they can't make a stand all the time. If you leave a mission in charge of a native missionary, no matter how trustworthy he seems, in course of time you'll find he's let abuses creep in."

Mr. Davidson stood still. With his tall, spare form, and his great eyes flashing out of his pale face, he was an impressive figure. His sincerity was obvious in the fire of his gestures and in his deep, ringing voice.

"I expect to have my work cut out for me. I shall act and I shall act promptly. If the tree is rotten it shall be cut down and cast into the flames."

And in the evening after the high tea which was their last meal, while they sat in the stiff parlour, the ladies working and Dr. Macphail smoking his pipe, the missionary told them of his work in the islands.

"When we went there they had no sense of sin at all," he said. "They broke the commandments one after the other and never knew they were doing wrong. And I think that was the most difficult part of my work, to instil into the natives the sense of sin."

The Macphails knew already that Davidson had worked in the Solomons for five years before he met his wife. She had been a missionary in China, and they had become acquainted in Boston, where they were both spending part of their leave to attend a missionary congress. On their marriage they had been appointed to the islands in which they had laboured ever since.

In the course of all the conversations they had had with Mr. Davidson one thing had shone out clearly and that was the man's unflinching courage. He was a medical missionary, and he was liable to be called at any time to one or other of the islands in the group. Even the whaleboat is not so very safe a conveyance in the stormy Pacific of the wet season, but often he would be sent for in a canoe, and then the danger was great. In cases of illness or accident he never hesitated. A dozen times he had spent the whole night baling for his life, and more than once Mrs. Davidson had given him up for lost.

"I'd beg him not to go sometimes," she said, "or at least to wait till the weather was more settled, but he'd never listen. He's obstinate, and when he's once made up his mind, nothing can move him."

"How can I ask the natives to put their trust in the Lord if I am afraid to do so myself?" cried Davidson. "And I'm not, I'm not. They know that if they send for me in their trouble I'll come if it's humanly possible. And do you think the Lord is going to abandon me when I am on his business? The wind blows at his bidding and the waves toss and rage at his word."

Dr. Macphail was a timid man. He had never been able to get used to the hurtling of the shells over the trenches, and when he was operating in an advanced dressing-station the sweat poured from his brow and dimmed his spectacles in the effort he made to control his unsteady hand. He shuddered a little as he looked at the missionary.

"I wish I could say that I've never been afraid," he said.

"I wish you could say that you believed in God," retorted the other.

But for some reason, that evening the missionary's thoughts travelled back to the early days he and his wife had spent on the islands.

"Sometimes Mrs. Davidson and I would look at one another and the tears would stream down our cheeks. We worked without ceasing, day and night, and we seemed to make no progress. I don't know what I should have done without her then. When I felt my heart sink, when I was very near despair, she gave me courage and hope."

Mrs. Davidson looked down at her work, and a slight colour rose to her thin cheeks. Her hands trembled a little. She did not trust herself to speak.

"We had no one to help us. We were alone, thousands of miles from any of our own people, surrounded by darkness. When I was broken and weary she would put her work aside and take the Bible and read to me till peace came and settled upon me like sleep upon the eyelids of a child, and when at last she closed the book she'd say: 'We'll save them in spite of themselves.' And I felt strong again in the Lord, and I answered: 'Yes, with God's help I'll save them. I must save them.'"

He came over to the table and stood in front of it as though it were a lectern.

"You see, they were so naturally depraved that they couldn't be brought to see their wickedness. We had to make sins out of what they thought were natural actions. We had to make it a sin, not only to commit adultery and to lie and thieve, but to expose their bodies, and to dance and not to come to church. I made it a sin for a girl to show her bosom and a sin for a man not to wear trousers."

"How?" asked Dr. Macphail, not without surprise.

"I instituted fines. Obviously the only way to make people realize that an action is sinful is to punish them if they commit it. I fined them if they didn't come to church, and I fined them if they danced. I fined them if they were improperly dressed. I had a tariff, and every sin had to be paid for either in money or work. And at last I made them understand."

"But did they never refuse to pay?"

"How could they?" asked the missionary.

"It would be a brave man who tried to stand up against Mr. Davidson," said his wife, tightening her lips.

Dr. Macphail looked at Davidson with troubled eyes. What

he heard shocked him, but he hesitated to express his disapproval.

"You must remember that in the last resort I could expel them from their church membership."

"Did they mind that?"

Davidson smiled a little and gently rubbed his hands.

"They couldn't sell their copra. When the men fished they got no share of the catch. It meant something very like starvation. Yes, they minded quite a lot."

"Tell him about Fred Ohlson," said Mrs. Davidson.

The missionary fixed his fiery eyes on Dr. Macphail.

"Fred Ohlson was a Danish trader who had been in the islands a good many years. He was a pretty rich man as traders go, and he wasn't very pleased when we came. You see, he'd had things very much his own way. He paid the natives what he liked for their copra, and he paid in goods and whiskey. He had a native wife, but he was flagrantly unfaithful to her. He was a drunkard. I gave him a chance to mend his ways, but he wouldn't take it. He laughed at me."

Davidson's voice fell to a deep bass as he said the last words, and he was silent for a minute or two. The silence was heavy with menace.

"In two years he was a ruined man. He'd lost everything he'd saved in a quarter of a century. I broke him, and at last he was forced to come to me like a beggar and beseech me to give him a passage back to Sydney."

"I wish you could have seen him when he came to see Mr. Davidson," said the missionary's wife. "He had been a fine, powerful man, with a lot of fat on him, and he had a great big voice, but now he was half the size, and he was shaking all over. He'd suddenly become an old man."

With abstracted gaze Davidson looked out into the night. The rain was falling again.

Suddenly from below came a sound, and Davidson turned and looked questioningly at his wife. It was the sound of a gramophone, harsh and loud, wheezing out a syncopated tune.

"What's that?" he asked.

Mrs. Davidson fixed her *pince-nez* more firmly on her nose.

"One of the second-class passengers has a room in the house. I guess it comes from there."

They listened in silence, and presently they heard the sound of dancing. Then the music stopped, and they heard the popping of corks and voices raised in animated conversation.

"I daresay she's giving a farewell party to her friends on board," said Dr. Macphail. "The ship sails at twelve, doesn't it?"

Davidson made no remark, but he looked at his watch.

"Are you ready?" he asked his wife.

She got up and folded her work.

"Yes, I guess I am," she answered.

"It's early to go to bed yet, isn't it?" said the doctor.

"We have a good deal of reading to do," explained Mrs. Davidson. "Wherever we are, we read a chapter of the Bible before retiring for the night and we study it with the commentaries, you know, and discuss it thoroughly. It's a wonderful training for the mind."

The two couples bade one another good-night. Dr. and Mrs. Macphail were left alone. For two or three minutes they did not speak.

"I think I'll go and fetch the cards," the doctor said at last.

Mrs. Macphail looked at him doubtfully. Her conversation with the Davidsons had left her a little uneasy, but she did not like to say that she thought they had better not play cards when the Davidsons might come in at any moment. Dr. Macphail brought them and she watched him, though with a vague sense of guilt, while he laid out his patience. Below the sound of revelry continued.

It was fine enough next day, and the Macphails, condemned to spend a fortnight of idleness at Pago-Pago, set about making the best of things. They went down to the quay and got out of their boxes a number of books. The doctor called on the chief surgeon of the naval hospital and went round the beds with him. They left cards on the governor. They passed Miss Thompson on the road. The doctor took off his hat, and she gave him a "Good morning, doc," in a loud, cheerful voice. She was dressed as on the day before, in a white frock, and her shiny white boots with their high heels, her fat legs bulging over the tops of them, were strange things on that exotic scene.

"I don't think she's very suitably dressed, I must say," said Mrs. Macphail. "She looks extremely common to me."

When they got back to their house, she was on the verandah playing with one of the trader's dark children.

"Say a word to her," Dr. Macphail whispered to his wife. "She's all alone here, and it seems rather unkind to ignore her."

Mrs. Macphail was shy, but she was in the habit of doing what her husband bade her.

"I think we're fellow lodgers here," she said, rather foolishly.

"Terrible, ain't it, bein' cooped up in a one-horse burg like this?" answered Miss Thompson. "And they tell me I'm lucky to have gotten a room. I don't see myself livin' in a native house, and that's what some have to do. I don't know why they don't have a hotel."

They exchanged a few more words. Miss Thompson, loud-voiced and garrulous, was evidently quite willing to gossip, but Mrs. Macphail had a poor stock of small talk and presently she said:

"Well, I think we must go upstairs."

In the evening when they sat down to their high-tea Davidson on coming in said:

"I see that woman downstairs has a couple of sailors sitting there. I wonder how she's gotten acquainted with them."

"She can't be very particular," said Mrs. Davidson.

They were all rather tired after the idle, aimless day.

"If there's going to be a fortnight of this I don't know what we shall feel like at the end of it," said Dr. Macphail.

"The only thing to do is to portion out the day to different activities," answered the missionary. "I shall set aside a certain number of hours to study and a certain number to exercise, rain or fine—in the wet season you can't afford to pay any attention to the rain—and a certain number to recreation."

Dr. Macphail looked at his companion with misgiving. Davidson's programme oppressed him. They were eating hamburger steak again. It seemed the only dish the cook knew how to make. Then below the gramophone began. Davidson started nervously when he heard it, but said nothing. Men's voices floated up. Miss Thompson's guests were joining in a well-known song and presently they heard her voice too, hoarse and loud. There was a good deal of shouting and laughing. The four people upstairs, trying to make conversation, listened despite themselves to the clink of glasses and the scrape of chairs. More people had evidently come. Miss Thompson was giving a party.

"I wonder how she gets them all in," said Mrs. Macphail, suddenly breaking into a medical conversation between the missionary and her husband.

It showed whither her thoughts were wandering. The twitch of Davidson's face proved that, though he spoke of scientific things, his mind was busy in the same direction. Suddenly, while the doctor was giving some experience of practice on the Flanders front, rather prosily, he sprang to his feet with a cry.

"What's the matter, Alfred?" asked Mrs. Davidson.

"Of course! It never occurred to me. She's out of Iwelei."

"She can't be."

"She came on board at Honolulu. It's obvious. And she's carrying on her trade here. Here."

He uttered the last word with a passion of indignation.

"What's Iwelei?" asked Mrs. Macphail.

He turned his gloomy eyes on her and his voice trembled with horror.

"The plague spot of Honolulu. The Red Light district. It was a blot on our civilization."

Iwelei was on the edge of the city. You went down side streets by the harbour, in the darkness, across a rickety bridge, till you came to a deserted road, all ruts and holes, and then suddenly you came out into the light. There was parking room for motors on each side of the road, and there were saloons, tawdry and bright, each one noisy with its mechanical piano, and there were barbers' shops and tobacconists. There was a stir in the air and a sense of expectant gaiety. You turned down a narrow alley, either to the right or to the left, for the road divided Iwelei into two parts, and you found yourself in the district. There were rows of little bungalows, trim and neatly painted in green, and the pathway between them was broad and straight. It was laid out like a garden-city. In its respectable regularity, its order and spruceness, it gave an impression of sardonic horror; for never can the search for love have been so systematized and ordered. The pathways were lit by a rare lamp, but they would have been dark except for the lights that came from the open windows of the bungalows. Men wandered about, looking at the women who sat at their windows, reading or sewing, for the most part taking no notice of the passers-by; and like the women they were of all nationalities. There were Americans, sailors from the ships in port, enlisted men off the gunboats, sombrely drunk, and soldiers from the regiments, white and black, quartered on the island; there were Japanese, walking in twos and threes; Hawaiians, Chinese in long robes, and Filipinos in preposterous hats. They were silent and as it were oppressed. Desire is sad.

"It was the most crying scandal of the Pacific," exclaimed Davidson vehemently. "The missionaries had been agitating against it for years, and at last the local press took it up. The police refused to stir. You know their argument. They say that vice is inevitable and consequently the best thing is to localize and control it. The truth is, they were paid. Paid. They were paid by the saloon-keepers, paid by the bullies, paid by the women themselves. At last they were forced to move."

"I read about it in the papers that came on board in Honolulu," said Dr. Macphail.

"Iwelei, with its sin and shame, ceased to exist on the very day we arrived. The whole population was brought before the justices. I don't know why I didn't understand at once what that woman was."

"Now you come to speak of it," said Mrs. Macphail, "I re-member seeing her come on board only a few minutes before the boat sailed. I remember thinking at the time she was cut-ting it rather fine."

"How dare she come here!" cried Davidson indignantly. "I'm not going to allow it."

He strode towards the door.

"What are you going to do?" asked Macphail.

"What do you expect me to do? I'm going to stop it. I'm not going to have this house turned into—into . . ."

He sought for a word that should not offend the ladies' ears. His eyes were flashing and his pale face was paler still in his emotion.

"It sounds as though there were three or four men down there," said the doctor. "Don't you think it's rather rash to go in just now?"

The missionary gave him a contemptuous look and without a word flung out of the room.

"You know Mr. Davidson very little if you think the fear of personal danger can stop him in the performance of his duty," said his wife.

She sat with her hands nervously clasped, a spot of colour on her high cheek bones, listening to what was about to hap-pen below. They all listened. They heard him clatter down the wooden stairs and throw open the door. The singing stopped suddenly, but the gramophone continued to bray out its vulgar tune. They heard Davidson's voice and then the noise of something heavy falling. The music stopped. He had hurled the gramophone on the floor. Then again they heard Davidson's voice, they could not make out the words, then Miss Thompson's, loud and shrill, then a confused clamour as though several people were shouting together at the top of their lungs. Mrs. Davidson gave a little gasp, and she clenched her hands more tightly. Dr. Macphail looked un-certainly from her to his wife. He did not want to go down, but he wondered if they expected him to. Then there was something that sounded like a scuffle. The noise now was more distinct. It might be that Davidson was being thrown out of the room. The door was slammed. There was a moment's silence and they heard Davidson come up the stairs again. He went to his room.

"I think I'll go to him," said Mrs. Davidson.

She got up and went out.

"If you want me, just call," said Mrs. Macphail, and then when the other was gone: "I hope he isn't hurt."

"Why couldn't he mind his own business?" said Dr. Macphail.

They sat in silence for a minute or two and then they both started, for the gramophone began to play once more, defiantly, and mocking voices shouted hoarsely the words of an obscene song.

Next day Mrs. Davidson was pale and tired. She complained of headache, and she looked old and wizened. She told Mrs. Macphail that the missionary had not slept at all; he had passed the night in a state of frightful agitation and at five had got up and gone out. A glass of beer had been thrown over him and his clothes were stained and stinking. But a sombre fire glowed in Mrs. Davidson's eyes when she spoke of Miss Thompson.

"She'll bitterly rue the day when she flouted Mr. Davidson," she said. "Mr. Davidson has a wonderful heart and no one who is in trouble has ever gone to him without being comforted, but he has no mercy for sin, and when his righteous wrath is excited he's terrible."

"Why, what will he do?" asked Mrs. Macphail.

"I don't know, but I wouldn't stand in that creature's shoes for anything in the world."

Mrs. Macphail shuddered. There was something positively alarming in the triumphant assurance of the little woman's manner. They were going out together that morning, and they went down the stairs side by side. Miss Thompson's door was open, and they saw her in a bedraggled dressing-gown, cooking something in a chafing-dish.

"Good morning," she called. "Is Mr. Davidson better this morning?"

They passed her in silence, with their noses in the air, as if she did not exist. They flushed, however, when she burst into a shout of derisive laughter. Mrs. Davidson turned on her suddenly.

"Don't you dare to speak to me," she screamed. "If you insult me I shall have you turned out of here."

"Say, did I ask Mr. Davidson to visit with me?"

"Don't answer her," whispered Mrs. Macphail hurriedly.

They walked on till they were out of earshot.

"She's brazen, brazen," burst from Mrs. Davidson.

Her anger almost suffocated her.

And on their way home they met her strolling towards the quay. She had all her finery on. Her great white hat with its vulgar, showy flowers was an affront. She called out cheerily to them as she went by, and a couple of American sailors who were standing there grinned as the ladies set their faces to an icy stare. They got in just before the rain began to fall again.

"I guess she'll get her fine clothes spoilt," said Mrs. Davidson with a bitter sneer.

Davidson did not come in till they were half way through dinner. He was wet through, but he would not change. He sat, morose and silent, refusing to eat more than a mouthful, and he stared at the slanting rain. When Mrs. Davidson told him of their two encounters with Miss Thompson he did not answer. His deepening frown alone showed that he had heard.

"Don't you think we ought to make Mr. Horn turn her out of here?" asked Mrs. Davidson. "We can't allow her to insult us."

"There doesn't seem to be any other place for her to go," said Macphail.

"She can live with one of the natives."

"In weather like this a native hut must be a rather uncomfortable place to live in."

"I lived in one for years," said the missionary.

When the little native girl brought in the fried bananas which formed the sweet they had every day, Davidson turned to her.

"Ask Miss Thompson when it would be convenient for me to see her," he said.

The girl nodded shyly and went out.

"What do you want to see her for, Alfred?" asked his wife.

"It's my duty to see her. I won't act till I've given her every chance."

"You don't know what she is. She'll insult you."

"Let her insult me. Let her spit on me. She has an immortal soul, and I must do all that is in my power to save it."

Mrs. Davidson's ears rang still with the harlot's mocking laughter.

"She's gone too far."

"Too far for the mercy of God?" His eyes lit up suddenly and his voice grew mellow and soft. "Never. The sinner may be deeper in sin than the depth of hell itself, but the love of the Lord Jesus can reach him still."

The girl came back with the message.

"Miss Thompson's compliments and as long as Rev. Davidson don't come in business hours she'll be glad to see him any time."

The party received it in stony silence, and Dr. Macphail quickly effaced from his lips the smile which had come upon them. He knew his wife would be vexed with him if he found Miss Thompson's effrontery amusing.

They finished the meal in silence. When it was over the two ladies got up and took their work, Mrs. Macphail was making another of the innumerable comforters which she had turned out since the beginning of the war, and the doctor lit his pipe. But Davidson remained in his chair and with abstracted eyes stared at the table. At last he got up and without a word went out of the room. They heard him go down and they heard Miss Thompson's defiant "Come in" when he knocked at the door. He remained with her for an hour. And Dr. Macphail watched the rain. It was beginning to get on his nerves. It was not like our soft English rain that drops gently on the earth; it was unmerciful and somehow terrible; you felt in it the malignancy of the primitive powers of nature. It did not pour, it flowed. It was like a deluge from heaven, and it rattled on the roof of corrugated iron with a steady persistence that was maddening. It seemed to have a fury of its own. And sometimes you felt that you must scream if it did not stop, and then suddenly you felt powerless, as though your bones had suddenly become soft; and you were miserable and hopeless.

Macphail turned his head when the missionary came back. The two women looked up.

"I've given her every chance. I have exhorted her to repent. She is an evil woman."

He paused, and Dr. Macphail saw his eyes darken and his pale face grow hard and stern.

"Now I shall take the whips with which the Lord Jesus drove the usurers and the money changers out of the Temple of the Most High."

He walked up and down the room. His mouth was close set, and his black brows were frowning.

"If she fled to the uttermost parts of the earth I should pursue her."

With a sudden movement he turned round and strode out of the room. They heard him go downstairs again.

"What is he going to do?" asked Mrs. Macphail.

"I don't know." Mrs. Davidson took off her *pince-nez* and wiped them. "When he is on the Lord's work I never ask him questions."

She sighed a little.

"What is the matter?"

"He'll wear himself out. He doesn't know what it is to spare himself."

Dr. Macphail learnt the first results of the missionary's activity from the half-caste trader in whose house they lodged. He stopped the doctor when he passed the store and came out to speak to him on the stoop. His fat face was worried.

"The Rev. Davidson has been at me for letting Miss Thompson have a room here," he said, "but I didn't know what she was when I rented it to her. When people come and ask if I can rent them a room all I want to know is if they've the money to pay for it. And she paid me for hers a week in advance."

Dr. Macphail did not want to commit himself.

"When all's said and done it's your house. We're very much obliged to you for taking us in at all."

Horn looked at him doubtfully. He was not certain yet how definitely Macphail stood on the missionary's side.

"The missionaries are in with one another," he said, hesitatingly. "If they get it in for a trader he may just as well shut up his store and quit."

"Did he want you to turn her out?"

"No, he said so long as she behaved herself he couldn't ask me to do that. He said he wanted to be just to me. I promised she wouldn't have no more visitors. I've just been and told her."

"How did she take it?"

"She gave me hell."

The trader squirmed in his old ducks. He had found Miss Thompson a rough customer.

"Oh, well, I daresay she'll get out. I don't suppose she wants to stay here if she can't have anyone in."

"There's nowhere she can go, only a native house, and no native'll take her now, not now that the missionaries have got their knife in her."

Dr. Macphail looked at the falling rain.

"Well, I don't suppose it's any good waiting for it to clear up."

In the evening when they sat in the parlour Davidson talked to them of his early days at college. He had had no means and had worked his way through by doing odd jobs during the vacations. There was silence downstairs. Miss Thompson was sitting in her little room alone. But suddenly the gramophone began to play. She had set it on in defiance, to cheat her loneliness, but there was no one to sing, and it had a melancholy note. It was like a cry for help. Davidson took no notice. He was in the middle of a long anecdote and without change of expression went on. The gramophone continued. Miss Thompson put on one reel after another. It looked as though the silence of the night were getting on her nerves. It was breathless and sultry. When the Macphails went to bed they could not sleep. They lay side by side with their eyes wide open, listening to the cruel singing of the mosquitoes outside their curtain.

"What's that?" whispered Mrs. Macphail at last.

They heard a voice, Davidson's voice, through the wooden partition. It went on with a monotonous, earnest insistence. He was praying aloud. He was praying for the soul of Miss Thompson.

Two or three days went by. Now when they passed Miss Thompson on the road she did not greet them with ironic cordiality or smile; she passed with her nose in the air, a sulky look on her painted face, frowning, as though she did not see them. The trader told Macphail that she had tried to get lodging elsewhere, but had failed. In the evening she played through the various reels of her gramophone, but the pretence of mirth was obvious now. The ragtime had a cracked, heart-broken rhythm as though it were a one-step of despair. When she began to play on Sunday Davidson sent Horn to beg her to stop at once since it was the Lord's day. The reel was taken off and the house was silent except for the steady pattering of the rain on the iron roof.

"I think she's getting a bit worked up," said the trader next day to Macphail. "She don't know what Mr. Davidson's up to and it makes her scared."

Macphail had caught a glimpse of her that morning and it struck him that her arrogant expression had changed. There was in her face a hunted look. The half-caste gave him a side-long glance.

"I suppose you don't know what Mr. Davidson is doing about it?" he hazarded.

"No, I don't."

It was singular that Horn should ask him that question, for he also had the idea that the missionary was mysteriously at work. He had an impression that he was weaving a net around the woman, carefully, systematically, and suddenly, when everything was ready, would pull the strings tight.

"He told me to tell her," said the trader, "that if at any time she wanted him she only had to send and he'd come."

"What did she say when you told her that?"

"She didn't say nothing. I didn't stop. I just said what he said I was to and then I beat it. I thought she might be going to start weepin'."

"I have no doubt the loneliness is getting on her nerves," said the doctor. "And the rain—that's enough to make anyone jumpy," he continued irritably. "Doesn't it ever stop in this confounded place?"

"It goes on pretty steady in the rainy season. We have three hundred inches in the year. You see, it's the shape of the bay. It seems to attract the rain from all over the Pacific."

"Damn the shape of the bay," said the doctor.

He scratched his mosquito bites. He felt very short-tempered. When the rain stopped and the sun shone, it was like a hot-house, seething, humid, sultry, breathless, and you had a strange feeling that everything was growing with a savage violence. The natives, blithe and childlike by reputation, seemed then, with their tattooing and their dyed hair, to have something sinister in their appearance; and when they pattered along at your heels with their naked feet you looked back instinctively. You felt they might at any moment come behind you swiftly and thrust a long knife between your shoulder blades. You could not tell what dark thoughts lurked behind their wide-set eyes. They had a little the look of ancient Egyptians painted on a temple wall, and there was about them the terror of what is immeasurably old.

The missionary came and went. He was busy, but the Macphails did not know what he was doing. Horn told the doctor that he saw the governor every day, and once Davidson mentioned him.

"He looks as if he had plenty of determination," he said, "but when you come down to brass tacks he has no backbone."

"I suppose that means he won't do exactly what you want," suggested the doctor facetiously.

The missionary did not smile.

"I want him to do what's right. It shouldn't be necessary to persuade a man to do that."

"But there may be differences of opinion about what is right."

"If a man had a gangrenous foot would you have patience with anyone who hesitated to amputate it?"

"Gangrene is a matter of fact."

"And Evil?"

What Davidson had done soon appeared. The four of them had just finished their midday meal, and they had not yet separated for the siesta which the heat imposed on the ladies and on the doctor. Davidson had little patience with the slothful habit. The door was suddenly flung open and Miss Thompson came in. She looked round the room and then went up to Davidson.

"You low-down skunk, what have you been saying about me to the governor?"

She was spluttering with rage. There was a moment's pause. Then the missionary drew forward a chair.

"Won't you be seated, Miss Thompson? I've been hoping to have another talk with you."

"You poor low-life bastard."

She burst into a torrent of insult, foul and insolent. Davidson kept his grave eyes on her.

"I'm indifferent to the abuse you think fit to heap on me, Miss Thompson," he said, "but I must beg you to remember that ladies are present."

Tears by now were struggling with her anger. Her face was red and swollen as though she were choking.

"What has happened?" asked Dr. Macphail.

"A feller's just been in here and he says I gotter beat it on the next boat."

Was there a gleam in the missionary's eyes? His face remained impassive.

"You could hardly expect the governor to let you stay here under the circumstances."

"You done it," she shrieked. "You can't kid me. You done it."

"I don't want to deceive you. I urged the governor to take the only possible step consistent with his obligations."

"Why couldn't you leave me be? I wasn't doin' you no harm."

"You may be sure that if you had I should be the last man to resent it."

"Do you think I want to stay on in this poor imitation of a burg? I don't look no busher, do I?"

"In that case I don't see what cause of complaint you have," he answered.

She gave an inarticulate cry of rage and flung out of the room. There was a short silence.

"It's a relief to know that the governor has acted at last," said Davidson finally. "He's a weak man and he shilly-shallied. He said she was only here for a fortnight anyway, and if she went on to Apia that was under British jurisdiction and had nothing to do with him."

The missionary sprang to his feet and strode across the room.

"It's terrible the way the men who are in authority seek to evade their responsibility. They speak as though evil that was out of sight ceased to be evil. The very existence of that woman is a scandal and it does not help matters to shift it to another of the islands. In the end I had to speak straight from the shoulder."

Davidson's brow lowered, and he protruded his firm chin. He looked fierce and determined.

"What do you mean by that?"

"Our mission is not entirely without influence at Washington. I pointed out to the governor that it wouldn't do him any good if there was a complaint about the way he managed things here."

"When has she got to go?" asked the doctor, after a pause.

"The San Francisco boat is due here from Sydney next Tuesday. She's to sail on that."

That was in five days' time. It was next day, when he was coming back from the hospital where for want of something better to do Macphail spent most of his mornings, that the half-caste stopped him as he was going upstairs.

"Excuse me, Dr. Macphail, Miss Thompson's sick. Will you have a look at her?"

"Certainly."

Horn led him to her room. She was sitting in a chair idly, neither reading nor sewing, staring in front of her. She wore her white dress and the large hat with the flowers on it. Macphail noticed that her skin was yellow and muddy under her powder, and her eyes were heavy.

"I'm sorry to hear you're not well," he said.

"Oh, I ain't sick really. I just said that, because I just had to see you. I've got to clear on a boat that's going to 'Frisco."

She looked at him and he saw that her eyes were suddenly startled. She opened and clenched her hands spasmodically. The trader stood at the door, listening.

"So I understand," said the doctor.

She gave a little gulp.

"I guess it ain't very convenient for me to go to 'Frisco just now. I went to see the governor yesterday afternoon, but I couldn't get to him. I saw the secretary, and he told me I'd got to take that boat and that was all there was to it. I just had to see the governor, so I waited outside his house this morning, and when he come out I spoke to him. He didn't want to speak to me, I'll say, but I wouldn't let him shake me off, and at last he said he hadn't no objection to my staying here till the next boat to Sydney if the Rev. Davidson will stand for it."

She stopped and looked at Dr. Macphail anxiously.

"I don't know exactly what I can do," he said.

"Well, I thought maybe you wouldn't mind asking him. I swear to God I won't start anything here if he'll just only let me stay. I won't go out of the house if that'll suit him. It's no more'n a fortnight."

"I'll ask him."

"He won't stand for it," said Horn. "He'll have you out on Tuesday, so you may as well make up your mind to it."

"Tell him I can get work in Sydney, straight stuff, I mean. 'Tain't asking very much."

"I'll do what I can."

"And come and tell me right away, will you? I can't set down to a thing till I get the dope one way or the other."

It was not an errand that much pleased the doctor, and, characteristically perhaps, he went about it indirectly. He told his wife what Miss Thompson had said to him and asked her to speak to Mrs. Davidson. The missionary's attitude seemed rather arbitrary and it could do no harm if the girl were allowed to stay in Pago-Pago another fortnight. But he was not prepared for the result of his diplomacy. The missionary came to him straightway.

"Mrs. Davidson tells me that Thompson has been speaking to you."

Dr. Macphail, thus directly tackled, had the shy man's resentment at being forced out into the open. He felt his temper rising, and he flushed.

"I don't see that it can make any difference if she goes to Sydney rather than to San Francisco, and so long as she promises to behave while she's here it's dashed hard to persecute her."

The missionary fixed him with his stern eyes.

"Why is she unwilling to go back to San Francisco?"

"I didn't enquire," answered the doctor with some asperity. "And I think one does better to mind one's own business."

Perhaps it was not a very tactful answer.

"The governor has ordered her to be deported by the first boat that leaves the island. He's only done his duty and I will not interfere. Her presence is a peril here."

"I think you're very harsh and tyrannical."

The two ladies looked up at the doctor with some alarm, but they need not have feared a quarrel, for the missionary smiled gently.

"I'm terribly sorry you should think that of me, Dr. Macphail. Believe me, my heart bleeds for that unfortunate woman, but I'm only trying to do my duty."

The doctor made no answer. He looked out of the window sullenly. For once it was not raining and across the bay you saw nestling among the trees the huts of a native village.

"I think I'll take advantage of the rain stopping to go out," he said.

"Please don't bear me malice because I can't accede to your wish," said Davidson, with a melancholy smile. "I respect you very much, doctor, and I should be sorry if you thought ill of me."

"I have no doubt you have a sufficiently good opinion of yourself to bear mine with equanimity," he retorted.

"That's one on me," chuckled Davidson.

When Dr. Macphail, vexed with himself because he had been uncivil to no purpose, went downstairs, Miss Thompson was waiting for him with her door ajar.

"Well," she said, "have you spoken to him?"

"Yes, I'm sorry, he won't do anything," he answered, not looking at her in his embarrassment.

But then he gave her a quick glance, for a sob broke from her. He saw that her face was white with fear. It gave him a shock of dismay. And suddenly he had an idea.

"But don't give up hope yet. I think it's a shame the way they're treating you and I'm going to see the governor my-self."

"Now?"

He nodded. Her face brightened.

"Say, that's real good of you. I'm sure he'll let me stay if you speak for me. I just won't do a thing I didn't ought all the time I'm here."

Dr. Macphail hardly knew why he had made up his mind to appeal to the governor. He was perfectly indifferent to Miss Thompson's affairs, but the missionary had irritated him, and with him temper was a smouldering thing. He found the governor at home. He was a large, handsome man, a sailor, with a grey toothbrush moustache; and he wore a spotless uniform of white drill.

"I've come to see you about a woman who's lodging in the same house as we are," he said. "Her name's Thompson."

"I guess I've heard nearly enough about her, Dr. Macphail," said the governor, smiling. "I've given her the order to get out next Tuesday and that's all I can do."

"I wanted to ask you if you couldn't stretch a point and let her stay here till the boat comes in from San Francisco so that she can go to Sydney. I will guarantee her good behaviour."

The governor continued to smile, but his eyes grew small and serious.

"I'd be very glad to oblige you, Dr. Macphail, but I've given the order and it must stand."

The doctor put the case as reasonably as he could, but now the governor ceased to smile at all. He listened sullenly, with averted gaze. Macphail saw that he was making no impression.

"I'm sorry to cause any lady inconvenience, but she'll have to sail on Tuesday and that's all there is to it."

"But what difference can it make?"

"Pardon me, doctor, but I don't feel called upon to explain my official actions except to the proper authorities."

Macphail looked at him shrewdly. He remembered Davidson's hint that he had used threats, and in the governor's attitude he read a singular embarrassment.

"Davidson's a damned busybody," he said hotly.

"Between ourselves, Dr. Macphail, I don't say that I have formed a very favourable opinion of Mr. Davidson, but I am bound to confess that he was within his rights in pointing out to me the danger that the presence of a woman of Miss Thompson's character was to a place like this where a number of enlisted men are stationed among a native population."

He got up and Dr. Macphail was obliged to do so too.

"I must ask you to excuse me. I have an engagement. Please give my respects to Mrs. Macphail."

The doctor left him crest-fallen. He knew that Miss Thompson would be waiting for him, and unwilling to tell her himself that he had failed, he went into the house by the back door and sneaked up the stairs as though he had something to hide.

At supper he was silent and ill-at-ease, but the missionary was jovial and animated. Dr. Macphail thought his eyes rested on him now and then with triumphant good-humour. It struck him suddenly that Davidson knew of his visit to the governor and of its ill success. But how on earth could he have heard of it? There was something sinister about the power of that man. After supper he saw Horn on the verandah and, as though to have a casual word with him, went out.

"She wants to know if you've seen the governor," the trader whispered.

"Yes. He wouldn't do anything. I'm awfully sorry, I can't do anything more."

"I knew he wouldn't. They daren't go against the missionaries."

"What are you talking about?" said Davidson affably, coming out to join them.

"I was just saying there was no chance of your getting over to Apia for at least another week," said the trader glibly.

He left them, and the two men returned to the parlour. Mr. Davidson devoted one hour after each meal to recreation. Presently a timid knock was heard at the door.

"Come in," said Mrs. Davidson, in her sharp voice.

The door was not opened. She got up and opened it. They saw Miss Thompson standing at the threshold. But the change in her appearance was extraordinary. This was no longer the flaunting hussy who had jeered at them in the road, but a broken, frightened woman. Her hair, as a rule so elaborately arranged, was tumbling untidily over her neck. She wore bedroom slippers and a skirt and blouse. They were unfresh and bedraggled. She stood at the door with the tears streaming down her face and did not dare to enter.

"What do you want?" said Mrs. Davidson harshly.

"May I speak to Mr. Davidson?" she said in a choking voice.

The missionary rose and went towards her.

"Come right in, Miss Thompson," he said in cordial tones. "What can I do for you?"

She entered the room.

"Say, I'm sorry for what I said to you the other day an' for — for everythin' else. I guess I was a bit lit up. I beg pardon."

"Oh, it was nothing. I guess my back's broad enough to bear a few hard words."

She stepped towards him with a movement that was horribly cringing.

"You've got me beat. I'm all in. You won't make me go
back to 'Frisco?"

His genial manner vanished and his voice grew on a sudden
hard and stern.

"Why don't you want to go back there?"

She cowered before him.

"I guess my people live there. I don't want them to see me
like this. I'll go anywhere else you say."

"Why don't you want to go back to San Francisco?"

"I've told you."

He leaned forward, staring at her, and his great, shining
eyes seemed to try to bore into her soul. He gave a sudden
gasp.

"The penitentiary."

She screamed, and then she fell at his feet, clasping his legs.

"Don't send me back there. I swear to you before God I'll
be a good woman. I'll give all this up."

She burst into a torrent of confused supplication and the
tears coursed down her painted cheeks. He leaned over her
and, lifting her face, forced her to look at him.

"Is that it, the penitentiary?"

"I beat it before they could get me," she gasped. "If the
bulls grab me it's three years for mine."

He let go his hold of her and she fell in a heap on the floor,
sobbing bitterly. Dr. Macphail stood up.

"This alters the whole thing," he said. "You can't make her
go back when you know this. Give her another chance. She
wants to turn over a new leaf."

"I'm going to give her the finest chance she's ever had. If
she repents let her accept her punishment."

She misunderstood the words and looked up. There was a
gleam of hope in her heavy eyes.

"You'll let me go?"

"No. You shall sail for San Francisco on Tuesday."

She gave a groan of horror and then burst into low, hoarse

shrieks which sounded hardly human, and she beat her head passionately on the ground. Dr. Macphail sprang to her and lifted her up.

"Come on, you mustn't do that. You'd better go to your room and lie down. I'll get you something."

He raised her to her feet and partly dragging her, partly carrying her, got her downstairs. He was furious with Mrs. Davidson and with his wife because they made no effort to help. The half-caste was standing on the landing and with his assistance he managed to get her on the bed. She was moaning and crying. She was almost insensible. He gave her a hypodermic injection. He was hot and exhausted when he went upstairs again.

"I've got her to lie down."

The two women and Davidson were in the same positions as when he had left them. They could not have moved or spoken since he went.

"I was waiting for you," said Davidson, in a strange, distant voice. "I want you all to pray with me for the soul of our erring sister."

He took the Bible off a shelf, and sat down at the table at which they had supped. It had not been cleared, and he pushed the tea-pot out of the way. In a powerful voice, resonant and deep, he read to them the chapter in which is narrated the meeting of Jesus Christ with the woman taken in adultery.

"Now kneel with me and let us pray for the soul of our dear sister, Sadie Thompson."

He burst into a long, passionate prayer in which he implored God to have mercy on the sinful woman. Mrs. Macphail and Mrs. Davidson knelt with covered eyes. The doctor, taken by surprise, awkward and sheepish, knelt too. The missionary's prayer had a savage eloquence. He was extraordinarily moved, and as he spoke the tears ran down his cheeks. Outside, the pitiless rain fell, fell steadily, with a fierce malignity that was all too human.

At last he stopped. He paused for a moment and said:

"We will now repeat the Lord's prayer."

They said it and then, following him, they rose from their knees. Mrs. Davidson's face was pale and restful. She was comforted and at peace, but the Macphails felt suddenly bashful. They did not know which way to look.

"I'll just go down and see how she is now," said Dr. Macphail.

When he knocked at her door it was opened for him by Horn. Miss Thompson was in a rocking-chair, sobbing quietly.

"What are you doing there?" exclaimed Macphail. "I told you to lie down."

"I can't lie down. I want to see Mr. Davidson."

"My poor child, what do you think is the good of it? You'll never move him."

"He said he'd come if I sent for him."

Macphail motioned to the trader.

"Go and fetch him."

He waited with her in silence while the trader went upstairs. Davidson came in.

"Excuse me for asking you to come here," she said, looking at him sombrely.

"I was expecting you to send for me. I knew the Lord would answer my prayer."

They stared at one another for a moment and then she looked away. She kept her eyes averted when she spoke.

"I've been a bad woman. I want to repent."

"Thank God! thank God! He has heard our prayers."

He turned to the two men.

"Leave me alone with her. Tell Mrs. Davidson that our prayers have been answered."

They went out and closed the door behind them.

"Gee whizz," said the trader.

That night Dr. Macphail could not get to sleep till late, and when he heard the missionary come upstairs he looked at his watch. It was two o'clock. But even then he did not go to bed at once, for through the wooden partition that separated their rooms he heard him praying aloud, till he himself, exhausted, fell asleep.

When he saw him next morning he was surprised at his

appearance. He was paler than ever, tired, but his eyes shone with an inhuman fire. It looked as though he were filled with an overwhelming joy.

"I want you to go down presently and see Sadie," he said. "I can't hope that her body is better, but her soul—her soul is transformed."

The doctor was feeling wan and nervous.

"You were with her very late last night," he said.

"Yes, she couldn't bear to have me leave her."

"You look as pleased as Punch," the doctor said irritably.

Davidson's eyes shone with ecstasy.

"A great mercy has been vouchsafed me. Last night I was privileged to bring a lost soul to the loving arms of Jesus."

Miss Thompson was again in the rocking-chair. The bed had not been made. The room was in disorder. She had not troubled to dress herself, but wore a dirty dressing-gown, and her hair was tied in a sluttish knot. She had given her face a dab with a wet towel, but it was all swollen and creased with crying. She looked a drab.

She raised her eyes dully when the doctor came in. She was cowed and broken.

"Where's Mr. Davidson?" she asked.

"He'll come presently if you want him," answered Macphail acidly. "I came here to see how you were."

"Oh, I guess I'm O.K. You needn't worry about that."

"Have you had anything to eat?"

"Horn brought me some coffee."

She looked anxiously at the door.

"D'you think he'll come down soon? I feel as if it wasn't so terrible when he's with me."

"Are you still going on Tuesday?"

"Yes, he says I've got to go. Please tell him to come right along. You can't do me any good. He's the only one as can help me now."

"Very well," said Dr. Macphail.

During the next three days the missionary spent almost all his time with Sadie Thompson. He joined the others only to have his meals. Dr. Macphail noticed that he hardly ate.

"He's wearing himself out," said Mrs. Davidson pitifully. "He'll have a breakdown if he doesn't take care, but he won't spare himself."

She herself was white and pale. She told Mrs. Macphail that she had had no sleep. When the missionary came upstairs from Miss Thompson he prayed till he was exhausted, but even then he did not sleep for long. After an hour or two he got up and dressed himself, and went for a tramp along the bay. He had strange dreams.

"This morning he told me that he'd been dreaming about the mountains of Nebraska," said Mrs. Davidson.

"That's curious," said Dr. Macphail.

He remembered seeing them from the windows of the train when he crossed America. They were like huge mole-hills, rounded and smooth, and they rose from the plain abruptly. Dr. Macphail remembered how it struck him that they were like a woman's breasts.

Davidson's restlessness was intolerable even to himself. But he was buoyed up by a wonderful exhilaration. He was tearing out by the roots the last vestiges of sin that lurked in the hidden corners of that poor woman's heart. He read with her and prayed with her.

"It's wonderful," he said to them one day at supper. "It's a true rebirth. Her soul, which was black as night, is now pure and white like the new-fallen snow. I am humble and afraid. Her remorse for all her sins is beautiful. I am not worthy to touch the hem of her garment."

"Have you the heart to send her back to San Francisco?" said the doctor. "Three years in an American prison. I should have thought you might have saved her from that."

"Ah, but don't you see? It's necessary. Do you think my heart doesn't bleed for her? I love her as I love my wife and my sister. All the time that she is in prison I shall suffer all the pain that she suffers."

"Bunkum," cried the doctor impatiently.

"You don't understand because you're blind. She's sinned, and she must suffer. I know what she'll endure. She'll be starved and tortured and humiliated. I want her to accept the

punishment of man as a sacrifice to God. I want her to accept it joyfully. She has an opportunity which is offered to
very few of us. God is very good and very merciful."

Davidson's voice trembled with excitement. He could
hardly articulate the words that tumbled passionately from
his lips.

"All day I pray with her and when I leave her I pray
again, I pray with all my might and main, so that Jesus may
grant her this great mercy. I want to put in her heart the passionate desire to be punished so that at the end, even if I offered to let her go, she would refuse. I want her to feel that
the bitter punishment of prison is the thank-offering that she
places at the feet of our Blessed Lord, who gave his life for
her."

The days passed slowly. The whole household, intent on
the wretched, tortured woman downstairs, lived in a state of
unnatural excitement. She was like a victim that was being prepared for the savage rites of a bloody idolatry. Her terror
numbed her. She could not bear to let Davidson out of her
sight; it was only when he was with her that she had courage,
and she hung upon him with a slavish dependence. She cried
a great deal, and she read the Bible, and prayed. Sometimes
she was exhausted and apathetic. Then she did indeed look
forward to her ordeal, for it seemed to offer an escape, direct
and concrete, from the anguish she was enduring. She could
not bear much longer the vague terrors which now assailed
her. With her sins she had put aside all personal vanity, and
she slopped about her room, unkempt and dishevelled, in her
tawdry dressing-gown. She had not taken off her night-dress
for four days, nor put on stockings. Her room was littered and
untidy. Meanwhile the rain fell with a cruel persistence. You
felt that the heavens must at last be empty of water, but still it
poured down, straight and heavy, with a maddening iteration,
on the iron roof. Everything was damp and clammy. There
was mildew on the walls and on the boots that stood on the
floor. Through the sleepless nights the mosquitoes droned
their angry chant.

"If it would only stop raining for a single day it wouldn't be so bad," said Dr. Macphail.

They all looked forward to the Tuesday when the boat for San Francisco was to arrive from Sydney. The strain was intolerable. So far as Dr. Macphail was concerned, his pity and his resentment were alike extinguished by his desire to be rid of the unfortunate woman. The inevitable must be accepted. He felt he would breathe more freely when the ship had sailed. Sadie Thompson was to be escorted on board by a clerk in the governor's office. This person called on the Monday evening and told Miss Thompson to be prepared at eleven in the morning. Davidson was with her.

"I'll see that everything is ready. I mean to come on board with her myself."

Miss Thompson did not speak.

When Dr. Macphail blew out his candle and crawled cautiously under his mosquito curtains, he gave a sigh of relief.

"Well, thank God that's over. By this time tomorrow she'll be gone."

"Mrs. Davidson will be glad too. She says he's wearing himself to a shadow," said Mrs. Macphail. "She's a different woman."

"Who?"

"Sadie. I should never have thought it possible. It makes one humble."

Dr. Macphail did not answer, and presently he fell asleep. He was tired out, and he slept more soundly than usual.

He was awakened in the morning by a hand placed on his arm, and, starting up, saw Horn by the side of his bed. The trader put his finger on his mouth to prevent any exclamation from Dr. Macphail and beckoned to him to come. As a rule he wore shabby ducks, but now he was barefoot and wore only the *lava-lava* of the natives. He looked suddenly savage, and Dr. Macphail, getting out of bed, saw that he was heavily tattooed. Horn made him a sign to come on to the verandah. Dr. Macphail got out of bed and followed the trader out.

"Don't make a noise," he whispered. "You're wanted. Put on a coat and some shoes. Quick."

Dr. Macphail's first thought was that something had happened to Miss Thompson.

"What is it? Shall I bring my instruments?"

"Hurry, please, hurry."

Dr. Macphail crept back into the bedroom, put on a waterproof over his pyjamas, and a pair of rubber-soled shoes. He rejoined the trader, and together they tiptoed down the stairs. The door leading out to the road was open and at it were standing half a dozen natives.

"What is it?" repeated the doctor.

"Come along with me," said Horn.

He walked out and the doctor followed him. The natives came after them in a little bunch. They crossed the road and came on to the beach. The doctor saw a group of natives standing round some object at the water's edge. They hurried along, a couple of dozen yards perhaps, and the natives opened out as the doctor came up. The trader pushed him forwards. Then he saw, lying half in the water and half out, a dreadful object, the body of Davidson. Dr. Macphail bent down—he was not a man to lose his head in an emergency—and turned the body over. The throat was cut from ear to ear, and in the right hand was still the razor with which the deed was done.

"He's quite cold," said the doctor. "He must have been dead some time."

"One of the boys saw him lying there on his way to work just now and came and told me. Do you think he did it himself?"

"Yes. Someone ought to go for the police."

Horn said something in the native tongue, and two youths started off.

"We must leave him here till they come," said the doctor.

"They mustn't take him into my house. I won't have him in my house."

"You'll do what the authorities say," replied the doctor sharply. "In point of fact I expect they'll take him to the mortuary."

They stood waiting where they were. The trader took a

cigarette from a fold in his *lava-lava* and gave one to Dr. Macphail. They smoked while they stared at the corpse. Dr. Macphail could not understand.

"Why do you think he did it?" asked Horn.

The doctor shrugged his shoulders. In a little while native
police came along, under the charge of a marine, with a
stretcher, and immediately afterwards a couple of naval officers
and a naval doctor. They managed everything in a businesslike manner.

"What about the wife?" said one of the officers.

"Now that you've come I'll go back to the house and get
some things on. I'll see that it's broken to her. She'd better not
see him till he's been fixed up a little."

"I guess that's right," said the naval doctor.

When Dr. Macphail went back he found his wife nearly
dressed.

"Mrs. Davidson's in a dreadful state about her husband,"
she said to him as soon as he appeared. "He hasn't been to bed
all night. She heard him leave Miss Thompson's room at two,
but he went out. If he's been walking about since then he'll
be absolutely dead."

Dr. Macphail told her what had happened and asked her to
break the news to Mrs. Davidson.

"But why did he do it?" she asked, horror-stricken.

"I don't know."

"But I can't. I can't."

"You must."

She gave him a frightened look and went out. He heard her
go into Mrs. Davidson's room. He waited a minute to gather
himself together and then began to shave and wash. When he
was dressed he sat down on the bed and waited for his wife.
At last she came.

"She wants to see him," she said.

"They've taken him to the mortuary. We'd better go down
with her. How did she take it?"

"I think she's stunned. She didn't cry. But she's trembling
like a leaf."

"We'd better go at once."

When they knocked at her door Mrs. Davidson came out. She was very pale, but dry-eyed. To the doctor she seemed unnaturally composed. No word was exchanged, and they set out in silence down the road. When they arrived at the mortuary Mrs. Davidson spoke.

"Let me go in and see him alone."

They stood aside. A native opened a door for her and closed it behind her. They sat down and waited. One or two white men came and talked to them in undertones. Dr. Macphail told them again what he knew of the tragedy. At last the door was quietly opened and Mrs. Davidson came out. Silence fell upon them.

"I'm ready to go back now," she said.

Her voice was hard and steady. Dr. Macphail could not understand the look in her eyes. Her pale face was very stern. They walked back slowly, never saying a word, and at last they came round the bend on the other side of which stood their house. Mrs. Davidson gave a gasp, and for a moment they stopped still. An incredible sound assaulted their ears. The gramophone which had been silent for so long was playing, playing ragtime loud and harsh.

"What's that?" cried Mrs. Macphail with horror.

"Let's go on," said Mrs. Davidson.

They walked up the steps and entered the hall. Miss Thompson was standing at her door, chatting with a sailor. A sudden change had taken place in her. She was no longer the cowed drudge of the last days. She was dressed in all her finery, in her white dress, with the high shiny boots over which her fat legs bulged in their cotton stockings; her hair was elaborately arranged; and she wore that enormous hat covered with gaudy flowers. Her face was painted, her eyebrows were boldly black, and her lips were scarlet. She held herself erect. She was the flaunting queen that they had known at first. As they came in she broke into a loud, jeering laugh; and then, when Mrs. Davidson involuntarily stopped, she collected the spittle in her mouth and spat. Mrs. Davidson cowered back, and two red spots rose suddenly to her cheeks. Then, covering her face with her hands, she broke away and ran quickly up the stairs. Dr. Macphail was outraged. He pushed past the woman into her room.

"What the devil are you doing?" he cried. "Stop that damned machine."

He went up to it and tore the record off. She turned on him.

"Say, doc, you can that stuff with me. What the hell are you doin' in my room?"

"What do you mean?" he cried. "What d'you mean?"

She gathered herself together. No one could describe the scorn of her expression or the contemptuous hatred she put into her answer.

"You men! You filthy, dirty pigs! You're all the same, all of you. Pigs! Pigs!"

Dr. Macphail gasped. He understood.

P. & O.

Mʀs. HAMLYN lay on her long chair and lazily watched the passengers come along the gang-way. The ship had reached Singapore in the night and since dawn had been taking on cargo; the winches had been grinding away all day, but by now her ears were accustomed to their insistent clamour. She had lunched at the Europe and for lack of anything better to do had driven in a rickshaw through the gay, multitudinous streets of the city. Singapore is the meeting-place of many races. The Malays, though natives of the soil, dwell uneasily in towns, and are few; and it is the Chinese, supple, alert and industrious, who throng the streets, the dark-skinned Tamils walk on their silent, naked feet as though they were but brief sojourners in a strange land, but the Bengalis, sleek and prosperous, are easy in their surroundings and self-assured; the sly and obsequious Japanese seem busy with pressing and secret affairs; and the English in their topees and white ducks, speeding past in motor-cars or at leisure in their rickshaws, wear a nonchalant and careless air. The rulers of these teeming peoples take their authority with a smiling unconcern. And now, tired and hot, Mrs. Hamlyn waited for the ship to set out again on her long journey across the Indian Ocean.

She waved a rather large hand, for she was a big woman, to the doctor and Mrs. Linsell as they came on board. She had been on the ship since she left Yokohama, and had watched with acid amusement the intimacy which had sprung up between the two. Linsell was a naval officer who had been attached to the British Embassy at Tokio, and she had wondered at the indifference with which he took the attentions that the doctor paid his wife. Two men came along the gang-way, new passengers, and she amused herself by trying to discover from their demeanour whether they were married or single. Close by, a group of men were sitting together on rattan chairs, planters she judged by their khaki suits and wide-brimmed double felt hats, and they kept the deck-steward busy with their orders. They were talking loudly and laughing, for they had all drunk enough to make them somewhat foolishly hilarious, and they were evidently giving one of their number a send-off; but Mrs. Hamlyn could not tell which it was that was to be a fellow-passenger. The time was growing short. More passengers arrived, and then Mr. Jephson with dignity strolled up the gangway. He was a consul and was going home on leave. He had joined the ship at Shanghai and had immediately set about making himself agreeable to Mrs. Hamlyn. But just then she was disinclined for anything in the nature of a flirtation. She frowned as she thought of the reason which was taking her back to England. She would be spending Christmas at sea, far from anyone who cared two straws for her, and for a moment she felt a little twist at her heartstrings; it vexed her that a subject which she was so resolute to put away from her should so constantly intrude on her unwilling mind.

But a warning bell clanged loudly and there was a general movement among the men who sat beside her.

"Well, if we don't want to be taken on we'd better be toddling," said one of them.

They rose and walked towards the gangway. Now that they were all shaking hands she saw who it was that they had come to see the last of. There was nothing very interesting about the man on whom Mrs. Hamlyn's eyes rested, but because she had nothing better to do she gave him more than a casual glance. He was a big fellow, well over six feet high, broad and stout; he was dressed in a bedraggled suit of khaki drill and his hat was battered and shabby. His friends left him, but they bandied chaff from the quay, and Mrs. Hamlyn noticed that he had a strong Irish brogue; his voice was full, loud and hearty.

Mrs. Linsell had gone below and the doctor came and sat down beside Mrs. Hamlyn. They told one another their small adventures of the day. The bell sounded again and presently the ship slid away from the wharf. The Irishman waved a last farewell to his friends and then sauntered towards the chair on which he had left papers and magazines. He nodded to the doctor.

"Is that some one you know?" asked Mrs. Hamlyn.

"I was introduced to him at the club before tiffin. His name is Gallagher. He's a planter."

After the hubbub of the port and the noisy bustle of departure, the silence of the ship was marked and grateful. They steamed slowly past green-clad, rocky cliffs (the P. & O. anchorage was in a charming and secluded cove), and came out into the main harbour. Ships of all nations lay at anchor, a great multitude, passenger boats, tugs, lighters, tramps; and beyond, behind the breakwater, you saw the crowded masts, a bare straight forest, of the native junks. In the soft light of the evening the busy scene was strangely touched with mystery, and you felt that all those vessels, their activity for the moment suspended, waited for some event of a peculiar significance.

Mrs. Hamlyn was a bad sleeper and when the dawn broke she was in the habit of going on deck. It rested her troubled heart to watch the last faint stars fade before the encroaching day and at that early hour the glassy sea had often an immobility which seemed to make all earthly sorrows of little consequence. The light was wan, and there was a pleasant shiver in the air. But next morning when she went to the end of the promenade deck, she found that some one was up before her. It was Gallagher. He was watching the low coast of Sumatra which the sunrise like a magician seemed to call forth from the dark sea. She was startled and a little vexed, but before she could turn away he had seen her and nodded.

"Up early," he said. "Have a cigarette?"

He was in pyjamas and slippers. He took his case from his coat pocket and handed it to her. She hesitated. She had on nothing but a dressing-gown and a little lace cap which she had put over her tousled hair, and she knew that she must look a sight; but she had her reasons for scourging her soul.

"I suppose a woman of forty has no right to mind how she looks," she smiled, as though he must know what vain thoughts occupied her. She took the cigarette. "But you're up early too."

"I'm a planter. I've had to get up at five in the morning for so many years that I don't know how I'm going to get out of the habit."

"You'll not find it will make you very popular at home."

She saw his face better now that it was not shadowed by a hat. It was agreeable without being handsome. He was of course much too fat, and his features which must have been good enough when he was a young man were thickened. His skin was red and bloated. But his dark eyes were merry; and though he could not have been less than five and forty his hair was black and thick. He gave you an impression of great strength. He was a heavy, ungraceful, commonplace man, and Mrs. Hamlyn, except for the promiscuity of shipboard, would never have thought it worth while to talk to him.

"Are you going home on leave?" she hazarded.

"No, I'm going home for good."

His black eyes twinkled. He was of a communicative turn, and before it was time for Mrs. Hamlyn to go below in order to have her bath he had told her a good deal about himself. He had been in the Federated Malay States for twenty-five years, and for the last ten had managed an estate in Selantan. It was a hundred miles from anything that could be described as civilization and the life had been lonely; but he had made money; during the rubber boom he had done very well and with an astuteness which was unexpected in a man who looked so happy-go-lucky he had invested his savings in Government stock. Now that the slump had come he was prepared to retire.

"What part of Ireland do you come from?" asked Mrs. Hamlyn.

"Galway."

Mrs. Hamlyn had once motored through Ireland and she had a vague recollection of a sad and moody town with great stone warehouses, deserted and crumbling, which faced the melancholy sea. She had a sensation of greenness and of soft rain, of silence and of resignation. Was it here that Mr. Gallagher meant to spend the rest of his life? He spoke of it with boyish eagerness. The thought of his vitality in that grey world of shadows was so incongruous that Mrs. Hamlyn was intrigued.

"Does your family live there?" she asked.

"I've got no family. My mother and father are dead. So far as I know I haven't a relation in the world."

He had made all his plans, he had been making them for twenty-five years, and he was pleased to have some one to talk to of all these things that he had been obliged for so long only to talk to himself about. He meant to buy a house and he would keep a motor-car. He was going to breed horses. He didn't much care about shooting; he had shot a lot of big game during his first years in the F.M.S.; but now he had lost his zest. He didn't see why the beasts of the jungle should be killed; he had lived in the jungle so long. But he could hunt.

"Do you think I'm too heavy?" he asked.

Mrs. Hamlyn, smiling, looked him up and down with appraising eyes.

"You must weigh a ton," she said.

He laughed. The Irish horses were the best in the world, and he'd always kept pretty fit. You had a devil of a lot of walking exercise on a rubber estate and he'd played a good deal of tennis. He'd soon get thin in Ireland. Then he'd marry. Mrs. Hamlyn looked silently at the sea, coloured now with the tenderness of the sunrise. She sighed.

"Was it easy to drag up all your roots? Is there no one you regret leaving behind? I should have thought after so many years, however much you'd looked forward to going home, when the time came at last to go it must have given you a pang."

"I was glad to get out. I was fed up. I never want to see the country again or any one in it."

One or two early passengers now began to walk round the deck and Mrs. Hamlyn, remembering that she was scantily clad, went below.

During the next day or two she saw little of Mr. Gallagher who passed his time in the smoking-room. Owing to a strike the ship was not touching at Colombo and the passengers settled down to a pleasant voyage across the Indian Ocean. They played deck games, they gossiped about one another, they flirted. The approach of Christmas gave them an occupation, for some one had suggested that there should be a fancy-dress dance on Christmas day, and the ladies set about making their dresses. A meeting was held of the first-class passengers to decide whether the second-class passengers should be invited, and notwithstanding the heat the discussion was animated. The ladies said that the second-class passengers would only feel ill-at-ease. On Christmas day it was to be expected that they would drink more than was good for them and unpleasantness might ensue. Every one who spoke insisted that there was in his (or her) mind no idea of class distinction, no one would be so snobbish as to think there was any difference between first- and second-class passengers as far as that went, but it would really be kinder to the second-class passengers not to put them in a false position. They would enjoy themselves much more if they had a party of their own in the second-class cabin. On the other hand, no one wanted to hurt their feelings, and of course one had to be more democratic nowadays (this was in reply to the wife of a missionary in China who said she had travelled on the P. & O. for thirty-five years and she had never heard of the second-class passengers being invited to a dance in the first-class saloon) and even though they wouldn't enjoy it, they might like to come. Mr. Gallagher, dragged unwillingly from the card-table, because it had been foreseen that the voting would be close, was asked his opinion by the consul. He was taking home in the second-class a man who had been employed on his estate. He raised his massive bulk from the couch on which he sat.

"As far as I'm concerned I've only got this to say: I've got the man who was looking after our engines with me. He's a rattling good fellow and he's just as fit to come to your party as I am. But he won't come because I'm going to make him so drunk on Christmas day that by six o'clock he'll be fit for nothing but to be put to bed."

Mr. Jephson, the consul, gave a distorted smile. On account of his official position he had been chosen to preside at the meeting and he wished the matter to be taken seriously. He was a man who often said that if a thing was worth doing it was worth doing well.

"I gather from your observations," he said, not without acidity, "that the question before the meeting does not seem to you of great importance."

"I don't think it matters a tinker's curse," said Gallagher, with twinkling eyes.

Mrs. Hamlyn laughed. The scheme was at last devised to invite the second-class passengers, but to go to the captain privily and point out to him the advisability of withholding his consent to their coming into the first-class saloon. It was on the evening of the day on which this happened that Mrs. Hamlyn, having dressed for dinner, came on deck at the same time as Mr. Gallagher.

"Just in time for a cocktail, Mrs. Hamlyn," he said jovially.

"I'd like one. To tell you the truth I need cheering up."

"Why?" he smiled.

Mrs. Hamlyn thought his smile attractive, but she did not want to answer his question.

"I told you the other morning," she answered cheerfully. "I'm forty."

"I never met a woman who insisted on the fact so much."

They went into the lounge and the Irishman ordered a dry Martini for her and a gin pahit for himself. He had lived too long in the East to drink anything else.

"You've got hiccups," said Mrs. Hamlyn.

"Yes, I've had them all the afternoon," he answered

carelessly. "It's rather funny, they came on just as we got out of sight of land."

"I daresay they'll pass off after dinner."

They drank, the second bell rang, and they went into the dining-saloon.

"You don't play bridge?" he said, as they parted.

"No."

Mrs. Hamlyn did not notice that she saw nothing of Gallagher for two or three days. She was occupied with her own thoughts. They crowded upon her when she was sewing; they came between her and the novel with which she sought to cheat their insistence. She had hoped that as the ship took her further away from the scene of her unhappiness the torment of her mind would be eased; but contrariwise, each day that brought her nearer England increased her distress. She looked forward with dismay to the bleak emptiness of the life that awaited her; and then, turning her exhausted wits from a prospect that made her flinch, she considered, as she had done she knew not how many times before, the situation from which she had fled.

She had been married for twenty years. It was a long time and of course she could not expect her husband to be still madly in love with her; she was not madly in love with him; but they were good friends and they understood one another. Their marriage, as marriages go, might very well have been looked upon as a success. Suddenly she discovered that he had fallen in love. She would not have objected to a flirtation, he had had those before, and she had chaffed him about them; he had not minded that, it somewhat flattered him, and they had laughed together at an inclination which was neither deep nor serious. But this was different. He was in love as passionately as a boy of eighteen. He was fifty-two. It was ridiculous. It was indecent. And he loved without sense or prudence: by the time the hideous fact was forced upon her all the foreigners in Yokohama knew it. After the first shock of astonished anger, for he was the last man from whom such a folly might have been expected, she tried to persuade herself that she could have understood, and so have forgiven, if he had fallen in love with a girl. Middle-aged men often make fools of themselves with flappers, and after twenty years in the Far East she knew that the fifties were the dangerous age for men. But he had no excuse. He was in love with a woman eight years older than herself. It was grotesque, and it made her, his wife, perfectly absurd. Dorothy Lacom was hard on fifty. He had known her for eighteen years, for Lacom, like her own husband, was a silk merchant in Yokohama. Year in, year out, they had seen one another three or four times a week, and once, when they happened to be in England together, had shared a house at the seaside. But nothing! Not till a year ago had there been anything between them but a chaffing friendship. It was incredible. Of course Dorothy was a handsome woman; she had a good figure, overdeveloped, perhaps, but still comely; with bold black eyes and a red mouth and lovely hair; but all that she had had years before. She was forty-eight. Forty-eight!

Mrs. Hamlyn tackled her husband at once. At first he swore that there was not a word of truth in what she accused him of, but she had her proofs; he grew sulky; and at last he admitted what he could no longer deny. Then he said an astonishing thing.

"Why should you care?" he asked.

It maddened her. She answered him with angry scorn. She was voluble, finding in the bitterness of her heart wounding things to say. He listened to her quietly.

"I've not been such a bad husband to you for the twenty years we've been married. For a long time now we've only been friends. I have a great affection for you and this hasn't altered it in the very smallest degree. I'm giving Dorothy nothing that I take away from you."

"But what have you to complain of in me?"

"Nothing. No man could want a better wife."

"How can you say that when you have the heart to treat me so cruelly?"

"I don't want to be cruel to you. I can't help myself."

"But what on earth made you fall in love with her?"

"How can I tell? You don't think I wanted to, do you?"

"Couldn't you have resisted?"

"I tried. I think we both tried."

"You talk as though you were twenty. Why, you're both middle-aged people. She's eight years older than I am. It makes me look such a perfect fool."

He did not answer. She did not know what emotions seethed in her heart. Was it jealousy that seemed to clutch at her throat, anger, or was it merely wounded pride?

"I'm not going to let it go on. If only you and she were concerned I would divorce you, but there's her husband and then there are the children. Good heavens, does it occur to you that if they were girls instead of boys she might be a grandmother by now?"

"Easily."

"What a mercy that we have no children!"

He put out an affectionate hand as though to caress her, but she drew back in horror.

"You've made me the laughing-stock of all my friends. For all our sakes I'm willing to hold my tongue, but only on the condition that everything stops now, at once, and for ever."

He looked down and played reflectively with a Japanese knick-knack that was on the table.

"I'll tell Dorothy what you say," he replied at last.

She gave him a little bow, silently, and walked past him out of the room. She was too angry to observe that she was somewhat melodramatic.

She waited for him to tell her the result of his interview with Dorothy Lacom, but he made no further reference to the scene. He was quiet, polite, and silent; and at last she was obliged to ask him.

"Have you forgotten what I said to you the other day?" she enquired frigidly.

"No. I talked to Dorothy. She wishes me to tell you that she is desperately sorry that she has caused you so much pain. She would like to come and see you, but she is afraid you wouldn't like it."

"What decision have you come to?"

He hesitated. He was very grave, but his voice trembled a little.

"I'm afraid there's no use in our making a promise we shouldn't be able to keep."

"That settles it then," she answered.

"I think I should tell you that if you brought an action for divorce we should have to contest it. You would find it impossible to get the necessary evidence and you would lose your case."

"I wasn't thinking of doing that. I shall go back to England and consult a lawyer. Nowadays these things can be managed fairly easily and I shall throw myself on your generosity. I daresay you will enable me to get my freedom without bringing Dorothy Lacom into the matter."

He sighed.

"It's an awful muddle, isn't it? I don't want you to divorce me, but of course I'll do anything I can to meet your wishes."

"What on earth do you expect me to do?" she cried, her anger rising again. "Do you expect me to sit still and be made a damned fool of?"

"I'm awfully sorry to put you in a humiliating position." He looked at her with harassed eyes. "I'm quite sure we didn't want to fall in love with one another. We're both of us very conscious of our age. Dorothy, as you say, is old enough to be a grandmother and I'm a baldish, stoutish gentleman of fifty-two. When you fall in love at twenty you think your love will last for ever, but at fifty you know so much, about life and about love, and you know that it will last so short a time." His voice was low and rueful. It was as though before his mind's eye he saw the sadness of autumn and the leaves falling from the trees. He looked at her gravely. "And at that age you feel that you can't afford to throw away the chance of happiness which a freakish destiny has given you. In five years it will certainly be over, and perhaps in six months. Life is rather drab and grey, and happiness is so rare. We shall be dead so long."

It gave Mrs. Hamlyn a bitter sensation of pain to hear

Hamlyn would have had difficulty in concealing her amusement.

"Mr. Gallagher's lived a long time up-country, if you understand what I mean, and of course it's lonely, and you know what men are, miss."

"I've been married for twenty years," she replied, smiling.

"I beg your pardon, ma'am. The fact is he had a Malay girl living with him. I don't know 'ow long, ten or twelve years, I think. Well, when he made up 'is mind to come 'ome for good she didn't say nothing. She just sat there. He thought she'd carry on no end, but she didn't. Of course 'e provided for 'er all right, 'e gave 'er a little 'ouse for herself, an' 'e fixed it up so as so much should be paid 'er every month; 'e wasn't mean, I will say that for 'im, an' she knew all along as 'e'd be going some time. She didn't cry or anything. When 'e packed up all 'is things and sent them off she just sat there an' watched 'em go. And when 'e sold 'is furniture to the Chinks she never said a word. He'd give 'er all she wanted. And when it was time for 'im to go so as to catch the boat she just kep' on sitting, on the steps of the bungalow, you know, and she just looked an' said nothing. He wanted to say good-bye to 'er, same as any one would, 'an, would you believe it? she never even moved. 'Aren't you going to say good-bye to me?' he says. A rare funny look came over 'er face. And do you know what she says? 'You go,' she says; they 'ave a funny way of talking, them natives, not like we 'ave, 'you go,' she says, 'but I tell you that you will never come to your own country. When the land sinks into the sea death will come upon you, an' before them as goes with you sees the land again, death will have took you.' It gave me quite a turn."

"What did Mr. Gallagher say?" asked Mrs. Hamlyn.

"Oh, well, you know what 'e is. He just laughed. 'Always merry an' bright,' he says and he jumps into the motor, an' off we go."

Mrs. Hamlyn saw the bright and sunny road that ran through the rubber estates, with their trim green trees, care-

fully spaced, and their silence, and then wound its way up hill
and down through the tangled jungle. The car raced on, driven
by a reckless Malay, with its white passengers, past Malay
houses that stood away from the road among the coconut
trees, sequestered and taciturn, and through busy villages
where the market-place was crowded with dark-skinned little
people in gay sarongs. Then towards evening it reached the
trim, modern town, with its clubs and its golf links, its well-
ordered rest-house, its white people, and its railway station,
from which the two men could take the train to Singapore. And
the woman sat on the steps of the bungalow, empty till the
new manager moved in, and watched the road down which
the car had panted, watched the car as it sped on, and watched
till at last it was lost in the shadow of the night.

"What was she like?" Mrs. Hamlyn asked.

"Oh, well, to my way of thinking them Malay women are all
very much alike, you know," Pryce answered. "Of course she
wasn't so young any more and you know what they are, them
natives, they run to fat something terrible."

"Fat?"

The thought, absurdly enough, filled Mrs. Hamlyn with dismay.

"Mr. Gallagher was always one to do himself well, if you
understand what I mean."

The idea of corpulence at once brought Mrs. Hamlyn back
to common sense. She was impatient with herself because
for an instant she had seemed to accept the little cockney's
suggestion.

"It's perfectly absurd, Mr. Pryce. Fat women can't throw
spells on people at a distance of a thousand miles. In fact
life is very difficult for a fat woman anyway."

"You can laugh, miss, but unless something's done, you
mark my words, the governor's for it. And medicine ain't
goin' to save him, not white man's medicine."

"Pull yourself together, Mr. Pryce. This fat lady had no
particular grievance against Mr. Gallagher. As these things
are done in the East he seems to have treated her very well.
Why should she wish him any harm?"

"We don't know 'ow they look at things. Why, a man can live there for twenty years with one of them natives, and d'you think 'e knows what's goin' on in that black heart of hers? Not 'im!"

She could not smile at his melodramatic language, for his intensity was impressive. And she knew, if any one did, that the hearts of men, whether their skins are yellow or white or brown, are incalculable.

"But even if she felt angry with him, even if she hated him and wanted to kill him, what could she do?" It was strange that Mrs. Hamlyn with her questions was trying now, unconsciously, to reassure herself. "There's no poison that could start working after six or seven days."

"I never said it was poison."

"I'm sorry, Mr. Pryce," she smiled, "but I'm not going to believe in a magic spell, you know."

"You've lived in the East."

"Off and on for twenty years."

"Well, if you can say what they can do and what they can't, it's more than I can." He clenched his fist and beat it on the rail with sudden, angry violence. "I'm fed up with the bloody country. It's got on my nerves, that's what it is. We're no match for them, us white men, and that's a fact. If you'll excuse me I think I'll go an' 'ave a tiddley. I've got the jumps."

He nodded abruptly and left her. Mrs. Hamlyn watched him, a sturdy, shuffling little man in shabby khaki, slither down the companion into the waist of the ship, walk across it with bent head, and disappear into the second-class saloon. She did not know why he left with her a vague uneasiness. She could not get out of her mind that picture of a stout woman, no longer young, in a sarong, a coloured jacket and gold ornaments, who sat on the steps of a bungalow looking at an empty road. Her heavy face was painted, but in her large, tearless eyes there was no expression. The men who drove in the car were like schoolboys going home for the holidays. Gallagher gave a sigh of relief. In the early morning, under the bright sky, his spirits bubbled. The future was like a sunny road that wandered through a wide-flung, wooded plain.

Later in the day Mrs. Hamlyn asked the doctor how his patient did. The doctor shook his head.

"I'm done. I'm at the end of my tether." He frowned unhappily. "It's rotten luck, striking a case like this. It would be bad enough at home, but on board ship . . ."

He was an Edinburgh man, but recently qualified, and he was taking this voyage as a holiday before settling down to practice. He felt himself aggrieved. He wanted to have a good time and, faced with this mysterious illness, he was worried to death. Of course he was inexperienced, but he was doing everything that could be done and it exasperated him to suspect that the passengers thought him an ignorant fool.

"Have you heard what Mr. Pryce thinks?" asked Mrs. Hamlyn.

"I never heard such rot. I told the captain and he's right up in the air. He doesn't want it talked about. He thinks it'll upset the passengers."

"I'll be as silent as the grave."

The surgeon looked at her sharply.

"Of course you don't believe that there can be any truth in nonsense of that sort?" he asked.

"Of course not." She looked out at the sea which shone, blue and oily and still, all round them. "I've lived in the East a long time," she added. "Strange things happen there."

"This is getting on my nerves," said the doctor.

Near them two little Japanese gentlemen were playing deck quoits. They were trim and neat in their tennis shirts, white trousers and buckram shoes. They looked very European, they even called the score to one another in English, and yet somehow to look at them filled Mrs. Hamlyn at that moment with a vague disquiet. Because they seemed to wear so easily a disguise there was about them something sinister. Her nerves too were on edge.

And presently, no one quite knew how, the notion spread through the ship that Gallagher was bewitched. While the ladies sat about on their deck-chairs, stitching away at the costumes they were making for the fancy-dress party on Christmas day, they gossiped about it in undertones, and the men in the smoking-room talked of it over their cocktails. A good many of the passengers had lived long in the East and from the recesses of their memory they produced strange and inexplicable stories. Of course it was absurd to think seriously that Gallagher was suffering from a malignant spell, such things were impossible, and yet this and that was a fact and no one had been able to explain it. The doctor had to confess that he could suggest no cause for Gallagher's condition, he was able to give a physiological explanation, but why these terrible spasms should have suddenly assailed him he did not say. Feeling vaguely to blame, he tried to defend himself.

"Why, it's the sort of case you might never come across in the whole of your practice," he said. "It's rotten luck."

He was in wireless communication with passing ships and suggestions for treatment came from here and there.

"I've tried everything they tell me," he said irritably. "The doctor of the Japanese boat advised adrenalin. How the devil does he expect me to have adrenalin in the middle of the Indian Ocean?"

There was something impressive in the thought of this ship speeding through a deserted sea while to her from all parts came unseen messages. She seemed at that moment strangely alone and yet the centre of the world. In the lazaret the sick man, shaken by the cruel spasms, gasped for life. Then the passengers became conscious that the ship's course was altered and they heard that the captain had made up his mind to put in at Aden. Gallagher was to be landed there and taken to the hospital where he could have attention which on board was impossible. The chief engineer received orders to force his engines. The ship was an old one and she throbbed with the greater effort. The passengers had grown used to the sound and feel of her engines and now the greater vibration shook their nerves with a new sensation. It would not pass into each one's unconsciousness, but beat on their sensibilities so that each felt a personal concern. And still the wide sea was empty of traffic so that they seemed to traverse an empty world. And now the uneasiness which had descended upon the ship, but which no one had been willing to acknowledge, became a definite malaise. The passengers grew irritable, and people quarrelled over trifles which at another time would have seemed insignificant. Mr. Jephson made his hackneyed jokes, but no one any longer repaid him with a smile. The Linsells had an altercation and Mrs. Linsell was heard late at night walking round the deck with her husband, and uttering in a low, tense voice a stream of vehement reproaches. There was a violent scene in the smoking-room one night over a game of bridge, and the reconciliation which followed it was attended with general intoxication. People talked little of Gallagher, but he was seldom absent from their thoughts. They examined the route map. The doctor said now that Gallagher could not live more than three or four days and they discussed acrimoniously what was the shortest time in which Aden could be reached. What happened to him after he was landed was no affair of theirs; they did not want him to die on board.

Mrs. Hamlyn saw Gallagher every day. With the suddenness with which after tropical rain in the spring you seem to see the herbage grow before your very eyes, she saw him go to pieces. Already his skin hung loosely on his bones and his double chin was like the wrinkled wattle of a turkey-cock. His cheeks were sunken. You saw now how large his frame was and through the sheet under which he lay his bony structure was like the skeleton of a prehistoric giant. For the most part he lay with his eyes closed, torpid with morphia, but shaken still with terrible spasms and when now and again he opened his eyes they were preternaturally large; they looked at you vaguely, perplexed and troubled, from the depths of their bony sockets. But when, emerging from his stupor, he recognized Mrs. Hamlyn he forced a gallant smile to his lips.

"How are you, Mr. Gallagher?" she said.

"Getting along, getting along. I shall be all right when we get out of this confounded heat. Lord, how I look forward to a dip in the Atlantic. I'd give anything for a good long swim. I want to feel the cold grey sea of Galway beating against my chest."

Then the hiccup shook him from the crown of his head to

the sole of his foot. Mr. Pryce and the stewardess shared the care of him. The little cockney's face wore no longer its look of impudent gaiety, but instead was sullen.

"The captain sent for me yesterday," he told Mrs. Hamlyn when they were alone. "He gave me a rare talking to."

"What about?"

"He said 'e wouldn't 'ave all this hoodoo stuff. He said it was frightening the passengers and I'd better keep a watch on me tongue or I'd 'ave 'im to reckon with. It's not my doing. I never said a word except to you and the doctor."

"It's all over the ship."

"I know it is. D'you think it's only me that's saying it? All them lascars and the Chinese, they all know what's the matter with him. You don't think you can teach them much, do you? They know it ain't a natural illness."

Mrs. Hamlyn was silent. She knew through the amahs of some of the passengers that there was no one on the ship, except the whites, who doubted that the woman whom Gallagher had left in distant Selantan was killing him with her magic. All were convinced that as they sighted the barren rocks of Arabia his soul would be parted from his body.

"The captain says if he hears of me trying any hanky-panky he'll confine me to my cabin for the rest of the voyage," said Pryce suddenly, a surly frown on his puckered face.

"What do you mean by hanky-panky?"

He looked at her for a moment fiercely as though she too were an object of the anger he felt against the captain.

"The doctor's tried every damned thing he knows, and he's wirelessed all over the place, and what good 'as 'e done? Tell me that. Can't 'e see the man's dying? There's only one way to save him now."

"What do you mean?"

"It's magic what's killing 'im, and it's only magic what'll save him. Oh, don't you say it can't be done. I've seen it with me own eyes." His voice rose, irritable and shrill. "I've seen a man dragged from the jaws of death, as you might say, when they got in a *pawang*, what we call a witch-doctor, an' 'e did 'is little tricks. I seen it with me own eyes, I tell you."

Mrs. Hamlyn did not speak. Pryce gave her a searching look.

"One of them lascars on board, he's a witch-doctor, same as the *pawang* that we 'ave in the F.M.S. An' 'e says he'll do it. Only he must 'ave a live animal. A cock would do."

"What do you want a live animal for?" Mrs. Hamlyn asked, frowning a little.

The cockney looked at her with quick suspicion.

"If you take my advice you won't know anything about it. But I tell you what, I'm going to leave no stone unturned to save my governor. An' if the captain 'ears of it and shuts me up in me cabin, well, let 'im."

At that moment Mrs. Linsell came up and Pryce with his quaint gesture of salute left them. Mrs. Linsell wanted Mrs. Hamlyn to fit the dress she had been making herself for the fancy-dress ball, and on the way down to the cabin she spoke to her anxiously about the possibility that Mr. Gallagher might die on Christmas day. They could not possibly have the dance if he did. She had told the doctor that she would never speak to him again if this happened, and the doctor promised her faithfully that he would keep the man alive over Christmas day somehow.

"It would be nice for him, too," said Mrs. Linsell.

"For whom?" asked Mrs. Hamlyn.

"For poor Mr. Gallagher. Naturally no one likes to die on Christmas day. Do they?"

"I don't really know," said Mrs. Hamlyn.

That night, after she had been asleep a little while, she awoke weeping. It dismayed her that she should cry in her sleep. It was as though then the weakness of the flesh mastered her, and, her will broken, she was defenceless against a natural sorrow. She turned over in her mind, as so often before, the details of the disaster which had so profoundly affected her; she repeated the conversations with her husband, wishing she had said this and blaming herself because she had said the other. She wished with all her heart that she had remained in comfortable ignorance of her husband's infatuation, and asked herself whether she would not have been wiser to pocket her pride and shut her eyes to the unwelcome truth.

She was a woman of the world and she knew too well how much more she lost in separating herself from her husband than his love; she lost the settled establishment and the assured position, the ample means and the support of a recognized background. She had known of many separated wives, living equivocally on smallish incomes, and knew how quickly their friends found them tiresome. And she was lonely. She was as lonely as the ship that throbbed her hasting way through an unpeopled sea, and lonely as the friendless man who lay dying in the ship's lazaret. Mrs. Hamlyn knew that her thoughts had got the better of her now and that she would not easily sleep again. It was very hot in her cabin. She looked at the time; it was between four and half-past; she must pass two mortal hours before broke the reassuring day.

She slipped into a kimono and went on deck. The night was sombre and although the sky was unclouded no stars were visible. Panting and shaking, the old ship under full steam lumbered through the darkness. The silence was uncanny. Mrs. Hamlyn with bare feet groped her way slowly along the deserted deck. It was so black that she could see nothing. She came to the end of the promenade deck and leaned against the rail. Suddenly she started and her attention was fixed, for on the lower deck she caught a fitful glow. She leaned forward cautiously. It was a little fire, and she saw only the glow because the naked backs of men, crouched round, hid the flame. At the edge of the circle she divined, rather than saw, a stocky figure in pyjamas. The rest were natives, but this was a European. It must be Pryce and she guessed immediately that some dark ceremony of exorcism was in progress. Straining her ears she heard a low voice muttering a string of secret words. She began to tremble. She was aware that they were too intent upon their business to think that any one was watching them, but she dared not move. Suddenly, rending the sultry silence of the night like a piece of silk violently torn in two, came the crowing of a cock. Mrs. Hamlyn almost shrieked. Mr. Pryce was trying to save the life of his friend and master by a sacrifice to the strange gods of the East. The voice went on, low and insistent

Then in the dark circle there was a movement, something was happening, she knew not what; there was a cluck-cluck from the cock, angry and frightened, and then a strange, indescribable sound; the magician was cutting the cock's throat; then silence; there were vague doings that she could not follow, and in a little while it looked as though some one was stamping out the fire. The figures she had dimly seen were dissolved in the night and all once more was still. She heard again the regular throbbing of the engines.

Mrs. Hamlyn stood still for a little while, strangely shaken, and then walked slowly along the deck. She found a chair and lay down in it. She was trembling still. She could only guess what had happened. She did not know how long she lay there, but at last she felt that the dawn was approaching. It was not yet day, but it was no longer night. Against the darkness of the sky she could now see the ship's rail. Then she saw a figure come towards her. It was a man in pyjamas.

"Who's that?" she cried nervously.

"Only the doctor," came a friendly voice.

"Oh! What are you doing here at this time of night?"

"I've been with Gallagher." He sat down beside her and lit a cigarette. "I've given him a good strong hypodermic and he's quiet now."

"Has he been very ill?"

"I thought he was going to pass out. I was watching him, and suddenly he started up on his bed and began to talk Malay. Of course I couldn't understand a thing. He kept on saying one word over and over again."

"Perhaps it was a name, a woman's name."

"He wanted to get out of bed. He's a damned powerful man even now. By George, I had a struggle with him. I was afraid he'd throw himself overboard. He seemed to think some one was calling him."

"When was that?" asked Mrs. Hamlyn slowly.

"Between four and half-past. Why?"

"Nothing."

She shuddered.

Later in the morning when the ship's life was set upon its daily round, Mrs. Hamlyn passed Pryce on the deck, but he gave her a brief greeting and walked on with quickly averted gaze. He looked tired and overwrought. Mrs. Hamlyn thought again of that fat woman, with golden ornaments in her thick, black hair, who sat on the steps of the deserted bungalow and looked at the road which ran through the trim lines of the rubber trees.

It was fearfully hot. She knew now why the night had been so dark. The sky was no longer blue, but a dead, level white; its surface was too even to give the effect of cloud; it was as though in the upper air the heat hung like a pall. There was no breeze and the sea, as colourless as the sky, was smooth and shining like the dye in a dyer's vat. The passengers were listless; when they walked round the deck they panted and beads of sweat broke out on their foreheads. They spoke in undertones. Something uncanny and disquieting brooded over the ship, and they could not bring themselves to laugh. A feeling of resentment arose in their hearts; they were alive and well, and it exasperated them that, so near, a man should be dying and by the fact (which was after all no concern of theirs) so mysteriously affect them. A planter in the smoking-room over a gin sling said brutally what most of them felt, though none had confessed.

"Well, if he's going to peg out," he said, "I wish he'd hurry up and get it over. It gives me the creeps."

The day was interminable. Mrs. Hamlyn was thankful when the dinner hour arrived. So much time, at all events, was passed. She sat at the doctor's table.

"When do we reach Aden?" she asked.

"Some time to-morrow. The captain says we shall sight land between five and six in the morning."

She gave him a sharp look. He stared at her for a moment, then dropped his eyes and reddened. He remembered that the woman, the fat woman sitting on the bungalow steps, had said that Gallagher would never see the land. Mrs. Hamlyn wondered whether he, the sceptical, matter-of-fact young doctor, was wavering at last. He frowned a little, and then, as though he sought to pull himself together, looked at her once more.

"I shan't be sorry to hand over my patient to the hospital people at Aden, I can tell you," he said.

Next day was Christmas eve. When Mrs. Hamlyn awoke from a troubled sleep the dawn was breaking. She looked out of her porthole and saw that the sky was clear and silvery; during the night the haze had melted, and the morning was brilliant. With a lighter heart she went on deck. She walked as far forward as she could go. A late star twinkled palely close to the horizon. There was a shimmer on the sea as though a loitering breeze passed playful fingers over its surface. The light was exquisitely soft, tenuous like a budding wood in spring, and crystalline so that it reminded you of the bubbling of water in a mountain brook. She turned to look at the sun rising rosy in the east, and saw coming towards her the doctor. He wore his uniform; he had not been to bed all night; he was dishevelled and he walked, with bowed shoulders, as though he were dog-tired. She knew at once that Gallagher was dead. When he came up to her she saw that he was crying. He looked so young then that her heart went out to him. She took his hand.

"You poor dear," she said. "You're tired out."

"I did all I could," he said. "I wanted so awfully to save him."

His voice shook and she saw that he was almost hysterical.

"When did he die?" she asked.

He closed his eyes, trying to control himself, and his lips trembled.

"A few minutes ago."

Mrs. Hamlyn sighed. She found nothing to say. Her gaze wandered across the calm, dispassionate and ageless sea. It stretched on all sides of them as infinite as human sorrow. But on a sudden her eyes were held, for there, ahead of them, on the horizon was something which looked like a precipitous and massy cloud. But its outline was too sharp to be a cloud's. She touched the doctor on the arm.

"What's that?"

He looked at it for a moment and under his sunburn she saw him grow white.

"Land."

Once more Mrs. Hamlyn thought of the fat Malay woman who sat silent on the steps of Gallagher's bungalow. Did she know?

They buried him when the sun was high in the heavens. They stood on the lower deck and on the hatches, the first- and second-class passengers, the white stewards and the European officers. The missionary read the burial service.

"Man that is born of woman hath but a short time to live, and is full of misery. He cometh up, and is cut down, like a flower; he fleeth as it were a shadow, and never continueth in one stay."

Pryce looked down at the deck with knit brows. His teeth were tightly clenched. He did not grieve, for his heart was hot with anger. The doctor and the consul stood side by side. The consul bore to a nicety the expression of an official regret, but the doctor, clean-shaven now, in his neat fresh uniform and his gold braid, was pale and harassed. From him Mrs. Hamlyn's eyes wandered to Mrs. Linsell. She was pressed against her husband, weeping, and he was holding her hand tenderly. Mrs. Hamlyn did not know why this sight singularly affected her. At that moment of grief, her nerves distraught, the little woman went by instinct to the protection and support of her husband. But then Mrs. Hamlyn felt a little shudder pass through her and she fixed her eyes on the seams in the deck, for she did not want to see what was untoward. There was a pause in the reading. There were various movements. One of the officers gave an order. The missionary's voice continued.

"Forasmuch as it has pleased Almighty God of his great mercy to take unto himself the soul of our dear brother here departed; we therefore commend his body to the deep, to be turned into corruption, looking for the resurrection of the body when the sea shall give up its dead."

Mrs. Hamlyn felt the hot tears flow down her cheeks. There was a dull splash. The missionary's voice went on.

When the service was finished the passengers scattered; the second-class passengers returned to their quarters and a bell rang to summon them to luncheon. But the first-class passengers sauntered aimlessly about the promenade deck. Most of the men made for the smoking-room and sought to cheer themselves with whiskies and sodas and with gin slings. But the consul put up a notice on the board outside the dining-saloon summoning the passengers to a meeting. Most of them had an idea for what purpose it was called and at the appointed hour they assembled. They were more cheerful than they had been for a week and they chattered with a gaiety which was only subdued by a mannerly reserve. The consul, an eye-glass in his eye, said that he had gathered them together to discuss the question of the fancy-dress ball on the following day. He knew they all had the deepest sympathy for Mr. Gallagher and he would have proposed that they should combine to send an appropriate message to the deceased's relatives; but his papers had been examined by the purser and no trace could be found of any relative or friend with whom it was possible to communicate. The late Mr. Gallagher appeared to be quite alone in the world. Meanwhile he (the consul) ventured to offer his sincere sympathy to the doctor who, he was quite sure, had done everything that was possible in the circumstances.

"Hear, hear," said the passengers.

They had all passed through a very trying time, proceeded the consul, and to some it might seem that it would be more respectful to the deceased's memory if the fancy-dress ball were postponed till New Year's eve. This, however, he told them frankly was not his view, and he was convinced that Mr. Gallagher himself would not have wished it. Of course it was a question for the majority to decide. The doctor got up and thanked the consul and the passengers for the kind things that had been said of him, it had of course been a very trying time, but he was authorized by the captain to say

that the captain expressly wished all the festivities to be
carried out on Christmas day as though nothing had happened.
He (the doctor) told them in confidence that the captain
felt the passengers had got into a rather morbid state and
thought it would do them all good if they had a jolly good time
on Christmas day. Then the missionary's wife rose and said
they mustn't think only of themselves; it had been arranged by
the Entertainment Committee that there should be a Christmas
tree for the children immediately after the first-class passengers' dinner, and the children had been looking forward to
seeing every one in fancy dress; it would be too bad to disappoint them; she yielded to no one in her respect for the dead
and she sympathized with any one who felt too sad to think
of dancing just then. Her own heart was very heavy, but she
did feel it would be merely selfish to give way to a feeling
which could do no good to any one. Let them think of the
little ones. This very much impressed the passengers. They
wanted to forget the brooding terror which had hung over the
boat for so many days, they were alive and they wanted to
enjoy themselves; but they had an uneasy notion that it would
be decent to exhibit a certain grief. It was quite another matter if they could do as they wished from altruistic motives.
When the consul called for a show of hands every one, but
Mrs. Hamlyn and one old lady who was rheumatic, held up an
eager arm.

"The ayes have it," said the consul. "And I venture to congratulate the meeting on a very sensible decision."

It was just going to break up when one of the planters got
on his feet and said he wished to offer a suggestion. In the
circumstances didn't they all think it would be as well to
invite the second-class passengers? They had all come to the
funeral that morning. The missionary jumped up and sec-
onded the motion. The events of the last few days had drawn
them all together, he said, and in the presence of death all
men were equal. The consul again addressed them. This matter had been discussed at a previous meeting and the conclusion had been reached that it would be pleasanter for the

second-class passengers to have their own party, but circumstances alter cases, and he was distinctly of opinion that their previous decision should be reversed.

"Hear, hear," said the passengers.

A wave of democratic feeling swept over them and the motion was carried by acclamation. They separated light-heartedly, they felt charitable and kindly. Every one stood every one else drinks in the smoking-room.

And so, on the following evening, Mrs. Hamlyn put on her fancy-dress. She had no heart for the gaiety before her, and for a moment had thought of feigning illness, but she knew no one would believe her, and was afraid to be thought affected. She was dressed as Carmen and she could not resist the vanity of making herself as attractive as possible. She darkened her eyelashes and rouged her cheeks. The costume suited her. When the bugle sounded and she went into the saloon she was received with flattering surprise. The consul (always a humorist) was dressed as a ballet-girl and was greeted with shouts of delighted laughter. The missionary and his wife, self-conscious but pleased with themselves, were very grand as Manchus. Mrs. Linsell, as Columbine, showed all that was possible of her very pretty legs. Her husband was an Arab sheik and the doctor was a Malay sultan.

A subscription had been collected to provide champagne at dinner and the meal was hilarious. The company had provided crackers in which were paper hats of various shapes and these the passengers put on. There were paper streamers too which they threw at one another and little balloons which they beat from one to the other across the room. They laughed and shouted. They were very gay. No one could say that they were not having a good time. As soon as dinner was finished they went into the saloon where the Christmas tree, with candles lit, was ready, and the children were brought in, shrieking with delight, and given presents. Then the dance began. The second-class passengers stood about shyly round the part of the deck reserved for dancing and occasionally danced with one another.

"I'm glad we had them," said the consul, dancing with Mrs.

Hamlyn. "I'm all for democracy, and I think they're very sensible to keep themselves to themselves."

But he noticed that Pryce was not to be seen, and when an opportunity presented asked one of the second-class passengers where he was.

"Blind to the world," was the answer. "We put him to bed in the afternoon and locked him up in his cabin."

The consul claimed her for another dance. He was very facetious. Suddenly Mrs. Hamlyn felt that she could not bear it any more, the noise of the amateur band, the consul's jokes, the gaiety of the dancers. She knew not why, but the merriment of those people passing on their ship through the night and the solitary sea affected her on a sudden with horror. When the consul released her she slipped away and, with a look to see that no one had noticed her, ascended the companion to the boat-deck. Here everything was in darkness. She walked softly to a spot where she knew she would be safe from all intrusion. But she heard a faint laugh and she caught sight in a hidden corner of a Columbine and a Malay sultan. Mrs. Linsell and the doctor had resumed already the flirtation which the death of Gallagher had interrupted.

Already all those people had put out of their minds with a kind of ferocity the thought of that poor lonely man who had so strangely died in their midst. They felt no compassion for him, but resentment rather, because on his account they had been ill-at-ease. They seized upon life avidly. They made their jokes, they flirted, they gossiped. Mrs. Hamlyn remembered what the consul had said, that among Mr. Gallagher's papers no letter could be found, not the name of a single friend to whom the news of his death might be sent, and she knew not why this seemed to her unbearably tragic. There was something mysterious in a man who could pass through the world in such solitariness. When she remembered how he had come on deck in Singapore, so short a while since, in such rude health, full of vitality, and his arrogant plans for the future, she was seized with dismay. Those words of the burial service filled her with a solemn awe: *Man that is born of woman hath but a short time to live, and is full of misery.*

He cometh up, and is cut down, like a flower. . . . Year in, year out, he had made his plans for the future, he wanted to live so much and he had so much to live for, and then just when he stretched out his hand—oh, it was pitiful; it made all the other distresses of the world of small account. Death with its mystery was the only thing that really mattered. Mrs. Hamlyn leaned over the rail and looked at the starry sky. Why did people make themselves unhappy? Let them weep for the death of those they loved, death was terrible always, but for the rest, was it worth while to be wretched, to harbour malice, to be vain and uncharitable? She thought again of herself and her husband and the woman he so strangely loved. He too had said that we live to be happy so short a time and we are so long dead. She pondered long and intently, and suddenly, as summer lightning flashes across the darkness of the night, she made a discovery which filled her with tremulous surprise; for she found that in her heart was no longer anger with her husband nor jealousy of her rival. A notion dawned on some remote horizon of her consciousness and like the morning sun suffused her soul with a tender, blissful glow. Out of the tragedy of that unknown Irishman's death she gathered elatedly the courage for a desperate resolution. Her heart beat quickly, she was impatient to carry it into effect. A passion for self-sacrifice seized her.

The music had stopped, the ball was over; most of the passengers would have gone to bed and the rest would be in the smoking-room. She went down to her cabin and met no one on the way. She took her writing-pad and wrote a letter to her husband.

My dear. It is Christmas day and I want to tell you that my heart is filled with kindly thoughts towards both of you. I have been foolish and unreasonable. I think we should allow those we care for to be happy in their own way, and we should care for them enough not to let it make us unhappy. I want you to know that I grudge you none of the joy that has so strangely come into your life. I am no longer jealous, nor hurt, nor vindictive. Do not think I shall be unhappy or lonely. If eve

you feel that you need me, come to me, and I will welcome
you with a cheerful spirit and without reproach or ill-will. I
am most grateful for all the years of happiness and of tender-
ness that you gave me, and in return I wish to offer you an
affection which makes no claim on you and is, I hope, utterly
disinterested. Think kindly of me and be happy, happy, happy.

She signed her name and put the letter into an envelope.
Though it would not go till they reached Port Said she
wanted to place it at once in the letter-box. When she had
done this, beginning to undress, she looked at herself in the
glass. Her eyes were shining and under her rouge her colour
was bright. The future was no longer desolate, but bright
with a fair hope. She slipped into bed and fell at once into a
sound and dreamless sleep.

The Best of the World's Best Books
COMPLETE LIST OF TITLES IN
THE MODERN LIBRARY

A series of handsome, cloth-bound books, formerly available only in expensive editions.

MISCELLANEOUS

MODERN LIBRARY GIANTS

A series of sturdily bound and handsomely printed, full-sized library editions of books formerly available only in expensive sets. These volumes contain from 600 to 1,400 pages each.

THE MODERN LIBRARY GIANTS REPRESENT A
SELECTION OF THE WORLD'S GREATEST BOOKS

G86 PASTERNAK, BORIS: *Doctor Zhivago*
G5 PLUTARCH: *Lives* (The Dryden Translation)
G40 POE, EDGAR ALLAN: *Complete Tales and Poems*
G29 PRESCOTT, WILLIAM H.: *The Conquest of Mexico* and *The Conquest of Peru*
G62 PUSHKIN: *Poems, Prose and Plays*
G65 RABELAIS: *Complete Works*
G12 SCOTT, SIR WALTER: *The Most Popular Novels* (Quentin Durward, Ivanhoe & Kenilworth)
G4 SHELLEY & KEATS: *Complete Poems*
G32 SMITH, ADAM: *The Wealth of Nations*
G61 SPAETH, SIGMUND: *A Guide to Great Orchestral Music*
G92 SPENGLER, OSWALD: *The Decline of the West* (one volume)
G91 SPENSER, EDMUND: *Selected Poetry*
G75 STEVENSON, ROBERT LOUIS: *Selected Writings*
G53 SUE, EUGENE: *The Wandering Jew*
G42 TENNYSON: *The Poems and Plays*
G23 TOLSTOY, LEO: *Anna Karenina*—tr. revised
G1 TOLSTOY, LEO: *War and Peace*
G49 TWAIN, MARK: *Tom Sawyer* and *Huckleberry Finn*
G50 WHITMAN, WALT: *Leaves of Grass*
G83 WILSON, EDMUND: *The Shock of Recognition*

MISCELLANEOUS

G77 *An Anthology of Famous American Stories*
G54 *An Anthology of Famous British Stories*
G67 *Anthology of Famous English and American Poetry*
G81 *An Encyclopedia of Modern American Humor*
G47 *The English Philosophers from Bacon to Mill*
G16 *The European Philosophers from Descartes to Nietzsche*
G31 *Famous Science-Fiction Stories*
G85 *Great Ages and Ideas of the Jewish People*
G89 *Great Classical Myths*
G72 *Great Tales of Terror and the Supernatural*
G9 *Great Voices of the Reformation*
G87 *Medieval Epics*
G48 *The Metropolitan Opera Guide*
G46 *A New Anthology of Modern Poetry*
G69 *One Hundred and One Years' Entertainment*
G93 *Parodies: An Anthology from Chaucer to Beerbohm and After*
G90 *Philosophies of Art and Beauty: Readings in Aesthetics from Plato to Heidegger*
G21 *Sixteen Famous American Plays*
G63 *Sixteen Famous British Plays*
G71 *Sixteen Famous European Plays*
G45 *Stoic and Epicurean Philosophers*
G22 *Thirty Famous One-Act Plays*
G66 *Three Famous Murder Novels, Before the Fact,* FRANCIS ILES, *Trent's Last Case,* E. C. BENTLEY, *The House of the Arrow,* A. E. W. MASON
G10 *Twelve Famous Plays of the Restoration and Eighteenth Century* (1660–1820): Dryden, Congreve, Wycherley, Gay, etc.
G56 *The Wisdom of Catholicism*
G59 *The Wisdom of China and India*
G79 *The Wisdom of Israel*